TIBET

**BEING THE RECOLLECTIONS AND ADVENTURES
OF THE HERMIT CALLED
SMALL EARS**

A NOVEL BY GIL ZIFF

Crown Publishers, Inc. • *New York*

Inquiries should be addressed to Crown Publishers, Inc.,
One Park Avenue, New York, New York 10016
Printed in the United States of America
Published simultaneously in Canada
by General Publishing Company Limited
Library of Congress Cataloging in Publication Data
Ziff, Gil.
Tibet: Being the recollections and adventures of
the hermit called Small Ears.
I. Title.
PS3576.I34T5   1981   813'.54   81-178
AACR2
ISBN: 0-517-544369
Book Design by Camilla Filancia
10 9 8 7 6 5 4 3 2

*For Sara, who was with me
through every word and saved me
from myself more than once*

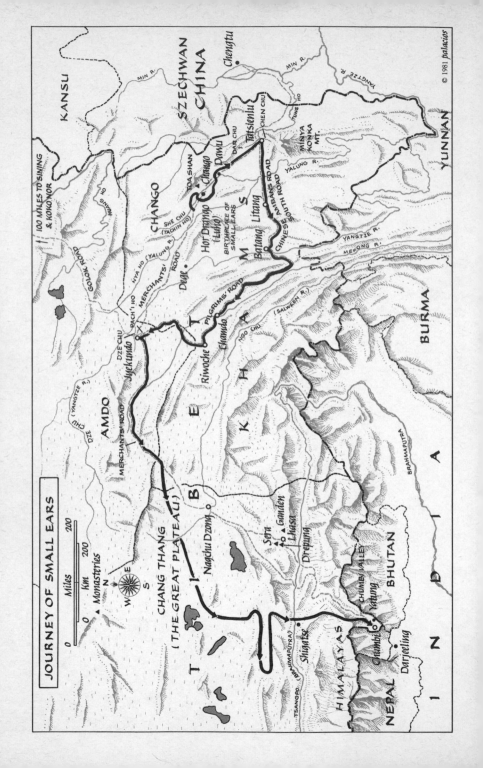

© 1981 palacios

Translator's Preface

The story of the hermit who lived with the *migou* abominable snowman first came to my attention in 1953. At the time I didn't put much credence in it.

It was told by a gregarious and boisterous Tibetan guide named Tsering Don Dop from the Khams province in eastern Tibet. Tsering guided me to the land of the Panik tribe on the northern banks of Koko Nor in Tibet, where I did my research on the Panik language. (See University of Bagnols Oriental Division Bulletin, Volume 87, 1954.) Aside from speaking many languages, Tsering's overwhelming asset was his enthusiasm as a guide. So I credited the story with his desire to amuse me, the foreigner, on a dark Tibetan night. But he insisted a hermit lived among the *migou*. He even claimed the hermit left a record of his adventures.

I would have forgotten it were it not for the meeting I had with my good friend and colleague Dr. Emile Lenoir at his home in Uzès, France, in 1962. He had just been given a Tibetan manuscript written in the Zhang Zhung language. He told me that from what he could piece together, the manuscript dealt with a lama who lived among the *migou*.

My thoughts rushed back to that cold Tibetan plain, the lukewarm buttered yak tea, and Tsering's dark eyes shining in the dim light of the fire.

"When I told you how I carried a mare and her foal out of a snowstorm," he said, "well, that was not altogether true.

"And when I told you why I dare not go to Batang, I said it

vii

was because I had defeated eight men in a fight. Well, it was actually four but they were Khampas so that's almost true.

"But no one makes jokes about the *migou*." He smiled. Then his expression changed. He looked at me seriously. "I assure you."

Now a renowned scholar was confirming Tsering's word, and even asking for my aid in the translation.

But how did Lenoir come to be in possession of the manuscript?

This is what he told me.

In the late winter of 1921 (the Year of the Iron Bird in Tibet) a tribe of nomadic herdsmen were driving their herds over the barren and desolate plain that lay south of the Nan Shan range and a tributary of the Huang Ho, the great Yellow River. They were bound for the Tibetan uplands to the east, where they expected to find summer pastures and good, nourishing grazing for their herds of yaks, sheep and goats.

They did not usually travel through this uninhabited region, since they feared both bandits and the lack of grazing land. That year, however, there were a number of disturbances in the south due to the almost perpetual conflicts between the Tibetan government in Lhasa and the Chinese government in Peking. They had heard that both parties in the dispute thought nothing of conscripting the nomads' animals for their own service, and indeed had even attempted to turn the nomads into soldiers.

Wishing to avoid this at all cost, the chief of the tribe, after consulting with the aged lama who traveled with them, decided to risk the northern passage, moving the animals as quickly as possible to reach safe grazing lands. However, the northern route proved to be much more perilous than expected. Raw nature had already made its claim on this part of the country.

They were lashed by snow, wind, hail and rain. Sometimes the earth they marched across turned into a huge bog, causing both man and animal to stumble along. The mountains that had seemed so close appeared to move farther away. Huddled together in their tents with their horses, they attempted to warm themselves, but the yak chips they used to heat their tents were often too damp to ignite.

Although the nomads were accustomed to hardship, the journey took its toll. Of the thirty-nine families—eighty-two people—in their party, almost a fourth perished on that inhospitable plain. The herd on which their existence depended was seriously reduced.

Perhaps the most severe loss was the old lama who traveled with the tribe. Early in the journey, his horse stumbled, causing the old man to break a leg. It was a nasty wound, the bone piercing his skin. He painfully set the leg himself and coated it liberally with yak dung but he could do nothing to stop the gangrene that steadily progressed and finally claimed his life.

Without their spiritual leader and guide, the tribe made slow, unsteady progress across the cold plain. They were too far to turn back or head south. They continued their trek across the harsh plain.

In the midst of this alkaline desert, they saw what from a distance appeared to be a religious shrine or marker. This cheered them a little. They welcomed this sight, for it proved that others had taken this same journey; other landmarks and guideposts were bound to appear.

But when they reached the object, they were greatly

disappointed and more frightened than before. It was like nothing they had ever come across in all their travels.

They saw flat stones, placed in a closely set oval, with the corner stones projecting out at the four points of east, west, south and north. These stones surrounded a much larger flat stone that covered what seemed to be a large hole in the ground.

Perhaps it did have some religious significance, but it was not a *chorten*, the pyramid-shaped clay altar which contains the remains of a holy lama or some other precious relic. Nor was it a *mani* pile. *Mani* piles abound throughout Tibet and are piles of flat stones on which the sacred formula is written. These are used to mark a religious place, a place infested with ghosts, or as landmarks.

Since burial is not practiced by Tibetans, at first they thought it might be an ancient burial ground. (Cremation is an honor for ranking lamas. Bodies are either left on the highest point of a mountain, cut up and fed to the vultures, or in the poorest circumstances simply thrown in a river, lake or stream.)

Fearing the spirits of the dead, the nomads immediately moved away from the site. They were convinced that it could only contain the remains of a foreigner, the Frenchman Dutreuil de Rhins, who was killed by Tibetans in this area in 1893. (They were wrong by about seven hundred miles; de Rhins died near the village of Gonka, some seven hundred miles to the west.) They remembered that although four Tibetans had been put to death for this act, their leader, a powerful lama, went free. This was no doubt the area known for its vengeful ghost. And it was probably for this reason that even the fiercest bandits did not enter this plateau without a very good reason.

They moved away quickly, but the chief had the courage to turn around to see if any ghosts were following. Seeing nothing, his curiosity overtook his caution. He was an intelligent man with great initiative; and while he would never think of spending a night near such an unholy spot, the next day he rode back with three of his strongest lieutenants. He was not sure that this was a burial ground, for no one in his tribe had ever seen anything like it. He was intent on finding out what it really was.

It took most of the morning and the efforts of men and horses, but they finally were able to remove the large flat stone that seemed to have been so carefully placed in the middle. They were careful not to disturb any of the surrounding rocks. While the chief had doubts that this was a burial ground, he did not wish to take any chances.

The hole that they uncovered was not particularly deep, coming up only to a man's waist. In it they found two lengthy manuscripts written on Tibetan paper. Like most Tibetan works, it was not bound, but had two heavy wooden boards in the front and back to keep the pages together. On one of the boards, half painted and half engraved, was the figure of a red tiger. The head was turned toward the tail, yet the tiger was in a crouching position as if about to pounce.

There was no telling how old these were. The papers were made from the daphne flower, which has the property of being poisonous to insects which eat paper, so everything was well preserved in the dry atmosphere of the plain.

Their discovery was seen as an auspicious change in their luck. Being devout Buddhists, they felt that they had come across some of the secret works of the Padmasambhava, the eighth-century Indian Buddhist missionary who was reputed to have buried works throughout Tibet, waiting for the time when human beings would be capable of receiving this precious enlightenment.

Unfortunately, only the dead lama had been able to read, but the nomads knew their sacred books by heart. They were sure that this was a part of it. But on closer inspection, comparing these pages with some from the volumes they already owned, they could find no similarities. Even the language was different. It was decided to move on to the next inhabited place where they could find a lama to translate these words. They loaded the books on wooden saddles and gave the responsibility of carrying them to two of their best yaks.

Four days later they arrived at Luho, a small and poor village of eight families. At one time it had been a spot for caravan stops, as there was a strong flowing stream nearby. But the stream had become alkaline as the surrounding plain slowly but steadily moved in and around it. The village did not have a monastery and there was only one old lama, who took it on himself to keep a small temple. They sent for him.

For all their hardships, the nomads were pleased and optimistic; they felt that they were lucky to have come across these holy words which no doubt were the key to many religious questions.

The lama, Riwa Narbung, was a member of the reformed, or Yellow Hat, sect of Tibetan Buddhism, as were the nomads. They told him of their remarkable discovery and how he would attain merit by reading these sacred works. But he insisted on a price for his services, explaining that he earned his livelihood by the dispensation of religious services. They arranged a small price, for the lama saw that there was not much to be made from these wretched people. He consented to come to the chief's tent and read the works.

As soon as he began reading, however, it was clear that these works were not what anyone expected them to be. The nomads, in their simplicity, believed that any written work was surely religious, but this writing had nothing at all to do with the sacred *Kanjur* or the commentaries of the *Tenjur*, which the nomads had heard read so many times on so many nights in so many tents.

The lama did not have to read long to find that this was not the work he expected it to be. Not being a man of great initiative, he dispatched a messenger to consult the authorities in Jyekundo, the nearest large town. He asked the nomads to stay just a few weeks more until word could get back about what to do. The nomads refused, stating that their animals would perish if they did not find grazing.

The lama directed them toward a small patch of grazing land, allowing them to use it on the condition that they leave these volumes in his care. They again refused, but promised to return in some weeks when both they and their animals had gathered fresh strength and health. To this they all agreed.

In the meantime, the religious authorities in Jyekundo were at a loss to know what to do; it seemed that only the authorities in Lhasa could handle it. They realized the importance of keeping the matter secret, for they had no idea what they had uncovered.

By the second meeting the Jyekundo lamas were already involved. Still nothing had been settled. No one would dare read the books. The lama asked the nomads to wait until word had been received from Lhasa. (If they left, they would be under the penalty of a million hells.)

By the end of a month, however, the nomads felt uncomfortable being in one place for such a long time. A number of them left, but since none had taken the strange books, they were not pursued.

When word reached Lhasa of the auspicious discovery in the northern wastelands, the secretiveness of the affair was soon ended. The three major lamaseries—Sera, Ganden and Drepung—all claimed that by rights these works belonged to them, although no one could say what they contained. Each lamasery dispatched its own agents to Luho.

Each knew of the others' doings. Spies were all around, as the rivalries of these monasteries were legendary. The expedition from the Sera Monastery was the first to reach Luho, but they arrived four days too late—the chief of the nomads, no longer able to wait, had taken off late one night with the books. He joined the rest of his tribe, who had been waiting for him some miles away. While smiling and civil to lamas, he was only waiting for an opportunity to sneak away.

The nomads had decided to fight the authorities, although it was not in their nature to take up arms. Fortunately, this did not become necessary. Time, wind and constant heavy snowfall covered their tracks. They waited near a small valley far from the village for the monastic soldiers to come, but they never arrived. The vast plain swallowed them up, and the lama had no idea where to look for them.

The lama of Luho was reprimanded for allowing them to escape and it was soon believed that the whole affair was something of a hoax. The nomads could never again march in that part of their country; they were soon forgotten, as were the books.

But the chief's curiosity again got the better of him. He

was determined to find out what these works were about. Some months later, the nomads found an obscure monastery of the ancient pre-Buddhist Bon sect near the border with Ladakh, India, in southwest Tibet. The news of the discovery had not reached this place. When the Bon lama saw the works, he put them to his forehead again and again, as if kowtowing. The nomads had come to the right place, for these works were indeed related to the Bon faith. The lama offered the nomads whatever they wanted if they would at least let him copy the words.

The nomads asked only that he read the words aloud to them.

Unfortunately, word of the discovery had reached the Chinese authorities, who were not always the last to hear of events in Tibet. The Chinese felt that if these were the religious works they were purported to be, they would be best in their hands; for in Tibet, the ones who control religion control Tibet.

It took two months for the Bon lama to read the books to the nomads; by this time, the Chinese, through their spies, had been informed of the little Bon monastery. A small regiment of soldiers was dispatched to the monastery, which housed sixty-four monks.

The soldiers found the place completely deserted. The Bon lama had heard from his spies of the imminent Chinese attack; he and the other monks had escaped just a few days before they arrived.

The Bon lama and his monks traveled with the nomads. Some of the priests became herdsmen, marrying into the nomad tribe (Bon lamas are not celibate). Every night, a few pages of the works were read aloud, until everyone knew them by heart. The books were then reburied in another spot far from the one where they had been found. Only the nomads and the Bon monks knew its location.

The books remained safely hidden for many years and their stories became the legends of this obscure nomad tribe.

Forty years later, after the Chinese invasion of Tibet, a grandson of the chief of the tribe escaped into Darjeeling in northern India. He was barely alive when they took him to the refugee field hospital but alive enough to remember the stories he had heard all his life. These stories concerned a hermit who lived among the *migou*.

Before he died, the Tibetan offered a fragmented description of this legendary creature to the Indian doctor in attendance, A. R. Singh.

"I am a herdsman, sir. I know about the *migou*. Any herdsman worthy of merit knows of the *migou*. Yes, I saw one. That the *migou* is something other than human, there can be no doubt. But there is much in his appearance which could easily be mistaken for human . . . the top of his head is slightly pointed and there is a tuft of white fur. One can easily mistake that for a nomad's cap. . . . He reminded me of a gold washer from the upper Ni Chu, who to protect himself from the bold wind and the hot sun, wraps himself in a thick black yakskin.

"We were grazing the upland slopes and now that winter was approaching, were descending into the valley. He was coming up. I saw him just below the snowline. He was watching us from a rhododendron bush. It was as if he was waiting for us to pass.

"I remember his fur was brownish red. The color was brighter around his fingers. In fact, they looked like they were on fire. I cannot say how large he was. His face appeared from behind the bush as I passed. It was flat and white. There wasn't any fur, only two bright green eyes that shone like pure turquoise. I still cannot say if the sharp white teeth he displayed were the beginnings of a smile or a snarl."

These Tibetan "tales" might have all been forgotten were it not for the foresight of the dying Tibetan nomad. Before he went on to his next rebirth, he told Dr. Singh the location of the hermit's works. He stressed that if Tibet was to be saved, they must be found.

At first Singh credited this fantastic tale to the ramblings of a dying man. Exposure, hunger and fatigue are known to work on the mind as well as the body and the man was barely alive when he was discovered. Singh didn't think too much about it and the matter would have ended were it not for a casual ironic twist.

Three weeks after the nomad died, Otto Krasna, of the Institut Suisse des Affaires Tibétaines, was touring the refugee camp. Krasna's work with the Tibetans in Switzerland was well known and had earned him the name "Lungdop Philing" or "gentle foreigner." As he passed the tent where the nomad had died, Singh told him the dying nomad's tale.

When Singh finished the tale, Krasna's face was white. "What is it, my friend?" Singh asked. "Are you not well?"

"I am fine," Krasna answered. "It is only that I heard a similar story from a Tibetan who now lives in Switzerland. And you say you wrote down the directions to reach these books?"

"I did," Singh smiled as he produced a number of pages on which the directions were written, "although I did not think too much about it at the time. But it was the dying man's wish, and I could do no less than to write down what he told me."

Krasna returned to Switzerland with a copy of the directions and, after a few weeks' search, found the Tibetan who had first told him the same tale. The Tibetan, Ang Dorje, was working in a hotel in Montreux, and he was only too happy for a chance to return on an expedition into the wilds of his native Tibet. Ang Dorje was not a member of the nomadic tribe, but he had heard about them and even knew some tribesmen. The directions looked authentic to him.

The mission was kept small and very secret so as not to attract attention.

On October 7, 1964, the small party penetrated Tibet from Chumbi valley. Their accomplishment was an adventure in itself, for seven months later, on May 11, 1965, they marched out of Tibet with the volumes intact.

Krasna made the first attempt at translating these books and brought them to Lenoir's attention. Both scholars had made considerable progress, overcoming seemingly insurmountable difficulties.

But it was clear they needed additional help to complete their task.

It was then that both Lenoir and Krasna decided to approach me. I could hardly believe my good luck. After Lenoir left the treasured work with me, I cleared my schedule and began the task ahead of me.

Sections of the text were written in the long-extinct Zhang Zhung language of pre-Buddhist Tibet, which made complete translation difficult. The invaluable help that my good friend Lama Dawu gave to this problem cannot be overestimated. Not only did the lama aid in the translation of Tibetan and

Sanskrit passages, but he devised the first working alphabet of the Zhang Zhung language.

Another source of confusion was the identification of certain towns, rivers, tributaries and mountains; Tibetans, Chinese, Mongolians and other ethnic groups in eastern Tibet name each spot in their own language, so any one place could have many names. To achieve order, I have called the places in question by the name used most commonly in the region. The name may be Tibetan, Mongolian or Chinese, and the mixture of languages may appear not to have rhyme or reason. The papers themselves reveal a blend of many tongues so I feel in this respect that I am faithful to the original.

The story, although essentially religious (as all Tibetan works are), deals with *migou,* also called yeti and the abominable snowman. He is a supernatural being, possibly a god, but that is only part of it. Most gratifying and perhaps more unusual is the glimpse of the many cultures within Tibet's mountain barriers at the turn of the century.

These were crucial years in Central Asia. England and Russia were involved in their great rivalry, each keeping an eye on the other while both kept an eye on Tibet. The Manchus would soon tumble from power in China, and Mongolia was also in a state of unrest. Tibet, remote, unsociable and aloof, would soon find the weight of world events breaking through the mountain strongholds, spilling twentieth-century politics on the roof of the world.

I also owe a special debt of gratitude to Gezony Jigme, my Tibetan teacher and friend, for reading over and making corrections on the first complete translation.

Also, I should not like to forget my Tibetan friends, who

rather than live under the Chinese communist thumb, have dispersed to the world's mountains and who, like I, wait with longing for the day when Tibet will once again fall under Tibetan rule.

May religion be victorious.

MARCEL DUPONT-DEINER
Saint Andre de Oliraques
Gard, France
September 1971

TIBET

The First Hermitage

I must tread lightly through this mountain wilderness. I am still on dangerous ground.

I have done battle with the mountain spirits both of the air and the earth. They have alternately been conquered and appeased. A fragile agreement has been reached and I will remain here.

This can change. At the slightest affront, the wind fiends can blow me off the mountain or bury me in ice. The glaciers can open up to swallow me and the poisonous breath of the earth spirits can suffocate me. Still, I am happy here. The place was well chosen.

A long time ago, I was in a hermitage on one of the mountains north of the city of Shigatse. I found what I believed would be a difficult place to reach. But I was continually disturbed by half-sincere students, pretentious monks and just the curious seeking a hermit's blessing.

I climbed higher on the mountain, found another cave and thought that here I could free myself from the illusory world that binds sentient beings through endless rebirths on the wheel of life. But somehow I was found again.

At first, I accepted visits. In most cases, however, I had confused hardiness with religious zeal. The fact that some of these monks had survived the ordeal of the climb in no way assured their commitment to religion. It was their physical rather than their mental stamina that got them up here. That had never been enough. Some of the warrior monks of Sera Monastery in Lhasa are said to have the strength of yaks, but this strength is seldom matched by a mind capable of receiving the full meaning of the dharma.

I withdrew again. I discouraged visits. If someone approached my cave, I either shouted him away or threw rocks if first warnings did not work.

Once four monks from a small monastery not far from Shigatse came tramping up the mountain. I watched them struggle up the narrow inclines. From the way that they were climbing I could tell that three of them were quite young and the fourth much older. It was the elderly monk who was hit by one of the stones I threw. It was then, as he fell back and slid some distance down the ice, that I realized that he was the elderly abbot of the monastery—a learned and good monk. I was sorry that my stone did not find a better mark. I had some admiration for this man. But what was done was done. The monks returned to their valley and I to my cave.

They told everyone that the old hermit had finally succumbed to madness.

So much the better.

Young Days in Khams

I have lost track of time. I have tried to bury the memories that rush back at me. They cloud my meditation. They distort my solitude. Memory is the rope that I have been unable to cut. It is the madness to which I have succumbed. I am compelled to relate, to chronicle, to think back.

That I can remember the name of the neighbor's dog, a tree on the south road leading out of Tatsienlu, the strong aroma of snuff that my grandmother so liberally used, or the fragile scent of a flower growing on the banks of the She Chu amazes me.

I remember the house where I was born. In the She Chu valley, scattered along rolling plains, between fields of barley, turnips and peas, were clusters of tall oak and walnut trees. Our mud-brick home, with its two floors and flat roof, from which many prayer flags fluttered in the wind, was built within one of these gatherings of big trees facing the lucky south.

A mud wall, some twenty hands high, the limit of power for our household gods, enclosed the farm and was broken only by a high wooden gate, also facing the south.

The house was partially hidden behind a small pear orchard just inside the gate, leaning toward the east. A wide, deep courtyard separated it from our house. The orchard was a gloomy place. The earthquake had uprooted some of the trees, forcing them to grow this way and that in a gnarled, tortured reach for the sun. Nevertheless, the trees somehow flourished, producing a fruit that was excellent enough to be sent to Chengtu, a good eighteen days' march over the mountains to the plains of China. This could be attributed to the special care the surviving trees received at my grandmother's hands.

A notched log in our stable led to a small, dimly lit hallway in which a butter lamp burned. All the rooms on the second floor could be reached from this hallway. The kitchen, directly east of the hall, was the biggest and warmest room and the place of family activity.

Near one wall, a large clay fireplace protruded from the wooden floor. Yak chips and evergreen shrubs were burned for cooking and heating.

Yak chips burned long and blue, filling the room with a dark greasy smoke that gave the walls the appearance of having been coated with black paint. Like any Tibetan, I became instinctively accustomed to this heavy smoke.

A hole in the ceiling, large enough for a healthy fat fox to pass through, allowed some light to enter the room and some smoke to escape. A large boulder covered the hole during the rainy season and throughout winter's heavy snows.

A small prayer wheel was attached near the opening and turned to the action of the rising smoke. Many nights, I fell asleep to the low groaning song it played as it turned its invocations toward the gods.

I was born with this skin, near the village of Hor Drango, the Horpa state of Chango, in the eastern province of Khams, on the ninth day of the fourth month in the Year of the Earth Tiger (1878). (Today it is called Romi Changku and it is in the Szechwan region of China.) I was the second son born to the woman, Drolmo Dorje, and the Bon priest, the Lama Gezong.

It was hoped that I would continue a long line of sons. There were three children before me. A brother died in the earthquake, and a sister died of smallpox (along with my grandfather) in that terrible year when the dreaded disease ravaged Khams. This was before I was born, but the tragedies of that time were well known to me.

Another brother left for the small Bon monastery in Bawang, some three weeks to the north, when I was six years old. We were not to see him ever again, as this monastery was located in an unlucky spot in the path of the Moslem-Chinese conflict. In the Year of the Fire Dog (1886) the monastery was sacked and burned consecutively by both warring parties.

Some days after I was born, my father placed me under the protection of our family deity, Tamlin, the red tiger. A small wooden amulet, encrusted with coral and turquoise and containing a tiny painting (made by a lama in the Bati Monastery) of the red tiger was placed around my neck.

Of my physical appearance, my ears were most conspicuous, being small and round. Although I was named Yungdrung by my father, the family priest, I was called Small Ears by all who knew me.

Though my ears were small, my hearing was not in the least impaired. I could hear the storm fiends gathering in winter; the green parrots fresh from India, chattering by the banks of the river in summer; and when the marmot sat on two paws in front of his mound issuing his weird screeching, I could hear him. I could even hear the incredible stillness that one encounters on the upland slopes, where yaks and sheep graze, and only occasional barking of the dogs shatters the silence. Such were my small ears.

When I no longer suckled my mother's breast, I was given a small wooden bowl for drinking tea. I consumed great quantities of tea daily. I kept it, along with a small goatskin bag of barley, in the ample folds of my sheepskin garment.

When I was older, the sheepskin was replaced by a brown robe made of thick, sturdy yak's wool, which was tied at the waist with a woolen ribbon that served as a belt. From this belt, I was able to hang a dagger, a flint box and a small box for religious relics. The sleeves were long, falling below my fingers. It was designed this way to keep my hands warm. The entire robe seemed too big for me, but of course it was not. Though I might have given the impression of being a walking tent, I was able to fit, within the copious folds of the robe, an entire shank of sheep. On warm days I would fold back the robe and be naked to the waist. Sometimes, I only exposed my right shoulder.

I wore a pair of high yakskin boots tied with bright woolen bands almost to the knee. When the sole was worn, I was taught how to sew on a fresh leather sole. The boots had no heels to catch the snow.

I wore the Khampa hat, which is made of many colors of wool with a fox fur lining.

My attire was not to change a great deal during my life.

I have never owned, or needed, much more than what I had. One must think of one's body as a garment which can be put on or taken off. Only then is there advancement toward enlightenment. Garments, like bodies, are transient, impermanent and subject to decay.

In my early days in Hor Drango, I learned simple but important responsibilities. I blew the fire with the goatskin bellows. I collected yak chips and shrubs for fuel. I stirred the food and sometimes went for water from the little stream—a small finger of the turbulent She Chu (in Chinese, Tachin Ho)—that flowed back to the river just beyond our home.

I felt out of place in Hor Drango. This feeling defied description. In essence, I felt that I belonged to another place away from the quarrels of men and in a landscape beyond Hor Drango.

Where this was, I could not say. Though the memory of a previous existence had been carefully etched on my mind, dust covered my eyes and I could not make out a series of images and phantoms that crossed my dreams.

Even after I had acquired the power of speech, a time when the memory of previous lives should be fading, mine remained, dimly lit in my mind like a smoldering yak-dung fire waiting for the goatskin bellows to bring it to life.

As I grew older, my feelings of belonging to another place increased. I had vague dreams of a place where the grass was thick and black as it rolled its way up into the mountains. These images were often broken by bright white flashes waking me wide-eyed.

Where this place was, or why I repeatedly kept seeing it in my visions, I could not say. Nor could anyone else offer any reasonable explanation.

When I told my mother, she attributed these dreams to a lack of fats in the food I was eating. She started to feed me more of the yak cheese that hung from long strips of yak leather strung around our home. This supplemented the parched barley, tsamba, which was our staple.

My father, who, after all, was a Bon lama, or priest, agreed.

"Your liver is rising," he said. "It must be pressed down with more fats. That will stop the dreams."

But I could see, even in the way he explained the dreams,

7

that he himself was not convinced that this was the answer.

Only Grandmother Dorje did not offer any explanation, although she would think on the matter for some time. And even after more fats were added to my *tsamba* and the dreams persisted, Grandmother remained silent.

Big Father and Little Father

My father's path was not always directed toward enlightenment. He became a lama by divine intervention. The story of how this happened would be too lengthy a digression to relate in its entirety here, and may be discussed in its time.

For now, we may think of him as a lama with a muleman's history.

Indeed, his longing for the old life never quite left him. He missed the ancient camaraderie of men and mules that one finds traveling the great tea roads around Hor Drango.

His longing for this caravan life became apparent when any caravan, large or small, passed below, winding its way through the mountains. From our cool pasture, Big Father and I watched until the last man, the last mule or yak disappeared into the next valley.

We saw many caravans, since our home was not far from the ancient north road. This is one of the two great roads connecting Lhasa, three months away, with Tatsienlu.

The great official road to the south is perhaps shorter, but the mountains are higher, and the hazards of travel more prevalent. So it was the north road, referred to as the Merchants' Road, that most travelers used. This ancient

Chinese road begins in Tatsienlu, passes Hor Drango going north and then heads west at Jyekundo down across the plateau.

Mongols from the Koko Nor region, as well as Tibetans and Chinese from the area, use this road. Yaks, men, mules, all things that move can be seen on the road.

Sometimes a caravan had a thousand yaks and mules. Mules marched along in single file while yaks thundered along in an unruly mass. As they rumbled by, they covered the red earth in a brown and gray mass. Brigands, including the Goloks, seldom attempted adventures with caravans like these; they were well armed and even occasionally included numbers of Chinese soldiers. Some carried loads of tea headed for inner Tibet. Others going east or north carried musk, deerhorns and rhubarb, all of which were in great demand in China.

Sometimes, lower in the valley, late in the afternoon, the sun brought deep contrast, and one could easily recognize the figures below. I sat with Big Father on some of these days.

"There goes so-and-so," he'd sigh. "You see how he walks favoring one leg. I was there when he fell with two of his mules into an icy ravine. Unfortunately, one of the unfortunate beasts fell on his unfortunate leg. . . . And there is another old mate, I am glad to see that he is alive. I heard that he was killed in a Golok raid. . . . And listen, you can hear so-and-so calling his mules. He has the loudest voice in Tibet. His roar is even more ferocious than the strongest of our dogs, but he actually is a very gentle man. . . ."

As I listened to him, I watched his dark eyes brighten around his long straight nose.

I, too, watched the roads and caravans. Like my father, I

9

felt a great deal awaited me on those traveled and untraveled roads.

I also looked forward to the return of my father's brother, Sangsang. He was a muleteer and always had tales of what adventures he encountered here and there in his travels.

Sangsang was called Little Father, for as custom demanded, he, too, was married to my mother. He was a happy fellow. Even under the grime of the road, one could see his soft, gentle eyes, his long, narrow face ready to break into a smile.

He was younger than Big Father by four years. His nose was somewhat flat compared to Big Father's and this, in a long Khampa face, made him appear even more the joker.

He always had something for the entire family when he returned from a caravan. Delicious Hami dates from Chinese Turkestan; coral and stones from the upper Yangtze valley; expensive, delicate dried apricots from Kansu province.

The cost of these gifts was apparently never considered, as Sangsang did not put much value in things.

Perhaps the only possession he treasured was a large coral earring, encrusted in silver, which hung from his left ear, as it is worn in Horpa country. Sometimes when he excitedly related some adventure of the road, he gently tugged at this earring to make a point. Sometimes he tugged at the earring as if to make sure it was still there.

At twenty-nine years he still had all his teeth, while Big Father had lost many; there were those who believed that he had made a deal with some demon to keep them. But I think not.

Perhaps he drank more *chang,* the strong barley beer, than his companions. When he did, which was often, he became aggressive and unpleasant. More than once he found himself groggily awakening in some bramble or mud puddle.

Each time it happened, it was the same. At first, he'd try to move but he had no control over his body. Although he was not a religious man, he knew that to sleep under the sun is to invite the demons who would bring with them fever and death. Eventually, as the sun began to flash across his face, he would get up with a mighty effort.

If his sheepskin muleteer's robe caught thorns, he'd pull them out. Even those attached to his skin did not bother him. Perhaps it was because between his skin and the pick of the thorn there was a thick layer of mud and grime; the accumulation of many trips across the high plateau and the lofty mountains. But he did not smell unpleasant. Living the outdoor life in the keen air, his body was constantly aired from head to toe.

He'd march away determined to find who it was that put him in such an uncomfortable situation the night before. At first resolved to his revenge, upon walking a little he would soon forget and begin laughing.

Unlike Big Father, he was never swayed by religion. He was religious only in the sense that his view of life was rigidly optimistic. He was a muleteer through and through; a poor man who had seen the suffering of existence but refused to acknowledge it. Such people are rare in this country and risk being branded as heretics. Still, for Sangsang, this attitude served him well. Perhaps this is what I admired in him. An easy laugh, happy, narrow eyes and a warm smile got him through many times that would stop a lesser man.

He had many opinions and he instilled in me a sense of pride in our Khampa background. As for the Khampa disposition, much has been said and much of that untrue. We

11

have been accused, for example, of being quick-tempered and rude.

Little Father had his ideas on the subject.

"Such accusations invariably originate from Lhasa," he said. "Only a Khampa would become a muleteer, they sneer. Mules serve men faithfully, but in Lhasa, they are not thought much of. The responsibility of caring for these animals has fallen on the Khampa. So if the Khampa is quick-tempered and rude, it is because of his dealings with a quick-tempered, rude beast."

Not to leave the mules without a spokesman, however, he had a strong statement to make in their defense as well.

"I offer no apologies for mules," he said. "Quite the contrary. I know them to be the most steady of animals. On caravans, they carry more than their share, asking little but an occasional bit of grazing, a drink of water and sometimes not even that. In spite of this, the mules and the Khampas who drive them have gained a reputation of being easily angered and arrogant. But this is Lhasa talk."

He had been to Lhasa a number of times. In fact, in his time he had been from one end of Tibet to the other; had made contact with the various races both in and out of Tibet and had known many women.

His travels enabled him to become acquainted with many languages. His Mongolian was so flawless that some believed he had been either a camel or a Mongol in a recent previous life. Sangsang spoke Turki and a little Hindi in addition to both the Khampa and Lhasa dialect. He could understand but could not speak Nepali and his Chinese was only passable. For this lack, he offered an excuse.

"Let the Chinese learn Tibetan." At this, Grandmother would nod her head in agreement.

12

My mother had a room of her own, which she only used when she slept with either of my fathers. As I have pointed out, my mother had two husbands.

Big Father and Little Father were very seldom home at the same time, so there was never any conflict about their both being married to my mother. In the event both men were there, a scarf or boot was tied to the door handle of my mother's room. This was a sign to whoever was outside the door that his brother was inside. It was observed by both brothers and I cannot remember anything but gentle words passing between them.

"Brothers," my father told me, "should not deny each other anything."

Uncle Sangsang preferred *chang* and arak almost more than anything, and so was a steady patron at the Chinese inn in Hor Drango. Sometimes I was sent to the village to stir him out of the inn and help him to his pony.

This was a greater responsibility than caring for the animals. Sangsang, oblivious to the dangers around him and not very cautious anyway, swayed in his saddle like a fresh-cut tree. The ride home was always a thrilling journey but one I did not look forward to. Particularly when we reached the bridge, where he would threaten not to pay his toll to the old man who claimed to subdue the *nags*, the underwater serpent-demons. He was a humorless old man who took his work seriously.

"My brother is a Bon lama," Sangsang would tell him. "A very important priest. Would he pay?"

I assured Sangsang that he would (as indeed he did) and so finally he offered something, but usually much more than he could afford. Such are the extremes of drinking *chang*.

A Strange Visit

My adventure began in the Earth Dog year. Big Father, a Bon lama, was away beating the drum in front of the tent of a recently deceased rich nomad. Sangsang was on the road.

The grass in the uplands was thick and lush, and while the days were not long, they were clear, bright and deep blue.

In the valley, nettles flourished from heaps of sheep dung. Yellow butterflies, as bright as the sun, jumped from heap to heap, feeding on the nettles. It was the time of year when the people, too, gathered nettles; a season that I always looked forward to. Some claim nettles to be poor people's food. This may be so, and that is not to say that there is not some virtue in the food of poor people. But I do not know of many, rich or poor, who would turn away from a bowl of nettles mixed in a soup with a little yak beef and butter.

We were more fortunate than others that year. The inevitable mudslides damaged only part of our barley crop. Our hearty turnips were spared altogether, which further proved the old adage that "even in the worst of times, one can always depend on the nourishment of turnips."

So it was more out of custom than necessity that my mother and I went to the fields surrounding our house.

I remember my mother; a jangle of precious metals, stones and jewelry. Each arm was heavy with bracelets of gold and silver and each ear was weighed down with large silver earrings. Around her neck she wore a rosary and an amulet which contained a strip of material on which the sacred Bon prayer had been written.

14

One could always hear her approach as the jewelry rattled and rang with her determined steps.

Her soft voice was a contrast to this loud music. She was always asked to sing at the festivals or any time a number of us gathered around the evening fire.

Mother's strong intelligent face was broad and red and surrounded her deep black eyes.

Can there be shades of black?

In the coldest months, when the bitter tooth of the god of the north was most severe, she rubbed yak butter on her face. This grease naturally attracted the soot from our fire as well as other floating particles. Still, through this mask of sorts, her deep black eyes shined brilliantly. Such was the blackness of her eyes.

Her long hair was worn in traditional Horpa fashion: two long plaits going down her back and gathered by a number of silver discs.

Now she carried a large iron hoop, which she swung back and forth over her head, felling the nettles before her.

I followed her with a basket to pick up the cut nettles. I heard the hoop pick up the wind. I watched the nettles fly up, just as the pheasant does at the footsteps of a stranger. Then, gently, they tumbled down, waiting to find their place in the straw basket. The smell of fresh green nettles was strong and sharp. It was a refreshing smell. I was able, at least for a while, to forget the confusing dreams that continued to fill my nights.

Mother and I worked together, exchanging verses of an old song that Grandmother had taught us. Both of us were so carried away by our own rhythm that we hardly noticed a very old woman coming toward us.

The old woman approached, slightly bent and extending her tongue in greeting, revealing a toothless smile. She leaned on her birch cane.

"I am on my way to Mount Omei," she said. "Perhaps my last pilgrimage."

"But Mount Omei is not this way," my mother told her. "It falls well into China."

"I am aware of that," said the old woman, as she used her cane to help her sit down on the soft earth near a heap of sheep dung.

She wore a rough, dingy, ragged gray robe tied at the waist with a piece of bright red material. The robe was lifted a bit in the front, revealing a pair of unusually fine boots of red and green with blue silk threads woven into the band. Bright red cloth came almost up to the knee. The boots suggested a rich noblewoman rather than an old beggar. Her hair was bright gray, almost the color of the single silver bracelet she wore on her right arm. Even the poorest of women have one silver or gold ornament which they always proudly display. A large wooden amulet hung around her neck. I could not make out what relic or statuette of a god (or goddess) it enclosed.

Because of these boots and some of her jewelry, she appeared not to be a woman without means. Yet, she did not strike one as being anything other than a beggar.

"No doubt, I am lost," she said to me. "This is Hor Drango?"

"The village lies along the great tea road," I told her.

She cocked her head a bit and squinted her old narrow eyes.

"Is poverty recent to your family?" she asked.

My mother put down the hoop and stopped her work.

"We do not scorn poverty," she said, "though we are

16

fortunate and not as poor as you would think. And we do not scorn the taste of nettles either."

"And you should not." The old woman raised a bony finger. "Did not the blessed poet Milarepa survive his hermitage on such nourishment?"

"Are you a nun?" I asked.

"I am a Tibetan. I have been everything. It makes no difference . . . Small Ears. It is Small Ears, isn't it?"

"It is," I answered.

She pulled off one of her boots. Although it was scuffed and soiled by what seemed to be much travel, one could see its fine quality. She rubbed the boot against her side and stretched her toes. Then she took off the other one. Satisfied that she had given her toes time to breathe, she proceeded to put her boots back on. She spoke as she did this.

"Yes, I have been everything. I have been to Lhasa, I have seen that place and I was a nun at one time as well. I do not remember which sect . . . would it interest you to know? Perhaps I can remember. I am hungry. Perhaps that is why I can't remember."

Then she stared off, appearing to be neither here nor there.

"You are welcome to share what we have." My mother broke her thoughts. "My husband is a Bon lama. He has gone north by way of the valleys to officiate with other lamas at the rites of a rich nomad. My mother has just returned from Tatsienlu and I'm sure would welcome the company of one of her own age. You may sit with us if you wish. And our flat roof is at your disposal, should you want to stay the night away from wild dogs. But I will say again, you are not going in the direction of Mount Omei."

"Yes, yes," the old woman said impatiently. "I am aware of

17

that. But I was told to come here. Yes, this is the right way."

My mother saw that the woman was becoming less coherent.

"As you wish. But we must continue our work," my mother said as she lifted the iron hoop.

"Yes, of course." The old woman smiled as she helped herself up with the aid of her cane. Then suddenly she turned toward me. Her tiny eyes widened, stretching her wrinkled face. "You know, I was told to come here."

Her eyes searched me up and down.

"This is Hor Drango, is it not?" she asked me again.

"It is," I answered again. "The two rivers junction just beyond."

"Yes," she mumbled to herself as she reached into her cloak and took out what at first appeared to be the skin of a small red bear. "Yes, this is where I was to come."

With the skin draped across both of her arms, she presented it to me the way one would offer a *kata*, the ceremonial scarf.

I watched my hands move toward the skin as if part of a dream. My arms were not attached to my body. They had a life of their own, reacting before my mind could.

I heard my mother's voice. "The skin of a bear," she said.

Then I seemed to hear a voice that spoke from another universe.

"Why do you wait?" the voice said. "The skin is yours. It was meant for you. Take it."

Only then did I realize that it was the old woman talking.

"Ah, now you have it," she said as I felt the skin fall into my hands. "And you know what it is, as well."

I couldn't answer. My tongue was buried in my throat.

"You know what it is," the old woman continued. "You know that it is not the skin of a bear. Why would I, an old pilgrim on the way to Mount Omei, carry a bearskin all the way across Tibet? You know what kind of skin it is."

I stood motionless. The skin was before me in my arms. I was unable to speak.

"Bearskin, indeed." The old woman laughed. "Bears were once humans who through their evil deeds have lost the power of speech. But that is not the case here. It is the skin of a *migou*," the old woman continued. "His very skin. The dreaded *migou* who wanders the inaccessible summits.

"See, look at it," she commanded. "Look at the skin of a *migou*. You see how the hair on the bottom goes up, while the hair on the top faces down? Do you know of any bears like that? No, of course you don't. And look at the red fur that yellows around the edges. There is no bear like that. It is a *migou*. You may take my word for it that I have given you the skin of a *migou* as I was told to do."

With that she grabbed the skin from me and placed it around my back as one would wrap a blanket. I felt myself becoming dizzy. My tongue felt deeper in my throat. I stumbled and barely caught my balance.

"When I was young," the old woman's tone became calm, "I was given the power to see. A magpie was robbing our barley on a daily basis. My father killed the bird. Now a magpie, at least in the region where I was born, is considered a wretched and unlucky bird. But its blood, when rubbed into the eyes, gives one the power to see what is not always apparent to others. And what I see, is that you must go to Chumbi. You must take the skin with you. I was told to come here and tell you this. And so I have. Now I must go. Perhaps

19

you can spare a handful of butter to see me on my way. It is merit. . . ."

I stared at the old woman, my head full of questions.

She sighed impatiently. "Perhaps a handful of barley?" she added, ignoring me.

"A pilgrim on pilgrimage can always depend on the generosity of the people in this region," my mother told her as she handed the old woman a handful of barley that she took from the bag she carried.

The old woman grabbed the barley as if she thought that my mother would change her mind. She put some of it into a bag she carried inside her cloak. Some she kept in her hand.

"I shall be on my way. I am going to Mount Omei. A pilgrimage. Am I going the right way?"

"You are not," my mother said, apparently having given up trying to find out anything from the old woman. "Mount Omei lies in China and it is well to the south."

"The south?" The old woman frowned. "But the dreaded lord of death, Yamantaka, resides in the south. Has it come to that? I think I shall look for a longer route."

Then she looked up from her cane and fixed her eyes on my mother. She had a wandering, disinterested look. She tossed a handful of barley into her mouth and chomped it quickly. Then she turned to me. "I can tell you this." She smiled gently. "You must go to Chumbi."

Then she turned and, hitting the bottom of her left boot as one would start a horse, she gracefully (if hobbling can be considered graceful) hobbled across the pasture, in the direction of the north.

As the old woman moved away from us, she suddenly broke out into song. Singing as loudly as a soldier in any Chinese

barracks, she slowly disappeared from our view. I remember
her song.

> I have a pair of fancy boots,
> As any eye can see.
> So anyone who wants these boots,
> Will have to take on me.

And then she was gone.

I held the edges of the skin tightly in my hands as I
wrapped it around my body. Somehow, the skin felt like a
part of me, as if I were meant to have it. I realized then that I
had not moved.

I saw my mother looking at me. She wore a confused,
worried expression. I remember her telling me to put the skin
in my cloak.

The *Migou* Skin

Grandmother picked up the skin and weighed it in her hands.
She stroked it gently at first and then tugged it as she would
the rope of a tethered yak.

She smelled it from every angle. It had a faint and
somehow familiar odor.

I watched her eyes float over the red edges of the fur. It
intrigued her. She was thinking about something, but as usual
I would have to wait until she was ready to tell me what it
was.

She was a small, stocky woman built more like a nomad
than a Khampa. She had a broad firm mouth, but it was her

21

penetrating eyes which spoke. One could tell from one of her looks her thoughts on a matter. A sharp glance was all that was needed to make a point.

She was named Draya Dorje by a lama, and I called her Ana ("grandmother"); she was called Raven Eyes by all who knew her—like most such names, however, never to her face.

Her hair was thick and long and fell down her back in many plaits that were brought together by a large silver disc. She wore a pleated apron, striped red, green and black, over her woolen *chuba*. On festival days, however, a very old, colorful silk apron was proudly worn.

Although she was old and had only a few of her teeth, she was not yet ready to sit in front of some sacred place and pray all day, as many women of her years did.

She had many opinions. Of the Chinese, she said: "The Chinese recruits rode into Hor Drango on the backs of frogs."

She did not hide her dislike of the Chinese, and insulting the horse was her Khampa way of insulting the rider.

If she was critical of the Chinese, she was equally at odds with Lhasa. Once a friend returned from a pilgrimage to that sacred city. My grandmother asked, "I have heard the Lhasa women do not take snuff."

"I did not see any, and I feel that they wouldn't," her friend replied.

"I have heard also that they adopt Chinese customs," Grandmother went on, "that they eat with chopsticks."

"I saw some who did." Her friend smiled.

"I think I will stay here in Tibet." Grandmother frowned. "I will remain a crude country woman who enjoys snuff and eats with her fingers."

And now I waited for this "crude country woman" to tell me about the strange skin.

"It is not a bear," she finally said. "That it is the skin of a *migou*," she continued, "who can say. . . ."

"But it is," I interrupted her.

"This may be so," Grandmother smiled, "and you seem to have assured yourself that it is . . . no, don't interrupt. You see, it matters little where this skin has come from. I did not see your old woman on her way to Mount Omei, but I am not so eager to take her advice. I am not so quick to trust this old pilgrim who came and went like a phantom and who talked in riddles. It is not unlike a demon to take human form to achieve evil. An old pilgrim comes to our home and gives you a skin. She instructs you to leave your home and travel somewhere to the other end of Tibet, and on the basis of this, you would leave everything and follow her instructions? No, I think it is better to wait for the arrival of your father, who is our lama. He, perhaps, may be able to throw some more light on the matter."

"Of course, we shall wait," Mother said. "This was never in question. But I too saw this old woman. I could not help but feel that what she said about the skin was true."

"I have no doubt that it is." Grandmother smiled. "But one person's truth may not be another's. In matters such as these one must proceed with caution."

"It is a *migou* skin," I repeated, not wanting to hear anything but what I wanted to believe.

"You are right." She threw me a quick glance with her raven eyes. "It is the skin of a *migou*. But my question is, why was it brought here? Why were *you* chosen to make a long journey? I will ask some questions first."

With that she handed me the skin. I folded it up neatly and placed it near me. I looked at Grandmother. She was sitting quietly, watching the fading fire.

the fire needs some more chips." Grandmother spoke to
without taking her eyes from the flame. I got up and threw
a few more chips into the fire. I watched the burst of blue
flame.

Somehow the events of the day seemed to burn in that
flame; a quick burst of fire that slowly faded away. I was
impatient for the return of Big Father. I was eager to begin my
journey. Like the fire, the events of the afternoon had been
cut out of time, and given a short life of their own. I had been
given my allotted time to nourish the flame, knowing it, too,
would go out.

I would have to make the best of the time that I had.

A Dream

A radiant light flashed across my face, penetrating my tightly
shut eyes. My eyes remained closed. I did not seem to have
the power to open them. Thin strands of rope had sewn them
shut, and although it would take little effort to break this
rope—only forcing my eyelids to open—I did not have that
power. I felt that even if I did, I would not, for to open my
eyes would risk the destruction of my vision. We are not
permitted, those of us whose karma has brought us to this
sphere, to witness the intricacies of cosmic events. And I
could not help but feel that on the other side of my tightly
shut lids, the side that looks out at the universe, something
was taking place.

It was on a beam of light that our precious Lord Shenrab
used to cross from the heavens into the body of a mortal

woman. Shenrab came to bring enlightenment to the struggling sentient beings who go through their allotted time on the wheel subject to suffering, blinded by ignorance.

Suddenly, a vision of a *dakini*—a skygoer, a female deity, very active and mischievous—wielding two swords in all her cosmic anger, crossed across the one eye that remained open—the mind's eye. And even here, I had to turn away. The *dakini* was terrifying as she came at me waving the sword. I felt my eyes burn and sting. The thin rope had been cut. I heard a voice saying, "I shall conquer ignorance." Whose voice was it? Was it mine?

My eyes opened. I was looking at a bright blue sky. Billowing clouds floated by. The sun was somewhere in this sky, but I was unable to see it. The brightness of this sky was radiated from the other side. It was a brightness the likes of which I had never seen.

"I know that I am dreaming," I said to myself. "This is surely a dream." I knew this, but it did not change the reality of the moment. I was overwhelmed with awe.

A cloud floated by and was quickly burned away by the blue-white brightness of the sky. It was not the sun. I knew the light came from somewhere else. And then, as the clouds seemed to gather above me into the center of the sky, I saw a tiny crack in the sky. The sky door was opening slowly. My protective diety, Tamlin, who is manifested in the form of a red tiger, was responsible for this. Even without the sweet fragrance of the morning offerings of juniper branches, the sky door was slowly being opened. I could not see beyond, but I knew that Tamlin was making it possible.

I heard a voice: "The King Srön Tsan Gampo, in a fight with the demon Pe-har, accidentally cut the rope that is attached to the top of his head and by which, when the time comes, the gods use to pull the spirit of man up to their heavens."

Yet another voice: "And so now man is confined to this sphere and condemned to tumble through the wheel of life."

Suddenly I felt myself being lifted up. I was floating like a cloud under the tiny hole in the sky door. A rope dangled in front of me, just out of reach. I jumped and twisted and attempted to grasp it, but it remained out of reach.

"Who are you, that you dare to attempt what kings and holy men have barely been able to do?" Another voice spoke to me. "What cosmic arrogance. To what ends has your ego brought you?"

"Am I destined to struggle for a rope that will remain always out of reach?" I asked.

"Who are you?" a voice answered my question with a question. "Who are you?"

"Indeed," I asked, "who am I?"

I awoke.

I heard the slow, monotonous groan of the prayer wheel send out its invocation to the gods. Bright moonlight fell into the darkened room, illuminating one part of the *k'ang*, the combination bed and stove. But there was another luminescence in the room. It came from right beside me, near my head. The *migou* skin seemed to be lit with a radiance of its own, a pulsating bright radiance that burned across its yellow edges to the red center of the skin.

"Who am I?" I heard myself ask.

There was no answer this time. Only the silence of night.

Then this, too, was shattered by the incessant barking of our dogs.

The Return of Big Father

It was in that blackest time just before the morning when the dogs erupted with loud and persistent barking. My heart jumped to my throat. It could be that Big Father had returned. It could also mean that there were bandits.

I jumped down the notched log to the stable, stepping on the neck of one of the sheep in my descent. This brought the most mournful cry to mingle with the fading sounds of night.

It also brought Grandmother to the top of the notched log. Sure that bandits were in our midst and taking every precaution to defend herself, she looked down into the stable, waving one of her heavy copper pots over her head with one hand, while the other struggled to lift the ladder.

"There will be no easy plunder here," she cried.

"It is I," I called out. I ran to the gently sloping walls of the stable. "Something is happening outside."

Still carrying the heavy pot in her hand, she descended the ladder and came to my side. The sheep scattered as she approached. We both peeked through the tiny peepholes in the wall.

"What is that?" Grandmother asked herself as we watched Mother unbolt the front gate that led to the compound.

As the door flung open, the horse, a large brown-and-white pony, took a few steps forward, stopped, pulled back and then repeated this slow march again. There was no mistaking the horse. Her name was Jarlo, the horse Big Father had purchased some years ago at the annual fair on Mount Tao Shan.

I could not understand why she moved in such an awkward manner. I thought she might be lame, but I soon realized that her rider was responsible for these mincing steps. Every few steps, he pulled back the reins. I was familiar with this style of riding. Little Father Sangsang had all but perfected it, when he returned from an evening's activity at the Chinese inn. The purpose of such unorthodox riding was simply to stay in the saddle.

As the sun climbed steadily behind the horse and rider, following them toward us, the first rays of light flooded the compound and I was able to get a better look.

I saw a long Khampa face, an extended chin and the long scarlet robes of a Bon priest. The rider wore no hat. Was it Big Father?

The rider rocked back and forth in the saddle and seemed to be fighting two battles within himself: to stay on his horse (which he was doing) and to keep his eyes open (which he was not doing). As the sun washed across his face, his eyes popped open with a wide, vacant stare.

Neither horse nor rider took the least bit of notice of the insistently barking dogs that ran and jumped about them. This was not threatening; they barked having recognized Big Father.

Mother pulled them away, half scolding them for greeting their master in such a ferocious way, at the same time praising them for keeping a good watch on our farm. Then she ran up behind the horse and rider and I could see an astonished look on her face.

She had recognized the horse and rider from afar, but now that they were close I could see that she, too, was puzzled by my father's strange behavior.

By this time, Grandmother had put down her copper pot

and I had opened the stable door. In that slow, halting manner, the horse approached the threshold, then stopped. Big Father ungracefully slid out of the saddle, catching one foot in the stirrup and almost bringing the horse on top of him. I ran over, attempting to help, but he waved his hand to keep me away. Finally collapsing on the hard ground, he laughed long and loud, looking at the end of his boots as a sitting baby looks at his toes.

Without a word, he struggled to get up. Again Grandmother and I tried to come to his aid and again he waved us away. Now standing on uneasy ground, he gently patted the horse's flank and handed me the reins.

If there were any doubt before, the smell of strong *chang* confirmed what all of us had already suspected. There was no denying that Big Father was totally and completely drunk.

I led the horse away from the stable door, immediately removed the saddle and watched Big Father stumble into the house.

I felt the animal's mane. She had not been ridden very hard, but she was an animal who was nourished by speed, one who loved to stretch her long legs. I could tell that the ride home had been something of an ordeal.

She pulled away from me, anxious to run around the compound, but I gripped the reins tightly as I led her to the back of the house, where the little stream rolled by. I watched her nose quiver as she picked up the scent of fresh water. We reached the water and she turned toward me. Are we truly home, she seemed to be asking. For some reason, I remembered the time she nearly bit off my fingers when I offered her some goat's meat. Then, plunging her face into the cold stream, she drank appreciatively.

I had questions. "Where have you been?" I asked out loud,

"and how is it that you return from the south with Big Father drunk?" She hardly took her head out of the water. When she had drunk her full, I led her back to the stable and carefully gave her a few handfuls of dried peas.

I took my responsibilities for the horses seriously; the relationship between a Khampa and a horse is a special one. Only when I was sure the animal was well settled in did I climb the notched log leading to the kitchen.

I found Big Father sitting near the last of the ashes from the previous night's fire. Mother and Grandmother sat on either side of him.

"The gods are victorious," he said, just before collapsing in a heap near the slowly dying fire.

Grandmother slapped her knee as she got up from her kneeling position. "This will not do," she said. "To sleep while there is daylight is a sure invitation for the demons of fever. We must not let him sleep. Besides, Small Ears has some questions."

"Shall I bring some water from the stream?" I asked.

Grandmother did not seem to hear me. She stood tapping her foot on the wooden floor. Her raven eyes flashed in the dim slow light of the weak fire.

"Shall I bring some water?" I asked again.

"For what?" She finally turned to me.

"It has always worked with Little Father," I answered. "It will wake him up."

Still thumping her foot, she hesitated for a moment. "No." Her foot stopped. "Not unless he is plunged into the stream will water be of any use. No, I have a better way. Come, help me remove his boots."

She struggled as we came to her side, and the three of us

30

ungently removed the first boot. As we did this Big Father roared like an awoken tiger, only to fall back snoring.

"I do not question his right to get drunk," Grandmother said as the first boot came off. Moving to the other foot, she lifted it as we tugged on the boot. "I do not even take issue with how drunk he is." Grandmother looked at Mother. The other boot came off. "But to sleep now is dangerous and he does not appear to be capable of appreciating this, so we must keep him awake. Besides, Small Ears has questions only a priest can answer.

"Now, Small Ears," she turned to me, "you must find some feathers."

"Feathers?" I asked, not understanding.

"Yes. Anywhere, in the stable, outside. We have chickens, so there must be feathers."

I looked at her, still not understanding.

"Go," her eyes commanded. "Bring me some feathers. And hurry."

When I returned with a handful of feathers, Grandmother was removing the dagger that Big Father carried in a sheath worn around his waist. Unmercifully, she applied the tip of the blade to the tip of Big Father's toes.

Big Father mumbled and sputtered as the blade dug into his feet. But Grandmother knew exactly what she was doing. The knife penetrated just barely enough to draw blood.

"Yes, family lama," she spoke to him like a child, "you are quite drunk." Then she took the handful of feathers and passed them over the toes she just stabbed. This brought muted giggles from Big Father.

"My husband once came to me like this," Grandmother

reminisced as she and Mother took turns with feather and knife on Big Father's toes.

Big Father alternated between groans and giggles, and there was no question but he was reviving.

"He has had enough." Mother looked sympathetically at Big Father, who was now holding his head as if to keep it on.

"Not yet," Grandmother insisted, applying the blade once more to the naked toes. This time she must have gone farther than before, because Big Father jumped up and, hopping on one foot, he grabbed the other with his hands.

"What is this torture you've devised for me, woman?" he called to Grandmother.

"Ah, what did I tell you." She smiled. "He is awake."

"Indeed I am," he grumbled. "But what has happened?" His arms didn't know where to go.

"My head! My feet!" he cried. "When did I get here?"

"You arrived this morning," I told him.

"This morning?" He looked puzzled. "But how? I don't remember."

"No small wonder, that," Mother chided him gently. "You were full of *chang.*"

"And Grandmother used the knife and feathers to make sure you do not sleep in the daytime," I explained. "It would bring demons."

"Of course," he said, limping about slightly. "I had to get home. This much I remember. Something has happened here, I know. I had to get home. But where was I? I cannot remember . . . my head."

"I will show you why you returned." Grandmother gestured to me to produce the *migou* skin. I handed her the skin and she tossed it at Big Father's feet.

"Migou," he blurted out, moving away from the skin.

"That is what the woman told us." Mother picked up the skin. *"Migou."*

Then each of us told him the story of the old woman and how she came and went. He listened carefully, but it was obvious that his head was still cloudy. Every now and then he rubbed his forehead or ran his hand over the patchy stubble under his chin.

As I finished my version of the tale, I could feel my fears catching up with me. The very telling brought out feelings in me that I had tried to submerge. It was not fright; one cannot avoid facing one's karma. It was more puzzlement, the demons of the unknown roaring through my mind like a quickly running stream.

"My first reaction," Big Father said at last, "is not to trust this old pilgrim."

"That is what I said," Grandmother interrupted.

"One must be wary of the counsel of strangers."

"I said that too," Grandmother interrupted again.

"This is as I have seen it," Big Father went on. "We have known for some time that a direction will pull you away from us. We didn't know where or when. We avoided it, thinking that things could go on exactly as they are. But the weight of one's karma is far stronger than one's will or even the love of one's parents. None of us can stop what has been already set in motion. The laws of karma are exacting. There are no accidents. No mistakes. You have been given the skin of a *migou*. Now you must travel until you find the *migou*. I know of no one who has ever been successful but nonetheless you must go."

Big Father looked at me. "You have reached the age of

33

fourteen. You have no choice but to follow this direction. You will be doing religion's work. This, too, I know. And who are we to interfere with religion's work?"

Grandmother sneezed as she applied snuff to each nostril. She knew that Big Father was right. Her eyes were watery. "The snuff." She attempted a smile. But we all knew that it was not the snuff that made her eyes moisten.

My Father, a Bon Lama

I learned a great deal from my father.

Above all, he taught me the ancient Zhang Zhung language of the Bon-po. When I was old enough to grasp objects in my hand, I was given my own *drilbu*, the tiny hand-bell used to drive away evil spirits. I was taught to turn a prayer wheel in the opposite direction from the way a Buddhist would turn it.

A memory leaps out: I see him through clouds of dust, the sweet thick smoke of incense; his hat is off, placed beside him like another dancer; his long hair falls this way and that as if taken by a wind fiend of its own. As he dances and chants to the quick music of his drum, perspiration lines his face.

Sometimes he danced for days around a corpse, making sure that the spirit had the proper instructions to reach the western paradise.

When praying, his voice rumbled, stretching each word into the next, forming a low, solemn chant. When he allowed himself to fall under a demon trance, he shrieked.

Other times his voice was deep, calm and clear, making it

difficult to believe that the same man was capable of producing such entirely different sounds.

As a lama of the Bon faith, he wore long scarlet robes and a long black conical hat topped by three peacock feathers. His small hand drum, made from two human skulls, was attached to a cloth belt around his waist.

A sacred dagger, used for destroying demons, adorned with three precious stones on the hilt, swung loosely from this belt as well.

In one hand, he carried the *dorje,* a small metal baton with a carved ball at each end, the symbol of the all-powerful thunderbolt.

In his other hand, Big Father carried the tiny *drilbu,* which he played constantly to drive away the evil spirits.

The most impressive article worn by Big Father was the yak-leather necklace on which two human tongues were strung. These were the tongues of the feared and dreaded *rolungs* (standing corpses): men who became mindless ghosts for one reason or another. A *rolung* can only march in one direction, and may be thwarted by tossing a boot at him. However, this will only change his direction, not his attitude. The touch of a *rolung* means certain and instant death. Only a lama who is as proficient as he is daring, and who is truly confident of his tantric skills, can stop a *rolung.* This is by no means easy to do. One must bite out the tongue of the unfortunate ghost so that the spirit is free to move to the next transmigration.

My father encountered *rolungs* on two occasions. The first was a nomad struck by lightning, the second a bandit who met a violent death.

These tongues were not only a source of considerable pride

and accomplishment, but were a warning to unfriendly lamas that Big Father's magic was strong and should not be taken lightly.

He was not of the class of lamas so prevalent in those days (and even today) who dance only to frighten people into giving gifts to their order.

Often he was asked to officiate at funerals. Having the power to receive spirits, he could plead for a merciful judgment from the king of hell. How much success he achieved in these rituals could not be known, since past lives are wiped from memory when one makes another turn on the oppressive wheel of life. The living, however, were satisfied that everything possible had been done for the departed.

His services as a magician were offered to anyone. He made no distinction in class, treating both rich and poor equally. For a brick of tea, a pair of boots, an Indian rupee, he would gladly beat the drum.

Like any Bon-po, he was very proficient in concocting poisons. However, this was done reluctantly and at great cost to the purchaser. Poisons, once made, have a life of their own and must be used. And as poisons were usually requested for political motives, my father hesitated. He was aware that a faction in power today can be a faction out of power tomorrow. Nothing is permanent. Poisons were risky, for they could easily be turned against their maker.

At one time, he had been a monk in the Bon *gompa* at Bati, on the banks of the Min River. Bati and its neighboring state, Bawang, are the last places on earth where orthodox Bon is still the state religion. He spent many months in Bati learning the rituals, chants and lore of the Bon faith.

Monastic life, however, did not suit my father. Fortunately, unlike the reformed sect, the Yellow Hats, he was not required to remain celibate. So he left the monastery, and married my mother. Soon he became a lama with a family; the father of a child with small ears.

Two Mulemen

Not totally recovered from his encounter with *chang*, Big Father sat behind the house on the banks of our little stream, quietly mumbling his prayers as his prayer beads fell between his fingers.

Grandmother occupied herself with polishing her new copper pot, while Mother and I worked in the barley field, removing some of the larger rocks that would obstruct the simple plow that passed over the terrain.

Everything seemed to be as it was, but it was not. My thoughts seemed caught in the atmosphere, as if trapped by invisible webs. Instead of stirring from my dreams, I found myself plunged even deeper into them. Compelled by habit, I went through the day's task.

But this was to change.

The following day, as I was returning from the fields—the sun was just beginning its descent from midsky, its warmth ebbing as it fell—I saw two riders coming toward our farm. From a distance, they made a striking pair. Each was physically an exact contrast to the other. One was tall, the other short; one fat, the other thin.

As their horses approached, the dogs barked. The riders were heading in our direction. I held the dogs back. As the riders neared, I saw the rough-and-tumble look, the confident swagger and the accumulated dust and grime of experienced caravan men.

The shorter one was unmistakingly Mongol. He was a sturdy fellow with narrow eyes and a broad flat nose that seemed to stretch from one end of his face to the other. His narrow eyes turned into thin slits when he laughed or smiled. I later found out that he laughed and smiled most of the time.

His companion gave the impression of being Khampa, but closer inspection revealed a full red beard of the sort seldom found on Khampa men. He had sullen, serious eyes that suggested dark intrigues had passed through his life. However, when he smiled broadly, any sinister aspect quickly faded into his shaggy red beard. A dingy white woolen cap on the top of his head testified that he was a Moslem.

Upon seeing them, I somehow found myself unable to move. Who can say how the gods signal us that something is about to happen? These men were riding into my life and would eventually take me out of Hor Drango. I was as sure of this as I was that the skin was *migou* and I would succeed where others failed before me to find the *migou*.

As they passed through the outer wall into the compound of our farm, I pulled the dogs back and attempted to calm them.

"Ho, small-eared child!" The short Mongol threw me a quick glance as he pulled his horse back. "Is this not the home of Gezong, the muleman turned Bon lama?"

Startled at his happy voice, I quickly recovered and, thinking of Big Father still reeling from the night before, I blurted out, "It is, but he is ill."

Laughing a long and deep laugh, the Mongol turned to his

friend and spoke in a language unknown to me. After hearing the shorter man, the taller laughed broadly. I noticed his long delicate fingers and wondered how they were able to do the difficult and dirty work that is required of caravan drivers.

The two men traded pokes at each other's ribs, increasing their mirth with each poke. Then the Mongol, still chuckling to himself and obviously not trying to suppress his laughter, dismounted, handing me his reins and riding crop.

"I would not be surprised," he smiled, "if the lama is not well." This brought fresh gales of laughter. "Take my riding crop, boy," he managed to get out between laughs. "It would be most ill-mannered to enter your home with a whip. And you may tell your father that Tiso Awa and Kareem Musa are here to inquire about his health."

The other rider dismounted and handed me the reins of his horse. Their horses, even had they been in good condition, were pitiful animals. Thin, low-backed and very old, they stood without moving; it seemed that any movement would be a great effort. Yet the way the men rode in, with dignity and self-assurance, suggested their horses were from a prince's stable. It was that muleman dignity that Big Father so often mentioned.

I was about to tie the reins to a post when Grandmother suddenly came rushing through the stable door. She had become suspicious of everything, and her cold greeting to these guests was not like her.

"What business do you have with the lama?" she asked with undisguised hostility as she stepped between me and the post. Grandmother flashed her raven eyes up and down the two men. Neither seemed disturbed or uneasy at her penetrating glance.

39

"Too many strange things have been happening here," she said. Then hesitating for a second, she grabbed the reins from me. She looked at the tall man again and tied the rope to the stake.

"Well . . . you are within the walls of our home and so deserve the protection of our household gods." Her tone changed. "Forgive me, for caution has gotten the better of my manners." Then turning to me, "Give the gentlemen's horses some water, and a little something to eat. Your father prays to the river *nags* by the stream behind the house. You may also tell him that his friends are here."

She gestured to the two guests to follow her. "To what purpose do you seek my son-in-law?" she continued in a friendly manner.

"None at all," the Mongol replied. "We were only concerned about his welfare. That he managed to return home safely last night is surely a blessing from the gods."

"Ah, so you know about that," she said as they walked through the stable door. "The fire is hot. Please forgive the initial fears of an old woman who has come to suspect the worst of things. Have you had a good trip?"

When I brought the horses to the stream, Big Father was mumbling his prayers in a low, droning voice, but he stopped when he saw me coming. "And whose wretched animals are these?" he asked, as he wrapped the beads around his wrist.

When I mentioned the name Tiso Awa, his face suddenly brightened.

"Tiso Awa?" he repeated the name. "And you say he is here?"

"With another muleman. A Moslem."

But Big Father wasn't listening. He was off toward the house, and I found myself having trouble keeping up with him.

"Old Tiso Awa. Flat Face," he mumbled to himself. "And he is here!"

Tiso Awa was an old and trusted comrade from Big Father's days as a caravan man. More than a little *chang* had passed between these two in those days—and quite a bit the night before.

When they saw each other, Big Father ran up to his friend and embraced him warmly, touching his forehead to his friend's in affection.

Strangely, the Mongol seemed a bit surprised at the warm reception, but I do not think anyone else detected this, certainly not Big Father. They seated themselves on yak-hair rugs around the *k'ang.* I walked around filling the cups with tea, as happy as my father to see these guests.

"But your friend has not said anything." Big Father looked at the Moslem, who was still smiling generously.

"His name is Kareem Musa." Tiso Awa extended a long arm as if to present his friend. The Moslem put his right hand to his heart and bowed graciously. "He is from Kotan in Turkestan. We've been together now for some time; perhaps even since you left the road."

Kareem turned to Big Father, smiling. "I must compliment you on your excellent Turki," he said in good Tibetan. "Last night your Turki was perfect."

Big Father looked confused. "Last night? How can that be, when I have just now seen you for the first time? Nor do I speak Turki."

"Ah, but you do," Tiso Awa insisted. "Or at least you did

last night, when you had drunk your *chang.* Do you not remember meeting us last night?"

Big Father's head fell onto his chest. "I would like to remember," he lamented, "but I cannot."

"I fear the new Gezong has forgotten the old one," Tiso mused. "The old Gezong was able to drink, remember and drive mules the next day. But you remember nothing."

"Nothing."

"Then," Tiso Awa said, puffing his sturdy chest up, "I will tell you what took place. You had ridden to the edge of the grasslands to say the rites for some rich nomad—or so you told us. However, the man's wealth was greatly exaggerated; you only received two fox skins for your services. One of these you traded for *chang* when we met you at a Chinese inn on the north road near Dawu. As to the other, I have no idea. But you did manage to drink like the old Gezong and broke into a perfectly civilized conversation with Kareem. And you rode south with us to another inn."

The Moslem smiled, looking up from his cup. He had something to add.

"Although I am not the most devout follower of the Prophet, given to drink among the other sins, I am still the son of Adam, and one who swears by Allah that all this happened." Once again the long fingers went to the Moslem's heart. "But when we woke in the morning, you were gone. We found you only because before you passed into the confusing world of *chang,* you told us of your new life here."

"Of course I drank a great deal." Big Father seemed to regain some memory.

"Like the old Gezong." Tiso Awa laughed. "What are old friends for, if not to share some drinks together, you kept

42

telling the innkeeper. And he was only too glad to keep pouring. And why not? You paid well."

"I remember that it was very important for me to come back here." Big Father scratched his head. "That much I remember."

"It was on my part that Big Father returned," I said. "I have been given the skin of a *migou.*"

"*Migou?*" The happy Mongol's eyes showed something other than mirth. Regaining himself, he leaned over to me, speaking in a low voice.

"You have such a skin in your possession? You do not fear it?"

"I don't know," I said. "I am to bring the skin to a place called Chumbi."

"'And you are alive as well," Tiso Awa continued. "Yes, we have come upon something here."

"That is not all," Grandmother volunteered, beginning to feel at ease with these men. "The skin offers the boy protection. Safety. It is worth a hundred charms. He must return the skin. He must find the *migou.*"

Kareem showed no fear at the mention of the skin. His expression remained serious. Finally he broke into a long speech, taking a breath between each thought.

"The place you seek, the Chumbi valley, is in the west."

Tiso Awa turned to Kareem and engaged him in a long conversation. Then both men nodded their heads in agreement.

Seeing my dismay, the Mongol turned to me. "We are not going to Chumbi ourselves," he seemed to apologize, "but we are going to Tatsienlu to meet the annual caravan from Shigatse to hire on as mulemen for the trip back. The trail

43

goes just north of Chumbi. Perhaps the boy can ride with us at least some of the distance."

This was too much to hope for. I was about to begin my journey. I looked at my mother, searching for her approval.

Her eyes were very sad, the blackness somewhat blurred. I was sure that she would discourage such a trip. Instead, she turned to Big Father.

"Does he have a choice?" Big Father asked and answered his own question.

"Well," said Tiso Awa, smiling at his friend and slapping his knees, "then it is settled. But now you must show us this unusual skin of a *migou*. I have never seen such a beast. Do I tempt the gods? Well. It's best to know what demons may await us on the road. Where is it? Show it to me."

I took the skin out of my *chuba* and laid it in front of Tiso Awa. He smiled nervously, looking at each one of us.

"So this is the skin of a *migou*," he said as I methodically opened the skin before him.

"Yes, that's what it seems to be." He began to laugh. "The skin of the dreaded *migou*."

His laugh became broader and we soon found ourselves laughing with him. Tiso Awa believed laughter bubbled under the surface of all of us, yet there was a strangeness in our laughter. I noticed Tiso Awa did not pick up the skin, but his companion did. Kareem looked the skin over carefully.

"No, it is not a bear," he said to himself, "nor is it the skin of any animal that I have ever seen. But a *migou* . . .?"

"It is without question," Big Father stepped in, "the skin of a *migou*."

"But how can you be sure?" Kareem asked. "Have you ever seen one of those creatures?"

"To see one with his skin on would certainly mean death," Big Father answered. "But I can assure you that this is the skin of one of those creatures."

"Perhaps," Kareem handed me back the skin, "but I suppose that I will never understand you Tibetans. Too many demons. Too many gods. Too complicated. If you were a follower of Allah, like myself, it would be much simpler. One prayer to one god. The true god. It's much simpler."

Big Father was always eager to get into a religious discussion and did not waste this opportunity.

"All that may be so." He smiled confidently. "But if the god you pray to is truly acting on your people's behalf, why is it that he allowed Moslem cities to be demolished, your women raped and your priests put to the sword? Why pray to such a god?"

"Ah, but there can be no discussion of all that," Kareem quickly came back. "The answer is very simple."

"And what is it?" Big Father asked.

"It was simply the will of Allah. One does not question the will of Allah."

And so the discussion came to an abrupt close because, according to Kareem, nothing was left to be said.

The Many Talents of Kareem Musa

Big Father took a reading of the stars and announced that two days hence would be the most auspicious time to begin my journey. The caravan from Shigatse, even if it had already arrived in Tatsienlu, would remain there for at least a month to conduct affairs. There was no particular hurry. And to begin a journey under a bad star is to offer too much temptation to the demons.

Besides, my prospective traveling companions did not have speed in their nature. They were accustomed to having the animals set the pace. Their own miserable horses could not take them out of Hor Drango, much less to Tatsienlu, without a few days of needed rest.

It was decided to keep my departure—and the reason for it—a secret. It would do no good to have the abbot of the Chango Monastery know of my plans. For any number of reasons he could have stopped me. For one thing, I had no identification papers, which are essential for a traveler between cities.

Kareem took care of this. Among his many talents, Kareem Musa was an excellent forger.

I was sitting near the pear orchard, contemplating what awaited me, when Kareem sat down beside me. He carried a small yakskin bag, which he proudly opened. He then spread the contents on the ground before me. I saw many seals and stamps of the Chinese magistrate in Sinkiang, official-looking documents signed by the ranking lamas of some of the bigger monasteries, beautifully written letters in Turki, even the seal of the king of Bhutan. All of these, of course, must have been forgeries.

Kareem gestured for me to choose one. "Which one would you choose?" I asked.

He shrugged his shoulders, and said something in his own language.

I closed my eyes and reached down, picking up a seal that lay close at hand. I handed it to Kareem.

His expression changed as he looked over my choice. He put the seal down and spat at his little finger. Apparently I had made a bad choice. *"Rus,"* he spit out, his hand going to his throat.

"I don't understand."

"Rus," he repeated, making a gesture of slitting his throat with his long fingers.

Then he reached down and picked up a seal. He looked at it and smiled. Taking a blank page of birch bark and a feathered pen from the bag, he began to write on the page. I watched his long fingers slowly move over the page, his eyes narrowing on his work. I wondered if being a caravan man was his first vocation.

After a while, he produced a very official-looking document written in Chinese. I do not know if he spoke that language; more than likely, he simply copied what looked official, with no idea what it meant.

He proudly held the paper up, smiling and well pleased with himself. I laughed at the blue ink which blended into his beard when he rubbed his hands over his face. Then he, too, laughed.

Later that night, when we were sitting around the fire, Kareem put the finishing touches on my papers.

"The papers are of no value without a seal." He smiled. "This is some of my best work."

Then he passed the paper around for all to see. When it reached Tiso Awa, he laughed broadly.

"You have nothing to fear," he said to me. "You will be traveling under the protection and goodwill of General Ka

47

Me Ting, who was the magistrate in Kashgar some five years ago."

Everyone laughed.

"Is this really his seal?" I couldn't help asking.

Tiso examined the paper again. "It is possible," he replied.

"But these are forgeries," my mother said.

"Some are, some aren't." Tiso picked up a handful of seals. "Some were stolen and some are copies, but there is not an official in Tibet who will recognize the difference. My friend is good at what he does. Do you see why I travel with him? The man is indispensable."

"And what about this one?" I searched for the first seal that I had chosen that afternoon.

Kareem made the same face as he had before.

"*Rus*," Tiso said calmly. "The seal of one of the czar's top ministers."

"Who is the czar?" I asked.

"The king of the Russians," Tiso explained. "Kareem hates the Russians. Such papers would be of no use in our country. His domain is over the mountains."

Kareem looked at me with the same bitter expression. I watched the word form in his mouth.

"*Rus*," he said, again making the gesture of slitting his throat. Then he bent down and began gathering up his collection. He was quick to observe that one of his treasures was missing.

It was the Russian seal and I was holding it, examining it, still intrigued that there were people such as Russians within our borders.

Kareem gestured for me to hand him the seal, which I did. He had become serious again.

Before I gave it to him, I noticed that one end had some red markings. Red is the color used by the clergy in Tibet. It could have been the red ink that Kareem used to do his work, but I don't think it was. It looked like blood.

I Prepare to Leave

I awoke with a start. Had I been dreaming?

I did hear the sounds of a single horse galloping off. But the dogs were not barking. I looked around. Everyone was sleeping. Perhaps I had been dreaming. I closed my eyes and allowed sleep to overtake me once again.

That morning the sky was gray; dark clouds hovered tenaciously around the mountain peaks. It would rain, but in the mountains it would snow. We would have to reach Tatsienlu before the passes were blocked.

I saw Grandmother in the compound, but as I was hidden behind the stable door, she did not see me. She walked slowly; her determined strong steps seemed heavy and old. When she realized that she was being watched, she attempted to change her pace. If the vitality had gone from her walk, it had not left her raven eyes. She threw me a quick sharp glance and spoke before I could.

"Soon you will be going to Tatsienlu," she said. "Even now, your father prays to the river *nags* for an auspicious day. Even now, he is reminding the *nags* of their agreement and obligation to protect us from disaster."

Grandmother looked up at the dismal sky and then at our flat roof. Mother was already there, preparing a bundle of juniper branches for the morning offerings to the local gods.

I could tell that there was something else on Grandmother's mind, but she would pick her own time to discuss it. I learned long ago not to press her, for she did everything in her own time. As she entered the house through the stable door, it began to rain. She did not seem anxious.

"I have been assured by your father that tomorrow will be an auspicious day to journey to the south."

I expected Grandmother to tell me what was on her mind after our morning prayers and tea. But she said nothing. I had to wait until the afternoon before I was to learn.

The rain came early in the morning and stopped almost as quickly as it started. It left the skies dark and gray with no sun to be seen.

I found Grandmother in the pear orchard sitting between two very old trees. One, partially uprooted, grew at a sharp angle away from the other, which was firmly upright. There was a space between these two trees where one could sit and imagine a dense forest on some distant mountain. It was a place I often visited. When I arrived, Grandmother was already waiting there. Looking at the fruits that were strewn about, some ripe, some not, she shook her head.

"The wind fiends," she said to herself and then to me. "The hearth god is behind this. He has not forgotten that a few days ago I allowed some snuff to blow near his domain. A sweet Kashmiri blend that he does not at all like. He has not forgotten. He has turned the wind fiends against us."

Picking up a green peach, she examined it carefully and then tossed it aside. She looked up at the darkening sky.

"Just a few days—if the gods do not send hail—the hearth god forgets an accidental slight, and the wind fiends will leave us alone."

Now she looked at me.

"Sit down," she commanded. "Across from me, where I can see you."

I did as she asked, and I waited for her to speak. She seemed to be searching for words. Finally, she pointed at me gently.

"If you eat any of these pears, you must make sure that the pits are given back into the earth spirits. See that you do not eat all the unripened fruits; it's not good for the tree."

It was apparent that this was not what she really wanted to talk to me about. I smiled and waited.

She was about to speak again but instead reached into her cloak for the snuff bag. Grandmother led a wholesome, religious life, allowing herself just one major indulgence: an overwhelming passion for snuff. She kept her supply of snuff in a stiff yakskin bag.

Rubbing the sides of the bag together and then carefully opening it, she placed small quantities on her finger. Then she applied it to each nostril. It was her own blend, and she was very proud of it.

Sometimes, very late at night or very early in the morning, I saw her poking through the ashes of the yak-dung fire. She mixed these ashes with her snuff; this, she claimed, was what made it so special. When she could afford it, however, she preferred to take her snuff undiluted. Unfortunately, she did not like the taste of snuff made from dry rhubarb leaves. Rhubarb was always plentiful, but she preferred the Szechwan variety, a small concession to the Chinese whom she disliked intensely.

She took a pinch of her own blend and inhaled strongly.

"You have not seen my cat, Chime, have you?" she asked, as her eyes became watery.

51

"I have. I saw him this morning. He was chasing a rabbit."

"He is just following his blood and has no time for an old woman like me. He knows you're leaving soon."

She took another pinch of snuff.

"Yes, Yungdrung," she looked at me seriously, "I am getting old. My body winds are in disarray; the hearth gods are turning the wind fiends against me. Yes, Yungdrung, it would be better for all if I leave now, with you. But this will not happen."

Grandmother enjoyed an adventure. She had made many treks through hazardous country, much of it inhabited by predatory nomads. Only the year before (the Year of the Earth Hare) she had visited a sister in Batang, a good month's march away. That same year she had accompanied Big Father on a pilgrimage to a Bon shrine which was near the edge of Khams province.

Her expression changed. A sharpness reappeared in her old raven eyes. She had exhausted all the small talk and now I would learn what was on her mind. Again, I waited for her to speak.

"When you were born," she began quietly, "it was your feet that first came out of your mother's womb. I stuck a pin in your little feet until you withdrew into the womb and came out in the correct manner. Perhaps the gods have a purpose for you, but I cannot say what it is."

Then she pulled me to her side and I fell into the folds of her aprons. Her long fingers reached into my black hair as if she were probing for lice, as she had done when I was younger. I could feel her heavy breath and smell the faint sweetness of snuff as her old rough hands searched and probed my hair. It was a warm and secure feeling.

"Who can say what purpose the gods have made for us," she comforted me. "One's karma is irrefutable. We are, all of us, powerless to interfere."

Nothing more of my impending journey was discussed that day. In fact, the day before I left my home is one memory I do not seem to be able to retrieve.

All I remember is waiting for night to come and morning to follow. I was frightened and wanted to stay home, but I couldn't fight the feeling that something, somewhere, was pulling me away from the place where I was born.

I had no concept of danger. My fear was the fear of separation. Soon, I would sever the binds that tied me to my family. I knew, as they did, there would be little chance of ever seeing each other again.

Big Father told me that I would be doing religion's work. From this one can easily gather the courage and determination to go on, he said.

This was true. Pilgrims crossed the rugged mountains, the windswept plains, the desolate valleys, to reach Lhasa, the holy city. Only with the force of religion could this be accomplished. Such pilgrims were not unusual, but they had made a choice. I had no choice.

I Leave Hor Drango

Morning came with a brilliant late-fall sun. The sky was deep blue and, except for a single white cloud that raced toward Toa Shan, the sacred mountain, like some lost intruder, the day was sparkling clear. It was an auspicious time to begin my adventure.

Under ordinary circumstances, my family and friends would have ridden out with me, even going so far as to take the first day's journey. There would be friends and people on the side of the road with gifts and good wishes and I would ride out of Hor Drango with some ceremony. Not this time. My family had already left to find a hidden spot where we would have our farewell celebration.

It was decided that my horse, Pempa, was too old to make the journey. Another horse had been chosen, a little brown mare with large floppy ears. Her belly was completely white, like the white bellies of the wild asses who live in small herds on the limitless upland plains. Though she in no other way resembled one of these cousins, she was given the name Kyang, which means wild ass. Perhaps there was some *kyang* in her blood after all. She was a spirited animal, who liked nothing better than galloping across an open plain.

Kareem Musa and Tiso Awa decided to keep their own horses. On appearance, the rest had done nothing to restore the vigor of these animals; they looked no better than they had the day they rambled onto our farm. But the Mongol insisted that they were never better.

The *migou* skin was neatly folded and placed in a yakskin bag, which I placed over Kyang's flanks. She pulled back as I tried to secure the bag in place. Whether this was caused by a desire to get started or some inborn fear of *migou*, I cannot say. Kareem came to my aid, speaking in gentle Turki to the animal, who seemed soothed by his voice.

Tiso Awa was already in the saddle, smiling impatiently as we came to his side. It was time to go.

We marched out past the pear orchard where my fantasies of *migou* were first born. I felt a cool chill crawl up and down my back. Now, I realized, there would be no games. I looked back once at the eerie orchard that had been so much a part of my life. A gentle wind ruffled the leaves.

"Ah, so it's you," I heard Grandmother's voice in my mind. "You are the one who stays in my orchard. And I thought it was demons. Well, you may help yourself to as much as you want, but you must be sure that the pits are put back into the ground."

Then the orchard disappeared behind us. Our horses moved past the heavy wooden gates. We approached a narrow path, barely wide enough for two riders. It was the only way to meet the great north road, which gleamed silver in the sun like a free-flowing mountain stream.

Smells were everywhere. Freshly burned juniper, sweet and gentle, mingled freely with the smell of recently harvested barley. We moved from one smell to another, guided as much by our noses as by our eyes.

After climbing a narrow incline, the road opened up, becoming much wider. Our nostrils were greeted by the smell of parched barley, *tsamba*.

Chenden Akung, a woman of immense size, hovered over an open fire near a tent that had been set up near the ruins of her farm. The Akung home was still buried in debris from the year's mudslides. Until the harvest was completed, there would be no attempts to build a new one. To build a home during the harvest would anger and confuse the gods, who on the one hand are asked to deliver rain for the crops, and on the other, are asked for sunshine to set the mud bricks. She looked like the beginnings of a large mountain as she quickly shook a large flat copper pot over the fire so as to parch, not burn, the barley. She had her back toward us and did not acknowledge us until her monster of a dog, Balu, sprang from seemingly out of nowhere, just missing Tiso Awa's foot with his heavy slaking jaws. Tiso Awa did not seem the least bit ruffled by this threat.

"I have seen dogs before." He laughed.

Then Balu, gathering all of his strength, released a roar that sounded like it came from one of the eight hells. Still unruffled, Tiso Awa moved his horse farther away from the angry dog.

"I have heard dogs bark before." He smiled.

I was not as courageous as my Mongol friend. The dog frightened me. I believed the animal was just warming up for an attempt at me.

Tiso Awa laughed, seeing the quick, jerking movements I made to avoid getting close to the dog. A nervous smile crossed my face as the dog tugged and strained on his leash.

"That is Balu," I told the Mongol. "He is the most ferocious of his kind, and certainly there are no animals in this valley who are considered more dangerous. I do not feel ashamed of being frightened."

The Mongol saw that I was serious and hesitated for a moment before speaking. No doubt, he thought he would have some fun with my fear, but he thought better of it. "I pray that your Balu will be the most dangerous encounter you meet on the road."

When we were well away from those clamping jaws, I turned and looked at Balu. "So, terrifying animal," I spoke softly, "who will you torment now? Who will be your new sport now that your neighbor Small Ears will not be here?"

By now, the big old woman had taken the rope in hand and brought the dog in. She squinted her eyes from the sun, trying to make out who the riders were. Even without the sun, the old woman's eyesight was very poor. Like Grandmother, she did not want any of her handicaps to be known.

"Ho, Sangsang," she called me, mistaking me for my uncle. "I was not aware that you had returned."

I bowed slightly in my saddle, content to let her mistake go. Then the old woman and her dog fell out of sight.

Just before reaching the north road, I had the sensation of being watched. It was not a totally uneasy feeling; the probing eyes, I felt, were not malicious.

I stopped my pony to look around. On the surrounding hills, livestock grazed peacefully. I saw nothing.

"Why are you stopping here?" The Mongol rode back to get me.

"I thought I saw a friend."

Tiso Awa looked around. Seeing nothing but grazing animals he shrugged his shoulders, turned and galloped up to his friend's side.

The Turkestani was well into the north road by now, marching toward the tent that my family had set up. I followed, not wishing to fall too far behind.

Farewells in the Family Tent

The family tent had been placed on a long narrow plain off the north road that led into a grove of apricot and pear trees. A stream that tumbled from the mountains had long since dried up; a dry rock bed remained. But the grass on the surrounding low banks was lush and hardy, and the horses were pleased to have something this good to nibble on at the beginning of a journey.

Grandmother was very discreet in choosing this spot, not wishing to draw any attention to my departure. It was almost halfway between our home and Hor Drango, on the west bank of the She Chu and well out of sight of the Chinese ferryman. In spite of outward politeness, it was easy to detect his resentment of my family. Not only did we avoid using his questionable services, but we had set a precedent for other Tibetans to follow. If he had known what was going on, he would surely have reported my departure to the monks at the Chango Monastery.

Nor did Gera Lama, the abbot of the Chango Monastery, disguise his contempt or his intentions with respect to my family. There was no telling what obstacles he could have put up if he had found a *migou* skin in my possession.

The old man who collected the tolls for the bridge was easily within our sight, as we were probably in his. But he was no problem; he had long ago withdrawn from mundane politics and commerce, devoting his life to the perfection of prayer and the hope of better rebirths. He could not have cared less what I did or where I went, providing, of course, that if I used his bridge I paid the proper toll.

The tent seemed strangely unfamiliar to me. I had seen it before at the annual harvest festival, which was held on the rolling plain that stretched out beneath Toa Shan's gleaming summit. Then, thousands of tents seemed to erupt from the earth: modest black yak-hair tents of the nomads; elaborate and ornate tents of rich nobles, made of heavy Chinese cloth and decorated with silk good-luck marks; the holy tents of the living incarnations, in front of which the people prostrated themselves to receive a blessing. (There were at least thirty incarnations in the Chango Monastery alone.)

Anyone who was in sight of the sacred peaks was sure to be at the festival. Some came to trade, some to race horses and wrestle, but most to picnic. Setting up a tent in the open air is a favorite pastime, a chance to see old friends and perhaps meet new ones. Old feuds were temporarily forgotten, although after much drinking of *chang* and arak, new feuds sometimes began.

Some people, like my father, came to the mountains simply to pray. There were as many prayers as there were lamas. All prayed for a good harvest and that the demon breath of the mountain *zidags* would not sweep the land.

The prayers were public, the tents proudly displayed. But now our tent, made of good Chinese cloth with the swastika, symbol of the *garuda* bird (representing the continuity of life), seemed more like a fugitive than the proud bearer of our family name.

But this is the way it had to be.

We could not let this hamper our day. Grandmother greeted us with outstretched arms, holding up a bowl of *chang*, on the rim of which three dabs of butter had been placed. As we dismounted, Mother and Big Father emerged from the tent where they were preparing the feast.

After grazing, our horses were tied up to a branch. I took the bowl from Grandmother, dipping my right forefinger into it, and throwing a drop to the gods in the four directions of the universe. This ceremony completed, I downed the bowl in two big gulps with a satisfied sound.

"Were you seen?" Grandmother asked nervously. "Did anyone see you come here?"

"Only the old woman Chenden Akung," I replied.

"And she took the boy for his Uncle Sangsang," Tiso Awa put in. "So we were not seen."

"Good," she said as she refilled our cups. "This is a safe place. Good shade. Isolated. We may get as drunk as we like and no one will have to know." Then she laughed, took out her snuff and passed the bag to each of us.

Only Grandmother and Tiso Awa took any. Kareem had some Szechwan tobacco that he was partial to, and he offered some of it. When it came to Grandmother, she made an unpleasant face.

"It will make your beard smell of tobacco," she said at Kareem. He pointed to the snuff and made a similar face.

We sat in front of the tent and the *chang* flowed freely. No one was allowed to have an empty or half-filled cup, as this would be bad luck. We talked about the late harvest caused by the recent mudslides, about the virtues and faults of *ladacki* mules in this part of Tibet, about the recent migration of Chinese to eastern Tibet, about gods and men, and about everything but our impending journey.

This would have been bad manners. This was no place for solemn thoughts, but rather a last chance to share tea and *chang* with my family. Only good and happy memories should come from this.

The late-morning sun threw heavy shadows on the uneven terrain. Inside the tent a great feast had been prepared. A whole lamb with the skin and entrails removed sat in the middle, surrounded by sacks of butter, bricks of tea, fresh apricots and pears and, to my screams of joy, delicious Hami dates. I thanked Grandmother as I reached for one of them.

Grandmother smiled. Sangsang had brought them and she was waiting for an occasion to serve them.

Kareem also reached for the dates, but his expression was not the same as mine. He was sad and I was sure that I even saw his sullen eyes moistening.

"Why is that?" I whispered to Tiso Awa, who was the Moslem's best friend.

"Ah," Tiso sighed. "Kareem has a wife in Hami, whom he is sure he will never see again."

"A pity," Mother comforted the Moslem.

"Oh, it's not so bad. He has plenty of other wives in plenty of other places." Tiso smiled.

"But none," Kareem said sadly, "is quite the same as this one."

"Hami," I said, "must be quite a place for beautiful women. Uncle Sangsang also speaks of a woman of Hami."

"Yes, but Sangsang is free to go there." Tiso grabbed a large piece of lamb. "Kareem cannot."

I wanted to ask why, but it seemed that neither man wanted to talk of the matter.

We stayed and talked and drank (except Kareem, who this time abstained from alcohol) until we almost forgot our reason for being there. Then it was time to go. Kareem had already left the tent to check the horses and he came back gesturing with his hands that the sun was getting lower in the sky. We could not stay there all day and the next; it was time to go.

I walked around to each member of my family, touching my forehead to theirs.

Big Father turned to me with serious eyes. The reality of my impending departure was only now beginning to be felt. I could see pride mixed with sorrow in his eyes.

"You are the son of a Bon lama," he spoke softly, "and so you go with the protection of our gods. Were you to remain here in this place of your birth, you would surely follow in my path. But this was not meant to be." He sighed deeply.

"My hope is that during these years with your Big Father," he continued, trying to change his expression, "you have learned something of our faith. While you have yet to consult the twelve sacred volumes of Shenrab which lie in the vaults of the Bati Monastery, you have read parts of them in the pages that I brought. You have learned the ancient Zhang Zhung language. You have been instructed in the proper procedure for making sacrifices and you have performed it without fault. You have learned something about medicine, if only by observing. You have seen firsthand the contempt in which our Bon faith is held. Do not expect this to be much different outside this province. You will ride out of here not complete, but with the foundation from which to build your experiences. Do not forget these things or your life here. Do not let it be said that you are the son of a Bon lama who does not know his father's faith."

This talk was directed at me, but everyone listened. Now there was nothing more to say. The only sound came from the sputtering yak-dung fire.

Then Big Father placed another amulet around my neck. There was a picture of a wild dog, surrounded by sacred writing which seemed to imprison the animal.

"This will protect you from wild dogs," Big Father explained. "The devourers of the dead who roam through the villages or the wild beasts that wander the plains. They cannot hurt you as long as you wear this charm."

Tiso Awa chuckled to himself. "I have already told the boy," he said, "that there are dogs that he could not imagine living in Tibet. Even more ferocious than that local dog you have here."

"If you speak of Balu," Big Father told him, "then it is doubtful that you will find an animal to match him for ferocity."

"Every region that I have been in has its Balu," the Mongol said. "So I have no doubt that your charm will be put to good use. But I am hearing the new Gezong again. Do you not remember an animal guarding a merchant's home in Shigatse? Now that dog . . ."

Big Father sighed and laughed. "How can I forget, although it was some time ago. I fear that I have been off the road for too long now. I would perhaps ride out with you if I thought more about it, but . . ."

He quickly changed his expression.

"But I have already consulted the stars and my karma does not lie on your road."

Mother walked up to me. In her hands she carried a small bag. "I have made your favorite little cakes." She smiled. "Although there is enough for a long journey I am sure that they will be gone before you reach Tatsienlu."

"And here," Grandmother stepped up. She reached into her robe and took out a number of *katas* rolled up into a small yakskin bag. They were of varying quality; most were of rough cotton, but at least one was Chinese silk. Grandmother held this one up and said, "You will know to whom to give this one." I looked at her, not quite understanding what she meant.

Then we embraced, and I could smell the sweet aroma of snuff that I associated with Grandmother. I felt her rough, gentle fingers pat one side of my face. She kept her hands there awhile and then, with a gentle final tap, she took her hand away.

Crossing the Turbulent She Chu

The road took a number of turns and eventually we found ourselves just outside the north gate of Hor Drango. The gate was still open since the sun had not yet set. Black yakskin nomad tents fringed the town. Even at this late time of day, there was a steady flow of people entering and leaving, trading, bartering and just gossiping.

Tiso Awa asked me if there were any way to avoid going through the town to pick up the road at the south gate. He was well aware of the danger of being discovered. I explained that the only way to do this would add much time to our trip. First, we would have to recross the She Chu at a muddy point well upriver. From there, we could follow the banks of the river downstream until it joined the Ma Chu somewhere below the village.

"And what harm would it be to ride through the town?" he seemed to ask himself.

"Probably none," I answered for him. "It is not unusual to see caravan men come and go through the town."

Tiso Awa turned to Kareem, who was also studying the situation. The two men spoke Turki; I could not understand them, but it appeared that Kareem was against going through the town. He looked up at the fast-descending sun, holding his hands over his eyes, and then motioned toward the She Chu.

"Kareem doesn't like it." Tiso spoke for his friend. "Nor do I. We'll strike out for the longer route now. Do you think that we can be well beyond the walls of your town by sunset?"

64

"That depends on how easy it will be to recross the river. There were heavy rains this year and even in drier times, crossing can be a tricky business."

We reached the muddy banks of the She Chu just before sunset, as the sound of the conch shell from the Chango Monastery, calling the monks to prayer, echoed through the valley.

To me it was a welcome sound. Only then did my feelings of uneasiness begin to fade. Gera Lama, although very powerful, could not put all of his energies into watching us. In spite of the fact that he used religion to cloak his power-hungry schemes, he was still the spiritual leader of the monastery, and so had more important duties to attend than watching our tiny caravan.

However, we were still far from being out of danger.

The turbulent She Chu quickly destroyed any optimism we might have had. The river *nags* were having their way. Great chunks of ice from the surrounding mountains jumped and crashed over the muddy bottom as they sped downstream. Whirlpools appeared and disappeared. Branches and tree trunks bobbed up and down, fighting the ice for space.

I looked at my traveling companions to see if they were still intent on crossing the river here. They were.

Earlier that day, far upstream, we had crossed the new bridge and paid the old lama. None of us wished to return to that spot, which would take us right back to where we started.

Kareem, forever impatient, was eager to move on. "Is it deep here?" the Mongol asked hopefully.

"Ordinarily it's not," I told him, "but the late rains have made it swell. I should say that it rises to my shoulders. But it is not the depth that worries me; I have already told you that this is a tricky place."

Tiso Awa looked over to the other side. It was not that far to cross, but it seemed like going to another part of the world.

"There is no other way," Tiso said flatly. Then he and Kareem dismounted and plunged into the river, holding the horses' reins. The horses balked and pulled back when they felt their feet sinking in the mud.

I stayed in the saddle and urged my horse on, but she had no taste for this adventure either. She struggled in the muddy banks and it was difficult to calm her.

"Save your strength," I whispered in one of her ears.

Finally, as luck would have it, she slipped on the mud and plunged into the stream. Now there was no easy turning back. She cried and protested as I urged her on. I watched a large chunk of ice flow by, barely missing her head, which she struggled to keep above water. Every step was slow and carefully placed, until all of a sudden she fell into a muddy pit which had been created by the force of the current.

The world turned upside down as I tumbled over her neck, headfirst into the icy stream. It felt as though hands were reaching out of the water to grip me and pull me down, but I managed to hold on to the reins. I grabbed tightly as the river rushed by, bouncing and turning me like one of the chunks of ice. All I could hear were the roar of the water and the sound of Kareem's whip as he cursed and pushed his horse along.

Another piece of ice approached. Still holding the reins, I ducked my head underwater. Icy water filled my nose and lungs but I was determined not to die until I had fulfilled my mission and, from this, I seemed to gather the strength to pull my horse along. Finally, I was able to feel the solid ground leading up to the other bank, and with one final lunge, I fell in between two thin willow trees on the other side.

I lay there coughing, panting and trembling with cold, no longer able to grip the reins. My horse weathered the ordeal better than I; when my two friends came to my side, she was quietly nibbling the short, nourishing grass that grew in profusion between some of the trees.

As I lay back, I realized that darkness had overtaken us. The sun had disappeared behind the mountains, and not far in the distance a bright full moon loomed over Toa Shan.

What enormous disappointment I felt when I saw the sacred mountain! I was exhausted, unable to move, yet I had not gone very far on my new adventure. The mountain, like the river, seemed to have a grip on me. I wondered if I would ever be out of the shadow of the sacred Toa Shan.

As I contemplated these thoughts, Tiso Awa reminded me of the more practical things that must be done. We had to assay our losses. Tiso Awa had managed to get all his things to the other side, but Kareem was not so lucky. He was very upset about the loss of a bag of tobacco. For him, this was very serious, particularly when I told him that the next village where we could find more was three to four days away. Even more important was the loss of his waterproof yakskin cape.

My own losses were not altogether as bad as they could have been. My first thought was for the *migou* skin. The saddlebag had been drenched, but as it had been tightly packed, the skin was not in bad shape. I stretched it out on a flat rock to dry.

The worst loss, however, was the delicious cakes that my mother had made. As I took them out of the saddlebag, they fell apart in my hands. Fortunately, my mother had been right, and the better part of them had already been devoured earlier that day, long before we were to reach Tatsienlu. Tiso Awa, who confessed a weakness for these little cakes and had eaten many of them, was very upset over the loss. He rummaged through the bag, and when the cakes crumbled in his hand, he threw them into the river.

"If we had offered a sacrifice before," he berated himself, "then maybe we would have crossed easier."

"Big Father offers sacrifices every morning," I told him. "I myself left many stones at different parts of the stream. The river *nags* here are angry but I think they were not acting on their own."

I pointed toward Hor Drango and the monastery.

"So you think it's his doing?" Tiso asked.

"While we are under the protection of Big Father, Gera Lama is reluctant to test his powers. But now we are on our own."

"Curse that bender of heretics." Tiso spat on his little finger. "Curse that Gera Lama." Then his bright smile returned. "We'll camp here tonight."

Kareem had already gathered some shrub wood and was starting a fire. "The horses are too tired to go on." Tiso smiled. In his own gentle way, Tiso was mocking me. He was not talking about the horses; he was talking about me.

But I was in no mood to argue. After we had some tea and lamb, I felt much better and wanted to tell Tiso that we could move on. But I hesitated, not wanting to wake him. I lay back and watched the sky swirl white around the sacred mountain.

All my life, this mountain had been the center of my

dreams. I tried to remember the times that I had spent there but my thoughts had changed sharply. The mountain seemed cruel and dispassionate now. I felt that I would never go beyond its grip. I was a prsoner, and Toa Shan was my jailer.

Somehow, I fell asleep.

A Gallop Out of Hor Drango

When we awoke the following morning, there was a fine mist in the air. The glorious weather of the day before seemed very far away. Looking toward the east, beyond the rim of rugged mountains, the clouds gathering over the plains of China were moved along by a gusting wind. There was no question that we would have rain that very morning, so Tiso Awa hurried us along, as rain could only slow our progress.

A new fire had been made by Kareem, who had been up for some time. I was to learn later that the Moslem slept very little, and when he did, it was usually with one eye open.

Smiling, he urged me to fill my bowl with the nourishing tea he had just made. Occasionally, he looked toward the gray east and then to his Mongol companion. Tiso Awa's usual calm and easy manner were not apparent. He made no secret of his dislike of rain and kept us from having a second bowl of tea, informing us that the rain would soon be on us and that we should keep moving.

"It may be good for your Tibetan crops," he forced a smile, "but it does nothing but hamper the caravan man."

By then he was impatiently waiting in his saddle for us to join him. Kareem understood his friend's sense of urgency, although he seemed to take a less serious view of the situation. As for me, I was only too eager to get moving.

I was reminded where we were when I heard the conch shell calling the monks to prayer in the Chango Monastery. In the distance, Toa Shan, with its mantle of white snow, loomed defiantly in the decidedly gray sky.

As I pulled up alongside my two companions, it began to rain. It was not a heavy rain, but there was enough of it to make the earth soft and muddy. As we marched on, my horse would every now and then catch a hoof in the mud; struggling to get loose, the hoof would only move deeper into the earth.

It was only then I really noticed what I thought was a dramatic change in my two companions. The usually happy smile had disappeared from Tiso Awa's face, while Kareem took a more optimistic view, and his sullen eyes even sparkled. It was as if they had switched personalities in the night.

Serious and determined, Tiso Awa looked straight ahead without saying a word. I felt that I could not talk to him. Somehow, I thought that he held me responsible for the bad weather.

I wanted to talk to Kareem but did not know what to say. I looked at the Moslem, who was munching on a piece of dry yak meat.

"I will have to learn Turki," I said to him.

He smiled. Nothing more was said.

The rain stopped just as my horse lodged her hoof in a muddy hole. There was nothing to do but dismount and pull her out. Fortunately, Kareem and Tiso Awa came to my aid. After we pulled the horse from the mud, I noticed that the Mongol's good-natured smile had returned.

"Everybody fears something," he said to me simply. "I do not like the rain, perhaps because I am Mongol and more at home on the arid plains. Kareem has a great aversion to ice, for whatever his reasons. And you, Small Ears, what fears do you carry in your heart?"

I thought for a bit. My demons lurked behind every rock or tree. I feared the unknown.

But such an answer was too simple. Who can ever know where his karma would take him? I didn't answer.

"You think on it for a while," Tiso said, and then, adding an afterthought, he looked at me gently. "You are right," he said. "You must learn Turki."

We rode on quietly, following the She Chu until the road led east away from its banks. The road brought us to an open plain dotted with settlements, much like the place from which we had come. Though not a very long plain, it was very wide, with a road that went right through the center and ended at a dense forest where it once again met the She Chu. We stopped on a narrow ridge to survey the situation.

"Down there," I pointed to the end of the plain, "lies the end of the Chango province. Beyond lie Dawu and Chala and places where I am not known."

Kareem, still upset about the loss of his tobacco, asked if there was any chance of trading with some of the inhabitants of these farms on the plain.

"Not likely," I told him. "These are the farms of Round Jigme, a sworn enemy of my family. Even if you could trade, I am sure he would have your very skin in the bargain."

"Are all these people loyal to Round Jigme?" Tiso asked.

"All. To be sure, there are some who find their fortunes tied up with his and others who live in fear of his wrath.

71

Either is dangerous to us, or at least to me. You may ride through unmolested, but not I."

"Then," said my Mongol friend, "we must find another road to take."

But there were no other roads.

The banks of the She Chu gave way at this point to the gorges and deep chasms that would take the river most of the way to Tatsienlu.

We saw some activity on the road. A number of small caravans emerged from the forest and moved slowly toward us. Unfortunately, they were going in the opposite direction from us, so there was no chance of attaching ourselves to one of them. One alternative was left.

"Are you eager to see what your horse is made of?" Tiso Awa smiled at me.

I knew he was talking about a mad gallop across the plain, and this thought filled me with as much apprehension as adventure. I was quite confident of my own mount, but I did not have the faith in my friends' horses that they did. Tiso detected this as I looked at his horse.

"Do not worry," he comforted me. "Our horses have rested well and Kareem will inform them of the excellent grass that awaits them in the forest on the other side."

I still wasn't sure. I looked at the gray sky. A slight drizzle was just beginning.

"The rain?" Tiso Awa looked at me. "It is not as bad as all that. My horse may not look like much, but she has been with me for some time. That in itself is unusual. And she is valuable. She knows how to avoid the marmot holes. You must have already noticed that she managed to avoid the same traps your horse fell into. Stay behind us. We'll lead the way."

Kareem understood, and his face lit up brightly at the prospect of a mad gallop through the last part of Chango territory. He smiled and gave me the thumbs-up sign.

"Besides," Tiso went on as we moved our horses down the narrow ridge that opened onto the plain, "I see no other way."

With that, he slapped his horse with his riding crop and horse and rider moved like an arrow, bounding over the plain. Kareem and I followed right behind as the mud splattered over our faces.

We were quickly approaching the first settlement. Wisps of black smoke curled over the flat roofs while the people were going about their work.

Kareem could not resist a warlike cry as we galloped by. An old woman working a small turnip field ran toward her house. Another group of women were sitting around a butter churn, no doubt gossiping, and at our approach they jumped up, running in every direction, calling for their children.

So this is how a Golok must feel when he goes out on a raid, I thought. I must admit that I was quite pleased with the feeling.

Except for an urge to overtake Tiso Awa's horse, my Kyang did not disappoint me. She stretched her fine legs in response to my moves, jumping here, zigzagging there.

Tiso was right: his horse was indeed valuable. We avoided the muddy pits and the marmot mounds that I feared. I would not say that she was a fast animal, but I was learning that speed is not the only quality to look for in a horse. When Tiso Awa told me that she had carried him all the way from Turkestan, I developed an even greater respect for his horse.

As we galloped over the road, one of the small caravans was slowly coming up the other side. It consisted of a party of monks, no doubt returning from a pilgrimage. None of the ten monks seemed to be of any high rank, and upon seeing our mad approach, they quickly made room on the road; a reverse of the usual situation, when one must make room for them. But our only thought was to reach the gorges of the She Chu, and so we felt we had the right of way.

How we must have looked, covered with mud, whipping our animals into a frenzied speed! I am sure that they thought we were demons fresh out of the bowels of hell.

As we passed another settlement along the road, I saw a fat, round man, waddling like a duck toward a stable. He was pulling three horses behind him, one of which seemed to be resisting; this only excited the man even more. I laughed to myself. This was none other than Round Jigme.

"Round Jigme," I called to Kareem, hoping he would understand. He did. He released the most blood-chilling scream that I ever heard. I found myself screaming as well.

Determined not to lose even one animal, Jigme struggled until he fell backwards in the mud. That was the last glance I had of this powerful man.

I laughed at the picture we must have made as we galloped by.

Not far off in the distance, the plain led into the forest. We could make out the narrow strip of road and the She Chu, which glistened like a silver cord above it.

We passed one old man, who took little notice of us and only shook his head when Kareem tried to frighten him with another cry. I recognized him as one of the patrons of the Chinese inn. No doubt he had seen the likes of us before.

We pulled our horses up just before the road led into the forest. I was out of breath with fatigue and laughter and found myself falling from the saddle into a pool of mud. This only made me laugh more.

My companions were covered from top to bottom with mud, and I knew I looked no different. Kareem's sullen eyes peered out from a mud-stained face while his mouth formed a big grin. Tiso, his usual happy self, jumped off his horse and joined me in the mud.

As we stood in the mud I said to Tiso, "Kareem makes a very believable bandit."

Tiso Awa, still laughing, looked at me. "Yes," he smiled, "he does."

But I detected something else in his laugh. I said no more.

We walked our horses down through the trees to where the road again paralleled the deep gorges of the She Chu.

At one point, I could not resist turning around to see the place we had left. I only saw the tops of trees and the glimmer of the plain beyond. The rain had stopped. Blue patches were beginning to appear in the broken sky, but Toa Shan had disappeared behind us.

That is how I left Hor Drango, the village of my birth.

Through the Dreary Gorges
of the She Chu

We marched for two days up and down the rocky gorges, the deep chasms of the turbulent She Chu. The ferocious voice of the river was all around us as it crashed and tumbled its way over its rocky bottom to its destination with the Tung Ho downstream, adding its set of demons to that of the larger river.

At times it was impossible to communicate over the roar. Only by the use of hand signals were we able to make ourselves understood.

Tiso Awa's surefooted horse led the way. Sometimes the road would narrow between giant rock facings, the river foaming and seething far below. Then we would have to march single file and put our confidence in Tiso's little pony.

The evidence that other travelers, less fortunate than ourselves, had passed through here was found from time to time on the rocky bottom. Once we saw three mules sprawled in twisted agony over some sharp, jutting rocks, their packs still firmly attached to their backs.

Tiso Awa remarked on this sight: "No doubt, they buckled when they reached this point. I can think of no animal more surefooted than mules, but when they panic, they quickly forget their natural abilities. A shame. But I blame their driver for this. He should have anticipated what could happen."

We found the driver just a short march away. The unfortunate man lay on a flat rock with one arm hanging over a dead branch that had lodged itself in the rocks and the other bouncing freely with the current of the river. He was far below us but I could still make out his face. He did not seem much older than I.

"Your turn to drive mules will come." Tiso Awa looked down, and then at me. "Remember this. No step can be taken without some risk, but this kind of disaster should never happen to an experienced muleman."

Tiso Awa wanted us to move as fast as we could without

bringing us to the brink of danger. He was eager to pass these treacherous gorges where so many lives had been claimed. They were damp and dark, and once again his Mongol heritage called out for the dryness of the sunny plain. He cursed the fine mist that was always with us, and at night he talked on and on about the arid plains, where "civilized man is at his best."

The weather paid no attention; we were in the midst of another world where there was never any sun and where the damp cold was a constant reminder of the malevolent intentions of the gods of this region.

Kareem, too, was anxious to leave this spot, but for a different reason. He feared bandits, and pointed out that any place within the gorges was perfect for ambush. His eyes always looked up and around the mountain wall in which we were enclosed. Sometimes he would stop suddenly and signal us to do the same. He would motion us to be still and then listen intently for something. All I could hear was the sound of the river. Kareem was obviously listening for something else. We waited. Then he would hesitate, bring his hand to his rifle and move on.

At the end of the second day's march, we were looking for a place to camp when we came upon a small clearing, much like a plateau, where we saw six men huddled around a burnt-out fire.

"Bandits?" I asked Kareem.

He brought his rifle up. Tiso Awa got his ready while I felt my heart jump to my throat.

Tiso motioned us to stop. There was something strange about this group of men. I noticed that no smoke rose from their fire and they seemed strangely silent.

Was this some sort of bandit trick? Why did they not ambush us before, when there were so many opportunities? And why would they let us come up to their camp at will?

Kareem volunteered to investigate. He jumped out of his saddle and, getting down on his hands and knees with his rifle slung loosely over his shoulders, he crept up to the camp.

He was only a small distance away from the men but they seemed to take no notice of his approach. We found out why when Kareem put the butt of his rifle to the back of one of the men. The man tumbled over, his face falling into the ashes of a long-burnt-out fire. Kareem jumped up quickly and called to his Mongol friend.

"They are dead," Tiso Awa explained to me. "Every one of them. Dead."

Kareem motioned us to come over. What we saw was the result of a ghastly slaughter at the hands of bandits.

Three of the men had bullet holes in the back of their necks. Another had his throat cut; when Kareem pushed him over, it seemed as though his head would roll away. Another, an old lama, had his own dagger thrust in his chest, and the last man, who may have been the leader of this ill-fated caravan, had the ummistakable marks of an ax on his head.

We walked around this gruesome scene. None of the men had boots, and everything else of value seemed to have been ripped away. The man with the ax mark was practically naked.

Kareem spit in anger as he looked over each man.

I was sure that he was repulsed by this awful scene of death, but Tiso Awa told me otherwise.

"He is upset," Tiso laughed, "because they left nothing. There is nothing else to take."

78

I looked at Kareem as Tiso revealed this information. He was going over each body to see what he could find. He glanced at me and smiled, his sullen eyes deep in concentration. When he came to the half-naked man, he lifted the blood-stained head.

"*Rus*," he said angrily.

"Was the man a Russian?" I asked.

"No," Tiso told me, "but there is evidence that at least one Russian was among these bandits. I know some of these Kalmyk Tartars. They are never without their ax."

When Kareem was satisfied that there was nothing to be taken, he walked away. I looked at Tiso Awa.

"Do you not understand?" the Mongol asked me. "Yesterday when we stopped it was because Kareem thought he heard some shots. No doubt the bandits came up upon these men as they were awakening. It seems that no resistance was offered."

"This pass will be haunted now," I said as I reached for the *migou* skin in my saddlebag. I was sure this would offer protection from the spirits.

"That is true," Tiso said. "We will leave at once."

"First we must make the beginnings of a *mani* pile," I told him. "We can use the burnt-out fire to pile the rocks. We must appease the spirits of this place, lest they follow us out of here."

"You speak like the son of a Bon lama," Tiso said as he began searching for rocks, "but you are right."

Night was coming and we still had not found a place to camp. Hurriedly, we built a *mani* pile in the center of the circle of dead men.

Then once again we depended on the surefootedness of

Tiso Awa's horse to lead us through the dark and away from this terrible place.

The Royal Line of Kareem Musa

We found a place to camp but did not light a fire, not wishing to inform the bandits who infested this area of our presence. The memory of such a mistake was still fresh in our minds and it was some time before I, at least, was able to shake off the feelings that some of the evil had followed us.

But moving quickly, a half-day's ride brought us to the mouth of the She Chu, where it falls into the Tung Ho. The river, although every bit as swift and treacherous here, was much wider, and the deep gorges gradually opened up into a swift, muddy stream with gently inclining banks.

It was a deceptively peaceful spot. The river was not very deep. Birds and yellow butterflies flitted from the grass, and every now and then a red fox inquisitively peered its head out of the bushes.

We threw stones into the river as offering to the *nags* who, in their serpent form, guard the treasures beneath the water. Even Kareem observed this custom, although I am sure he did not think it as important as we did.

Coming downriver, we discovered that the river seemed to have stopped in its course. We came upon a clear, still pool.

Kareem threw a rock in the water and we watched it slowly but steadily sink into the muddy bottom, until all that was left was a tiny bubble.

"A bad spot," Tiso Awa remarked. "Once I saw a horse

and rider disappear as quickly as that rock. The Tung Ho is full of places like this. The *nags* wait for their victims."

We decided that this would be a good place to camp, since the river formed a natural barrier on one side, while to the east the mountains rimmed a long plain. From here we could see in all directions, and if the bandits were to come, Tiso Awa devised a plan that would lead them into the soft mud. But we did not have to put the plan in use; no one came.

We made a fire and had the first warm tea in two days. For the first time, I felt that I could do something without having to look over my shoulder. But Kareem insisted on keeping a good watch himself. His eyes wandered nervously in every direction. Still not satisfied, he began to explore the area.

It was then that I learned more about my Moslem friend from Turkestan, and some suspicions that I had were revealed to be true. Tiso Awa told me the story.

"You know, of course," he said quite calmy, "that Kareem Musa is a bandit."

This did not shock me, and I said nothing.

"You did know," the Mongol continued, "but there is more to the story than that. Kareem is the son of a village chief. The blood of many centuries of royalty from the Chagatai Khanate flows through his body. He claims descent from the soldier-ruler Said Khan. Otherwise, tell me of another in his profession who can write with such a fine hand? You saw his work on the passports."

Tiso Awa paused to sip his tea. "No, writing and in such a fine hand does not fall into the bandit's ordinary skills. He writes. He speaks Turki, Russian, Urdu, Mongolian and even Hindi, which only some of the noblemen in Turkestan are able to speak. You see already that he is no ordinary bandit."

81

He reached for another bowl of tea and cleared his throat. "Why would a nobleman take up such treacherous work, you are asking." Tiso went on. "Why does any turn to such a life? There was nothing left to do. Kareem Musa is from the region of Bukhara, which falls at the extreme northwest of Turkestan, near the Russian border.

"For years, the Russians were building forts along the border. After this they began sending Cossacks to colonize Turkestan. The Cossacks were cruel and brutal. These peasants were an unruly lot; the dregs of Russian society, hating everything and everyone and each other and not knowing the reasons why. No, they were a people you would not want in your country.

"Some peasants came into his village, drunk and loud, and killed two men who offered resistance when they tried to drag off some Turkestani women. Kareem was thirsty to avenge this outrage, but his father was of a more peaceful nature, and also well aware that the Cossacks were backed with Russian rifles and more dangerous artillery.

"Not only that, but Khudayar Khan himself, ruler of Bukhara, had befriended the Russians. Bukhara already had Russian flags flying. Resistance would be disastrous.

"This only angered Kareem Musa more. Still, when asked by his father to go speak to the Russians, he could not disobey.

"The Russians temporarily had their headquarters on the Russian side of the Amu Darya River. It was a small detachment under a crude Cossack, Colonel Danilov. He received Kareem very warmly and apologized for the acts of his subjects. He informed Kareem that every effort would be made to find the whereabouts of the four women who were stolen from their homes and that the criminals responsible for such an act would be severely punished.

"When Kareem returned to his village, the Russian soldiers had already left. Not a person was left alive—not Kareem's parents or his wife or any of his children. All dead by the Cossack sword.

"The Russians, through one of their many spies, had heard that Kareem's original intention was to ride out against them. An example had to be made to show the Turkestanis that the Russians were not only there to stay, but would do everything to ensure their position.

"As for the Chinese, who also claim the territory, they would do nothing to offend the Russians. The magistrate, a petty man, far from the edicts of Peking, was on the best of terms with the Russians. Two dogs on the same leash, eh?"

He paused again. "The Russians could have easily murdered Kareem when he was within their midst, but they wanted him to return to see what defiance would bring. That was their mistake. They did not understand these Turkestanis.

"Kareem was immediately branded an outlaw; as the edict read, 'The Bukharan rebel and evil perpetrator of the destruction of villages.' They were accusing him of destroying his own village, hard as that is to believe. They said he wanted his father's position.

"Kareem took to the hills, where friendly peasants, recognizing his royal line, cared for him at great risk to their own lives. The Chinese, the Russians and Khudayar Khan's personal guards from Kokand were all looking for him. Spies of all sorts abounded.

"Meanwhile, Colonel Danilov put the second phase of his

plan for conquest into action by attempting to turn one tribe against another, then coming in after the bloodletting as the great mediator. It is not a happy place, this Turkestan.

"But Khudayar Khan was a disliked, unfeeling ruler. A revolt was inevitable. Kareem Musa assassinated Khudayar Khan when he was a guest of the Russian army.

"Another time, a detachment of Chinese soldiers rode out of Kashgar, which is a long way from Bukhara. Forty armed soldiers were being transferred farther east where some other troubles were erupting. They never arrived. Only Kareem knew their fate.

"Two days later, four Ukrainian peasants were washed ashore on the Turkestani side of the Amu Darya. And a few days after that, ten Cossacks rode into Shahrisabz strapped to their saddles. Not one had his head.

"Kareem had raised the sword of Islam, and he had only just begun. Later, Kareem was at the hill fortress on the Dengil-Tepe oasis where the Russians suffered their severest losses. He was also there, unfortunately, when the Russians returned under General Skobelev. Colonel Danilov, Kareem's enemy, was now a major-general. This time Kareem witnessed the slaughter of thousands of his countrymen, including women and children; he was not surprised.

"He later fought with the dervish Khan Tore in the Fergana valley and was also part of Ishan Madali's Sufi brotherhood that attacked the Russian garrison of Andizhan with some success. But he left Madali because he had no taste for a holy war. His war was one of vengeance."

All this meant little to me; these battles were far away. But Tiso Awa was very impressed. He had become Kareem Musa's chronologer, and when Kareem wasn't around, he enjoyed telling me of some of the Turkestani's exciting battles.

Kareem himself never discussed any of this, although he did not discourage Tiso Awa from talking about it.

Kareem returned. He was smiling at me, and in his smile I found it difficult to believe all that had happened to him. But not in his eyes. There, the fires of hatred and revenge burned clear. I was glad that this man counted me among his friends.

"I must check the north passage," he said as he left us again.

"But what happened?" I asked after he left. "How did he arrive here as a caravan man?"

"Betrayal," Tiso said flatly. "He was betrayed by one of his own men who thought he could rise to the leadership. He failed to recognize that he was dealing with Russians and Chinese. The entire band, including the traitor, Mohammed Tagar, was captured and executed. Only because of the warning of Moslem holy men did Kareem not return that fateful night. But he has no reason to be happy. The holy man also told him that he would never have the head of Danilov. This privilege had already been assigned to someone else. There are many like Kareem. That is his real sorrow."

"Everyone must follow his karma," I said knowingly.

"That may be good enough for you," Tiso looked at his friend, "but I do not think it's good enough for him."

"And what of your story, Tiso Awa?" I asked.

"My story?" He put a hand to his chest. "My story is not important."

A Close Call

We entered the uninhabited country beyond Koja by a narrow ravine which ran parallel to a rapidly moving stream that tumbled from the mountains above. Here we were forced to move single file and cautiously as the elements swirled and howled above and below us. To the sounds of the wind fiends were added the oaths of the two mulemen, each in his own language (as their horses were only familiar with those tongues) so that I felt immersed in a chaotic abyss from which I would never emerge. But my companions took little notice of this. To them, there had been worse places and worse times and I felt myself carried along by their confidence as well as my own desire to survive.

Above, the wind fiends shrieked and howled, occasionally penetrating the ravine in angry attempts to dislodge our animals and plunge us into the waiting stream. I was sure that we had walked directly into the trap of these demons. We dismounted and, in a single file, led our horses along the way.

The snow and the rain that had been so treacherous before when we were above the ravine did not have the power here. Somehow the mountains above afforded some protection from their wrath. But if this was a blessing, it was a curse as well.

We followed the ravine for a long time and were coming out to where the stream widened as it rushed along to its meeting with the great copper river, the Tung Ho. Here, we saw what fate would have been ours had we not passed quickly through these parts. Great boulders and rocks fell away from the mountains and crashed into the ravine, just narrowly missing the last of us to emerge. Had we been there just a little bit later, our fate would have been sealed under a mass of rocks and debris. The ravine had, in effect, disappeared.

We looked at each other but no one said anything.

The weather had not changed and we walked from one danger into another. Before us lay a vast white expanse. Snow was falling in great white flakes.

It was then that I realized that coming out of the ravine I had somehow lost my horsehair goggles, which could offer the only guidance through this sea of white. How this happened I cannot say. Perhaps in the excitement when my horse plunged one foot into the water, I threw them with my waving hands. Perhaps a demon took them, realizing how important they were. I was embarrassed to reveal their loss to my friends, as I felt that I had already been a burden to them. With my eyes only partially opened, I attempted to lead my horse through the storm, but even all my desire could not overcome the fury of the elements. After stumbling two or three times, I found myself alone. I held tightly to the reins, praying that my horse could lead me back to the others. The cold was penetrating to my very bones and I could feel heavy crystals form on my eyelids. I wanted to move but did not know in which direction to go. Everything around me was the same—white. I thought it ironic that I was seeking the origin of the *migou* skin, a creature who was at home in the snow and who somehow was tied into my karma, yet I could not face the snow myself. I cried out for help, huddling against my horse for warmth. But all I could hear was my own voice returning to me.

I still had the *migou* skin. I wondered if I could put it to use to guide me through this. Anxiously, I fumbled through my saddlebag until I could feel the warm fur against my hand. My horse was beginning to panic and I had all to do to keep her from running off, but I managed to get to the skin. Then, still holding the reins tightly as if they were extensions of my fingers, I clumsily wrapped the skin around me and sank to the cold hard earth.

I pulled my horse closer, calming her as best I could but not really believing that there was any hope for either of us. She sensed this, but whether out of loyalty or lack of a better alternative we lay there huddled up together, I in my *migou* skin and she in her horse skin. Soon the white turned to black and I was asleep.

I was awoken unceremoniously by a jab in the ribs, and then another. I opened my eyes. The snow had stopped. An occasional flake stirred up by a soft breeze floated before me. I looked into Kareem Musa's sympathetic face.

"Ha, your *migou* skin saved you." He laughed. "It is perhaps your luck."

"It is just as you said it would be, Small Ears." Tiso Awa's head appeared above me. "A magic skin that will be your protector."

I attempted to get up and I could still feel the reins of my horse tightly in my hands. My horse stumbled to her feet and shook herself off.

"Here, foolish boy." Kareem tossed me my horsehair goggles. "These were found just a short distance from you. Why did you not tell us that they were lost? What harm would it have been to lead you out of this on a rope?"

"What would I tell your mother," Tiso Awa asked in a stern voice, "if you were lost? How could I return on a caravan with the news of a son's death? Would you dishonor us by making us the bearer of bad news?"

Tiso Awa was angry. I had never seen him like that before. I wanted to reply but I knew that anything I said would only fuel his anger. He looked at me with narrow eyes and I felt that this look was surely enough payment for the prideful sin that I had committed.

"I . . . I . . . please forgive me," I stuttered. "It was . . ."

"It was a foolish thing to do." Kareem finished my sentence.

The Mongol turned and walked away. I began to follow, thinking of what I could say, but Kareem stepped in front of me.

"No," he said, "let him go. You can only add to his anger at this time. Thank Allah that you are still alive and settle for that."

Then he smiled. I nodded and struggled to hold back my tears.

"We were never very far from you." Kareem pointed to a large boulder behind which I could see the first feeble smoke of a yak-dung fire. "We took shelter behind that rock. Even with our own goggles it was impossible to penetrate very far."

I looked around, my eyes spanning in every direction. I had no idea what day it was or how many days I had been there. The sun cast a brilliant red shadow on the white snow as it disappeared behind the mountains, taking the day with it.

We walked to the boulder where Tiso Awa was struggling and cursing the fire that would not start. All the yak dung that had been collected was too wet to burn. And although the wind had brushed off the snow, there was little that could be used to start a fire. I sat down near Tiso Awa, trying very hard not to look at him.

"There will be no tea and no fire." Tiso was talking to himself but making sure that we could all hear him.

I released the reins of my horse and she joined the other two animals as they foraged in the diminishing light for a few blades of grass that managed to find their way to the surface.

Tiso Awa looked at the horses and threw one more yak chip into the smoldering fire that was quickly losing its power. Then he lay back.

"At least the horses will have some nourishment," he said. "I prefer them to camels, who at night have to have their food brought to them. And this from a Mongol."

Then he turned over and pulled his sheepskin up to his chin. He was very tired, as we all were.

"How long was I there?" I asked Kareem Musa. "How long did I lie there?"

"Not long," the Turkestani answered, and then he too fell back and was soon asleep.

But as fatigued as I was, I found sleep difficult. I sat up near the dead fire and watched the stars take their place in the sky. The moon lodged itself over one of the mountains as if perched on the white tip. Somewhere off in the distance I thought I heard the voice of a *migou* calling out. Was it calling me? I wondered. Or was it just the wind finding its way through the mountains. These were the kinds of thoughts that filled my mind until I was irresistibly over-whelmed by sleep.

Another Close Call

The next morning, we rode out under a dark gray sky. The last of the evening stars had faded into the sky and the sun had not yet begun its climb over the mountains. The morning air was chilled and damp and Tiso Awa was noticeably disturbed by this. As he did every morning that I rode with him, he cursed the Tibetan weather.

But he was in brighter spirits than usual for some reason, and gave us a song praising the dry arid reaches of his homeland in Mongolia.

"Look around." He waved his hand. "Do you see anything that can be used to start a fire? Perhaps by midday you will find a dry yak chip or a shrub or wood. You know, I have always been amazed at how far the Tibetan has advanced although his morning tea is served in the afternoon."

It was good-natured banter and Kareem, who would not be outdone, sang the praises of his homeland, although there was a certain melancholy in his song. Kareem could not openly return to Turkestan, where there was a price on his head.

I was content to listen to my two companions. Of course, I knew a song or two myself, but I felt my voice to be weak in comparison to my friends', and I felt that there was much to be learned from their songs.

However, upon prodding, I sang a song that my grand-mother had taught me. It was about the Chinese, and while my voice may not have been worthy of the song, both men applauded loudly and we laughed for a good long time. I still remember that song

> Chinese soldiers on backs of frogs
> Ride into Horpa land.
> They eat with sticks, in Dendru house,
> Tibetans eat with hands.

And so we rode out of the darkness and into the daylight, each of us with a song. I could feel the sun rising behind us as we approached a long narrow plain where the river divided into two smaller streams. One turned west and disappeared into the mountains; the other traversed the plain almost to its end, holding close to the mountains which rose abruptly like the walls of a town.

I had calculated—and Tiso Awa's horse agreed—that the westerly direction would be an unlucky one that day. So we continued to follow the river as it bounded over the plain.

Kareem was very cautious and more than a little bit apprehensive about either route. He insisted that we keep to the mountain side of the stream and be forever vigilant.

"What an ideal spot for a bandit attack." He stroked his long red beard with one hand as the other swept over the land. "Should we find ourselves in the middle of this plain with only this stream to our back, we would be lost for sure."

Tiso Awa agreed. "A lesson here," he turned to me, "to survive as a muleman, one must always think as a bandit. It is not often we have the luxury of a large caravan to protect us. In those times, one must put one's mind into that of a brigand and so stay one step ahead of danger."

"As for me," Kareem laughed sarcastically, "such thinking is not difficult."

If this plain was a bandit's dream, it was a herdsman's dream as well. The narrowness of the valley and the height of the surrounding mountains sheltered it from the harsh weather. A strong wind roared through the mountain canyons but puffed itself out over the plain so that hardly a leaf rustled. Here and there a thin but sturdy willow tree appeared by the stream's edge. It was late fall, but even so, there was rich brown-green grass and flowers of purple and red growing near heaps of yak dung. No doubt one of the nomadic tribes used this place as their summer pastures, and I could not understand why the region remained uninhabited.

"Brigands." Kareem answered my question with a word.

Somehow the word did not strike the fear in me that it once would have. I felt very safe with these two men who were wise and experienced in dangerous travel.

Finding yak dung to begin a fire was an easy task, as it lay all around us. As I was gathering some, I came upon a large rock that at first I thought had fallen from the mountain above. However, on closer inspection I noticed that wood had been piled neatly in a stack against it. The nomads had placed it there for use the following winter. I wondered what tribe they were to have no fear of the dangers contained on that plain.

I did not touch the wood, for it could have meant life or death to a nomad family in the winter. Besides, yak dung was plentiful and in some ways preferable: it did not burn as brightly and so was less apt to attract the attention of bandits.

I told my friends about the wood and they agreed that I had done the right thing. While neither was above taking what was not their own, they thought that to steal some wood from hapless nomads was too undignified an act.

We hovered around the fire and I was about to consume my second bowl of tea when Kareem suddenly looked up. His red beard glistened in the sunlight and his brown eyes were wide open. He cocked his head a little to one side and then began to kick earth on the fire.

"Get the horses, quickly," he commanded as the rifle swung from his shoulder.

I jumped up without questioning. The horses were peacefully grazing nearby and I rushed to fetch them. From the distance, I could hear the rumble of horses. I looked around but could not see from which direction they came.

As I brought the horses back, I tried to reason where they were coming from. Tiso Awa already had his gun poised. He told me to take the horses up into the gradually climbing foothills where they were to be hidden behind a heap of large boulders. Then my two friends joined me behind the rock.

"Perhaps it's a herd of wild yak," I reasoned innocently, "or the nomads coming to their pastures."

"Not likely." Kareem smiled.

Then, from the other end of the valley, we could see a group of riders coming toward us. I held my breath involuntarily and bent down a little bit more.

The riders were far away but they were closing in fast. I could see them splashing over the stream and coming directly at us.

Kareem patted his rifle and spat contemptuously. I could see that he was eager for some encounter. He was not easily bullied.

As the riders came closer, we were able to make out who they were. There were four of them, mounted; they were leading two ponies loaded down with what appeared to be supplies. Their horses were the biggest that I had ever seen, and even from a distance, I was overwhelmed by their imposing size.

"They're Lolos," Tiso Awa whispered. "Those are Szechwan ponies. The Lolos are the only ones who can really handle such an animal."

I had heard stories about Lolos but I had never encountered any. They were a tough and proud race of warrior bandits who for centuries had been a thorn in China's side.

It was well known, even in Hor Drango, how the generals

had sent division after division into the Lolos' mountain retreats to rout them out. But the soldiers seldom returned. The Lolos lived in an inaccessible mountain area south of the city of Tatsienlu, and although I was told they carried on commerce in that town, none dared approach them the wrong way.

I must admit that I was frightened and I am sure my companions were too, but neither showed anything more than a determination not to be slaughtered.

They were almost on us now. We were able to make out their features.

The leader was a woman. She was an imposing figure, and on her mount she seemed even more frightening. She wore a gown of dark purple with a band of bullets across her chest. This seemed to be more decorative than anything else. Her head was turbaned in black cloth coming down almost to her eyes, giving them a sinister, cruel look.

"She is a Black Bone Lolo," Tiso Awa whispered. "One of the royal stock."

The woman brought her horse to an abrupt halt near the pile of wood that I had seen earlier that day. She instructed the three men who rode with her to dismount, which they did. They were dressed in white gowns, except for one who wore the gray-blue tunic of a Chinese uniform. I couldn't tell whether he had at one time been a soldier or whether the uniform had been taken from a dead soldier.

The woman was very surly with the men. When she saw that there was not much more than the wood to be had she seemed to get angry with them. I could barely make out her speech, although I could detect similarities to my own tongue.

The wood was loaded on one of the horses, while one of

the men took a jug from another. He wiped the top with his hand and handed it to the woman. She took a few long swallows, wiping her face with her hand afterwards, and handed it back to the man.

We had not been detected, but the gods were in a humorous mood. Tiso Awa's horse rambled down the mountain from the other side and, following her nose, began to nibble at the tufts of grass on the plain. Kareem and Tiso Awa swore under their breath and made their rifles ready.

The horse walked quietly toward the woman, who seemed as surprised as we were at his wretched appearance. She laughed but her smile did not soften her bearing; it gave her face a cruel twist.

Two of the men came toward Tiso Awa's horse. They sized her up and down, laughing. Tiso Awa's horse, who even on her best days did not give a regal appearance, seemed all the more puny compared to the Lolos' animals.

One of the men took the horse by the reins and led her toward the Lolo woman. Tiso Awa suppressed his anger. This horse meant a great deal to him.

But he had no need to worry; after the Lolos had a good long laugh, the woman ordered the horse to be released. She seemed to be saying that it would bring disgrace on her, should she take such a wretched creature.

Tiso Awa breathed a silent sigh of relief, but Kareem kept his rifle on the woman. The Lolos were about to leave when one of the men stopped and turned around. Apparently, he thought he saw something. As the others were riding off, he called to them.

Fortunately, the woman would have no delay. The man

looked directly at the rocks that were hiding us. Then he looked around and called the woman again.

Now she was getting angry. She instructed the man to join them and stop wasting time. He turned and rode off, and soon the four riders and two packhorses were off across the plain.

"They have stolen the wood," Kareem said. "In the winter, they will come back for the nomads."

When they were safely out of sight, Tiso Awa climbed down from the rocks and approached his horse, who was calmly nibbling at the grass. He scolded her for a long time but she went on doing exactly as she pleased, which surprised no one.

The House on the Taja Road

Two more days' march through the narrow gorges of the Tung Ho brought us just above the tiny village of Taja, which sits on a vast open plain at the southern mouth of the gorges.

As we penetrated the chasms, the rugged rocky tops of the surrounding mountains gradually gave way to thick forests of evergreen and poplars. There was a noticeable increase in activity.

We saw Chinese woodcutters on the high slopes. They rolled their logs into the Tung Ho, which would carry them downriver. Much as we did not like the Chinese presence, it meant that if the Chinese felt safe enough to work these forests, they did not fear brigands in the area.

Many tea caravans, their yaks loaded with tea, were headed north for the roads that would take them to central

Tibet. This too was a good indication that we were not far from our first destination, Tatsienlu, where the tea trade flourished.

We also saw at least three detachments of Chinese soldiers ride by. They were from the garrison at Tatsienlu, where the Chinese magistrate of these provinces made his headquarters. One of these parties of soldiers stopped us to see if all our papers were in order; they rode on after carefully examining Kareem's well-forged papers. I had no idea what they were looking for.

The road to Taja was an unhappy one, lined from one end to another with decrepit and deserted buildings in all states of decay. Once this was a thriving area where a great deal of trade had taken place, but it had fallen victim to a system called *ula.*

An *ula* is like a passport but much more. The holder of such a document is usually a noble (Chinese or Tibetan), an official or a highly placed lama. With this document, they are entitled to secure what horses and provisions they want from the peasants they pass en route. They are not required to give any payment, usually take the man's best animals and invariably use the subterfuge of "official business." It is easy to see how this privilege can be abused.

The peasants had been taken advantage of to the point that it was a great hardship to continue living near the road, under the constant threat of *ula.* A dwelling near the road became a curse, and more and more peasants abandoned their homes and moved to the hills. The land may not have been as good, but they escaped the exactions of the much-abused and hated *ula.*

Now their houses stood in crumbling decay as a grim

reminder of the power of greed. There are many such deserted towns throughout the country; even in Hor Drango, a number of old houses are in abandoned ruin.

But nowhere have I seen so many deserted houses; nowhere were the results of *ula* more evident than on the road to Taja. It was easy to understand why. Taja and its road were in the most unfortunate position. Any "official" taking the north road could not avoid passing this spot before entering the gorges from the south.

It was a sad and dreary picture, and the light rain that had followed us all morning through the gorges did little to brighten things.

We rode through quietly under the heavy gray sky. It seemed we all felt the same remorse about the road to Taja and had no wish to speak and arouse the dormant ghosts who once lived here.

As we were passing by one of these old houses, the light rain of the morning gradually increased. And then with a suddenness that sometimes happens in these places, the sky opened up and the rain fell hard and heavy. The thunder god added his voice to the wind and the rain and we were forced to seek some shelter. The rain was so heavy that we could hardly see in front of us and so loud as it attacked the earth that we could barely hear each other

Tiso Awa, who was at the head of our tiny column, directed us to an old house not far off the road. It was a house much like any of the others on the road, with a flat roof and two stories. From its size I gathered that a wealthy peasant may have once lived there. But time and weather had already taken their toll. The flat roof had all but caved in, its tiny altar jutting up from the rubble like the beginnings of a mountain. The wall facing the canyon was nearly completely leveled by the winds; another wall had many holes in it from the wind and the weather and seemed to be in its last days. But it was the closest house for us to take refuge and we were sure that none of the other houses on the Taja road were any better.

As we approached the house, the stable door swung freely from one hinge as if not ready to give up its job of protecting the land and home. Then, even over the wind, rain and thunder, I was sure I heard something. Something that should not have been there. Kareem, too, noticed something and stopped with the rain pouring down on him.

"What was that?" I shouted over the noise. "It sounded like running."

Kareem looked at me as I looked at him.

"Come," Tiso Awa was already leading his horse into the stable. "The stalls are in surprisingly good condition. Do you not know enough to get out of the rain?"

We both hesitated but then followed him inside.

"I heard something," I told Tiso Awa as I put my horse into one of the stalls.

"You always hear things in these houses." Tiso smiled. "It is usually nothing more than the wind. Or perhaps," he pointed up to the caved-in roof, "you heard that family of bats snoring."

There were about forty bats living out their slumbering days, attached to the roof.

I laughed, but I wasn't convinced, nor was Kareem. He stood in the middle of the floor surveying the house.

"Well," Tiso Awa said as he sat down on the earth floor, "this is as good a spot as any to sit out this Tibetan rain. And

I for one intend to make the best of it." He took out a bag of snuff.

Just then, there was another sound. This time it seemed to come from above. Tiso's hands dropped to his sides as he looked up.

"I did hear that," Tiso looked at me with his expression changing, "and unless these bats wear boots, there is something or someone up there."

He got up and walked over to the wooden stairs leading to the rooms above. This was at one time a wealthy home to have had such stairs built.

"There is only one way to find out what this is about." He began to climb the steps. "Only one way."

The rifle fell from his shoulders. As he took another step a frightened voice suddenly came from behind us.

"Not another step," the voice said. "Please. Not another step."

We all turned toward the open stable door. In the doorstep was a Chinese soldier dripping with rain, waving his rifle. He seemed very nervous. He was a short fellow with tiny eyes and large lips. He nervously kept biting his bottom lip as he waved the gun at us.

"Please," he motioned us to a corner with his rifle, "move over there."

We obeyed, having no idea what he had in mind. My eyes glanced to my pony and to the saddlebag carrying the *migou* skin. What did I have to fear from Chinese soldiers, I thought to myself. I am just a young caravan man on the way to Tatsienlu. This skin is something I found on the road. If I were discovered, that is what I would tell them. But what had I to fear?

Even as these thoughts crossed my mind, I could not help feeling terribly afraid. Tiso Awa and Kareem Musa were as calm as ever and I believe that I successfully hid my apprehensions.

"Who are you?" The Chinese soldier looked at Tiso Awa. "What do you want here?"

"Want?" Tiso looked back at him. "Only to get out of the rain. We are caravan men headed for Tatsienlu to sign on with a caravan. Our papers are all here. Let me show you. . . ."

"No," the soldier interrupted, waving his gun. "Keep your hands where they are."

Tiso Awa turned and whispered to me, "It's becoming clearer what this is all about." Then he turned to the soldier. "Well," he said in an exasperated voice. "What do you want of us?"

Suddenly we heard the sounds from upstairs again.

"Well," Tiso said calmly.

"I want you to leave," the soldier blurted out in a nervous tone.

"Leave?" Tiso's voice mocked him. "We intend to leave as soon as the rain stops."

"Now," the soldier cried.

Tiso turned to me again. "Yes, I understand," he whispered.

"What are you saying?" the soldier asked angrily.

"I told my friend that I have heard only wonderful things about the Chinese soldiers and that surely one would not drive us out into the rain when there is enough room here for all of us." He looked up to the second floor. "All of us," he repeated. Then, with a sly sideways look, he added, "You

102

are part of the Chinese garrison in Tatsienlu, are you not?"

"You are taking a big risk, caravan man." The soldier approached Tiso, who did not change his expression.

"You are nervous and you wave a rifle but I assure you that you have nothing to fear from us." Tiso looked him right in the eyes. "We only stopped here to get out of the rain."

"A big risk." The Chinese soldier bit his bottom lip, but Tiso Awa went on anyway.

"You are a deserter," he told the soldier, "but why fear us? We have as much use for your army as you have."

The rifle barrel was under Tiso Awa's chin. He calmly moved it away.

Just then, the sounds from above became louder and a figure descended the stairs—a young Tibetan girl, very pretty with long black hair that fell to her waist and intelligent eyes that were red from crying.

"Ah," Tiso smiled at her, "the other soldier."

"Forgive my husband," she said as she walked over to the soldier and took his gun. "It was not loaded anyway."

She turned to the soldier. "Foolish man," she said in a way that Tibetan women talk to their husbands. "You would drive these men out into the rain. Can you not tell the good from the bad?"

She addressed us. "I am sorry. You must understand that in our position, we can not trust anyone. But the truth is that we have had nothing to eat for two days. Can you spare us something?"

The Chinese Soldier's Sad Story

After consuming a meal of buttered tea and *tsamba,* all of us sat around the large *k'ang.* It was in good working order despite the house that was falling down around it.

The bats had flown away for the night, and now that human beings were taking their home, we doubted whether they would return to a smoky house.

Outside the heavy rain had stopped and only a light misty rain fell. It was getting colder as we gathered around the *k'ang.*

Hsi Teng, the Chinese soldier, sat back with his legs crossed in front of him, very grateful for the food that we gave him and his wife. His nervousness was still obvious as he continually bit his bottom lip, but every now and then he managed a somewhat relaxed smile. He told us the unhappy circumstances that had brought him to this place.

"I am not what you think," he began as the snuff was being passed around. "I am not a coward. But neither am I a soldier. I am, or at least I was, a farmer. With my father, we had a small farm not two days west of Chengtu in Szechwan. It was not an easy life but I was content to accept what was thrust upon me and I would have remained content were it not for the Moslem insurrection and a certain Captain Cher Eh Feng. . . ."

Kareem suddenly looked up and I could see the anger in his eyes. "You marched with that dog?" He spoke each word slowly.

"I did." Hsi Teng's head went down.

Suddenly it was very quiet.

"But I had no part of the massacre of Urimachi," the soldier was quick to add. "I assure you of that. No one was more disgusted than I at the horrible things that took place in that wretched place. I will not deny that some of your brothers may have fallen at my hands, but they were soldiers, and in war some soldiers must die. Is that not right?"

He looked around to everyone but no one answered.

"The fact is," he continued, "that after the second siege of Urimachi, when the Moslems offered such stiff resistance, Captain Cher Eh Feng marched through many villages gathering recruits to throw into battle.

"I was, if you will, ripped away from my farm by this scoundrel. Had my father been younger, he too would have been 'recruited.' We were told that our time in service would only be for the duration of the Urimachi siege. Then we would be allowed to return to our homes.

"But this was not the case. After two weeks of heavy fighting, Urimachi finally fell and the captain marched in gloriously. The people there had no illusions as to their fate and many women had already committed suicide."

The siege of Urimachi and the subsequent destruction of the entire town were well known in the region. In places where Moslem unrest was still strong, the name Urimachi had become the battle cry. The Chinese soldier did not have to give details.

"But as I said before," Hsi Teng bit his lip again, "I did not take part in any of the slaughter—much to my own undoing. The lieutenant who led our detachment was going to shoot me on the spot. As I waited for the bullet, the captain himself interrupted. 'Why kill able men even if they are cowards,' he said. 'There is plenty of use for them in the western provinces where they are sure to meet more unpleasant deaths at the hands of the barbarians.'

"Ten of us were transferred here, under guard. Two men escaped. I do not know what happened to them.

"In Tatsienlu I served under the corrupt General Rang Fa. We were never paid, although funds from Chengtu arrived monthly. We were treated like dogs, and there was little chance of escaping back to China.

"What could I do? I resigned myself to a new life at this far outpost of the empire.

"Then," he pointed to his wife, "I met Tashi. She made me feel very happy in spite of the wretched conditions. I had to face the jibes and ridicule of my comrades, but what did I care what they said. 'Marry a barbarian woman with big feet,' I used to hear. 'They don't work and one night she is sure to slit your throat.'

"I could take all this as long as we were together in Tatsienlu. A number of years had passed and I had given up all hope of returning to China. But the army had other plans for me, and I was to be transferred once more to Chengtu.

"I did not want to go. I pleaded with the captain and offered a substantial bribe which, I might add, he took. But nothing changed.

"I could not take Tashi back with me, for she would surely fall ill and die in the lowlands of China and be subjected to the most cruel insults from the people. But I could not leave her either. And I will not. There was nothing to do. So here we are."

"Where will you go?" I asked.

"We will go toward Lhasa," Tashi spoke up. "As yet, there

is no Chinese army there. But I too have run away. I was promised to a man of my village whom I do not love. But all the arrangements had been made, the contracts drawn. They are looking for me as well."

"You understand our positions, sirs," Hsi Teng lamented. "We can neither return to China nor is it safe to stay in Tibet. We are plagued by misfortune."

A Happy Surprise for Kareem

Hsi Teng finished his story. No one noticed that the rain had already stopped. Through the breaks in the beams above, I could see the clouds swiftly move by, followed by the first blue light of dusk, while in the distance a wall crumbled under the weight of water, sounding at first like the grumbling of a yak.

The old house seemed solid enough, although heavy drops of water bounced from every exposed beam. For a time, it appeared that the rain had stopped outside only to return inside.

Kareem found himself under heavy attack by the rain, having lost his invaluable waterproof cape to the She Chu. He finally conceded victory to the elements once again, and walked over to one of the stalls where his horse stood contentedly. She was pleased that there would not be a full day's riding and I'm sure was secretly blessing the rain.

With firm, rough hands, Kareem shoved the rump of the animal to one side so he could get into the stall as well. The animal resisted at first but then gave way. Kareem, first looking up to make sure he did not pick a rainy spot, rolled out his sheepskin and lay back.

"What do you expect of us?" he asked from his stable bed. "Do you think that you are the only ones who have a sad tale to tell?"

"We ask nothing of you," the Chinese soldier answered, biting his lip nervously. "Nothing more than what you have already done for us. You have given my wife and myself nourishment for which we are grateful. I know that to be alive is to suffer. I accept this."

Kareem laughed sarcastically. "I am going to sleep," he announced.

"My friend is usually more understanding," Tiso Awa apologized for Kareem Musa. "It is the loss of his tobacco to the river *nags* of the upper She Chu and the absence of his evening pipe which have made him less tolerant to the hardships of others."

"Is it tobacco you need?" the soldier asked, his voice brightening.

"We have tobacco," Tashi called out.

The red-bearded face appeared from behind the horse. "You have tobacco?" Kareem's tone had changed.

"We do," the soldier answered proudly as he reached into his dingy uniform and lifted out a long clay pipe, followed by a small goathide bag containing tobacco.

"I have managed to salvage this much of my life," the soldier said as he displayed the pipe and tobacco.

By now, Kareem had moved to his side, and although he had picked a particularly wet spot, he did not seem to mind. He grabbed the pipe from the soldier without ceremony. Examining it carefully from every angle, he turned to the soldier. "The tobacco," he demanded.

The soldier did not hesitate. For the first time, I could see

108

the beginnings of a genuine smile cross his face. "I am happy," he watched Kareem load the pipe, "that we have found a way to repay the kindness you gentlemen have shown us. Could I do any less than offer you what we have?"

Then his smile faded. "But I must apologize for the quality of the tobacco. An inferior blend by your standards, I am sure."

Kareem lifted a small piece of burning wood from the fire with the help of two branches. Only after the pipe was lit did he realize that he was once again in the path of the rain. He moved slowly.

"It will do." He took a long puff as he came to my side.

"It is the Szechwan variety," the soldier continued, anxious to please. "Not very expensive. But you must know that a soldier's pay, even when he is paid, does not amount to much."

"Enough of your laments." Kareem looked sharply at the soldier. "Your tobacco will do."

Then I found the pipe in my hand. I hesitated, because although from time to time Grandmother used to give me some of her snuff, I had never actually smoked a pipe. But how could I refuse? What kind of caravan man would they think me if I did? I thought back to Hor Drango and the Chinese inn, where caravan men gathered around a pipe. These thoughts brought me to my grandmother and her snuff.

I felt all eyes were on me as I inhaled deeply on the pipe. It was harsh and strong and I wondered if it was indeed the quality of the tobacco.

I watched the smoke curl up before my eyes, adding to the smoke already filling the room. Thoughts of the home and the people I had left emerged from the faint gray wisps of smoke. Suddenly, the realization that I had left all that behind and would probably never see my home or family again went through me like the sharp point of a Golok lance. I longed to be at the foot of Toa Shan once more, although only days before I had felt a prisoner of the mountain. I missed the comforting touch of Grandmother's long fingers as she probed my hair for lice. I had emerged from the gorges of the She Chu but I did not feel that I had grown in any way. And now I felt a stranger in the midst of strangers.

All this flashed quickly before my mind's eye and presently I was jolted back to reality by the sound of coughing. I realized that I was making the sound.

Attempting, with little success, to subdue the coughing, I handed the pipe to Tashi, who looked at me the way my mother used to when she knew that I was not being completely honest.

"Have you been traveling the caravan road a long time?" she asked good-naturedly. "Tell me, how long has it been?"

Everyone laughed.

"It is more like days," I admitted between coughs and sputters.

"Ah, an honest caravan man." Tiso Awa smiled and patted me gently on the back. "You will be a rarity among your kind."

More laughter.

Then once again, I found the pipe in front of me. I was determined not to cough, but determination was not enough; another long round of coughing followed the two small puffs I took from the pipe. This was followed by dizziness which I believe I was able to conceal from all but Tashi.

"You men may sit here with your pipe," she said, as she

began to climb the stairs to the second floor. "I plan to get some rest before tomorrow comes."

This was the way I felt but I would not be the first man to suggest it. Tiso Awa came to my rescue by announcing that he, too, was going to sleep, and I quickly took advantage, forcing a long yawn.

We left Kareem and his new friend, the Chinese soldier, to their pipe. Kareem shifted himself again as the water seemed to single him out for torture. But as with everything else, the sullen Turkestani accepted and made little of it. After all, at least he had a pipe to smoke.

Tashi left us and climbed the notched log to the second floor of the crumbling house. Tiso Awa yawned and walked to his horse. He took a sheepskin from a saddlebag and searched the ground for a dry spot, finally settling down near his horse. I followed him.

Kareem Musa and Hsi Teng smoked and talked well into the night. I know this because I slept very restlessly. The insects had multiplied as a result of the rain and while they never were able to keep me awake before, it seemed that I needed little excuse that night.

I awoke just before dawn. Kareem, who had moved away from the falling drops of water the night before, was sleeping quietly near a muddy puddle, undeterred by the water. But Hsi Teng was still sitting by the fire, although it, as well as his pipe, had been cold for some time. I moved around and saw that the soldier's eyes were closed. He was sleeping in a sitting position. It was very strange, for he was not meditating, just sleeping.

Later that morning, I helped Tashi make the tea by bringing the water from the nearby stream. "Your husband sleeps sitting up?" I asked her.

"Yes," she said sadly, "don't you know why?"

I admitted my ignorance.

"You know that he served under Captain Feng? That dog of a man is without a heart. He is as cruel if not crueler to the men who serve him than he is to anyone else. When my husband refused to take part in the massacre, Feng took immediate steps before sending him to Tatsienlu. He was thrashed with heavy boards until the skin fell from his back. The wounds do not heal fast."

More Talk of *Migou*

The morning promised rain, and it was not long in coming. Pushed along by the strong winds, the clouds gathering in the east, on the plains of China, were soon above us with threatening grayness. The rain from the day before had left its mark on the terrain, leaving numerous deep puddles, muddy and difficult to cross.

We did not have to go very far to find water for the horses, but the mud caught their hoofs and only after much exertion, sloshing and struggling released them. There was also the added discomfort of hungry insects, who appeared in great numbers on the rain-drenched plain. It was bad for us and even worse for the horses, who made no attempts to disguise their discomfort.

When Tashi and I brought the horses back into the stalls, they seemed relieved for they had no wish to continue the journey that day, even if we did.

Tiso Awa came over to examine his brown-and-white

pony, brushing the insects away. "I care less for this Tibetan weather than you do," he whispered in the animal's big floppy ear. "But what can we do?"

He seemed to be waiting for the horse to answer, and then turned to us and answered himself. "We can stay here," he decided. "There is no point in pushing our animals where they have no desire to be pushed. We'll wait until tomorrow." He smiled, looking at his horse. "That's better, isn't it?"

Nobody objected. Kareem and Hsi Teng resumed the positions they had the night before, Kareem stoking the fire into a bright blaze. Neither looked up; they seemed happy that the decision had been made for them.

"Do you think it's safe for us to remain as well?" Tashi asked her husband. "I feel we are too close to the garrison at Dawu."

"Dawu," her husband waved his hand, "is a good day's ride from here. They only have a sergeant in charge of that garrison, and I know him to be a woman who needs no small excuse to find a reason to stay where he is. This rain is a major inconvenience and I doubt he would attempt a search under these conditions. Besides, where do you suggest we go?"

She sat down by his side, took a *tsamba* bowl from her gown and said no more. But her sympathetic eyes were anxious and it was evident that she did not stop worrying.

"Your face troubles me." Her husband looked at her. "What is better to do than nothing at all?"

"Spoken like a true Szechwanese." Tiso Awa laughed.

"In my country," the soldier went on, encouraged by the reception, "one does not need to find excuses for loafing." He turned to Tiso Awa. "How do you plan to arrive in Tatsienlu?" he asked directly.

Tiso helped himself to some buttered tea. "Do you have a route to propose?" he asked.

"We can only tell you what route to avoid," Tashi said. "We ourselves did not come through Tcheta pass."

"Tcheta pass," the soldier continued, "lies beyond the Dawu valley and it is the last major mountain barrier that must be crossed to reach that town from the north. But this is a well-traveled road and so liable to be swarming with Chinese soldiers."

"Dawu was my home," Tashi said longingly, "and I can tell you that at this time of year, there will be as many as ten caravans waiting for the rains to end so as to reach Tatsienlu. When the clouds finally are lifted, there will be a mad bunching up of caravans eager to get across."

"So it is settled." Tiso smiled broadly. "We will avoid Tcheta pass."

"No, no, no," Tashi exclaimed emphatically. "That is the way you must go. It is the only safe way."

"Good." Tiso Awa smiled again, seemingly taking all of this talk very lightly. "We will take Tcheta pass."

Tashi looked at her husband. It appeared that she was hesitant to talk about the other route. The Chinese soldier bit his lip and then looked at each one of us.

"But you must be aware of the dangers," he said, "even on Tcheta pass."

"Dangers?" I asked.

"Migou," Tashi answered flatly. "In the region between here and Tatsienlu there have been migou sightings."

The words went sharply through me. "Have you seen a migou?" I asked anxiously.

114

"No." Tashi shuddered. "We have not seen them, but they are there. We heard them."

I moved closer to the fire. My excitement was obvious and Tashi was more than a little surprised at my reaction.

"Mind you," her husband continued, "if there are *migou* there, they are sure to be on Tcheta as well. No one can be sure. But this much we can say—*migou* are wandering the forests beyond Koja."

"Then that is where we must go." I turned to Tiso Awa.

"The boy does not fear them," Tiso Awa explained. "His father, a Bon priest, has given him confidence."

"Only fools would follow a child into the mouth of a dragon," Tashi spoke strongly. "I do not know what charms your father has prepared for you, but I am sure that you have never seen or heard a *migou*. Otherwise you would not speak as you do. We have heard them."

"You have never heard them," Hsi Teng shook his head, "otherwise you would not be so eager to see them."

"I'm not afraid," I said proudly.

"But I am," Kareem suddenly spoke up. "You have a skin which you feel offers you protection, but I have no such thing."

"A skin?" Hsi Teng asked.

"I do not depend on skins for my protection," Kareem went on, "but on the mercy of Allah, who has a purpose for all things that are done. Trust in Allah."

"In your country," Tashi came to my defense, "perhaps that is the way to enlightenment." She turned to me. "But surely you must be aware of the dangers a *migou* can bring. You would be better off to throw the skin away or give it to a monastery. Do not confuse bravery with foolishness, Small Ears. Only evil demons and their kind are involved with such an animal. I have told you that we have heard the *migou.*"

"I cannot cast the skin off," I explained to her, surprised at my own voice. It was as if Grandmother were speaking through my voice. It was with that tone of finality, that no more can be said or discussed or proposed, that I spoke of the skin and how I came to possess it. When I had finished my story, both Tashi and Hsi Teng, although unable to touch the skin, at least looked at it.

Kareem once again put things in their place. "It is his protection," he said.

I folded the skin up once more and placed it in my saddlebag, which I used as a pillow. There was nothing more to be said.

However, later that night, when I thought everyone was asleep, I noticed Tashi sitting alone at the door to the house. The moonlight was bright. It glistened on her black hair, which seemed to absorb every ray.

Quietly, I came to her side. "You are troubled," I said, "but things will turn out fine."

She tried to smile. "And you are still determined to face a *migou?*" she spoke softly.

"I have no choice," I replied. "You must tell me where."

"You see there," she pointed toward the south, where in the distance one could barely make out the tops of the Dawu Monastery, "beyond the Dawu valley. From there one road leads to Tcheta and Tatsienlu. Another, the one that we took, does not go directly, but passes two small villages, Olosu and Koja. You'll find nothing there except for a few small houses, and with these rains, they may have been washed away. But there is a vast uninhabited region beyond Koja. High timber country and very rough. When we left

116

Tatsienlu, we did not have the luxury of time, nor were we willing to be spotted among the caravans waiting to cross Tcheta. That is why we took this route and that is where we heard the *migou.*"

More of Tashi

The rain continued for three days. It was not the heavy, drenching rain of the first days, but more of a thick mist of low clouds that gave the surrounding landscape the appearance of perpetual dawn.

It was enough to discourage Tiso Awa, who had assumed the responsibility of making decisions for our small caravan. Each morning he went outside, only to come back shuddering and cursing the Tibetan weather. Finally, he'd announce that it was not a good day to continue.

Kareem was content to abide by his decisions. He had found a new friend in Hsi Teng, he had a pipe and tobacco and claimed to need little else to see him through life.

Hsi Teng and Tashi had no place to go; no destination called them. Their only aim was to avoid the Chinese soldiers, who, everyone knew, would sooner or later come by the house. For the moment, this did not distress Hsi Teng.

I, it seemed, was the only one who was eager to keep moving. But I did not press the issue. As the son of a Bon lama I could calculate a series of unlucky days, and to travel on any one of them could prove disastrous.

Nevertheless, I could not conceal my impatience. Tiso Awa was aware of this. Though he had only to point out that these were unlucky days to travel, he humored me by explaining that his horse had not yet given him the word to go.

"She will not go into this weather," he politely explained. "There is, I am sure, a little Sikkimese mule in her family, for have you ever known an animal to be as stubborn as she? And she will not go."

I could understand why. In the early mornings, I took the animals out to graze on the scant grass that popped up in between the puddles and holes that covered the plain. They liked this, and for the first time they had a healthy if thin appearance.

I found that a routine began to settle in and my life had changed little from the way it was in Hor Drango. I was still responsible for the feeding and the watering of the horses. I paid particular attention to Tiso Awa's mount, hoping that favorable treatment might convince her it was time to move on.

I did the chores usually left to women and children— stirring the pot, fetching wood—and in the process came to know Tashi quite well.

She was in many ways a remarkable woman. Her family in Dawu was very wealthy, one of the noble families, and she was comely as well. She admitted things were difficult, but she had made the choice. She chose a poor Chinese soldier who offered her a life of running and what I falsely mistook for despair.

"You say that your karma will lead you to the *migou*," she told me, "and this is how I feel about my man. I do not fool myself into a belief that if the gods see love, they will make things right. But I know, just as you cannot avoid what waits for you, I cannot avoid my feelings for my husband."

Yet even with this attachment to him, she did not accept the usually passive role assigned to Chinese women. She ordered her husband around, telling him what he could and could not do, and in every way was a Tibetan woman. She was, in fact, very much like my grandmother.

I began to look forward to those early mornings when Tashi and I went out with the animals for water. She had done and seen a great deal in her time and appeared as eager to share her experiences with me as I was to hear them.

She knew Tatsienlu quite well, having lived not far from the town for most of her life. She told me about the great monasteries that were there and the golden spires on top of the castle of the king of Chala.

She spoke very well of the king. "He has managed to resist the Chinese advance into his region. A very reliable and strong man. Neither the monks nor the Chinese will make a move without consulting him. Yes, in Chala there is a real king."

It was quite different in Hor Drango, I told her. Although we had a king, he had little more than weak authority; rather than pity him for his fall from power, I was taught to scorn him as a weakling.

"Do not be so quick to judge," she told me. "Power, like all things, is impermanent. It is subject to the same stresses and whims that anything is. And as death follows life, power decays and disappears."

I listened to her arguments. As she was a devout Buddhist, I could understand her feelings. But this did not change my opinion of the king of Hor Drango, whom I still viewed as ineffectual and cowardly.

Then she asked me many questions about my life in Hor Drango and what drove me to the caravan roads in the company of these two mulemen. When I told her about my attraction to *migou* and how I could not explain it, she asked why it was that my father, a Bon lama of some power, could not predict or explain what karma awaited me.

"He has tried," I explained, "to work out my future from the stars and has even consulted other powerful lamas on my behalf, but, for some reason, when it comes to me, all the answers become cloudy. I cannot explain it."

The horses were watered now and we were leading them back to the house. She stopped.

"I hesitate to build up your hopes," she said, "but there is someone in Tatsienlu who may be able to help you. But it is difficult."

"You must tell me," I pleaded.

"There is one in Tatsienlu who is more powerful than the monks, the Chinese, even the king."

She gestured me to sit down near a large boulder and came to my side as we let the reins of the horses fall so that they could graze on the fresh grass popping up in every available part of the land.

"He is the oracle Sung," she went on. "You have heard of him, I'm sure."

I confessed that I had. But I was unaware of his reputation.

"Then it is only the mountains that separate our provinces that have contained his fame. In this part of the country, he is well known. General Fa is a steady visitor to Sung, as are all the nobles and people of wealth in Tatsienlu. That is the problem: he is not an easy man to see. I cannot say if he will see you. And if he does, how will you pay him? He demands a high fee for his services."

120

"I will find a way," I said. "But how do I find this Sung?"

She laughed. "Find him? Anyone in Tatsienlu can point out the dwelling of the oracle Sung. Seeing him is another matter."

"I will find a way," I said determinedly.

"I think you will." She laughed. "I have a friend in Tatsienlu who may be able to help. Her name is Rinchen Dorje and you will find her place near the second bridge not far from the tea warehouses. She, too, is well known in Tatsienlu. Tell her that you have seen me, and that should be a beginning. But come, the horses are wandering away. We must bring them back or your friends will think that they have been devoured by tigers. Come, bring the horses."

I wanted to ask more but Tashi, like Grandmother, had a way of terminating a conversation so that little more could be said or asked. Her mind had now turned to our immediate duties and I could see that it would not be moved.

We started toward the house, but Tashi stopped at one of the other deserted houses before we reached our own. She disappeared inside but soon emerged with a load of wood under her arms.

"Here we are fleeing the Chinese soldiers," she said, "fugitives with nowhere to go, and yet we have the luxury of wood for our fire. Even so, I have only taken the wood that I found lying about. This house, I am sure, is haunted and I would not disturb the way things are."

As we approached our crumbling house Kareem Musa was scolding Hsi Teng in loud and certain terms. The argument revolved around the way Hsi Teng allowed his wife to treat him.

"You are Chinese," he was saying. "The Tibetans I shall

121

never understand, but you are Chinese. How do you let a woman tell you what to do?"

Hsi Teng made no attempt to defend his actions and only shook his head with a smile. This was, perhaps, because he saw his wife at the door. He tried in vain to quiet his friend, but Kareem went on about the unfair way his friend was being treated. When Tashi and I entered, Kareem took little notice, and even when she threw a quick, penetrating glance, Kareem continued.

She was very calm. She approached Kareem with the wood under her arms and then ceremoniously dropped it just near the Turkestani's feet.

"He does not have it so bad," she said, as if she took little notice of what she had done. "I still gather the wood and the water and do all the work that is expected of me." Then she bent down and threw a piece of wood into the fire.

Kareem grunted. He wanted to say something but hesitated and finally grunted again. He would never understand Tibetan women but decided not to make an issue with this particular one.

They looked at each other eye to eye, neither blinking nor flinching, and finally Kareem reached for another cup of tea. He was defiant but so was Tashi. Meanwhile Hsi Teng heaved a long sigh of relief.

"Look," he pointed to his wife's large feet, attempting to change the subject, "would you have me with a Chinese woman? They have little feet and do not work well. I am much better off with this Tibetan woman."

He attempted a laugh as Tashi gently took his cup and filled it with tea. Then she handed the cup to her husband.

"See," he tried again, "see how much better off I am?"

Tashi allowed him that.

So it went for three days. Then, very late in the evening of the third day, I was stirred from my sleep by Kareem.

"Come, Small Ears," he said to me, "Tiso Awa's horse has given the go-ahead. We're leaving."

I jumped up. Kareem's pony was already loaded and Tiso was in the process of getting his mount ready. I looked around. It was very dark and colder than it had been. I rubbed the sleep out of my eyes and walked over to my pony.

"We're going?" I asked in disbelief.

By now Kareem and Tiso had already led their mounts outside the door. Then I realized that it was snowing. Large heavy flakes were falling in great gusts. I understood now why they had chosen this moment to go.

The snow was the first we had seen. It promised an early winter. If Tatsienlu was to be reached, it must be now, or all the passes would be buried. We had no provisions for a longer stay.

Hsi Teng and Tashi were standing by the door. He was shivering.

"Which way will you go?" he asked.

"This may not continue," Tiso replied looking around. "We will not attempt Tcheta pass, but we will take the other route."

"And you?" I asked quietly, as I brought my pony outside.

"We will find a place." He smiled.

"I know that you will." I looked at Tashi. But this was not altogether true. I felt that they would know more hardship before they found their place. It did not take oracular powers to see this, for they were people living on the edge of an abyss. Movement in any direction could plunge them into disaster.

"Come, Small Ears," Tiso Awa called to me. "We must ride as far as possible before afternoon, when the winds will come up."

Now I, who was so eager to leave, was the last one to march out. As I walked my pony toward the other riders, I heard heavy trudging on the newly falling snow. Hsi Teng ran up behind me and came to Kareem. Shivering and breathing very heavily, he took a small bag of tobacco from his uniform.

"My wife said I should not," he looked at the Turkestani, "but I don't always listen to her. I am sorry thát it is still the Szechwan variety but . . ."

Kareem took the bag.

"Thank your wife." He smiled, for he knew that Tashi herself had sent her husband.

"And if you see any soldiers," Hsi Teng said as he walked back, "please do not reveal us."

"You have nothing to fear on that account," Kareem said angrily. "Have you learned nothing of us in this time?"

"Yes, of course." Hsi Teng bit his lip. "But my wife . . ."

Then we turned and marched toward Tatsienlu.

The fine mist of days before had become icicles lashing at our faces. But this was the lucky day for which we had been waiting.

The Ride to Tatsienlu

Tiso Awa was right. It did not snow for very long, it lasted only into early morning. A brisk ride across the plain brought us to the first of the mountains. Although it was not particularly high, it was quite steep and somewhat treacherous. It took most of the day to climb. Beyond it, mountains piled on mountains, some with their snow-capped crowns burning red in the falling sun.

We were eager to make as much progress as possible, racing the sun as it began its descent over the mountains. Even well-known routes are dangerous to travel at night. None of us had ever been to this region before. As we watched the flat plain disappear behind us, it was with some apprehension.

To compound our difficulties, the stream that we had been using to guide our route fell away from the mountain and plunged into a deep roaring chasm. There was no discernible path through the heavily timbered forest that lined the lower parts of the mountain. The horses stumbled and protested, and at one point Tiso Awa's mare refused to go on any farther.

Any other time, perhaps, the Mongol would have indulged this animal he thought so much of, but now he would have none of it. He struggled and pulled her up the steep ridges, calling her every conceivable name.

We finally reached a small clearing where a forest of dwarf rhododendron bushes gave way to evergreen and pines. Tiso sat down, exhausted.

"She is as stubborn as a Sikkimese mule," he lamented. "And I doubt whether she will enjoy better rebirths if this is how she repays the kindness I have offered."

"She fears something." I came to the horse's defense.

"Nonsense," Tiso Awa replied flatly. "She fears work."

As we penetrated deeper and deeper into the dark forest, I had the uneasy feeling something was about to happen. There were things in this forest that were not easily explained.

125

We saw musk deer on spindly legs, foraging around the brush. As we passed them, they took little notice of us. One curious fellow even followed us for a while before he found another succulent bush to dine on.

I wondered why in an area so rich in timber we did not encounter one Chinese woodsman or see any evidence that some had been there. But I kept my question to myself.

We continued to climb, with only the sounds of the river crashing below us and our own breath attempting to take in as much air as possible.

Upon reaching the summit, we saw a pile of stones and a prayer flag with tufts of wool snapping in the early evening air. This was evidence that others had climbed this pass. They had issued the familiar prayer, "The gods are victorious," and laid a stone on a pile of stones to thank the gods and mark that they had been there.

Only one who did not value his life would attempt to descend an unknown mountain by moonlight, so we made camp.

Fortunately, we could build a fire for there was a little shrubbery around and Tiso Awa had instructed me to collect some yak chips while we were on the plain in anticipation of starting a fire. Even so, it was a difficult task, since the wind rambled and caused mischief on this desolate summit. But Tiso Awa, determined not to be denied his bowl of tea, began to dig a hole in the ground with his hands. When he was satisfied that the hole was deep enough, he placed some shrubbery and the yak chips inside and began the fire with his flint box.

"This is a Mongolian fire," he explained. "The winds off the dry Mongolian plain are just as treacherous as these that roam the summit of the mountains. One must be prepared for everything."

I will admit that, in spite of all my apprehensions, I cannot remember being so nourished by a bowl of tea as I was that night on the summit of the mountain near Tatsienlu.

We talked for a while around the fire and Tiso Awa gave us another of his songs. Sleep came later as a welcome friend.

But it did not last long. Shrieking laughter was pounding in my ears. I jumped up.

I looked around. My friends were awakened by the same noise. It seemed to surround us—now over here, afterwards over to the other side. It was the strangest cry, and with it came an even stranger and somewhat familiar odor.

The shrieking came closer and then moved away as if it were a voice with wings. It was a cry, yet it was not mournful or plaintive. It was a voice that seemed to be attempting to form words yet it was not a voice, but something carried by the wind. It was a single cry coming from one being and then it was many voices in unison. It was unlike anything I had ever heard. It was unmistakably the cry of the *migou*.

Kareem grabbed his rifle and slowly turned around, trying to discern from where the sound came. Meanwhile Tiso Awa ran to the horses, who were trembling with fear. His own horse broke away, but seeing that the only way to go was down, she ran around in circles until Tiso calmed her.

I did not move. I listened. I understood now that I had expected this. After all, was this not the reason that this route was chosen?

I sat there, unmoving, a statue, listening.

Suddenly something moved in the brush below us. I saw a bright red flame erupt from Kareem's rifle. I wanted to stop him, but I was speechless. It mattered little anyway, for soon there was another movement on the other side. And then, as suddenly as they had begun, the sounds faded away and only the voice of the wind could be heard.

"So, Small Ears," Kareem said as he brought his rifle to his side, "we have heard the voice of the *migou*."

"It could be nothing else," Tiso Awa agreed as he gently patted his mare. "It is an experience that I shall never forget."

"I do not think that they would do us harm," I said finally.

"Your *migou* skin will protect you," Kareem patted his rifle, "but I must rely on more earthly things."

"This explains why not many have been here." Tiso Awa lay down again. "This explains the behavior of my mare."

"I still do not believe that harm would come to us," I said.

"Nevertheless," Kareem pulled the sheepskin over him as if nothing had happened, "tomorrow, in the safety of daylight, I will see if it was a *migou* or a rabbit that disturbed our sleep tonight."

I wanted my friends to stay awake and talk to me, but it was not long before they were asleep. No doubt this was an experience they would not soon forget, but with the matter-of-factness of men accustomed to danger, they did not care to dwell on it.

"Get some sleep, Small Ears," Tiso Awa said to me before he fell asleep.

But sleep would not come easily. I was much too excited to take this with the calmness of my companions. I sat there with my eyes wide open.

As I stared at the forest that surrounded the summit I saw two bright green glistening objects between two trees, picking up the reflection of the moon. They were eyes and they were looking right at me. I stared back. It was as if those eyes lodged between two trees were a life unto themselves; burning like green fires. We stared at each other until there was no sense of time, no today, yesterday or tomorrow. Who can say how long I looked into the eyes of the *migou?*

The morning after, nothing was found. The wind had erased any footprints in the snow.

We passed the village of Olosu, which we found deserted. And then we rode by Koja, which, as Tashi predicted, had been literally washed away.

Very little was said that day. We were all very eager to get to Tatsienlu.

My First View of Tatsienlu

I was not prepared for Tatsienlu. When one comes face to face with one's images and expectations, one often finds that the mind's eye has distorted for its own purposes. One expects things to fall neatly into place, but reality, like a splash of cold water, clears the eyes and wakes the senses. Such were my impressions on first glancing toward the city of Tatsienlu.

With Kareem ahead of us, we were climbing a steep mountain. In the southwest, the majestic peaks of Minya Konka rose in confident arrogance, dwarfing even the tallest mountains in the area. Minya Konka had been our guide for some days now; it is a beautiful mountain and home to a very powerful deity which the people of Tatsienlu, Chinese as well as Tibetans, hold in great esteem. The mountain appears to be an afterthought of the gods. Surrounding it are two smaller mountains, each with its snow-white summit high in the clouds. But Minya Konka rises above these, sharp edged, proud and eternally cold. One cannot help but feel that one is always in the shadow of Minya Konka.

When Kareem, who was first to reach the summit of the small mountain, called me to his side, I was sure it was to show me another view of Minya Konka.

"Look here, Small Ears," he called.

I followed, leading my horse behind me. First I passed a *mani* pile, and I did not fail to place a stone on the already large heap. Though this was not a very high mountain, the gods here must also be recognized. We still had to go down the other side and I wished to do so on the best of terms with the gods.

Kareem waited impatiently for me to fulfill my religious obligations. Although he did not place a stone himself, he respected our beliefs and I am sure he felt much better, or at least safer, when Tiso Awa and I asked the gods to make sure that he was afforded the same protection we asked for ourselves. But of course he would never admit this, even to himself, and now he waited impatiently as we thanked the gods.

"Small Ears," he called, "there will be time for that. Look here."

I climbed to the summit with Tiso Awa following me. It was wide and rocky with a few brave poplar trees defiantly standing here and there in the mountain wind. It was almost sunset, and off in the distance, Minya Konka blazed red in the diminishing daylight.

Kareem was his usual matter-of-fact self as he led us across the summit.

130

"What is it?" I asked, trying to keep pace with his long strides.

He took us to the edge of the northern incline.

"There," he pointed down. "It is Tatsienlu."

His woolen cap came off as if he were paying homage to the city. "You may take your last long look at Minya Konka, for it cannot be seen within the walls of Tatsienlu."

The evening prayers from the monasteries were just beginning. The sound of the conch shell and trumpets as long as two men bounced back and forth off the narrow valley's walls, while sweet juniper smoke, burning from practically every flat rooftop, drifted up the valley, filling our nostrils. Tatsienlu was not as big as I had imagined it would be but much bigger than anything I had ever seen. It spread out from end to end in a narrow valley, surrounded on all sides by extremely steep and rugged mountains, discouraging daylight from entering.

From our vantage point, the entire valley could be seen. If the town was smaller than I expected, it was only because it had no more room to grow. It had already extended to the foot of the mountains, climbing in some places with fields of mustard and barley. In the eastern part, which was just below us, herds of yaks and sheep grazed peacefully with only the herdsman's shrill cry occasionally disturbing their contemplation.

Two rivers met at the northern tip of the town and united in strength and force; it rushed through the city, bisecting it like a knife. Three bridges brought the two halves together. The bridge closest to our view was near the north gate; it was wooden. Just outside, large groups of pack yaks and mules mingled in the night air, waiting for the morning when they would be loaded and sent out to all parts of Tibet. The south gate, which was on the right bank, was a hub of activity as porters carrying enormous loads of tea rambled back and forth. Some already relieved of their loads were seeking out the inns and teahouses where they would spend the night. Only the bridge in the middle of the town did not appear busy. I was to learn later a great deal of activity took place there. General Fa and the *amban* representing the celestial government in Peking had their official quarters on the right bank of that bridge.

Perhaps the most striking aspect of the town from our position were the golden spires and domes of an enormous palace. They glimmered in the last of the sun in such a way that the whole section of the town became a white blur.

"It is the castle of the king of Chala," Kareem told me as he saw my eyes fixed on that spot. "The spires are part of his private temple."

I was speechless. Only monasteries, I believed, could be built so high and powerfully. For this building suggested power.

The monasteries, too, were impressive. There were four of them, representing both the reformed Gelugpa sect—the Yellow Hats—and the ancient Nyingmapa Red Hats.

Tiso Awa pointed out each one to me. The Gelugpa monastery, on the south bank, was the largest and seemed to be a fortress city unto itself. I was sure that this was where the oracle Sung made his home, for I had been told that he belonged to that sect. The other monasteries, while not small, seemed no bigger than monasteries I had seen in other places.

"You see those high walls surrounding that house." Tiso Awa pointed toward the south bank. "That is the Chinese garrison. Only a fool or a soldier would settle in the path of disaster. But you can be sure that General Fa does not reside there. Only poor unfortunates like our friend Hsi Teng."

Kareem studied the garrison carefully. His cap went back to his head. He rubbed his curly red beard and was deep in thought.

"We are on the verge of our goals," he said somewhat mysteriously. I didn't understand what he meant, but Tiso Awa, who was in the Turkestani's confidence, quickly discouraged any questions.

"We will camp here," he said, "and tomorrow we will pass through the gates of Tatsienlu."

The sun finished its descent, and as it did, the mountains lighted up with the campfires of herdsmen, woodcutters and other travelers who would have to wait till morning to pass through the gates of Tatsienlu.

The south gate was the first to be closed. Traditionally, the god of fire enters by the south gate, and Tatsienlu, much of it built of wood, was often plagued by fires. I was told that before the earthquakes, there was a thriving community on the south bank, and there were even vineyards, but all that had been destroyed and any sensible Tibetan refused to move back there. But the Chinese, eager to get a foothold in town, were migrating and moving in, though reluctantly.

We soon added our fire to the many scattered throughout the mountains.

The prayers and devotions of the monks had given way to other night music as each teahouse attempted to outdo the others with noisy laughter and the angry quarrels that often erupt when caravan men gather. Barking dogs, wandering the narrow streets, cried mournfully as they vainly searched for something to eat. Once in the middle of the night I heard a shot ring out. Neither Kareem nor Tiso was awakened by it, but I was not asleep. I was thinking about tomorrow morning and the words of Kareem Musa.

"We are on the verge of our goals," he had said.

I knew what brought me here: I was to see the oracle Sung to find out what paths life had waiting in store for me. I had been given a skin and instructed to take it back to the *migou*. I knew I had to do this. I didn't know why.

Tiso Awa and Kareem Musa were here to find a caravan going in any direction but Turkestan. This, at least, is what they had told me. But Kareem's preoccupation with the Chinese garrison made me wonder. I had seen him, by the dim firelight, take a piece of paper out of his bag of papers and seals. It had lines and words on it that at first made no sense to me. He examined the paper very carefully, making a few more lines and figures. I realized then that it was a map of the Chinese garrison. I don't know if he noticed me or not, but in a while, he folded the paper neatly and put it back into his bag and went back to sleep. I lay back on the woolen rug which also served as a saddle blanket. I wondered what was going on, but my mind was already full of my own affairs, and then I, too, was asleep.

Kareem Musa's Mission

I was not completely surprised when Tiso Awa stirred me up before the dawn to announce that Kareem Musa would not accompany us into the town.

134

The Moslem was already seated by the fire. His horse was saddled and tied up near a small tree. He was sipping his tea calmly.

"Kareem has other business," Tiso Awa said as we came to the fire. "Other matters make it impossible for him to enter Tatsienlu."

"At least not now." Kareem smiled.

I already suspected what these other matters were, but I kept these thoughts to myself.

"Small Ears, it is better that you deny knowing me or anything about me." Kareem spoke softly. "You have never seen me. You do not know me. I tell you this for your safety as well as my own."

I pretended not to understand, which made Kareem laugh.

"Yes," he used his woolen cap to tap his knee excitedly, "yes. Like that. You don't understand. You know nothing. That's perfect."

"But you do understand," Tiso Awa asked me, "don't you?"

This was spoken more as a declaration than a question.

"Do you really think that you can take a garrison of more than two-hundred-twenty men?" I asked somewhat skeptically.

"Take the garrison?" Kareem laughed again. "See, he doesn't understand everything. What good would a garrison in Tatsienlu be to me? No, Small Ears, that is not my plan, although if it were, I am sure I would have no problem. According to my friend Hsi Teng, there are many who would desert rather than fight if given the chance. But I am afraid that these men would be of no use to me either dead or alive."

Now I was confused. They could see the bewilderment on my face. "I don't understand," I said.

"Perfect." Kareem laughed again. "That look must be frozen on your face when anyone mentions the name of Kareem Musa, prince of Bukhara, Allah's avenging angel."

"And as you have already become involved in this little matter of espionage, I shall feel free to call on you for help."

"I will help," I looked into Kareem's eyes, "but if I am going to put my life in danger, I should like to know the reason why."

"It's better that you don't know," Tiso Awa said softly.

"Besides," Kareem Musa added, "you have your *migou* skin to protect you. What have you to fear?"

Tiso Awa forced a laugh.

"Still," I was not giving up, "I would be of much more value to you if I knew what I was doing and why. You must put me firmly on your side."

The two men looked at each other. I waited.

"You are determined to find out," Tiso Awa asked, "aren't you?"

I didn't answer. Tiso Awa looked at Kareem Musa.

"I hope we are making the right decision," Kareem said as he tossed his rifle over to me.

"Look at that," he said. "A sentimental favorite. An antique."

I picked up the rifle and examined it. It was a standard rifle, probably from Dege in the Khans with an elaborate handle and a long iron barrel with carvings; one that anybody would be proud to own.

"A beautiful thing to behold, but practically worthless in battle. Now let me tell you something."

He paused and took out his pipe and tobacco. As he stuffed the bowl, he continued talking.

"General Fa, who has won many a ruthless victory through cunning and deceit, has yet to conquer the Lolos. He is an arrogant man and this disturbs him greatly. Moreover, it disturbs Peking, even though many generals before him have been less successful against these barbarians. One reason—or excuse—he gives is that his men are not well armed. This is true, but then neither are the Lolos. So much for excuses."

He lit his pipe. "But Fa still has some influence. He is the son of a rich landlord in Kansu province. In that city, his family, with the help of some foreigners called Germans, attempted to start a textile factory. It was not a success, but Fa's family lost nothing by it. When these Germans abandoned the project, the factory was turned into a firearms factory. It makes excellent copies of Russian rifles. A shipment will be arriving in Tatsienlu within the month. It would be no problem to gather enough men to attack this caravan, and the thought has occurred to me, but this would be suicide. Such a caravan will be well protected. The idea is to get these guns once they are in the garrison of Tatsienlu. And this," he took out his long Turkestani scabbard from its sheath, "will be done quietly."

"We did not tell you all this before," Tiso Awa said, "because we were not sure that you would be able to stand the general's torture if he found out you knew anything."

"I would never betray you," I said.

"I don't think you will." Kareem put his sword back into its sheath with a quick move. "And I will not deny that it has crossed my mind to make sure that you can't. But that is not

137

my mission. Besides, it was you who one way or another protected us from the *migou,* and how could I bring myself to kill a friend?"

"You would have killed me?" I asked, a little shocked.

"Of course," Kareem answered calmly. "But I will admit that it would not have been easy."

I wanted to ask if it was because I was too alert to be taken or if it was because Kareem considered me a friend, but I knew I would not be satisfied with either answer so I remained silent.

"Then this was the reason we did not take the Tcheta pass?" I asked. "You had no desire to be seen?"

"And this is the reason that I befriended that soldier as well." Kareem smiled. "He had much useful information, though here too, I will admit that I developed an affection for the fellow—and his tobacco."

"And this is the reason," Tiso Awa concluded, "that you must deny ever knowing Kareem Musa."

I swore once again that the Turkestani's secrets were safe with me.

The sun was coming up. Tiso Awa and I left Kareem Musa and began our descent toward the eastern gate of Tatsienlu. As we rode lower and lower into the valley, I could see Kareem Musa disappearing into the mist behind us. Minya Konka slowly became a white peak and then it, too, was gone.

On the way down, we passed a number of cultivated fields of barley and turnips. We passed a long plain where a herdsman and his son were bringing up their yaks and sheep. It was a steep climb and the surefooted yaks were moving faster than usual as they could smell the fresh grass above.

The rainy season had ended and the grass was rich and lush. When the herdsman saw us, he seemed surprised and, while his son watched the herd, he ran up to us.

He asked the usual questions. Who are you? Where do you come from? Where are you going?

He became very excited when we told him where we came from.

"Do you mean that you came here through the region around Koja?"

"We did," Tiso replied.

"Then the gods were with you." The herdsman rubbed his head. He was a tall fellow with a long narrow face, innocent and gentle. The beginnings of a beard covered his chin, giving his face a dark look, making his eyes seem like narrow openings.

"You are lucky indeed," he said again.

We had no doubt that he was referring to the *migou*, but he was not.

"A very dangerous thing to come through the forest of Koja. Very dangerous."

"You mean the *migou?*" I asked.

"That too?" He looked even more surprised. "Then if it is *migou*, they are better off there. You are lucky that you did not see any of the king's men. No one but he and his family can hunt those grounds. That is the king's land. No one is allowed there."

"We did not know."

"Did you not see the body of a man hanging from one of the trees?"

"We did not," I replied.

"A man was caught there last week. He claimed he was

139

lost, but he had already killed three musk deer. He was hanged on the spot."

"We saw no one," I said. "We did hear the *migou*, though."

"Then," the herdsman rubbed the top of his head again, "my advice to you is to forget that. Do not mention where you have been. Don't bring up the *migou* either. If they are in the king's forest, that is where they should be. You were lucky this time. The king is still in his summer grounds south of Tatsienlu. But my advice is that you forget what route you took."

I asked the herdsman if he knew anything about the oracle Sung and where he could be found.

"What business do you have with him?" he asked.

"I must see him," I replied flatly.

"Then you must wait in line." The herdsman laughed. "After all the Chinese dignitaries and the nobles of Tatsienlu have had their turn, perhaps he will see you. Now this will not be this year. Or the next."

"I did not expect that it would be easy."

"Perhaps in a life yet to come, you will be able to see him." The herdsman continued to laugh. "That is something. You come through the king of Chala's private land and survive to ask an audience with Sung. Who knows, you may even get to see him."

"Does he reside in the monastery?" I asked.

"Sung? In the monastery?" The herdsman shook his head. "Not him. He has too much of a taste for worldly things for that. His house is near that of General Fa's, on the east side of the middle bridge. You may tell him that Dendru the herdsman sent you."

And with that he turned, still laughing; he shook his head and went to join his herd.

Through the Gates of Tatsienlu

We entered Tatsienlu through the east gate. It is a high, wooden gate heavily ornamented with Chinese characters, although it leads directly into the Tibetan section of the city on the left bank of the Dar Chu. A wooden-framed tower had been built just inside the gate, and here we encountered Chinese soldiers whose job it was to make sure that no trader either entered or left the town without paying the necessary taxes demanded.

They stopped us and questioned us about our business in Tatsienlu. We told them that we were mulemen who had come to find a caravan going toward Chumbi. From our road-worn appearance and the condition of our ponies, it was obvious that we had nothing of value except our own skins. Nevertheless, there was a Chinese lieutenant of the officious type who, not being satisfied with the falsified passports we carried, insisted on inspecting our saddlebags.

We were powerless to resist. In fact, his search would have turned up nothing, for what we told the officer was essentially true. Still, I did not want the *migou* skin to be found. It would require too much explaining and one can easily become entangled in the complex laws and regulations enforced on traders.

The officer was about to reach for my saddlebag. I held my breath. Then, as luck would have it, a minor altercation broke out near the gate.

A Chinese trader was caught attempting to leave town with a stack of fox skins. Apparently, he had not claimed them all but hid a number under the saddles and packs of each of his seven mules. It had been obvious to the soldiers from the height of the packs and the unsteady balance of the burdened mules. But the trader, an old, wise-looking man, insisted he did not know how this had happened. He also singled out one of the soldiers as the ruffian who, on the trader's last trip to Tatsienlu, was among the bandits responsible for stealing another load of fox skins. The soldier, of course, denied everything, and the argument gained momentum, with all the parties accusing each other of everything.

Tiso Awa and I looked on without a word. The officer took his hand from my saddlebag just before reaching in and straightened his hat, giving him an official but stupid appearance. Then he marched over to the argument, which by now had developed into a first-class brawl, the old Chinese showing remarkable strength as he had his hands around a soldier's throat—ironically, not the soldier he accused.

Tiso Awa explained to me what was going on. "The old man is asking why he should pay a tax to this son of a thousand fathers when as soon as he is far enough away from the city the goods he paid such a high tax on are taken from him."

As they pulled the old man off the soldier, I was beginning to feel sorry for him, but Tiso Awa told me that it was not necessary.

"The real cause of this, I believe, is that the old man did not pay these soldiers off, as is customary. A foolish move, for now he will be required to make a bigger payoff to the

142

magistrate when his case comes up. Magistrates live higher than soldiers, you know."

The young lieutenant was now in the thick of it, trying to separate the warring parties. His hat was thrown off and one of his soldiers, in the passion of battle, accidentally stepped on it, crushing it into the damp morning earth.

Tiso Awa turned toward me. "Come, Small Ears," he said, "we have business to conduct."

He took his pony and began walking into the city.

"What about the officer?" I asked as I ran to catch up to him.

"What about him?" Tiso smiled. "He has already forgotten two innocent mulemen."

So we marched into Tatsienlu, heading toward the main avenue, which ran from east to west along the entire length of the city and the river.

I felt somewhat apprehensive about meeting this ambitious young lieutenant again, but Tiso Awa had not given it a second thought and scolded me for concerning myself with something of so little importance.

"Look around you," Tiso Awa waved his hand in a sweep, "do you know where you are?"

One cannot fully appreciate Tatsienlu until one is within its walls. The city is draped in a perpetual mist as the foam of the Dar Chu thunders down from the north to meet the torrential Chen, coming up from the south. The rivers tear their way through the town, sputtering, splashing, tumbling. Even at the farthest ends of the city walls one cannot escape the roar of these two mighty rivers as they crash over their rocky bottoms.

Trade is carried on at almost a shout. The hand signals

which one finds all over Central Asia are in full force here.

One encounters a conglomeration of languages and races in the streets of Tatsienlu. Stocky, bronzed-faced nomads, fresh from the plain, jewel-studded daggers at their sides, and their women, weighed down with heavy spangles, moving proudly behind them; men of the Horpa states, my own people, towering over the crowd, each one trying to outdo the other, the ubiquitous jade earring dangling from the left ear; Chinese traders from Shensi and Szechwan in their dark blue coats, arguing over the price of a piece of Lhasa cloth; Tibetans from Lhasa and even farther west, some in sheep-skin gowns and others, the more wealthy, wearing luxurious Chinese silk; musk and rhubarb traders arranging and rear-ranging their stock to make it look more appealing; tall, unsmiling and mysterious Lolos, making the most of their reputation as they swagger through the streets (but like most everyone else, they are here to trade); Nepalese, some with their white caps tipped slightly on their brown faces, selling all matter of articles from the outside world.

And in the midst of all this, there are the ever-present monks. Some in saffron-yellow gowns, others in deep red, depending on their sects. Here, too, were the Bon lamas who, like my father, had no monastery, but who, with their black conical hats and bell and *dorje* in hand, were available to dispense any lama service.

Somehow, all these different people came here to Tatsienlu. They crossed icy mountains, windswept plains, tree-less deserts, mighty rivers to gather in this town surrounded by steep mountains.

Kareem Musa was right, for within the walls of Tatsienlu one imagines that beyond the surrounding mountains the world falls off into nothingness. To look up, all one can see is the sides of steep mountains and, if one were not to leave Tatsienlu, one would never know that only a little bit to the south Minya Konka rises rugged and snowcapped above everything.

In the valley, all these elements brush against each other in a mingling of colors, odors and tongues. No one smell pervades; sweet juniper burned on the rooftops in the morning air mixes with the smells of yaks and sheep and open fires which the Chinese use to cook their meals.

As we passed one narrow street, a strong, almost overwhelming odor filled our nostrils. This was the street of leather tanners. There they sat, in what morning sun the mountains allowed to enter, working at their craft.

A young Moslem with a thick bushy mustache, his white turban and gown stained with blood, was coming up this street. Over his shoulder hung a large wooden bucket which was filled to the brim with something white and apparently sticky. He was obviously one of the Moslem butchers.

"I thought that the butchers were near the south gate," I said to Tiso Awa.

"They are," Tiso told me. "He is bringing sheeps' brains to the tanners. They use them to soften and lighten the leather."

We passed a number of wooden houses which were slightly built up on planks. Except for the flat roofs, they seemed to be more Chinese than Tibetan style.

We arrived at the north bridge, which was not very far from the walls of the city. It was a wooden bridge, partially covered on both banks with a small tower in a state of bad repair on the eastern bank. The bridge was known to the locals as the Chinese General's Bridge. Some prominent but now-forgotten general had built it many years before to facilitate the movement of his troops in either advancing or retreating as the battles against the hostile tribes of the lower Min River were waged. As the general himself was to use this bridge, it was well constructed and planned. Unlike the south bridge at the other end of the city, it was not subjected to the ravages of the river after the heavy summer rains.

The tower was now deserted except for a family of bats that spent their slumbering days there. They appeared at night, flying over the walls of the city, searching for mice or an occasional rabbit.

The wall met the bridge on the west bank resembling two fingers next to each other; on the other side, the land expanded to cover a wide area of Chinese shops and a small customs station.

The only attraction on the other side was the palace of the king of Chala. This three-storied building with its lofty pinnacles and gilded roofs dominated the area and could be seen from anywhere in the city.

Except for some merchants coming and going over the bridge and a few Chinese soldiers ostensibly making repairs, the traffic was very light. A Chinese soldier, naked to the waist, sat at the foot of the old tower in true Szechwan fashion, oblivious even to the flies that were attracted to the bright red watermelon he was enjoying. A pile of seeds rose by his side; the accumulation of many days' work on the bridge. In fact, wherever the Szechwanese soldiers gathered, watermelon and their seeds were always there.

Tiso Awa chuckled at this, recalling a story that he had heard about a Chinese commander who, finding his troops greatly outnumbered in a skirmish with bandits, reverted to eating watermelon, the only supply they had in abundance. The commander had decided that if he was to be defeated, he would at least allow his men to enjoy their favorite earthly pleasure before they fell to the sword. The bandits, seeing the rinds and piles of seeds surrounding the camp, assumed that a larger detachment was there to rout them and passed the camp up. The attack never came; they were saved by watermelon.

"This is the version I heard from a Chinese," Tiso Awa smiled, "so you may take that at its worth."

I wondered if that commander was the same who built this bridge, and whether the soldier who sat at the foot of the tower was paying homage to one of his country's noble warriors.

It was at the General's Bridge that Tiso Awa decided that it would be best to part company. We both had our own affairs to attend to and he thought it best that from now on we should not be seen too much together.

"I am, after all, a spy," he whispered to me, making sure the soldier and a companion were not looking. "I wish that you were not involved in all this, Small Ears, but I fear that you are. Your aid may in some ways be needed."

"You can rely on me," I said reluctantly, for I really had no wish to become involved in these intrigues.

My horse was in a very tired and broken state. Tiso Awa decided to take the animal, promising that after a few days' rest and some nourishment, she would be able to fetch a decent price.

I was sad to see this horse go. She had served me well and faithfully, seldom complaining in spite of the many hardships she had endured. But I had no need of an animal in Tatsienlu. I knew that the wily Mongol would get a better price than I could for the animal, but I asked him to choose his purchaser with care.

"You need not fear for the horse," he smiled, "I realize what a horse means to a Khampa."

I assumed that he would sell the horse to a Khampa and this made me feel much better.

I gently twisted one of the animal's black ears, brushed a few flies away, and handed the reins to my friend.

"I will contact you in some days after my business arrangements are put in order," he said to me as he took the reins.

"How will you do this?" I asked. "How will you find me?"

"You needn't fear on that account." He smiled and whispered with a wry laugh to his voice, "You forget, I am a spy. It is my business to know what's going on."

With that, he turned around and marched over the bridge, passed the Chinese soldier engrossed in his watermelon, and disappeared down one of the narrow alleys on the east bank of the Dar Chu.

Like it or not, my involvement with these revolutionaries was deepening. I only hoped that it would not impair my search for the oracle Sung—the main reason I was in Tatsienlu.

The Officer with Sandals
at the Middle Bridge

I passed the north bridge, where women with heavy loads of tea on their backs were bustling back and forth. There are no male coolies allowed to work within the gates of Tatsienlu, nor are yaks allowed to come into the town. Just outside the north gate the yaks graze peacefully, waiting for the journey that will take them to central and western Tibet.

I made my way through the narrow streets of Tatsienlu toward the middle bridge, where I had been told by the herdsman that Sung could be found. I passed a busy street where a great deal of commerce was taking place. The trade was mostly in copper and gold pots from Dege; raw woolens from the Lhasa area; musk and rhubarb, although for the latter there seemed to be more of a supply than a demand; and some nomads were selling radishes and turnips. Anyone with anything to sell or buy must have been there. Most of the traders were Chinese, but there was a liberal sprinkling of Tibetans among them. Over the years, there had been such an intermingling of these races that a Chinese could have been a Tibetan and a Tibetan a Chinese. The clients represented every imaginable race.

I stopped at the foot of the street just to watch the action of trade going on. Even at the annual fairs and horse races, I had never seen such a gathering of things and people.

But this trade, while important, is deceiving. For it is tea that makes Tatsienlu the city it is, and these transactions are carried out in quiet efficiency within the large teahouses that line the right bank of the Dar Chu.

I arrived at the middle bridge. It was not as active as the other bridges, but there was a large number of people coming and going. Most of them seemed to be of the noble class or part of Chinese officialdom.

I was briskly pushed to the side—almost into the angry torrent—by a Chinese soldier who was making way for some high official. I did not know who it was, as he or she was in a closed sedan chair of Chinese origin and carried by two thin coolies. I was sure a Tibetan could not have been inside. For in Tibet, only the Dalai Lama and his regent are given this honor. Tibetans don't believe one man should carry another.

It was an entire entourage: first a group of soldiers on horseback rode by, clearing the way, followed by the sedan chair, and behind it a group of foot soldiers marched by, though in a very unmilitary way. I waited for them all to pass and then continued on my way, crossing the wooden bridge.

When I reached the other side, another soldier stopped me. He was a short fellow with bulging froglike eyes and a narrow mouth. He seemed bored with his job and asked me questions that he must have asked many times.

"What are you doing here?" he asked, as if he were about to fall asleep.

"I am here to see the oracle Sung."

My answer apparently took him by surprise.

"Sung, is it?" He looked me up and down. "Who said that you can see him?"

I thought for a moment. I could see that my directness took him off guard and he wasn't sure whether to let me pass or not. I continued this direct approach.

"It is of vital importance that I see him."

This was a mistake. He was, of course, familiar with that response. Had I said General Fa or some other high official had given me permission he would not have believed me anyway. But now it was done.

"You better move on." He waved the point of his rifle at me. "You'll get in trouble here."

I was determined. I pointed to a large three-story house with a pagodalike roof and an enormous wooden door.

"Is that his house?" I asked. I would not be pushed away so soon.

"That is the house of General Fa, but what business is it of yours? Move on now. Move on before you get into trouble."

Another soldier, less sympathetic-looking than the first, came limping out of the large house. He seemed to be in charge, although he was not a very high-ranking officer. I was surprised at his limp, since his legs appeared to be normal, yet every step seemed painful. I also noticed he was wearing sandals.

"What's going on here, Ping?" he asked the soldier.

"This boy is here to see Sung," the frog-eyed soldier answered.

This brought a laugh from the second soldier. "Do you have a pass to see the oracle Sung?" he asked me sarcastically.

I thought for a moment. Why hadn't I asked Kareem to prepare something for me? My hesitation in answering settled that question.

"Just what I thought," he sneered maliciously.

"I told you to move on or you would get in trouble," the frog-eyed soldier whispered.

"I only wanted to see his house."

151

"That's all you want?" the sandaled officer asked with a hint of sarcasm. "Come, follow me. I'll show you."

I didn't trust this fellow. I looked at the frog-eyed soldier. He seemed to be motioning with his bulging eyes that I would be better off not following.

"Well?" the second soldier waited. "Are you coming?"

"I . . ."

He grabbed the rifle from the frog-eyed soldier and with all his force butted me across the ribs. "If you're not going to come with me, then you better move on."

I felt my legs crumble under me as I doubled over in pain. Spots of light flashed before my eyes and somehow I gathered the strength not to cry as I fell in a heap on the wooden bridge.

"See that this filthy barbarian is off the bridge, Ping," the officer said, tossing the rifle back to the soldier. Then he turned around and limped back to the house.

Ping helped me up. "I told you that you would get in trouble," he said. "They're a bad lot, that lieutenant and his bunch. You are lucky that you didn't go with him."

"I just wanted to see where Sung lives," I groaned as I stumbled to my feet.

Ping helped me up and pointed to a small flat-roofed house near the larger one.

"That is his house but it will do you no good to know that, for he would not see you even if he were there."

"He is not there?" I asked.

"Sung just left in that party—he was in the sedan chair. He is going to meet General Fa at the mineral baths near the south gate. But I have told you too much already. Go, before you get hurt badly."

I wanted to thank him but knew it wouldn't matter.

Just then the officer stepped outside the door again. Only then did I realize how drunk he was.

"You better go." Ping started butting me with his rifle. However, he did not have his heart in it. It was more of a show for the officer. He even threw in a few "filthy barbarians" as he pushed me over to the other side of the bridge.

I do not know what would have happened to me if I had followed the officer. I only remember his cold, glaring eyes. Cruelty, it seemed, was matter-of-fact to him. Cowardice, I discovered later, was his other virtue.

Finding Rinchen Dorje

I remembered that there was a woman, Rinchen Dorje, who could help me. I decided to find her.

As I came back toward the north bridge, three women porters were coming toward me, laughing and joking. They were small women, with thin arms and rigid backs. Like the other women in town, they made every attempt to display their charms in the best light. Each wore a short gown that came up almost to the knee, and while they wore no jewelry, their hair was full of coins and jewels. Their wealth, it seemed, was worn on their head. They were all very young and one of them was quite pretty, with her flashing black eyes and childlike smile.

"Good day, ladies." I took off my hat extending my tongue in greeting.

153

This was received with a gale of giggles. The pretty one smiled at me, and, in a very unusual accent, returned my greeting.

"I was told that I could find Rinchen Dorje in Tatsienlu," I said.

There was another burst of giggles. Again the pretty one spoke for her friends.

"Do you speak Chinese?" she asked.

"A little bit," I answered.

She started to say something in Chinese but I could barely follow. I'm sure that familiar look of bewilderment that Kareem admired so much crossed my face. The women continued to giggle.

"I am the only one who speaks Tibetan." The woman returned to that language. The other two women thought this was hilarious. "But I only speak a little," she continued. "Are you related to Rinchen Dorje? A cousin?"

I thought for a moment. "A friend." I smiled.

The other two women were eager to know what was being said.

The pretty one explained what was going on to her friends. They were really having a good time.

"Do you know this woman?" I asked, becoming somewhat impatient.

"Who in Tatsienlu does not know Rinchen Dorje?" The pretty girl smiled at me. She pointed toward the north gate.

"Do you see the castle of the king of Chala?" she asked.

How could I not? As the Minya Konka had been my guide outside Tatsienlu, the king's castle was visible from all parts of the city.

"I do," I replied.

"Well, just beyond the back wall of the castle, you will come to a street where you will find a number of teahouses. When you get there, ask for Rinchen Dorje."

Then, laughing, she turned away and the three women walked down the street giggling just as I had met them.

A couple of long winding streets where half-naked children and dogs ran up and down brought me to the gates of the castle. In the mountains, one could feel the size and strength of this building, but from within Tatsienlu, it was even more magnificent. I thought back to the king of the Chango tribe in my own Hor Drango and how, deprived of his power, he lived in a half-burnt-out castle that once must have looked like this.

As I walked toward the rear wall of the castle, a nomad in a dirty sheepskin was coming out the large door. He was a short and stocky man with a round face and tiny eyes. His sheepskin robe was covered with blood, much of it fresh. He was bleeding from the mouth but did not appear to be in any pain.

"The king is in." He smiled. "He's back from the summer grounds."

I noticed that his mouth was missing most of its teeth.

"Today he removed these three demons for me."

He displayed three teeth proudly in his grimy hand.

"The king did this for you?" I asked.

"Yes," the nomad smiled broadly, "and he will do it for you also if you wish."

"No." I returned his smile. "I still need mine a bit longer."

"Well, should you need them removed, the king will do it for you."

Then he looked at me quizzically. "You are not here to see

the king?" he asked. "If it's begging you are here for, you must come back when the king dispenses charity to all beggars. Come back on the fifteenth day of the month."

"I am not here to beg," I insisted.

"The king is generous, but it is also merit to give, is it not?"

"It is." I was becoming impatient. "But I am seeking Rinchen Dorje. Do you know her?"

"You are not from Tatsienlu?" he asked. Then, answering his own question, he said, "I have not seen you before. Are you a relative of Rinchen Dorje?"

Again this question.

"A friend," I answered again.

"A friend and you do not know where to find her?"

"I am not from Tatsienlu, as you said."

"Of course, of course," he muttered to himself. "The fourth teahouse just inside the north wall. You'll find her there where the women coolies congregate. I was not aware that she had any friends."

Now I began wondering who was this woman that everyone knew and who may not have had any friends.

"You better not waste her time," the nomad warned me, "she's a busy woman."

I thanked him as he turned and, taking proud steps, walked away from me. "A friend of Rinchen Dorje," he was muttering to himself. "This is very funny."

I followed the man's instructions and walked down the narrow street. The street was thronged with the women coolies and they all turned and looked at me as I walked by.

I reached the teahouse where I was told I could find this woman. Low tables had been placed outside where a few women were sitting and chatting. They stopped abruptly as I came to the doorway. Two wide doors remained open so that I could see a large square room inside. In the back of the room, there were stairs leading up to some other rooms. The room below was full of these coolies. I saw no other man around.

The women all stared at me and all the conversations came to a halt. The only sound that could be heard was the river, which flowed somewhere nearby.

Finally, one of the women spoke. She was sitting at a table with two others sipping wine and it appeared from her looks and tone that she had been doing it for some time.

"Are you lost?" she asked me.

This prompted a roar of laughter that drowned out even the sounds of the river. I could feel heat rushing to my head and I am sure that I must have looked quite flushed. I wanted to wait for the laughter to subside before asking for Rinchen Dorje.

"Let the boy speak," someone called out.

"He is so cute," another spoke in Chinese that I could understand.

"Look at those tiny ears," still another said in Tibetan. "Give him to me."

I suddenly became very frightened. I began backing out of the door slowly.

"Let the boy speak." Another voice rang out like a gunshot. The room became quiet. I stopped.

"I said, let the boy speak." The voice came from a large woman sitting with another at the table near the stairs. She had an extremely red and round face with big red cheeks and tiny eyes that almost disappeared under the rolls of flesh. Her mouth was very small, yet her voice was strong and deep.

"What do you want here?" She looked me up and down as she slowly brought a bottle of wine to her tiny lips.

"I was told that I can find Rinchen Dorje here." I tried to smile.

"You have found her." The woman put the bottle down. "I am Rinchen Dorje. But I do not recall having any business with you. What do you want?"

"I was told by Tashi Lungpa that you can help me."

"Ah, has that foolish woman changed her mind about that miserable husband she has? Is she ready to come back to work?"

"I do not think so," I answered. "She hopes to escape the soldiers. I cannot tell you where she is."

"What do I care where she is," she interrupted, but I could see that she really did care. "When she comes to her senses then I will take an interest in her affairs. But what did she say I could do for you?"

I looked around at all the women. Rinchen Dorje understood and sent the two women at her table away.

"Well," she asked in a gruff voice, "do you women have nothing to do but to gawk at this child?"

Thankfully, the hum of conversation and laughter returned.

"Sit down here," the big woman motioned me, "beside me. Have some wine. It's the best, honey wine. I have a special stock of it that I get from the Lolos."

A young servant girl immediately came to the table and handed me a cup. All this was happening so fast that I had little time to think.

The wine was strong and it burned my throat. I was not going to let this show.

"Good, eh?" She poked me in the ribs. "My own stock. You won't find anything like it in Tatsienlu. But you did not come here to drink wine with an old woman. What did Tashi Lungpa say that I can do for you?"

I wanted to tell her everything, but first I had to find out some things.

"Who are you, Rinchen Dorje?" I asked.

She laughed, her little mouth opening as wide as it could. "Who am I?" She smiled. "Who are you?"

"I am Yungdrung from the village of Hor Drango in the Horpa state of Chango."

"Ah," she took another sip of wine, "from beyond the mountains."

"That is who I am and in my village, which is not very large, everyone knows me. I am called Small Ears. But here in Tatsienlu, which to me seems the center of the universe, you are known by everyone. Everyone."

"Of course, everyone knows Rinchen Dorje here," she said without modesty, "but you do not know who I am? Well, that's to be expected from one who comes from beyond the mountains.

"I have often asked myself the same question. Who am I?

"Well, I shall not belittle my position in Tatsienlu. Do you realize that not a brick of tea, not a bale of Lhasa wool can move within the walls of Tatsienlu without my consent? All these ladies you see around you, all the women at the south gate who are at this moment carrying bales of tea to the various houses, all of them work for me. Even the king of Chala must ask my permission if he wants something done.

"Who am I? I have had six husbands. The first and the third ran away. The second and the fifth I sent away. The other two died, the cowardly wretches. I drink at least two bottles of *pikue* wine a day, and if I don't nothing moves in Tatsienlu. My law."

She stopped and laughed as she took another gulp of the sweet wine.

"Do you know the oracle Sung?" I interrupted.

"That pig." She frowned. "Of course I know him. What do you want with him?"

"I was told that he could give me some direction toward my karma."

"Toward your karma? You are young. Sung certainly can be of no help to you. And what is all this nonsense, anyway? Why can you not just live like the rest of us, not knowing what tomorrow will bring? Why are you special?"

"It is not easy to explain," I replied, as my hand went into my robe to touch the bag with the *migou* skin. "I was given the skin of a *migou*."

"Given the skin of a *migou*?" She looked at me skeptically. "For what purpose?"

"I don't know. It was given to me and I was told to bring it to a place called Chumbi, a town at the confluence of two rivers, as your Tatsienlu and my Hor Drango are, but I do not know where it is or why I am supposed to go there."

"So you think that scoundrel Sung will help you, eh? Well, I would not count on it. A very arrogant man, that Sung. And greedy. He will not talk to you unless you are at least noble."

"Can you talk to him?" I asked. "Do you know him?"

She laughed. "Of course I can talk to him," she answered, "but even his own monastery was glad to be rid of him. He had an enormous argument with the abbot. Claimed that there was not enough to be made from staying in the

160

monastery. The truth is that some of his Chinese friends were afraid to go outside the south gate to the monastery. So he decided to come to them. He stays close by General Fa's. Lives in the garrison. Every afternoon they ride out of town together. You did not see them near the north gate?"

"I entered Tatsienlu from the east."

"Ah, the Chinese gate. You don't find many Tibetans there. Too low. Too close to the plains of China. I have witnessed many unhappy scenes at that east gate when a Chinese soldier returns home without his Tibetan wife. She would die in China and he refuses to stay here. My fifth husband was a soldier. But I shed no tears over his departure."

"Did he run away?"

"No, I sent him away. But getting back to Sung: I will not deny that he does have the power to see ahead. Who am I to question the gods when they randomly choose a human to deliver their message? But in Sung they made a bad choice. I care little for these lamas anyway. One is like the other to me. I once said to the king of Chala, 'I will keep these Chinese in line and you will take care of the monks.' That is how we divided Tatsienlu. Now Sung is a special case. He is the responsibility of both of us. Here, have some more wine."

"I would still like to see him."

"I expected you would." She pushed the bottle to my lips. "I will see what I can do. But I make no promises. You are a determined young man. You carry the determination of your faith."

"Yes, I am a Bon-po. My father is a lama," I admitted.

"Well, whatever you are, it's all the same to me. But Sung is different. He does not tolerate Bons. You will stay with me.

Tonight we will burn juniper branches on the roof.

"Are you hungry?" she asked. "Lising, Lising! Where is that girl?"

The servant girl came running up with tiny steps.

"She's useless," Rinchen looked at me, "too weak to carry the loads. Too slow to be a servant."

The girl seemed no more than my age and was a mixture of Tibetan and Chinese. She was extremely thin with gaunt eyes. She bowed her head as Rinchen spoke to her in her commanding voice.

"Bring this man some food. What do we have? Bring him a bowl of tea. And some lamb meat. You do not take rice, do you?"

"I never have," I answered.

"Very expensive. Too Chinese, eh? Well, we have some. You can try it. And Lising, take something for yourself. A stupid girl. She won't eat unless she's told."

"What can I have?" the girl asked in a frail voice.

"Anything. Anything. You're such a stupid girl. Well, what are you waiting for? The man is hungry."

I consumed an excellent meal, but the rice did not appeal to me and I turned gladly back to my *tsamba.*

Rinchen Dorje watched me eat and seemed to be enjoying everything as much as I was.

We talked all afternoon, and before I knew it, the sun was on its way down.

I followed the large woman up to the roof of the inn where an altar like the one on top of my home waited for the juniper branches to be burned for the gods. Somehow I felt very much at home here. I liked this big red-faced woman. I was sure that she would be able to arrange everything. She was barking out orders, laughing, threatening and laughing again in one breath. She had the presence of an oncoming storm.

I offered to show her the *migou* skin, but she declined.

"What good would that be?" she asked. "I have already consented to help you."

She was a follower of the Nyingmapa sect and except for her levity with certain lamas, she seemed to follow all the precepts of that faith actively. There was a solemnity and respect given to the simple evening ceremony of burning juniper branches that reminded me of my home in Hor Drango.

Later that evening, Lising showed me to a small room on the second floor. There was one tiny window and a small low table near one wall. Sheepskin and woolen rugs had been spread out on the floor.

I opened the door and I could see Rinchen sitting with a Chinese and a rich Tibetan. They seemed to be arguing. I closed the door.

Somewhere outside, the river thundered by.

The conch shells and the trumpets from the monastery were silenced and once again the mournful dogs wandered the streets looking for something to eat. Only a few dim stars were out, but the moon was almost full. In a few days it would be the fifteenth of the month, when the moon has finished a cycle, and the town of Tatsienlu would be even more alive with processions and festivals. And I would be there.

I wondered where Tiso Awa was spending the night. I thought about Kareem Musa, who was awaiting word to strike while he hid in his mountain stronghold. I thought about Tiso Awa's horse and Tashi and her Chinese husband. I had been in Tatsienlu only one day, and already I was closing in on the path that would lead me to my karma.

I do not know how long I slept, but suddenly I was aroused by some unrestrained giggles. I opened my eyes. Standing over me was the pretty girl that I had met that afternoon on the bridge. She was removing her loose-fitting robe. I watched it drop below her knees. Then she lay down beside me. She was strong and muscular, yet her body was soft and sweet. I do not know if she came to me on her own, or if she was instructed to do so by Rinchen. I did not think to ask.

Rinchen Dorje and Her Women Porters

I woke up to a crash. The girl from the bridge had already gone. She was replaced by Lising, who was putting fresh charcoal into the *k'ang* with less grace than a wounded yak. I was convinced, at that moment, that the gods of chaos had sent her into the room for the sole purpose of torturing me with her clatter and noise. She went about her work taking no notice of me, and managed to make the most possible noise with the wooden buckets and the copper brazier of the *k'ang*.

Her gaunt face and tiny thin body were covered with charcoal dust. She had an intensity about her work that bordered on fanaticism. When I told her that I would no longer need the *k'ang* that day, as I did not plan to spend my time in Tatsienlu in a little room, she continued what she was doing as if I hadn't spoken. If she heard, she did not care.

164

Only the powerful voice of Rinchen Dorje calling her made her drop everything. The bucket fell to the floor with a loud clatter and charcoal dust swirled all over the floor. Apparently, she only heeded the voice of her mistress. She ran to the door, taking quick little steps, and was gone.

Now I was up. I looked around me. The sun, which had such difficulty penetrating the mountain walls of Tatsienlu, peered into the tiny window in dim shafts. Somehow the moon did not have this problem, and it seemed that the nights in Tatsienlu were brighter than the days. I was not sure if it was night or day, but the chatter of the women outside and the deep voice of Rinchen Dorje barking orders reminded me that another day had begun.

I peered through the door. Rinchen was assigning the women coolies their day's work. The room was packed with women. Some sat outside on the single step leading into the tea room. They were chattering, giggling, arguing, and above them all, Rinchen stood in uncontested majesty and dominance. She was like Minya Konka, which towers over everything around it.

It was not just her physical size; there were, after all, women of all shapes and sizes congregating around her and some were bigger than she. It was more of a confidence or arrogance which she seemed to enjoy. Lising was at her side, handing her a bowl of tea. Rinchen paused every now and then to take a sip. Some women were raising their hands and shouting, trying to get her attention, but she took each one in her own time.

I looked for the lovely girl from the bridge who had spent the night with me. It was difficult to spot her in this crowd. She was not as tall as some of the women, having apparently

165

less Khampa blood than Chinese, and if she was there I could not find her.

I waited until most of the women had cleared the room. Little by little they filed out with their assignments, walking together toward the south gate, where the male coolies (and some females) waited with the enormous bales of tea they had brought from Yaan and Youchou. Rinchen's women would take these loads to the various teahouses of the city to be repacked for yak transport. Each knew exactly where she was going and to what teahouse each bale belonged. There was already too much confusion at the south gate for the women to be assigned their loads there, so everything was arranged in Rinchen's house by drawing lots.

Only a few women remained in the room and my girl from the bridge, whose name I never heard, was not among them. When most of the women had gone, the big woman took the same place at the little table that she had had the night before.

A woman whose face was badly scarred from smallpox was talking to her. She seemed most distressed. I could not understand what was going on as they mostly spoke Szechwanese, but I gathered that she was not at all pleased with her assignment.

Rinchen was listening to her patiently but seemed unmoved. She watched me from the corner of her tiny eyes as I came down the stairs. In spite of the enormous bulk of this woman, or maybe because of it, every feature on her face was small. But she had the most uncanny control of her little agatelike eyes. She continued to listen to this poor woman wail her tale of woe, acknowledging my entry at the same time.

"Ah, Small Ears," Rinchen said in Tibetan without taking her eyes from the woman. "Sit down here next to me. Give Lising your *tsamba* bowl and have some tea. You have missed the morning lighting of juniper branches for the gods— among other things—but I trust you've slept well."

I thanked her and reached into the folds of my garment for my *tsamba* bowl, which I handed to the servant girl.

The woman with the scarred face had said all that she would. Now Rinchen spoke to the woman with measured words, sympathetically but firmly.

The woman's eyes filled with tears but, realizing that this would not affect the big woman's decision, she slowly began walking toward the street with her head hung low. She stopped at the door one more time, in a last pathetic attempt to make her point, but Rinchen was losing her patience and she barked her away.

Then she turned to me. "Ah, Small Ears," she said, "you have no idea how difficult this is for me every morning. I have often debated the king of Chala over who has a more difficult task. Has that stupid servant girl brought you your tea yet? Lisang, Lisang!"

I had just given the girl my bowl but Rinchen was a woman who got quick results. Suddenly a bowl of tea was thrust into my hands.

"And bring me some wine," Rinchen commanded the girl. "You will have some wine with me. It is the best thing in the morning."

I sipped my tea and declined her offer of wine. The tea was strong and good. It was obviously the best quality and I must admit that I had never had this kind before, as the price was always too high. But here in Tatsienlu, in the home of

Rinchen Dorje, there were only the best of things.

Rinchen took a long gulp from the bottle and wiped her mouth with the back of her hand. "As I was saying, the king and I have this perpetual debate. He rules the entire state of Chala, which extends well beyond Tatsienlu, two weeks west to Batang. All the tribes within these boundaries are under his domain. He must mediate conflicts between them and please the Chinese while making sure that he does not give up any of his power. He must also keep the monks, who in these parts tend to be a severe lot, in tow. No easy task, I would say.

"Me, on the other hand, I am in charge of the women coolies. Just a group of women, you might say. But it's not easy. I get them all here in Tatsienlu. One woman will not work with another because of an ancient dispute over some tribal pasturelands. Most of these women have already left their tribes and know as much about the dispute as they do about building a palace. Makes no difference. These are strong, deep feelings that go beyond simple tribal conflicts.

"Then there are others who will not work in a certain teahouse because it is haunted by demons. This, of course, I must take seriously as I would not wish to send any of my women to untimely deaths. But I don't assign the loads. I only supervise the drawing.

"That woman I just sent out is a particular problem. A very sad story. First her husband, a Chinese soldier, was killed by the Lolos. He was part of the last detachment to enter their territory. Then the small house she had near the south gate was burned down. Now no one would take her in, for who wants to be contaminated by the god of fire? I, however, did, and got her work in one of the teahouses. Sadly, there was a fire there too. Not too much damage but now nobody will give her work. What can I do? It's a world of suffering, Small Ears. Look around you."

I was about to speak, but she wasn't finished. "You have been to Sung's house?"

"I was near his home yesterday," I confessed. "I met a very unpleasant officer." I rubbed my ribs, which still ached slightly.

"Ah, Small Ears, you have met Lieutenant Chu," she said to me. She put down her tea and reached for the bottle of wine at her side. "He is a most unpleasant fellow but is a well-known weakling and should be easy to avoid. Sung keeps him around for the very reason that he is such an unpleasant man."

"Was he injured in battle?" I asked. "He wore sandals and limped."

Rinchen laughed ironically. "Battle, you say?" She smiled. "You might call it that. The man is a coward. He does not have the courage to do what he should do. And this, of course, makes him even more miserable."

"And what should he do?" I asked.

"He should do the only thing left for him to do," she replied. "Take his own life. You are not aware of his story?"

"No," I answered. "Is it well known?"

"Everyone in Tatsienlu knows of the coward Chu." She took a long gulp from her wine bottle. "Last summer Chu was in charge of a division of forty-three men that went into Lolo country to do battle. He was the only one to come out alive. One other soldier survived long enough to return to Tatsienlu, but I believe the Lolos intended this."

"What happened?"

169

"Chu marched his men directly into a Lolo trap. That, of course, could happen to any soldier, but a real soldier would have stood and fought. Chu did not. According to the soldier, when the battle began, Chu told his men to hold their ground, while he attempted to get away. He received a wound in the shoulder and, realizing that he was surrounded and unable to escape, decided to give himself up along with all his men. But the Lolos detest cowardice, and Chu was a coward they had no use for. Half of his men were killed and the other half taken prisoner and made slaves. For Chu, a special punishment was needed to repay his cowardice.

"The Lolos do not wear boots or sandals. To them, this is a sign of weakness. According to the soldier, they burned the soles of Chu's feet. They had no wish to have a coward as a slave, and killing him would have been too easy and too final. That is why he was spared. They even allowed him a horse to ride back to Tatsienlu. Of course, he told an elaborate tale of bravery and courage, but he did not know that one soldier had witnessed the whole incident and escaped.

"Chu, of course, can never return to Chengtu with such a mark against him, but he believes that, here in Tatsienlu, no one in his home province will ever hear his story. He is wrong. Traders as far away as Mongolia know of the lieutenant and his bravery. He is laughed at and ridiculed by most in town and it was only Sung, who was looking for a savage dog, who allowed him to serve. You see, this Sung is a very wily trader himself. He knows how to make use of everything."

"Sung was on his way to the baths at the north gate when I was there," I said.

She rubbed her chin methodically. "I expect that he would

170

rather not be confronted. But Chu has already seen you."

"Will that be a problem?" I interrupted.

"He is the least of our problems, Small Ears. One of my girls will see to it that he gets sufficiently drunk tonight and have no wish to face the following day."

"I would not have you send one of your girls to that monster on my part," I said.

"Don't worry," she smiled, "my girls can handle themselves. Besides, she will be paid well. I like this, Small Ears. I am beginning to smell the game and I like it. I will ask Min Su. Yes, I am sure that when I tell her the circumstances she will agree. You know her, or at least she knows you. She came here last night asking for you."

"Yes," I replied. "I think I do know her."

Surely, Min Su was the girl from the bridge. If one were to choose someone to distract a man's mind, one could not make a better choice.

But the matter of Lieutenant Chu had already been settled for us. A short woman coolie came running up the street and burst into the room.

"Have you heard, have you heard?" she called to Rinchen.

"What is this?" the big woman came back. "Is the Shigatse caravan here already?"

"No, no." The woman caught her breath. "Lieutenant Chu. Lieutenant Chu has been murdered. Stabbed many times. Right in front of his house. Tsien Li did it."

"And what has happened to her?"

"She has attempted suicide. She swallowed a good deal of opium. She is at the missionary doctor's right now but I doubt whether they can save her."

Rinchen sighed. "Well, she has had her revenge. This was

171

the woman you saw here this morning, Small Ears."

The woman coolie smiled. "So much for that dog, Chu."

"Yes," Rinchen smiled, "so much for Chu. In any case, I have some news. I have contacted Sung," she said. "But I do not wish to build your hopes too high. I decided to find out if he was aware of your arrival. A direct approach. He says he was. He did not realize it was you on the bridge yesterday, but he will see you."

"But this is wonderful news," I said eagerly.

"I feared you would think that." She sighed. "I told you that it is unwise to build your hopes on this man. I don't trust him. In any case, he has been contacted. He says that it would be impossible for you to see him in his quarters. Having Chinese officers and princes among his clients, it would not look good to have a peasant boy under the same roof. It would disturb his business."

"I do not care where I see him."

"No, but he does," Rinchen said. "He goes to the baths five *li* from the south gate tomorrow morning. He suggested a meeting place near a small grove of walnut trees. I know the place. It is well hidden and since these walnuts belong to his monastery you can expect to be alone."

"But this is wonderful," I repeated.

"I'm not so sure," she mused, partially to herself. "He wanted to know what payment you intend to offer."

"Anything he wants." I smiled.

"Don't be a fool, Small Ears," she chided me. "Offer him your boots, or some gold, or a turquoise earring, but do not offer him anything he wants. Never make such a foolish offer."

She took another long gulp and handed me the bottle. "Here, have some wine," she offered.

This time I took a long gulp and then another.

"I would not be overly optimistic about this, Small Ears." She looked at me. "I know this Sung." The bottle came back to my hands. "Yes, I know this Sung," she repeated.

A Dangerous Meeting

Filled with anticipation, I could not sleep that night, and I was approaching the south gate well before the lamas had begun their morning services.

The walnut grove was not difficult to find. Leaving the south gate in the company of a number of tea coolies, I followed the road past the missionaries and along the Chen Chu.

I found a small patch of green grass near one of the old walnut trees whose branches made an arched cover to the slowly lighting sky. Here, I waited for the sun to come up and for the oracle Sung.

I thought of all the questions I would ask him and what I would use to pay him. What would he ask for, I wondered; besides the silk *kata*, what could I possibly give him?

The sun was beginning to appear over the mountains in the distance, casting a bright yellow light on the landscape. My anticipation grew as the sun rose.

Rinchen had been kind enough to prepare a few corn cakes for me and I munched on these nervously. In no time, they were gone.

Presently, I realized that the sun was well above the mountains. I could hear the prayers from the monasteries, mingled with the damp morning air.

There was a hazy shadow, like some low-lying cloud, surrounding the grove, and when it had been burned away by the sun, it occurred to me that we were well into morning. The prayers having been said and the incense burned, I could hear the activity of town life well under way beyond the walls not far from the grove.

I wondered if Rinchen had been accurate in her instructions. I got up and looked around, not knowing what I expected to see.

Up until that time, I only saw the endless flow of coolies leaving and coming from the south gate, but no sign of the oracle or his party.

Now I was more anxious than ever. Thinking that I could get a better view of who was coming from the south gate, I was about to climb one of the old walnut trees. Then, as if coming from hell itself, an enormous black dog with one tan ear, a tan tail and black paws came rushing through the bushes, directly for my throat. I did not hesitate. Holding on to one branch, I swung myself up the tree, just barely avoiding the clamping jaws of the animal. The dog barked furiously, losing its deep voice only to take a breath as he jumped and ran about the tree. Even with the amulet Big Father had given me, I was afraid.

Soon, I heard the voices of men. They were not calling the dog away but seemed, on the contrary, to be encouraging his ferocity. Three *dop dop* monks with faces painted black emerged from the bushes waving clubs. These are monks who neither take examinations nor study the dharma. They live to fight. Their hair is long, their skirts are short and their ferocity is well known. The tallest of the three was in the lead. He had cold unsympathetic eyes and thick, almost white lips. It seemed to me that he was foaming as much as the dog. His followers were equally angry-looking but seemed to be under his instructions.

"There he is," one of them yelled.

"We've got him at last," the other called out.

The head monk did not say anything. He came to the trunk of the tree, waving his large wooden club, and looked up at me.

"So," his frightening voice boomed out, "you are the one who has been stealing our walnuts."

I clutched the charm that was to protect me from wild dogs and this gave me some confidence. "You have made a mistake," I called down. "Call away your dog."

"Call away our dog." One of the monks laughed. "Why should we do that?"

"We have caught the thief," the other said. "Sung was right. He said that we would catch the thief today."

"I tell you that you made a mistake," I called down.

"We made no mistake," the largest of the three grumbled. "If you are not the thief, what are you doing here? Come down now and take your punishment."

"I will not come down with that dog," I said.

"The dog?" the master of arms said. "The dog is nothing compared to what we have in store for you." He waved his large club threateningly.

"But this is a mistake," I cried. "I am not your thief."

"Then I'll ask you," the leader said, "what are you doing here?"

I could not answer and I felt that they knew it. I wondered if they were in on this with Sung, or merely being used.

"No answer, eh?" he grunted.

175

"You can't stay up there forever," the smallest of the three said as he began swatting the trunk of the tree.

"Pull the dog away and I will come down." Then one of them pulled the dog back and I descended the tree. When they saw me come down, they seemed a little surprised.

"A boy?" one of them questioned the others.

"A thief," the leader said flatly.

"You have made a mistake. I have taken nothing."

"What shall we do with him?" the tiny monk asked.

"It is customary to remove the right arm and gouge out the right eye if this is the first offense." The head monk smiled. "And as this child seems to be in possession of all his parts, it must be the first offense."

"Then on the second offense," another laughed, as he held the dog just close enough that I could feel the animal's hot breath, "hot oil is poured into the open wound of the gouged eye."

"I feel that he will commit these crimes again." The leader looked at me. "Why wait? Why not make him unable to steal from now on?"

I wondered if they were making fun of me or if they were seriously going to do what they said. I knew that before this punishment was inflicted I must appear publicly before the lamas. I felt that if my case were heard, they would believe my story. But I could not be sure.

So I ran. I ran as fast as I could, not stopping to look back to see if I were being followed. The dog took after me and I could hear him at my heels. But he did not chase me far. Out of breath, I watched the south gate rising and falling in front of me. A swarm of coolies with their enormous loads were just passing the gate and I fell into the middle of them. I cursed this Sung, and one of the coolies, seeing my fright, asked me, "Have you seen a bear?"

"Yes," I answered, "it was a bear."

When I reached the place of Rinchen Dorje, I expected the soldier monks to be waiting. But only Rinchen was there. She was quietly sipping her wine while going over some business affairs. When I told her what had happened, she was not at all surprised.

"I expected he would do something like that," she said, "but there was no stopping you. In any case, I've enlisted the aid of a good friend. His name is Joba Tunak and he is the head of the tea packers guild. He will be here tonight."

"Somehow I expected those monks would be waiting for me here," I said.

"Here?" She laughed. "They wouldn't dare. Now have some wine."

I sipped the wine slowly. I was becoming accustomed to its taste. "It was my fault," I said. "I should have known better. I should have been more careful. I should never have gone to the walnut grove."

"Well, there will be other days." She smiled.

"That's just it." I looked at her. "Today was not an auspicious day. I knew it wasn't. And Sung knew it as well. Today was not an auspicious day but I went ahead anyway. I will never do that again. I will never go against the gods. The next time, I will choose the day."

"Somehow," Rinchen looked at me curiously, "I believe that you will."

Joba Tunak and the Tea Packers Guild

It was not difficult to spot Joba Tunak and it was even less difficult to be aware of his presence. He brought with him the overwhelming odor of untanned leather. It was as if he had brought the whole street of tanners with him. But this seemed to be a badge that he wore proudly. He was, along with Rinchen Dorje, one of the most powerful people in the town. And like her, he was well aware of his power.

Rinchen had described him as a passionate and understanding man. He had no use for Sung or the likes of Sung and would be glad for any opportunity to prove it. She also told me that he was not a man who could be easily bullied, and when the occasion called for it, he was able to take decisive and sometimes violent action.

Some years back, a nephew of his tried to set up a competitive guild of tea packers in Tatsienlu. Joba Tunak, who had taught the nephew the trade, was more hurt than angry at this lack of loyalty. But he made no attempt to impede his nephew's affairs, realizing that most of the packers would remain loyal to him and that his nephew would soon come to his senses and forget this foolishness. He even was willing to speak to his nephew, although many thought he was bending over too far to accommodate the boy's mother, Joba's sister.

The boy, however, wanted nothing to do with his uncle and as the packers in his employ went back to Joba Tunak, he became more and more morose and vengeful. He set about an elaborate plan to murder his uncle by administering a very

178

strong poison into the soles of his uncle's boots. He was caught, however, while performing the act. When the boy was brought before his uncle with the accusation and evidence in hand, Joba Tunak asked the boy if all this were true. The boy denied everything, but Joba Tunak knew that it was true and forced the boy to swallow his own poison. The lama who had made the poison was also caught and dealt with by the members of his own order.

Would he have killed the boy if he had told the truth? Of course. There is a special place in hell for murderers as well as one for liars. As the boy had failed to avoid the former, he was at least given the chance to avoid the latter. This he did not take.

The affair had a profound effect on Joba Tunak. He had already been a deeply religious person and having to take any human life disturbed him greatly. His life was now devoted to the acquiring of merit to make up, at least in part, for the sin he committed in this life.

There was a melancholy serenity in his eyes. One would never think he could be involved in intrigues. He was a perfect counterpoint to Rinchen. One wondered what tied them together beyond trade. She, loud and boisterous with her hand waving a bottle of Lolo wine, and he, sitting calmly in deep contemplation and oblivious to the noise and raucousness surrounding him.

Physically, he was about half the size of the woman. He was mostly bald, except for the rim of white hair that circled his large ears. His nose was longish and slightly flat at the end; he had a tiny mustache and a wide mouth on which one would always hear the familiar prayer.

One may think that trade was the only attraction that

brought together this big woman and this serene man, but this was not the case. They seemed to have a genuine respect and admiration for each other. When Rinchen placed the bottle of wine before him, Joba Tunak only smiled and gently pushed it away as it appeared he had done many times before, and would do many times again. It was like watching a familiar lama play, a ritual, an expression of friendship that was not to change.

"What shall I do with this monk who wears the clothes of a tea packer?" Rinchen asked. "He will not drink wine or take snuff, and considers laughter a sin."

The beginnings of a smile appeared on Joba's mouth. "You failed to mention that I take no tobacco either." His serene eyes looked up.

"That is not all I failed to mention," she came back. "I have given this fellow first choice with any of my girls. Even I would consent to marry him but he will not have it."

Joba held his tea tightly in his hands. "How could I ever please a woman like you?" he asked with a wry smile. This brought a roar of laughter from the big woman. However, Joba Tunak's expression of calm was fixed. I was sure that he did not consider laughter a sin.

"Come," he said, "let us get down to business. I intend to put as many as forty packers to work tomorrow. I received word from a messenger this morning that a consignment is only one day from the south gate. Now if you can provide . . ."

"Wait, my friend, there is something else I must talk to you about first. You see this boy before you. He has come all the way from Hor Drango to see the oracle Sung."

"But that's quite impossible, you know," he interrupted.

"Sung will only see nobles or Chinese." He turned to me. "Has this foolish woman not told you that you are wasting your time?"

Before I could speak, Rinchen answered. "You of all people should realize that all things are possible."

Joba looked up from his tea. "But how can I possibly help you?" he asked.

"I had hoped the oracle Sung could help me and with your aid, I might see him," I answered.

"Sung will need at least sixteen packers for tomorrow if I am not mistaken," Rinchen said. "If Small Ears can be among them, he might have an opportunity to speak to Sung."

"That is true." Joba went back to his tea. He paused. "That is true, but it is not as easy as you would expect. Sung is most demanding and exact. I do not believe that this will work."

Rinchen brought the bottle of wine down on the table with a crash. "Have you given up already?" She was angry.

"Not at all," he answered calmly. "I said I do not believe it will work; I did not say that we could not try."

My face broadened and this seemed to please the old man.

"And if it is to work, why must it be in such haste? Give me a few weeks at least so you can develop the proper odor and learn something about the craft. If I were to send you to his warehouse tomorrow, you would be discovered in no time, in spite of what this foolish old woman tells you. I know Sung. He has even complained about some of my best people." He paused, and I could see his sad eyes brighten. "I have never cared much for Sung. I do not think he will help you, but you seem determined."

"I am."

"Yes, I see you are. Although you do not have time to learn the craft, it is important you know something about it. I am sure that you will be discovered, but anything that displeases Sung is calculated to please me. Of course we will try."

Rinchen suggested that Min Su, the girl from the bridge, show me how the trade was carried on, but Joba Tunak thought it was a bad idea. "She is much too pretty," he said. "She cannot help but attract attention."

Rinchen reluctantly agreed and I felt a little disappointed. I looked forward to seeing this lovely girl again.

"One of my best men, Thundup, will make an ideal guide," Joba Tunak suggested. "He is one of the best packers in Tatsienlu. He is fast, efficient and knows his craft. Even more important, he is not well known here. He does not frequent the teahouses but lives quietly with his wife near the north gate."

"Thundup?" Rinchen asked. "I do not know him."

"And if he is not known by you," Joba smiled, "there is little chance he is known to the oracle Sung."

The Business of Tea

Tea, along with rupees (known as lama-head coins), is the currency of Tatsienlu and most of Tibet. Yet I was never aware of the process by which tea comes into the country. In my village of Hor Drango, we had no choice but to purchase our tea from the Chango Monastery. As in most parts of Tibet, the tea trade is a virtual monopoly of the monasteries.

During the Moslem uprising and the tribal conflicts that coincided, the tea trade was seriously affected, with the result of an enormous increase in price. This, at least, was the reason given when my mother used to go to the lamasery to trade for tea. (Grandmother refused to have any transactions with the lamas.) But it was no secret in Hor Drango that the monks, under the business guidance of the truculent Gera Lama, had been hoarding tea for some time in anticipation of trouble.

However, here in Tatsienlu, where the tea trade centered and where all the tea coming into Tibet must first pass, I was able to observe firsthand how the tea came to Hor Drango and how with each subsequent step the price increased. Even so, I realized that the Chango monks were making an enormous profit.

In Hor Drango, the tea came in large bricks. Some were wrapped in untanned leather hides. The tea inside was snug, closely packed and watertight so even if a *gam* (a leather-encased brick containing six smaller bricks) should fall into a torrent, as often happened, the tea inside was protected, dry and usable. Every brick was packed in Tatsienlu.

Although I had no intention of becoming either a porter or a tea packer, Joba insisted that I learn something about the trade so my disguise would be convincing.

It would have been unwise to be seen walking the streets of Tatsienlu in the company of my two new friends, for the town is not very big and gossip was one of its more active pastimes. Should the oracle Sung find out that I now had two allies, both strong and powerful, I have no doubt that he would have taken more effective steps to avoid me.

While neither of my friends liked the oracle, both were

aware of the many spies in his employ. For the most part, Sung was neither loved nor hated by the majority of the people. Like the tea trade that passed through their town, Sung was another part of town life that was simply accepted.

Thundup: Tea Packer and Christian

The next morning, I met Thundup at his home near the north bridge. He lived on a narrow street that ended at the northern walls of the city. Children, some half-naked, were playing on the street, running back and forth, chasing the stray dogs; except for an occasional hard pull of the tail, the dogs did not seem to mind.

Three children stood outside the front door of the one-story wooden-frame house. There were two little girls of eight or nine and a small child. The girls had enormous brown eyes dominating their ruddy dark faces. When I approached, they looked at me with vacant stares, quickly moving out of the way. I watched them run down toward the wall with their brother behind them, falling every now and then, picking himself up and running to his sisters, laughing, while a black-and-white dog, caught up in the game, barked continuously at his side.

Thundup stepped outside to greet me.

"I am Small Ears," I said simply.

He looked me up and down without a word. He was tall with extremely curly long black hair plaited with a silver ring. His eyes were sympathetic. In addition to the two amulets he wore around his chest, there was another one that I had never seen before: two crossed sticks tied to a leather chain. He noticed that I could not take my eyes from it.

"I am a Christian," he said in a strong, proud voice.

I had no idea what a Christian was, but I knew that I would be learning a lot more in Tatsienlu, so I merely smiled.

"Come inside, please." He finally waved his hand toward me. "My wife has already gone to work at the mission but we will have some tea. Please." He pushed a horsehair cushion toward me.

He waited for me to sit down and then pulled up a cushion for himself. I looked around the room, the only room in the dwelling. The k'ang, as usual, was in the middle of the floor, and the furnishings were sparse: an old wooden chest, a flat bench near the east wall, and a section of the room lined with thick woolen blankets where the family slept. There was an altar table facing the south wall and on it were three unlit butter lamps and another vessel which contained grains of barley. But there was no image of any god or goddess, or of the Buddha, on the top of the altar table. Once again, there were the crossed sticks.

He watched me as I glanced around the room. "My wife insists that there is room in the mission and that we can move in there at any time, but this has always been my home and I would not feel safe living outside the town walls," he said as he took my *tsamba* bowl and filled it with tea.

"I was told that you were not from the region," he said. "Missions, Christians—these are the things that the outsiders are bringing to Tibet. It is religion. The cross is our sign for the Lord Jesus Christ who gave his life on the cross. You seem confused."

I was.

"Well, it's not important now. I will show you everything." And that he did.

After finishing two or three bowls of warm tea, we proceeded toward the south gate, avoiding the main avenues of the town. I asked him about his children and why they were not with their mother.

"I have no children," he replied. "Those children you saw were not mine. They are not even brother and sisters. They are the unfortunate results of marriages between Chinese soldiers and Tibetan women, as I was. I never knew my father. My mother died when I was six years old. I wandered the streets like them before Joba Tunak took me in and taught me the trade. He still takes orphans in. The children you saw know that they can always have a morning bowl of tea at our house. They have even been offered a place to stay at the mission, but like me they would not feel safe living outside the town walls."

We passed a number of warehouses, customs stations and Chinese administrative buildings. Then the south gate loomed before us.

Rinchen's porters, with brick tea piled on their shoulders in two neat rows, were moving back and forth. Some of the porters were sitting outside the gate waiting for the go-ahead, while others, already relieved of their loads, marched toward the center of town and the teahouses where they would rest, waiting for loads of Lhasa wool to bring back to China. There was a constant flow of porters coming from Yaan and Youchou with their giant loads of tea and other porters leaving for China with even heavier loads of raw Lhasa wool, musk or rhubarb.

Once inside the south gate, the long trek of the tea porters came to an end. Now they could relax in the teahouses and arrange for loads of wool or musk to take back to China. Some of them sat by the side of the road munching on flat corn cakes, while others, leaning on their steel-tipped canes, chatted with each other about the long journey they had just completed.

Then it was the women's turn to carry the loads, for once inside the gates of Tatsienlu, only the women served as porters. They mingled with the crowd of men, looking for their assigned loads. The Chinese porters, who had left their homes, were searching for familiar faces to give them some news of their home province. Occasionally, a woman would break down in sobs upon learning of some fresh tragedy that had befallen her family. I saw two women with tears streaking down their faces picking up their giant loads of tea and marching solemnly toward town. I wondered what bad news they had heard.

"Very often," Thundup told me, "they do not hear the worst of it. I am sure that many sad stories are left untold, for no one wishes to collect bad luck by being the bearer of bad news."

Chinese soldiers in their dull blue-gray uniforms moved in and out of the crowd, making sure that all the taxes had been paid and attempting to be as official as possible. For the most part, the porters paid little attention to them. The porters were not responsible for the business arrangements, only for the transference of goods.

It was early morning on a bright, clear fall day. The south gate was a beehive of activity and I wondered how in all this chaos things were moved to their right places. But Thundup explained to me that everyone knew his assignment and very seldom was there a mixup.

"This is nothing," he went on. "In a few days' time, the

caravan from Shigatse will be here. After that, the Sikkimese caravan. The season is almost on us. Then you will not believe the number of people who come to town. Women from all the outlying districts will be here to seek work from your benefactor, Rinchen, and even with these there are still never enough hands to do all the work. There won't be a place to stay in Tatsienlu. The teahouses, the temples, the streets will be overflowing with people. What you see today is nothing at all."

For me, it was something. It was the center of all activity.

"Come, Small Ears," Thundup took my hand, "we will be working for a Dege merchant today."

I looked over the crowd for my girl from the bridge but was unable to find her. We marched down one of the narrow avenues toward the center of town, following three or four women as they strolled along.

"I believe they are headed for the Dege lamasery's warehouse," Thundup said. "I know of only two warehouses down this street and the other one is already filled to capacity. This is good, for I know the head packer who is usually assigned there. He is a good friend of mine."

"Is he a Christian too?" I asked.

"No," Thundup laughed, "I believe I am the only Christian among the packers and this is probably because of my wife. It makes her happy."

Down another narrow street we marched, loud with the noise of the teahouses, the arguments of the mule drivers, the grunting of yaks and complaints of mules.

Finally, we arrived at a large three-story wooden-frame building. Numerous prayer flags fluttered on the flat roof. Except for this, the building was very much in the Chinese style, with ornaments and characters written up and down the enormous wooden doors.

The doors were open. They led to a wide, spacious courtyard which the building surrounded. Inside there were men and women in the various stages of repacking tea for yak transport. Mounds of brick tea were piled high and covered with large skins which had been sewn together. A few men sat cross-legged on the earth, sewing up skins in what seemed to be a frenzied pace. They worked as if possessed by a spirit, hardly looking up from their untanned skins and only occasionally stopping to catch a breath. Near them, already packed cargoes were spread out drying in the sun. A group of monks were examining them.

Directly opposite the doors, on the other side of the courtyard, were two more doors which led down a narrow path to a fenced-in pasture where horses and mules grazed quietly.

Without missing a stitch, one of the men called out, "Thundup, you were assigned here today?"

"Has your wife given you permission to work here?" another man called out good-naturedly.

There were a couple of chuckles and scattered laughter. "And who is the boy?" the first man asked, casting me a quick glance. He had only three teeth, one on the bottom.

"This is my friend Small Ears." Thundup pushed me in front of the first man. "I was hoping that he could learn the craft. He would like to join our guild."

"This is not such easy work," the practically toothless man said as he put down the skin. "But like anything, it can be learned."

He reached for my hands and examined them carefully as if

he were inspecting a piece of gold. Then he sucked in his breath and, with his head cocked slightly to the left, asked, "Farmer?"

"Yes," I admitted.

"And what has driven you to Tatsienlu?" He continued to study me. "The Goloks? Taxes? Chinese?"

I hesitated. How could I tell him that it was the skin of a *migou* which had brought me to Tatsienlu, that I was here to see the oracle Sung.

"If it's a feud that has brought you here," he said sternly, "then you will find no anonymity among us."

"I assure you it's not," I interrupted.

"Well, what matter," he sucked in his breath through his three teeth. "Thundup has taken your part and that should be good enough."

Thundup smiled at me.

"I have not had that much to do with Christians yet." The old man sat down in his cross-legged position. "So I have not yet learned to distrust them."

"But," Thundup smiled, "you have known me for many years. Even before I became a Christian."

The old man looked up with a bit of a smile. "Yes," he said, "I have." Then he turned toward me.

"Thundup has explained everything to you?" he asked. "We are paid two and a half rupees for each of the packed goods. You may also take your money in tea. Bad work, of course, is not paid for. In fact, if any tea is lost en route due to inferior workmanship, that packer is liable. But this has not happened yet. We have a well-deserved reputation that we uphold. Do you think you can be part of it?"

"I will try," I answered.

"Then we may begin." He smiled. "I am Lozang," the old man touched his fist to his chest, "but I am known here as Sparrow Mouth."

He showed his three teeth proudly. "And you can see the reason why." He laughed. "And can you hear with such tiny ears?"

"I can hear," I came back, "as well as you can sip tea with your sparrow mouth." He laughed again.

"I must leave you for a while." Thundup took me by the shoulders.

"Where will you be?" I asked, hoping not to lose the company of this Christian.

"Where will he be?" The old man looked up in disbelief. "He will be conducting his affairs."

Thundup tried to smile. "Yes," he said. "That's what I will be doing."

"At the teahouses!" another of the packers exclaimed. "He will be drinking *chang* and conducting affairs."

This brought about a roar of laughter from everyone, but Thundup did not seem to mind; in fact, he was laughing along with everyone else.

"Maybe I should become a Christian too," another packer near the load of tea called out. "Then I wouldn't have to work either."

Toothless Sparrow Mouth turned to the man. "Get back to work," he demanded. "Our friend Thundup was lazy before he was a Christian."

After Thundup was gone, Sparrow Mouth said to me, "He is at once the best tea packer and the laziest man in Tatsienlu."

191

The Christian Outsider

Since Tatsienlu was not as large as I thought, it was not long before I was well acquainted with the town. I had been fortunate in finding both a friend and an adviser in Rinchen Dorje. She was well connected to all the politics that prevailed and I felt confident to be guided by her.

For reasons I did not completely understand, she avoided seeing me publicly. She claimed to have as many enemies as friends in Tatsienlu, and I assumed she did not wish to place me in the line of fire of some of her intrigues. She did not consider the oracle Sung a friend or an enemy, but admitted that an underlying hostility existed between them.

I remained with Thundup and his Christian wife. At first I thought that if I was to stay unseen and unnoticed, it would be much harder to accomplish this in the company of these Christians. But wisdom prevailed, for the couple did not participate in the mainstream of town life and for the most part little attention was paid to their comings and goings.

I found the missionaries had precious few converts to their faith, and the majority of them were not Tibetan. Anyone, I judged, who joined this new religion would be looked on as somewhat of a rarity and the gossip mills would always be astir.

Some of the missionaries had been in Tatsienlu for some time, and after their initial presence was felt, most people either forgot about them or accepted them as just another part of the town's life. The gossip turned back to the price of silver in Litang, two weeks to the west, and to some of the provocative interrelations between certain citizens. That year there was talk of another outsider, a woman missionary who attempted unsuccessfully to penetrate Lhasa. And, of course, there was always talk about the tea trade, which dominated the life of the town.

These Christian outsiders were a mystery to me. I was led to believe that they walked freely about the town with the same anonymity as any ten tea coolies, but I had never seen one. My curiosity was sparked, and when I heard that the Christians counted among their number a very powerful and well-liked doctor, I thought that here at last was a chance to find out more about my karma without having to see the oracle Sung. I was told that the Christians accepted anyone and everyone, and always offered help.

When I confronted Rinchen with these thoughts during one of our private meetings, she laughed and for a moment I felt anger at being ridiculed.

"No, Small Ears, I am not laughing at you," she said. "But unless you have some particular ailment, I doubt whether these Christians can help you. They are not the kind of doctors that you think they are."

"Do you know any of these outsiders?" I asked.

"I know them all and I knew the ones who were here before but are now gone," she answered. "A confusing situation was created among them. They all claim to be Christians, but no sooner does one Christian explain his doctrine than another follows and says, 'No, don't listen to them, listen to us.' And no sooner do they leave when another arrives and says, 'No, listen to us.' Much too confusing for me. But in Tatsienlu we have all types of these outsiders: French at the south gate, English at the groves of

193

the north gate. They claim not to agree on too much but their relationships remain cordial. Perhaps they would do better to convert each other."

Now I laughed. "But they are good doctors," Rinchen added. "I know a number of people who were treated by them, although they would never admit it publicly."

Thundup and his wife, Dorje Prahna, were most hospitable hosts. She was a small woman with a soft voice and understanding eyes. They had lost two children in infancy and she saw my arrival as providence and the answer to her prayers. Both her husband and I pointed out that my visit would be a limited one, but she was going to make the most of it. She was not actively remorseful about these unfortunate deaths, as they had happened some time ago and "they had found a better world next to the Lord Jesus," as she put it. Still, every now and then I could see the sadness welling up in her, particularly when she watched me. Once I was stirring the coals of the k'ang and I found her eyes on me. She stared grimly. I felt a bit uncomfortable but continued stirring.

"Do you know," she finally said to me, "my son died of smallpox. Even the mission doctors were unable to save him." Then she continued her work. Nothing else was ever said about the death of her children.

While I stayed with this quiet family, I always had enough tea, and I was never cold. Still, I remember that my first meeting with one of the Christian outsiders was much less than auspicious.

Late one afternoon, I went back to Thundup's after having worked the day at one of the larger merchant's houses, helping Thundup with a particularly heavy work load. I marched back and forth from the street of tanners, down a narrow alley, over the south bridge toward the south gate and the street of the butcher's. Here I collected fresh hides and brought them back to the other end of town. Thundup sent me on before him, claiming to have some business to attend to, and told me he would see me later that night. I knew that this business was to drink a great deal of *chang* with some of his friends, for although he was a convert to Christianity and had abstained to some degree from these drinking bouts, he still had an inner calling that wished for the companionship of men and *chang*. Having worked a particularly long day, I could well understand this desire. Had I not been so exhausted I no doubt would have joined him. Naturally, I was not to tell his wife of these goings-on, for it would do nothing but upset her. Naturally, she was well aware of her husband's un-Christian behavior, but said nothing as long as it did not become an everyday occurrence, as it had been in the past.

When I reached their house, I noticed that the door was slightly ajar and I could smell the warm tea brewing on a fresh flame. Assuming that Dorje was already home, I thought nothing about this and entered the room.

Darkness was descending fast upon the town and the mustard lamps in the house were not lit. As I entered the room, I was immediately taken aback in fright by a large bearded black figure hovering over the dim fire.

The eyes of this figure did not appear human, nor had I ever seen anything like them on any of the fiercer deities or even in the *migou*. They were eyes on top of eyes. The two eyes in front seemed to be made of glass, while behind them were two more eyes of the most piercing blue.

I was sure that some demon had come to the Thundup home. I was also sure it was because I was there. I backed out of the door and slammed it shut, hoping to contain the demon in the room until I could find a lama to expel it by magic. But as I shut the door, the figure rose and lunged at me, or at least that is the way it appeared.

Two of the street children were coming by and I told them that I had captured a demon in Thundup's house and that they should run for help while I contained the monster. They did not seem to care, and I was sure that I even heard them laugh at me.

Meanwhile, light tapping began on the other side of the door, and a voice with the most peculiar accent told me to please open the door.

Naturally, I did not. I would have remained there as long as necessary. I only hoped that Dorje had not already fallen victim. Then I saw her talking to the children at the end of the street. She came down toward me taking quick steps, seemingly agitated.

"What are you doing?" she said when she got within earshot. "What are you doing?"

"Run for help," I said. "I have captured a malevolent force in your house."

"Run for help?" She came up to me and took my hand from the latch. "Why do you keep the good father in there like that?"

"The good father?" Obviously she was familiar with this creature, for she did not appear to be in the least frightened. In fact, she now forcibly removed my hand from the door and flung it open.

The good father emerged chuckling and smiling. I could not detect evil in this laugh, and when he stepped out into the last of the sunlight, I saw that he was a man. He wore black robes and a crossed figure that I had seen before. But he was a man unlike any I had ever seen. His hair was yellow, as was his beard, which was cut quite short. I watched him remove the first two of his eyes, which he then held in his hand. They were held together by a series of wires. I jumped back in amazement.

"Thank you for rescuing me," he spoke first to Dorje, who was apologetic.

"I am sorry, Father," she said. "The boy did not know."

Was this man her father? I was more confused than ever. "Please," he went on in a much softer voice than I would have imagined, "there is no harm done. There is no reason to apologize."

Now he put his two front eyes back on his face by extending the wires over his ears. I was speechless and intrigued.

"These are spectacles." He smiled at me, noticing my expression of amazement. He removed them once again and gestured for me to take them and put them over my eyes. I did so reluctantly, and when they were in place, everything seemed hazy and in motion. I handed them back quickly, which made both him and Dorje laugh.

"You are a missionary?" I asked.

"I am," he answered with a smile. "I am with the mission just outside the south gate."

"Are those the eyes you use to detect metal in the earth?" I asked.

"Who told you that I could do that?" he asked.

"These people from beyond the mountains," Dorje said, "have many beliefs."

"Well," he turned to me, "I cannot do what you say but I will not harm you."

"Come inside," Dorje took me by the shoulder, "and we

will have some tea. Where is my husband?"

I followed them inside the house and we sat down around the *k'ang*. "He had some matters to attend to," I answered as each of us reached for our *tsamba* bowls and helped ourselves to tea. The tea had been prepared by the missionary, and like his fluent Tibetan, it surprised me that he knew so many of our ways.

"Matters to attend to." She looked at me disappointedly. "On this of all days."

"Don't worry, Dorje," the missionary comforted her. "He will be here."

"Yes," she lamented. "He will be here filled with *chang*. He knows how important this is to me."

"We cannot push him," the man said.

"What is all this talk?" I asked. "Is this man your father? What is the importance of today?"

"In my faith," the man spoke, "the priests are called father, just as in yours they are called lamas. As for today . . ."

"As for today," Dorje interrupted, "we were to make arrangements for our marriage."

"But are you not married already to Thundup?"

"Yes," she answered, "he is my husband, but we have not been joined together in the eyes of the church. I had hoped that we would have the first Christian wedding in Tatsienlu. Once we are really married, then perhaps I will be able to have more children."

"The church cannot guarantee this," the priest said to her.

"I have faith, Father," she retorted.

But her faith was not to be rewarded that night. We sat around drinking our tea and the good father answered many questions I had about the outsiders and their world. He also spoke of his god and the bliss one can achieve by following him. But my path had already been laid out for me, and it did not include embracing another religion. It was religion itself that had brought me to Tatsienlu.

This did not disturb the father. He seemed as curious about my religion as I was about his. Occasionally, he was unable to disguise his negative opinions of my religion, but he quickly apologized for this.

"I am not attempting to convert you," he said. "But there are many things in your faith that my god would find abhorrent. But there are as many things in mine you would find the same way. Am I right?"

He told me that his extra eyes were used to help him see better and that in Chengtu and Lhasa there were Chinese and Tibetans who also utilized these means of seeing better. He was an extremely intelligent man, I thought, and quite courageous to come among an unfamiliar people. He had made a special point of learning the language, although he apologized for not speaking it better. But I was amazed that he did so well.

"I have been in your country close to eight years now," he confessed. "I consider it my country now."

When I asked him if he longed for his homeland, as I did for mine, he was unable to hold back his emotions, and I could see that there was some part of him that he had left behind. He quickly recovered, though, and said how happy he was to be here. "You cannot understand what it is like to be in a place such as this," he smiled, "where religion is the profession of all."

So we spoke well into the night. Every now and then Dorje

would go to the door and look outside for her husband. But as time wore on, she tired of this and sat quietly and despondent near the fire.

Thundup did not return until well into the night and was in no condition to discuss a marriage.

Dorje was very upset, but the priest took it all philosophically. He had been warned that it would not be an easy task, and he did not seem altogether surprised.

He stayed overnight and in the morning, finding Thundup still unable to conduct his affairs, he left for his mission outside the south gate.

"You are welcome to stay with us anytime," he said to me before he left. "And I will pray for you."

I thanked him, for any prayers are of value. I learned later on that in the eight years he had been here, the mission had made few converts and some of these, like Thundup, did not remain loyal to the faith. But if there was one thing that the priest did not exhibit, it was a sense of defeat or failure. He had a contagious optimism and a warm good humor that would carry him through these dark valleys he meant to penetrate.

Thundup and Dorje never married in his church as far as I know, but one need feel no pity for the priest. Though certain lamas ridiculed him and were very hostile, in the end, I am sure, he had his own way. For I saw in him an inner light that no amount of abuse could ever extinguish.

The Lama Butcher

I was with Thundup for some time, and it was not long before I too exuded the familiar smell of untanned leather. I also became familiar with his routine. He frequented a particularly out-of-the-way teahouse that was stuck between two warehouses. Here, he consumed great amounts of *chang*, which he claimed fortified him for a day's work.

"It's an inconvenience," he told me, "but it's one I must live with. I cannot publicly drink *chang* without offending my wife. So I privately drink *chang* when most are working. She knows and I know. But so far this arrangement has worked. But it is an inconvenience."

Thundup was a patient and understanding instructor. He did not believe that within a few weeks I could learn a trade which he had spent most of his life in perfecting.

In the beginning my chores were extremely basic. It was some time before I even touched one of the long steel needles used to tie up the bricks of tea. In the meantime, I was sent, every other day, to the street of butchers, where I collected the untanned hides used for sewing the bricks together.

The street of butchers was an interesting place. Large yak carcasses were hung and displayed on the street, while the Moslem butchers went about their work in the cool afternoon breezes, oblivious to the flies and insects which swarmed the area. The butchers were mostly of the Moslem faith, as Tibetan Buddhists abhor the taking of animal life. But the large monasteries used the services of the butchers as much as everyone else. As the Moslem law forbade anything to do with pigs, the assignments for butchering pigs were given to a former lama. And as more and more Chinese settled in the area, he did a brisk and profitable business in pigs and yaks.

The lama was a short, fat man with a large red face and almost red eyes, which gave him a somewhat demonic appearance. His bloodstained gown, his two large knives, always fresh with blood, which hung from a belt around his wide middle, and his deep, low voice, made him appear even more frightening.

When I came to collect the yakskins that were neatly piled up in front of his shop, I tried to make the most possible haste, to avoid a confrontation with him. He was feared by most of the children in Tatsienlu and was said to be an example of virtue that had gone wrong. He would carry the accumulated sins of this life into all of his lives to come.

But the lama butcher did not pay much attention to this. Indeed, he seemed to enjoy his role as an evildoer, and every time I came by his shop he made sure that he laughed as I nervously piled the yakskins up and carried them on my head.

Why I should have feared this butcher and not the dreaded *migou*, who in most aspects was much more frightening, I could not explain. But, so did everyone else. There was a belief that the butcher was still adept at the black arts, and while he was not liked, everybody carefully avoided offending him. If somehow he managed to gain possession of something belonging to you—such as a strand of hair or a toenail—you had no choice but to negotiate with him or pay another lama whose powers were stronger.

I had no doubt that my father's magic was much stronger than his, for my father had discouraged the powerful monks at the Chango Monastery from their adventures for years. But Hor Drango was many days away, and my father could not know what was happening here.

The Lama Butcher's Surprise

One morning I passed the lama butcher's shop and found him standing in the door waving what seemed to be a woolen cap.

At first I thought nothing of it. But when I realized that it was the cap of my friend Tiso Awa, my heart sank deep in my body. I felt my knees weaken and the load of skins fell from my head.

The butcher came to my side, still dangling the cap in his big hands. "Do you know Tiso Awa?" he whispered as he helped me pick up a skin. I did not answer. If he needed information, he would not get it from me.

"I asked you if you know the Mongol?" he said in an impatient voice. I pretended not to hear him. Instead of increasing his anger, this only made him laugh.

"So, am I to be judged?"

I didn't know what to do. I had no idea where my friend was or how the lama butcher had come into possession of his cap. I only knew that he would get no information from me. The last of the skins was picked up and placed on top of the load.

The butcher looked up and down the street to see if anyone was watching. The street was busy with people coming and going. People were too busy with their own affairs to concern themselves with the lama butcher. "I have one more skin for you." The butcher smiled at me as he tossed Tiso Awa's hat from hand to hand. "I have it inside."

I felt a surge of bravery born of outrage. If this lama butcher had harmed my friend, I felt it would be up to me to seek revenge. My words were carefully chosen.

"My father is a powerful lama," I challenged him. "Tiso Awa is a good friend of his as well as a friend of mine. If you've harmed him . . ."

The red-faced butcher laughed out loud, but then, realizing he could be heard all around, muffled his laughter with Tiso Awa's cap. He appeared very secretive. "Come inside." He smiled with a slight twist to his lips. "I will show you your friend Tiso Awa. Come inside, please. Leave those bundles, a servant will take them inside."

I hesitated, but I had no choice except to follow. One thin shaft of sunlight, like a single blade of grass, was able to penetrate the inner darkness. Like many of the houses in Tatsienlu, the butcher's had a single floor with one large room. I could not make out what was in that room but I stepped into the darkness. There was a musty odor and a cold dampness that, judging from the location of the house near one of the raging rivers, I assumed was constant.

Large yak and sheep carcasses hung from hooks near the door, in various stages of carving. At the other end of the room, I could make out a small table with an altar and a small statue of a deity, which surprised me.

There was one small window on the left side of the room. The butcher walked over to it and removed the cloth that was hanging over it.

The river roared outside. Another shaft of light fell into the room, settling near the *k'ang* on the middle of the dirt floor. Next to the *k'ang* I saw Tiso Awa, sitting calmly with his *tsamba* bowl in his hand, quietly sipping tea.

"So we've found you at last," Tiso Awa said. He smiled as he gestured for me to sit down next to him.

I was still cautious. I knew that the lama butcher must have a good many tricks at his disposal, and this could be a demon disguised as my friend.

"I assure you that it is I," Tiso Awa spoke, seeing my apprehension.

The lama butcher looked on patiently. "I have not harmed your friend," he finally sighed.

"What are you doing here?" I asked.

Tiso Awa looked up from his bowl of tea. "Have some tea," he said, "and I will explain everything. You are right to be suspicious. One cannot be too careful. Tell me, have you seen the oracle Sung yet?"

"I have not," I confessed. "I hope to accomplish this by becoming one of the tea packers assigned to his warehouse."

The lama butcher laughed out loud. "Why would you go to so much trouble to see this man?" he asked in a knowing way. "Do you really believe that you will be able to fool a man who has the power to see into the future? You must know that he is the most exacting employer and that you will be discovered in no time. Ah, such an elaborate plan."

"I hope to gain entry at least." I found myself becoming more at ease.

"You could not have devised such a scheme on your own." The red-faced butcher looked at me. "This is too much. I see the hand of Rinchen Dorje in this. Only she could devise a complicated method such as this."

"You are right," I said to him, "it was her plan."

I wondered how he knew. Was he in possession of some magic that penetrated my mind?

"I suggest that you abandon this foolish plan," he exclaimed. "And when I see Rinchen Dorje next time, I will suggest it to her," the lama butcher said.

"Do you see Rinchen?" I asked, becoming more and more surprised at the lama butcher.

"All the time," Tiso Awa spoke up.

"Yes, of course I see her," the butcher continued. "I even have tea with her, or wine as my mood demands—except when she offers that sickening *pikue* honey wine. We are on

205

the best of terms. She has called upon my services from time to time, and not, I may add, as a butcher." As he spoke, I felt the *tsamba* bowl leave my lips. What would happen now could not be stopped. "So far we have not been subjected to the gossip that passes along these streets," he continued, "but your plan is already well known in almost every quarter of town. I am sure that Sung is well aware of your intentions. Why did Rinchen not come to me if she had a problem of this nature?"

I was becoming more confused. The butcher asked me for my *tsamba* bowl and this time I handed it to him.

"But what are *you* doing here?" I turned to my friend Tiso Awa.

"Jamtzen, the lama butcher, is involved with our plan. He is one of our people in Tatsienlu."

"Very little happens in this town that I am not aware of." The lama butcher smiled proudly.

"It is too late, Small Ears." Tiso Awa looked at my anxious face. "You are already involved in this business and now you must help us see it through."

"But what can I do?" I asked.

"The guns will arrive from Kansu in three days if all goes as planned," the butcher spoke, "and then Kareem Musa must make his move. There are, unfortunately, two elements working against us. The first is the Moslems themselves. I know them. They have no desire for another outbreak in Tatsienlu. These are not fanatical Salar Moslems, they are White Caps. They are still licking their wounds from the last revolt. Now if the trouble were to begin in Sining, as it did before, most of the followers of Islam would rally to the cause. It was in Sining, not Tatsienlu, where the grand mufti was executed by the Chinese. What these Moslems want here is only to be left alone, and I know of some among them who would gladly turn our friend over to the Chinese. But they can be dealt with." His hand went to one of his knives.

"The other problem, however, is not so easily handled," he continued, "and I am not sure what action to take. Kareem Musa will have to decide. You will have to carry our message to him. Should I leave the city walls, I am immediately known. Tiso Awa must remain here in hiding until the moment comes. Only you are left to bring Musa the word."

"And what is that?" I asked.

"Lolos," Jamtzen said flatly. "They, too, are interested in these rifles, and according to the reports that come to me, they plan a similar raid."

"You must get that information to Kareem Musa," Tiso Awa commanded me. "And you must do it soon. No one will suspect you when you leave the gate. Kareeem Musa hides near the forest where you left him. But leave by the south gate. We are not known there and it is busier. Go to Kareem Musa. Get his instructions."

"Does Rinchen know of all this?" I asked.

"Of course," Jamtzen laughed. "Rinchen offered me the information about the Lolos."

"And why are you involved in this?" I asked Jamtzen.

"I do not know the Russians, I care little for the Chinese—not enough to lose my head over, mind you. My motives are pure. I expect to be well paid for my help."

"And you will be," Tiso Awa added.

"Come, come." The red-faced butcher looked at me. "Am I to be judged again?"

"I cannot judge you," I said flatly, "but when the time comes, you will be judged."

"I shudder at that prospect," the butcher mocked me, "but I already have so many sins on my hands, will it make a difference if there is something to be made of them? But you, Small Ears, you must want something too. We do not expect you to risk your head for nothing, after all. There must be something that you want."

"Leave the boy alone," Tiso Awa spoke sternly to the butcher.

"I was only trying to be of help," he continued to mock me.

"Can't you see that he does not like you?" Tiso Awa came back.

"Nobody likes the lama butcher," he laughed, "but the lama butcher can arrange things in Tatsienlu. The lama butcher can arrange it so that this boy gets to see the oracle Sung and you can stop all this foolishness with Rinchen's games."

"You can do that?" I asked. I was sure that he could.

"Aha!" He smiled. "So there is something you want. I knew that there was."

Trouble on the Bridge

Tiso Awa gave me a bag of tobacco to take to Kareem Musa, who had somewhat comfortable lodgings near an old shepherd's hut north of the city, near the incline of a very steep mountain. I would have to circle the walls of the city, keeping at a safe distance so as not to be seen.

As the south gate is the one that leads to China, I would need a passport and a reasonable explanation for my journey. The passport had already been prepared by Kareem Musa, and Tiso Awa told me that the Moslem considered it some of his best work. As it turned out, it was never put to the test.

I passed through the south gate among a throng of coolies. The soldiers merely waved us on, taking little notice of the Tibetan boy with the small ears and the load of yakskins.

The Luting bridge spans the Dar Chu at one of its widest points. It is ten *li* south of Tatsienlu, not far from the summer palace of the king of Chala. Another customs station was situated on the north bank. The bridge is one of the oldest in the area and one of the few built entirely of stone. I had no plans to cross this bridge, for this could involve inspection and questions. Just before reaching it, I took a quick turn to the west, down a narrow incline that ran parallel to the Dar Chu.

I hadn't realized that I had been carefully observed by some Chinese soldiers. Seeing me turn off before reaching the bridge must have aroused their suspicions. They no doubt believed that I was trying to avoid them to escape paying the duty demanded for this station. I could not imagine that they knew anything more.

I placed my load of skins by my side and relaxed by the water's edge, biting into a flat corn pancake that Rinchen Dorje had prepared for me. Suddenly, two Chinese soldiers emerged from behind a small grove of willow trees. One was an officer of medium rank. He had a large nose and an intelligent face which was partially shaded by the rim of his cap. His uniform was impeccably clean and he had an aristocratic bearing. The other was somewhat crude, with the beginnings of a straggly beard and an unkempt, almost slovenly manner. His dull blue uniform had various stains on it and his thin eyes looked vacant and tired. He was undoubtedly a regular user of opium.

The officer approached me first, using the butt of his rifle to tap my feet and make me aware of his presence.

"What are you doing here?" he demanded.

"Why, I'm resting." I tried not to act surprised.

"You think you can pass through here without paying the tax?" the crude soldier growled.

"I am not crossing the bridge. These skins are for the Christian mission," I lied. "I'm taking them there after I rest."

The officer looked at me. I could see that he did not believe me but he wasn't quite sure.

"I know of no shipment to that place." He shook his head. "We are usually informed of who goes by here. There is nothing about this shipment."

"It was a late order, I think. But see here," I said, trying to act angry, "I have a passport. I was told to bring these skins and that's all I know."

"You tried to pass without paying the tax." The crude soldier put the point of his rifle to my neck, not allowing me to produce the passport.

The officer moved it away with his riding crop. I breathed easier. "Private Shu gets a bit too eager when he thinks someone is trying to pass without paying the tax." The officer smiled. "Sometimes I can't control him. You understand. He is devoted to his duty as a soldier. Now you do realize that something must be paid."

"But I've done nothing," I pleaded. "I have nothing."

I stood up. "He's lying," the crude soldier sneered. "Let me break his nose."

The officer tried to act as if he were losing his patience. "Do you call avoiding the tax owed to the government nothing?" he said sternly. "Now you must realize that we have to maintain some order on this border."

"I tell you that I have no intentions of crossing the bridge," I attempted to explain.

"I say we cut off one of those small ears." The other soldier wiped his sweaty hands on his uniform.

"You see," the officer said as he turned to me, "what can I do?"

The soldier began looking through the skins, spreading them all around the bank. Any attempt to stop him would have done little good. Finding nothing among the skins, he approached me.

"Maybe he has some tobacco." He wiped his sweaty hands again. I had made the foolish mistake of carrying the tobacco in a bag attached to a leather strap around my neck. He smacked my face with the back of his hand and almost took my head off.

"I am a Manchu," the officer said, "but what can I do when one of my soldiers becomes overzealous?"

"Ha, what's this?" The soldier smiled as he lifted the bag of tobacco. He tossed it to the officer, who smelled it and then put it in one of his pockets.

"Is this all he has?" he asked the soldier.

"It looks like it," the other answered.

"Well," the officer turned to me, "you see, you had the tax all along."

"I would still cut off an ear." The soldier laughed.

"I must apologize for Private Shu," the officer smiled at me, "and I also must compliment you on your taste in tobacco."

It was useless to protest.

"Consider yourself lucky that it was men of our sympathetic nature who discovered you." He cocked his hat. "Others might have demanded more than a bag of tobacco. I trust you will take this into consideration the next time you attempt to cross the bridge without paying the tax. You are free to pass now."

I picked up the skins and placed them on my head and began walking toward the bank of the Dar Chu, hoping to follow it some of the way before catching up with Kareem Musa. "Hey, barbarian," Private Shu hollered, "you are going the wrong way."

"The bridge is the other way," the officer called to me. "You may pass now."

I debated with myself for a moment. Perhaps the best course would be to cross the bridge so there would be no question about my meeting with Kareem Musa. I turned around and attempted a smile at the two thieves. The officer waved his hand, gesturing for me to pass him.

As I passed him, Private Shu, who had been waiting nearby, gave me the full force of his rifle butt on the back of my legs. I stumbled for an instant but managed to maintain my balance as I crossed the bridge.

It was the middle of a bright morning. The sky was cloudless and deep blue. The breeze was hot and dusty. I waited for the afternoon, when the two soldiers would be relieved of their post. When a throng of coolies came by I lost myself in their numbers, crossed the bridge again and set out for Kareem Musa.

Kareem Musa at His Hideout

I found Kareem Musa not far from where I had left him, in the mountains north of Tatsienlu. He had chosen a place in the northern end of the valley in one of the high mountain passes that were seldom frequented by either caravans or grazing animals. It was a small plain that at one time may have been much larger, but over the years landslides had claimed more and more of the plain for the mountains. Now it was a treeless, desolate place with large boulders and rocks strewn about. Not a single tree or shrub grew here, since earth covered by landslides can seldom be used again. A stream plunged from the slopes but had been confused by the behavior of the mountain and made a strange zigzag pattern as it trickled to the plain below. There was a *mani* pile on one of the passes to the top, but it had not been visited recently.

There was also an old roofless herdsman's hut which had escaped the ravages of the mountain and which gave evidence that at one time herds had grazed here. That seemed some time ago. Kareem Musa had set up his lodging near the little hut.

Although the rains that summer had been heavy, the Turkestani did not concern himself with the danger of landslides. It was this very danger, he believed, that made this such an ideal place to work out his plans. Herdsmen and their flocks, women from the town looking for firewood and Chinese soldiers were all discouraged from climbing up to Kareem's hideout. "Besides," he pointed out, "it is not written that I should die on this mountain."

This spot's major advantage was the magnificent view it commanded of the entire valley leading into Tatsienlu. Any caravan from the north had to pass in view, and while it would be quite visible, Kareem could not be seen.

Wood was plentiful on the surrounding slopes. The mountain itself, like the ones to the east and west, was much too steep to hold any snow, but snow was falling on that little plain when I approached Kareem. To the south all the mountains were snowcapped. It was early afternoon and patches of already fallen snow were scattered over the plain.

I climbed up the slope, following the instructions that Tiso Awa had me memorize; I left a stone on the *mani* pile. I came upon Kareem Musa deep in thought, oblivious to my arrival as well as to the light snow that fell around him. He was like a monk in the midst of meditation. No one near would have thought he was planning to rob the Chinese garrison.

His back was toward me and I thought how easy it would be for an enemy to strike him from behind. But I had underestimated my friend. He had been watching me for some time.

"Ah, Small Ears," he said, his back still toward me, "I shall not be long."

He had a map spread out in front of him. I watched him make a few more marks on it before he carefully folded it and placed it in the folds of his robe. Then he turned around and faced me. The wind had reddened his face, and with his long red hair and red beard speckled with snow he looked like a steppe fox caught in his lair. Only his sharp brown eyes had not been affected by the climate. They shined brightly, and intelligently.

"There is some tea brewing." He smiled warmly, pointing

214

toward the hut. "How was your journey? Do you bring news from Tatsienlu? What about my tobacco?"

When he mentioned tobacco, I felt a twist in my stomach that was not due to hunger. I knew that it would not be easy to tell him that there was no tobacco.

"Well, you must tell me everything." He took his *tsamba* bowl from his robe as he sat down near the fire. "And I have some news for you as well."

With a large copper ladle he filled his bowl and then gestured me to hand him mine. He could detect my uneasiness.

"Do you bring such terrible news?" he asked.

I didn't answer. He continued to talk.

"I assume that you have not yet seen the oracle Sung." He attempted to soothe me. "I expected you wouldn't. But things have happened here, Small Ears. Two nights ago, I was visited by your friends."

He handed me back my *tsamba* bowl and I took a sip of tea.

"My friends?" I asked.

"*Migou*," he said flatly. "They were here—or perhaps one was here. It is difficult to say how many there were."

"Did you see them?" I asked anxiously.

"Praise Allah, I did not. But I heard them, and in the morning—here, you can see for yourself."

He reached over toward the hut and showed me a saddlebag which had been ripped down the middle.

"All they took was the meat." He tossed the bag over to me. "I am sure that it was the smell of cooked meat that attracted them. But they are good thieves, I will say that for them."

Two other saddlebags had been ripped open, their contents

215

strewn about. One contained a pair of boots and the other two bricks of tea.

"They only took what they wanted," he said, "and I am thankful that they were not in the mood for Turkestani."

I wanted to know everything about the *migou.*

"I do not have the familiarity with these creatures that you have, Small Ears," he laughed, "but I will admit that I was thoroughly frightened. I remained in this little hut hoping that they would remember that I was your friend and that the smell of fresh Turkestani did not stir their appetites. I was afraid. I would never admit this to anyone else, but I was afraid."

"I am sure that they would do you no harm," I assured him.

"You are right. It is written that I should not perish on this mountain. I have no fears of Chinese soldiers, landslides or anything else, but when I heard them screeching, just on the other side of the thin rock wall, I was afraid. But now, Small Ears, I have told you everything. What terrible news do you bring from Tatsienlu?"

I hesitated again and I could see that Kareem was becoming impatient.

"Tell me," he insisted, "what is it?"

"The Lolos have found out about the shipment," I told him, hoping that I was breaking the worst of the news first.

"The Lolos?" He laughed broadly. "Of course they know about the shipment. It would surprise me if they didn't. Yes, that could create some problems. It would be easier to steal these rifles from the Chinese than from the Lolos. But there is something else, isn't there? Hand me my tobacco and I shall light my pipe while you reveal these terrible things."

I knew that now there was no avoiding reality.

"Well, where is it?" Kareem was coming to the end of his patience. "I instructed Tiso Awa to get me some tobacco. Did he forget?"

"The tobacco was taken from me at the Luting bridge by two Chinese soldiers," I blurted out, surprised at my own directness.

He stared into my eyes. I could feel the tension building up behind his red beard, his eyes blazing with anger and disbelief.

I bowed my head to avoid looking at him.

"Stolen?" he said finally.

"Yes," I muttered.

"Who were these dogs?" He spit out each word. "You must give me a description of them so I can take special care to make sure that they are repaid for their adventure." I expected him to reach for his sword, but he remained remarkably calm.

I began describing the soldiers and the incident at the Luting bridge. I could see in his eyes that he was making a mental note of everything, interrupting me every now and then to ask a question.

"Are you sure he was a captain?"

"Yes, he wore the epaulets of that rank."

"It must have been Captain Feng. I've heard of him. A Manchu. Not easily bribed, but a thief nevertheless."

We sat there with the light snow falling around us. It was perfectly still and I could almost hear the snowflakes as they fell from the sky.

"I know these bullies," he said finally, "and I know what to do."

Now his hand went to his scabbard. With that his anger

subsided, and the matter seemed closed, at least for the time being. He had acclimated himself to the loss of his tobacco and was already planning his revenge.

"Now, is there any other tragedy that I must know about?" he asked calmly.

"There is," I answered. "I have met the lama butcher Jamtzen."

"A detestable but useful man," he interrupted.

"I did not like him," I responded.

"There are few who care for him," Kareem said, "but in spite of what you think, he is capable of trust. What does he say?"

"The butcher said that you can expect no help from the Moslems of Tatsienlu. They have no taste for revolt now and want nothing more than to carry on business in Tatsienlu."

"This does not surprise me either." He rubbed his red beard. "I did not expect them to take up arms. What good would a bunch of fat merchants be to me in battle? I had only hoped that they would donate some of their wealth to the cause. A few small, well-placed bribes to the Chinese soldiers would make matters much easier for us."

"He said nothing of this," I said. "Are you sure he can be trusted?"

"One can never be sure of anything, Small Ears," he smiled, "but the lama butcher is on our side. He stands to profit. When we drive the Russians back across the river, I have promised him an important position in my government."

"I still don't trust him," I said, "but I will carry your instructions to him."

"I will have to think about that," he said, rubbing his beard

218

again. "If only I had my pipe"—he stamped his foot into the earth—"the thinking would be much easier. Well, I shall accept this loss and make amends when the time comes. In the meantime, you will remain here with me until tomorrow. The darkness falls early and it would be dangerous to descend the mountain."

"There is one more thing," I said.

"Tell me."

"The lama butcher said that he could get me an audience with the oracle Sung. Can that be?"

"It is possible," he comforted me. "There is little that happens in Tatsienlu which he does not have a hand in. I do not know your Sung or anything about him, but I do know Jamtzen, and I have found him to be a man of his word."

The snow gave way to a light misty rain. Kareem reached for another bowl of tea.

"Yes," he smiled, "if he is nothing else, he is a man of his word. But now you must tell me all that you saw of the Chinese garrison. I want nothing left out."

The Chinese Soldier's Fate

I was dreaming.

I was dreaming that I was climbing Toa Shan in the company of Kareem Musa and Tiso Awa. We were approaching the summit, which flashed brilliantly white with snow.

Or was it Toa Shan that we were climbing?

I was aware that we had left the shadow of that mountain some time ago, yet here I was again, as I had been so many times in the past, climbing to the snow-mantled summit of this mountain of my days in Hor Drango.

Kareem Musa had lost his horsehair goggles and was struggling up, blinded by the snow, which had become white hot from the rays of the sun.

I remember thinking this is a dream, for only in dreams can these things happen.

I took my own goggles and handed them to Kareem Musa. I was surprised at my ability to see without them.

"I do not need them," I reassured Kareem Musa.

"Yes." He smiled at me, his red beard contrasting sharply with the white snow. "But what do you hope to find when you reach the summit?" he asked.

I was about to answer him when I found myself being stirred out of my sleep.

I opened my eyes slowly. The dream was over. My eyes squinted in the bright morning sun. The sky was an impeccable blue without a single cloud to mar the path of the sun.

Once again, I saw Kareem Musa's red-bearded face, now against the bright blue background of the sky.

"Get up, Small Ears. Hurry," he was saying anxiously.

I gathered my energy and stood up, barely able to shake off the sleep and the dream. But the hard, unsympathetic light of day soon brought me to reality.

"Look at this," Kareem was saying to me.

"Have we been discovered?" I asked. "Must we flee?"

"No, no," he answered. "Come here. Look at this."

I followed Kareem Musa across the rock-strewn plain that fell off to the east into a steep, rocky incline. From here I could see the valleys that led into the north gate of Tatsienlu.

I was reminded of the days in Hor Drango when Big Father and I watched the caravan roads. The day was perfect, as the sun made deep contrasts in the valley below.

But it was not a caravan that we saw riding toward Tatsienlu in the valley below—it was a small company of eight mounted Chinese soldiers. The last rider was pulling three walking prisoners with a rope that was tied to the hands of each one. A woman stumbled alongside the prisoners. She was not bound, but seemed to be following this band of her own accord. I recognized her as Tashi, the Tibetan woman from Dawu. One of the prisoners was her husband, Hsi Teng, the deserter from the Chinese army.

"What will they do to him?" I asked, as the sounds of the small company clomped their way below us.

Kareem Musa laughed ironically. "Do you have to ask?" he said. "Don't you know?"

"I liked that Hsi Teng. I am sorry to see this."

The company moved below us, turning toward the east and the next canyon before arriving at the north gate of Tatsienlu.

"The other two are bandits," Kareem Musa said. "Their heads will no doubt hang in wicker baskets at the gates of the city. If our friend Hsi Teng is lucky, his will be there too, as an example to deserters. Otherwise, he will be sent back to his home province to face execution."

"If he is lucky?" I asked.

"The execution of a deserter does not have the swiftness of a blade across the neck. I witnessed such an execution near Hami. The poor fellow was tied to a post. Then archers came out, from his own regiment. They shot their first round of arrows and then sat down to a meal and an ample supply of strong drink. Then they shot their second round and returned to their feast. The poor fellow did not die until this had gone on for some time. No, if he is lucky, Hsi Teng's head will hang at the gates of the town."

"But there must be something we can do," I said, knowing there was not.

"Small Ears, I would risk my life to save this farmer if there were some chance of success." Kareem rubbed his beard nervously. "But there is nothing we can do."

We watched them disappear into the next canyon, and when they could no longer be seen, Kareem Musa said again, "Nothing."

Then, with the matter-of-factness that seemed to come so naturally to this Turkestani, he turned to me.

"But now we must think of saving ourselves, Small Ears, for neither of us have come this far to be turned back. I have thought about the matter of the Lolos and the lack of support from the Moslem community. I have also thought about your Sung and what must be done about him. The time for action on all these matters is near." Then he laughed to himself.

"You have a plan?" I asked.

"Not completely," he answered, rubbing his beard again, "but you may inform our friends in Tatsienlu that the sword of Allah will once more be unleashed. You can count on that."

I thought this attitude and his words were bravado to prepare himself for a big battle. I knew that if Kareem Musa were to succeed, he would need the coordination of an able front force in the city. He, too, seemed to be aware of this. I also knew that time would not wait for him to take action, and that without a plan of some sort all his hopes would be destroyed.

But Kareem Musa was calm, and it seemed that pressing him on the matter would make little difference. He would not be stampeded into initiating a plan based on expediency. The red-faced bandit was a shrewd and careful strategist. He had already demonstrated not only sly and resourceful cunning, but also a bravery that came from well-laid schemes. He would not fail this time, and I would have to accept that. I regretted only, as I am sure he did, that there was not enough time or resources to rescue the Chinese deserter. The message I was to bring to Tiso Awa and his agents was that "the time was near." I could not press him for anything more.

"And what of your Sung?" he asked me calmly as I started the fire for tea.

"He is not easy to contact," I confessed, "but I will do it."

"You told me that he was a frequent visitor to the baths outside the north gate. What else can you tell me about him?"

"Only what you already know," I said.

Again he rubbed his beard nervously and I could see that something was crossing his mind.

"You may tell the lama butcher that he can expect a visit from me within days." Kareem smiled at me. I thought that he meant me to understand this smile, but I did not. I could never intrude on his thoughts. I knew that he would only tell me what he wanted me to know.

"Yes," he repeated, "I will be coming into Tatsienlu. You may tell the butcher that. And you may tell Tiso Awa. Tell them that the time is near."

Another Incident with the Lama Butcher

When I marched back into Tatsienlu the following morning, I thought my worst fears for the Chinese soldier had been realized.

I was greeted by two heads hanging in wicker baskets at the south gate of the city. His was not one of them. I asked one of the mule drivers at the gate if he knew what had happened.

"They caught them yesterday," he answered, surprised I didn't know.

"But weren't there three of them?" I asked.

"Oh," he answered, "the other one. They were going to take him back to Chengtu. A deserter. These are only bandits." He pointed to the heads.

"But what happened?" I asked impatiently.

"Killed himself," the mule driver said calmly. "He and that Tibetan wife of his. Both dead. She brought the poison. You look upset. Did you know them?"

"No," I lied, not knowing why.

Then I marched to Thundup's house, trying to hide my tears.

Thundup asked me where I had been. I told him that I thought I might have had an opportunity to see the oracle Sung near the baths of the north gate, so I went there. This was not totally untrue—I had been near the north gate—but I doubt whether it would have made a difference to Thundup. Whether he believed me or not did not matter. He had no way of knowing that I was involved in a plot to obtain rifles, and I doubt that he even knew that rifles were being delivered to the city.

As far as he was concerned, I was an able extra hand to help him in his work, and he was more upset that I had missed a day's work than anything else. This was by no means a mercenary motive; I was not being exploited by the Christian, for he felt that I was learning a valuable trade. He was also aware of my desire to see Sung and he knew of Rinchen's elaborate and complicated plan that required me to have a good knowledge of the packer's trade. The work that I was doing had been done without me and would be done after I left. But with the big annual caravan coming in from Shigatse and another from Sikkim, Rinchen's plan had to be put into effect soon.

"Did you see him?" he asked.

"No," I answered.

"Well," he shrugged his shoulders, "you have missed a day's work for your troubles. A batch of skins awaits you at the lama butcher's."

This was perfect, I thought; he was sending me to the very person I wanted to see. Still, I could not show how pleased I was and made a sour expression.

"You don't like the lama butcher, do you?" he asked.

"No," I answered.

Did he suspect something? Did he know my mission with the lama butcher? These thoughts crossed my mind.

"Does anybody like him?" I asked.

He laughed broadly. "If I were a true Christian, I would forgive my enemies. We are, after all, all sinners, are we not?"

I didn't answer.

"At least this is what our Lord Jesus teaches us," he continued, "but I suppose that I am not a real Christian because I cannot find a place in my heart for this lama butcher. No, I do not like him either. But business is business. He supplies us with skins to wrap the tea and so we are forced to deal with him. And if not him, it would be another butcher."

I agreed. I was sure now that Thundup did not suspect that I wanted to see the lama butcher.

Once again I made my way through the narrow streets of Tatsienlu, walking toward the south gate, crossing the south bridge and then another turn to the street of butchers. When I arrived at the lama butcher's home, he was in the process of carving a yak. All the innards were being placed in a transparent sac which came from the stomach. These would be hung for some days and then sold, being a great delicacy among the Tibetans.

He rubbed his bloodstained hands on his robe when I reached his shop and, with a sly smile, said, "We missed you yesterday."

Then he looked around and came to the door. His red eyes wandered up and down the street.

"I suppose you will not come inside for the skins," he said.

"Do you think that is a good idea?" I asked.

"No, I suppose not," he said to himself. I could see that he was anxious. "Wait here," he said. "I will bring them out."

He went back inside and emerged with an armful of skins, which he placed in front of me.

"Wait," he stopped me from picking them up, "there is more." He walked inside his dark room again and came out with more skins. "I have to count them," he said. "I do not want to cheat your Christian friend."

As he bent down and began counting the skins, he motioned me to come near him. "You may check my count," he said, smiling. When I got next to him, he whispered, "So, what have you learned from the Turkestani?"

"He said that he will see you within days and that the time is near."

"I hope it is soon." He smiled. "I fear that some of the Moslems are aware of our plan and would save their own skins by handing our friend over to the Chinese."

I suspected that this was his own plan for I still did not trust him, but I said no more.

"Is that all he said?" he asked. "What of the Lolos?"

"That was all he said," I answered, fearful of giving him any more information than necessary.

"Well," he said, getting up, "you do not agree with my count. You think that I am trying to cheat you."

I couldn't understand why this sudden change of mood until I saw three Chinese soldiers coming up the street. This was obviously for their benefit.

"You wretched, ungrateful boy," he hissed, "you would accuse me. A man of honor. You think I need your meager trade. I do not have to take this kind of abuse from the likes of you."

The Chinese soldiers stopped near the lama butcher's house and watched the scene with obvious pleasure.

"Ah, I will ask these gentlemen," he said, pointing to the soldiers, who were laughing. "You know me. I am many things, but I do not cheat in business, yet this ungrateful child would accuse me. Gentlemen, I do have a reputation."

Then he turned to me. "If you are so sure that you are being cheated," he growled, "you may turn me in to the authorities. They will find me innocent."

The soldiers did not say a word, but only laughed; and when the lama butcher ran into his house and came out with a yak-tail whip, they laughed even more.

He began striking me with the whip. I wondered if he was really enjoying this, as he did not seem to hold back his blows. "Here," he cried, "take your skins. And tell your master that I do not want to see you again here. I do not have to put up with these accusations."

Then he turned to the Chinese soldiers. "Would any of you gentlemen care to count for this stupid boy?" he asked. "Settle the matter right now."

They all declined but continued laughing. They had been told that it was not wise to become involved in the internal conflicts of barbarians. As these were everyday occurrences, they became spectators and usually enjoyed the show. Since this episode was going no further, they moved on.

I lifted the skins on my head as the lama butcher lashed me every now and then with his whip, cursing me and my family. He was very good at this ruse.

As I marched down the street, he followed me for a few steps to let out a few more epithets.

It was only when I arrived back at Thundup that I found out how devious this red-eyed lama butcher was.

"But you are two skins short," Thundup said to me. "I will take this up with that scoundrel of a lama."

Then he laughed. "Do not be upset," Thundup said. "You are not the first that he has tried to cheat. What do two skins matter?"

The Chinese Moslem

For the next two days I worked with Thundup in a large tea-house belonging to the great Red Hat monastery in Kansu, where I saw and learned the art of packing tea. I was already familiar with needles and leather, as I had used both to reinforce my boots. But there was a definite style that developed from practice in tying up the great bales of tea so that they could stand up to the rigors of the hard trail into inner Tibet.

Thundup was pleased with my progress and told me that I would soon have the responsibilities of a full member of the packers guild, assuming I would be accepted. I decided to be paid in tea. The payment for each bale that was packed was four bricks of third-standard tea. I would get two bricks; the other two went to the guild. I was told that when I became a member I would only have to give one and a half bricks to the guild.

I was happy to receive the pay I did. Nevertheless, I knew that much more awaited me outside the gates of Tatsienlu. Whether or not I would see the oracle Sung was becoming even less important. I would still try very hard, but I was becoming more and more aware that the time was coming near to move on. The dreams of high passes closed by mountain snows had begun again, and I took this as a signal.

Still, I shall not forget the satisfaction of receiving my first pay. I strutted through the streets of Tatsienlu like a proud Horpa merchant who has just consummated some large business venture. But if I thought that I was a rich Horpa merchant, this was not the impression I gave to others. I am sure that I looked like just what I was: someone from the outlands of Tatsienlu who was at once impressed and overwhelmed with the intricacies of the city, and an easy mark for unscrupulous merchants.

I remembered what Tiso Awa had once told me of this city: "They would think nothing of taking all your possessions here. They are good at cheating, and to many it is not so much the prize as it is the game. And what a game they can play on you."

This knowledge was absorbed and taken into consideration. I was suspicious of any business ventures.

I was walking over the middle bridge on my way to see Rinchen to tell her of my plans for leaving, when I was stopped on the bridge by a round fat Chinese with a white turban.

"Can I interest you in some precious stones?" he asked, his whole face lighting up with a smile. "Corals, green jade from China, blood-red agates . . ."

He held up a handful of jewels and I must admit that they seemed to be of good quality. But I would not be easily taken.

"No." I moved his hand away.

"Perhaps a new earring," he went on. "The best quality. The agate was handpicked by me."

"I do not need anything," I said. This was true, but the merchant was persistent. He followed me across the bridge.

"You appear to me to be a Khampa," he said. "Am I correct?"

"I am," I answered proudly, "but what difference does that make?"

"My good friend," he answered, "there is a difference.

Even a poor Moslem dealer in precious stones such as myself would not risk incurring the wrath of your kind. No, my friend, I value my life more than my business."

I continued walking. He continued following.

"I am not interested," I said flatly.

"But sir, where are you going in such haste? Do you think that I would take my most precious prizes out here on the street where they can be viewed by thieves and dogs? Please, do me the honor of having tea in my miserable house and I will show you things you never imagined."

I stopped and turned to the round Chinese. His eyes looked up at me with quiet yearning; although a Moslem, he wore a sublime expression like a Buddha.

"You have nothing that I want," I said.

"But you are wrong." He smiled. "I have exactly what you want."

I turned again and continued walking, but the merchant was persistent. I was sure he would follow me to Rinchen's if I did not buy one of his jewels.

"Yes," he continued to berate me, "I have stones and jewels and all manner of things. A gift, perhaps. Something you can only find in Tatsienlu. Pearls. Amber. Please do me the honor of sharing some tea in my wretched hovel. It is not often that I can please an important customer like yourself. Please."

"I have no time," I said, still not understanding his persistence.

"Allah has been kind to me, sir." He looked up to the sky. "Do you see? We are near my home."

He pointed to a two-story house built up on some flat rocks and not in the least miserable. Obviously this merchant was prosperous. I wondered what he wanted with me.

"Now you must not refuse me," he said. "I must show you my most treasured prizes."

I was about to refuse him but I realized he would only persist. Besides, I was now intrigued; I could not understand what he wanted with me. I stopped walking.

"Then you will take tea with me?" he asked pleadingly.

"Yes," I answered defeatedly, "but not for long. I have affairs to conduct."

"Of course, of course," he beamed, "but I am sure you will not be sorry."

A servant came to the door and bowed to his master.

"Are the displays of jewels ready yet?" the turbaned Chinese asked.

"Yes, they are all awaiting you. And this," he turned to me, "must be Small Ears."

"How did you know my name?" I asked, becoming a bit apprehensive.

"By the size of your ears." The servant laughed.

I was inside the door now. It was a large room with low seats and many wall hangings. Rugs were spread out on the floor and I could see a stairway of good workmanship leading to some rooms upstairs.

The round Moslem's face changed expression. He looked directly at me. "Then you are Small Ears?" he asked.

"Yes," I answered, "but what is all this?"

"I had to be sure," he said flatly. "Now, if you will follow me, please."

"Won't you tell me anything?" I asked.

"You will find out soon enough, my good friend." He smiled. "Now if you will follow me. Rasheed will bring us some tea upstairs. It is much better there. More private."

232

The servant disappeared into another room while I followed the merchant up the stairs.

"I am Abdullah Sema," he said.

He led me to the second floor, where there was a narrow hallway with three closed doors. We came to the door at the far end.

"It is I, Abdullah Sema," he called out before opening the door.

The room had no windows and the few mustard lamps that burned gave only a little light. It was dark and damp with a stale odor. It had obviously not been used for some time. It was a storage place where extra grain, the Moslem's festival tent and some old saddles were stored.

"Please." Abdullah motioned me inside.

Tiso Awa sat near a dim mustard lamp sewing his boots. He did not rise at my entry, but acknowledged me with a broad smile that flattened his face. He had surrounded himself with piles of blankets and saddlebags and it appeared that he would repair each one in its time.

"Well," he said as he motioned me over. "A great deal has happened."

"The rifles?" I asked. "Have they arrived?"

"The rifles?" Tiso Awa looked up from his work. "There are no rifles. They won't be coming from Kansu, Small Ears. War has broken out once again in Kansu. The rifles remain there. Everyone fears the rebellion will ignite here. Tatsienlu fears a revolt of fat merchants. But come, our friend Kareem Musa has something for you in the other room."

As I followed him across the hall, I was full of questions but Tiso Awa said nothing more. He pushed the door open and waited for me to enter.

As my eyes became accustomed to the light, I saw Kareem

Musa at one end of the room. He was brandishing his sword over two men sitting before him.

"Ah, Small Ears." Kareem laughed. "Found again. Now you must tell me which of these dogs is your oracle Sung. The other I will kill right now."

I glanced quickly at the prisoners. They were neither tied nor bound, but the specter of the Moslem's large servant who quickly came to the door, armed with a fairly modern weapon, seemed to discourage any thoughts of escape.

One man was Chinese. He was very red, with white hair. He had very high cheekbones and almost no chin from which, nevertheless, a full white beard protruded. He wore only a cloth around his waist and sat with his arms wrapped around his shivering body.

I looked at the other man and could not mistake his presence. It was the oracle Sung. He was much younger than I expected him to be and much fatter. His red tunic seemed too small for his large body. He appeared to be a man in his twenties, but in that time he had obviously denied himself nothing. His lips were thick and a black mustache was almost hidden under his large fat nose. His attitude was one of confident arrogance, as if anytime he chose, he could easily walk out the door and onto the streets of Tatsienlu. But this was not true. The large Moslem at the door kept a careful eye on the oracle.

"We captured them at the baths outside the south gate," Kareem said. "There was no time to take the clothes that would identify them. As it was, we were forced to kill two soldiers. An unpleasant business."

"But Sung is not an ordinary man," I said. "It is not the garments he wears which make him special."

"Very true, Small Ears," Tiso Awa spoke as he reached into his *chuba*, taking out a walnut, which he cracked open with the palms of his hands. "Then you can tell us which of these two fish has the inner radiance you speak of."

I looked at the fat one. "So you think it's him." Kareem Musa smiled. "So do I."

"You have no idea the time we had capturing this one." Kareem Musa smiled again. "I can only think of one animal who is more outraged at his captivity and that is the camel. Hey, oracle, were you a camel in another life?"

The oracle did not respond.

The old Chinese merchant forced a laugh, hoping Kareem would appreciate a sense of humor, but Kareem ignored the old man.

"Will you talk to this boy?" Kareem asked the oracle.

There was no response again. Kareem nodded toward the door. We stepped into the hallway; Tiso Awa followed.

"You think that I captured the oracle Sung for you, don't you, Small Ears?" Kareem said. "But this is not the case. Oh, you shall have him, and I assure you that he will talk. But it is for me, not for you, that he is here. You see, I discovered the one weakness of General Fa. And that weakness is the oracle Sung. It is well known that General Fa will not make a decision without first consulting the oracle Sung. Such blind dependence, particularly in a military man, can mean disaster. Fa has never made a decision on his own. Now there's the pressure of an impending invasion. What kind of decision can he make? Cut off the head of a tiger and his claws are useless. No, Small Ears, as long as we hold Sung, we have Fa."

"What will you do with him?" I asked.

"It will not be easy." He smiled. "But after you have had your time with him, we will take him to Kansu. I go to help my brothers."

Then he turned to Tiso Awa. "And this fool," he frowned, "refuses to come with me."

"He is going to Kansu," Tiso defended himself. "I am not traveling in that direction." Then he reached into his goatskin robe and took out a handful of rupees.

"Here." He handed them to me. "Your pony. That was the best I could do. You Khampas are not so easy to do business with."

"But this is more than I would have expected." I smiled.

"I have some bad news as well," Tiso Awa said. "Some time after you left me, my horse died."

"Died?" I asked. Somehow I thought this animal was invincible.

"Just died," he repeated. "She stopped, waited for me to dismount, and then just died in the middle of Tatsienlu."

"She was old." I tried to comfort him.

"Much older than you would imagine," he lamented. "It will be a long time before I come across such an animal again."

"Where will you go?" I asked. "What will you do?"

"I will find a caravan," he said confidently.

Kareem motioned us to come into the room again. He walked over to the oracle Sung, looking him directly in the eyes.

"Will you talk to this boy?" he asked in a gentle voice.

The oracle did not answer. He looked straight ahead without blinking and with unchanged expression.

Kareem turned to me.

"He won't talk now, but he will," Kareem said confidently.

Then he motioned for the large Moslem guard to take the two prisoners to the back courtyard of the house.

"You wait here," Kareem said to me. "When he is ready to talk, I will call you outside."

I sat down on a pile of rugs and waited.

It wasn't long before I heard shouting, and then, even though muffled by the roar of the river, I heard a loud splash as if a large rock had been thrown in the water of the Dar Chu. Shortly afterward, the large Moslem guard returned and motioned me outside.

There was Sung, sitting under a large oak tree of undeterminable age and in its way very much like the oracle himself. The tree had roots growing both in and out of the water. Defiant to the erosion of time and age, it seemed to grow at its own will, sometimes shaking in the night wind like the rattle of a prayer wheel and then finding a kind of perfect stillness that only nature bestows on her own. But it was defiance, in the face of inevitable disaster, which characterized the tree. For there was little doubt that time would have its way someday and the old oak would plunge into the river. And there, under its large branches, sat the oracle, with the same expression of defiance that he had worn before.

I did not see the Chinese merchant anywhere. But I did not think to ask about him. Perhaps, I did not want to know his fate.

"I think that he will talk to you now." Kareem Musa smiled and then turned and headed back toward the house. "I am sure that the river Dar will help his divinations. So I will leave you."

The message was clear, and if Sung had any doubts about

Kareem Musa's threats he was not anxious to test them.

Images of the old Chinese gripped my mind, but were quickly broken by the oracle's strong voice.

"You understand," he suddenly spoke, "that I am not able to invoke any of the protectors of the faith from this wretched place. I need my temple, where there is already the energy of many divinations rebounding from the walls. But here," he waved his hand, "the gods can wander at will and I may never be able to go into a trance and so . . ."

"I know all this," I said somewhat disrespectfully, and surprised at my own arrogance. "But you understand that you cannot go back to your temple. Not just yet, anyway. Besides, I have a feeling that you have already seen what you can tell me. You no longer need to go into a trance or invoke the eight protectors of your faith. I have a feeling that you were aware of my coming here and so tried to avoid me, but I do not know why."

The oracle's expression changed to one of smiling surprise. "You do not need my help," he smiled, "you are already very perceptive."

"Perhaps I am," I said as I took the *migou* skin from the folds of my cloak and tossed it at the oracle's feet. "But perhaps you can explain to me what this is all about."

He picked the skin up slowly and ran it through his fingers, as if testing the quality or telling his beads. Then he put the skin on his lap, folding his hands over it.

"A *migou* skin?" he asked and answered his own question. "The wild man of the mountains."

"I was told that it is the skin of a *migou*," I said. "It was given to me by an old woman pilgrim who was heading for Mount Omei but lost her way and passed through my village. I am to take it to the Chumbi valley."

238

"Chumbi," the oracle said. "That is easy. I am surprised that you did not know of it. Ask any caravan man. Chumbi falls well beyond these mountains, past the great plateau and almost to the very limits of Tibet. A caravan man should have known that. So you see that you really do not need me. Go and tell your Turkestani friend that the interview has been concluded and . . ."

"You are still reluctant to answer my questions," I interrupted. "But I will call Kareem Musa when I am through, not when you are."

"Very well," the oracle sighed, "that savage you call your friend leaves me little choice."

"No choice," I said flatly.

He seemed startled at my words, and I found myself braver than I ever would have imagined.

An oracle, it must be understood, is more than a ranking lama but is a "God mouth." He is a human bridge to the gods.

A memory leaped out at me. I remembered when I was much younger my father took me to Bawang. The oracle of Bawang who has his temple on the banks of the river Min was going to give his predictions. This was an event that always had a great deal of pomp and ritual. The oracle of Bawang wore elaborate Chinese silk gowns and a gold- and silver-lined tiara. He sat above the people on a little stool on top of an altar. The sides of his temple were painted with the deities in their most hideous and frightening poses in both their male and female energies. An orchestra of drums, long trumpets, *drilbu* and cymbals sat to the right of the oracle and after the invocation to the gods, the oracle, who in this case was a boy not much older than I, went into a trance in which his facial and physical appearance twisted and contorted until one found oneself facing one of the fierce deities represented on

239

the temple walls. The oracle shook and jumped and removed his sword, swinging it over his head while he babbled in the language of demons. Three monks had to hold him down lest he do harm to himself and, when finally calmed, another monk asked him questions that had already been written on little sheets of paper which were carefully folded. I remember feeling the presence of forces from beyond in that little temple and how eager I was to find out what was in store for me. However, when my questions came, the oracle was coming out of the trance. It was as if my very questions had brought him out.

I spoke to the oracle afterwards.

"I wish that I could help you," he told me, "but you must know that even the gods have secrets."

Now here I was, again facing an oracle.

It was a chilly night in spite of the bright orange moon that hovered over the rim of the surrounding mountain. The sky was bright with shining stars, as if the whole universe were converging over Tatsienlu to witness this audience. I felt this a reassuring, if not auspicious, sign.

How different this was, I thought, from my last encounter with an oracle. Sung, who had been spirited from the baths, was given a bright maroon robe which was too small for him. He did not wear gold or silver and his head was bare. An amulet with a magic mirror hung across his wide chest, the only evidence that he was an oracle. But I did not need visible evidence, for I could not help but feel his enormous energy rush through the cold night air.

He shifted his position slightly as if this were a sign that he was ready to speak. There was still defiance in his tiny red eyes, but there also seemed to be acceptance. Rather than flow against this meeting like a rock that sits in the path of the rushing Dar Chu, he would flow with it, seeing it to the end.

"You are right," he began softly. "I do not need a temple to tell you what I know. I have been awaiting your arrival but I have avoided you. I have avoided you because I have no desire to look at the things you will make me look at. But neither you nor I nor even the goddess Tara with her great wisdom and compassion can change what is meant to be. I do not know your name, but you are called Small Ears."

I nodded in agreement. I had no intention of telling him my real name lest he use one of his demons against me.

"You were born in the Year of the Earth Tiger. Your birth was confusing and here you must help me. When you were born, you either had no desire to see the world or you wanted to jump in feet first. This is not clear."

"I have been told this by my grandmother," I said, "and my father, who is a Bon lama, has also spoken of it."

"You are impatient as well." The oracle looked at me critically. "I am attempting to put things in order and so I am bound to cover some old ground.

"You will arrive in the Chumbi valley in the Year of the Female Wood Dragon. Before you arrive, war will develop in the Chumbi valley. Many Tibetans will die. The invaders will come from across the oceans and penetrate even to Lhasa. The Dalai Lama himself will be forced to flee to China. It will be a bad time. A very bad time.

"This skin has been given to you to take back to Chumbi. It is of no small significance. Although you are a Bon-po, you have been given the task of returning it to save religion. When the skin goes back to the place from which it came,

241

the *migou* will come to religion. You have studied Bon-po ritual with your father. You know your own faith well. But you have not accepted Buddha's dharma. Still you must know what you are not accepting. One should study with many teachers. One lama, no matter how great, is not enough for a lifetime."

He paused as if he were waiting for me to speak.

"Are you to be my teacher?" I asked.

"Me?" He laughed with a hint of sarcasm. "No, never! But your lama will come and you will study religion and teach it to the *migou*. So even if a time comes when good words are crushed and religion is in danger, it will always survive in the mountains. You are a Bon-po. I cannot say why you have been given this task. But in our country, the defense of religion is the occupation of all, is it not?"

He stopped and put his hands together, closing his eyes as if to receive further visions. What he was telling me was, for the most part, already etched in his memory. Now he was straining, it seemed, to complete the images.

"I have told you what I could," the oracle added bluntly. "You have a patron god or goddess, I am sure. Pray to whoever it is. Guidance will come.

"I am tired," Sung continued. "Call that savage Turkestani and tell him that the audience is completed. I have told you everything you need to know. I really do not care if it is enough; I have told you everything. Perhaps when you reach Chumbi, there will be more answers or more questions. That is not my concern."

He appeared to be telling the truth and there was a bleak sadness in his telling which I attributed to sincerity. But I had so many unanswered or unasked questions, and as I fired them at the oracle, he merely waved his hands in front of me as if to say enough, enough.

Finally I said, "This does not concern me; I suppose that it is just a matter of curiosity, but I will ask it anyway." I paused. He looked up at me. "Why do you befriend the Chinese?" I asked. "They are our enemies. They are the lion's paw on the neck of Tibet. You even allow men to carry you in a sedan chair."

The oracle laughed sarcastically. "You are indeed a naive peasant boy, aren't you?"

"Perhaps I am," I admitted.

"Perhaps?" He laughed again. "You are. But then this is probably the reason that you have been assigned the karma you have. Look, my small-eared Khampa, see how much I will make from this audience. See how empty-handed you came. Not even a silk *kata*."

He was right. I had not even thought to observe the usual customs. It didn't seem necessary. After all, our meeting was not voluntary.

Still, he was a "god mouth," so I reached into my bag and took out the silk *kata*.

"Put it back." He smiled and waved his finger east and west. "Give it to someone who will appreciate it."

"I will give you the money from the sale of my horse."

He laughed. "You may keep that too," he said. "It is not worth my time. You are Tibetan and so pay what a Tibetan pays. The Chinese are where the money is to be made."

"Have you no fear for future rebirths?" I asked. "You must know that merit cannot be measured by wealth and that every sin will be held in account when you make another turn on the wheel of life."

"You are right. No doubt, I will have to pay for this life with the next. But I do not think about it. The Perfect One, the Buddha, said that no matter how far one goes, to whatever remote section of the planet, one cannot escape the responsibilities of one's sins. But I am young. I am barely twenty years old. I have a lifetime ahead of me to accumulate merit. But for now, the Chinese pay. The Tibetans do not.

"Now get that Turkestani out here and see what he wants to do with me."

The City Prepares for War

There was a great deal of activity in Tatsienlu that night. The rumors of the impending Moslem invasion had set the city on the verge of panic. In the teahouses, Chinese merchants who had not already boarded up their shops were trying to enlist the aid of friends and relatives to help them before the invaders arrived. Entire families congregated by the south gate, waiting for the morning. Then it would be opened and they could seek the shelter of the Yellow Hat monastery, whose monks were preparing for war.

General Fa remained in seclusion, ostensibly planning the defense of the city. It was not yet known that his spiritual and military guide, the oracle Sung, was in enemy hands. And although his army was ill-coordinated and leaderless, he was intelligent enough to keep the abduction of Sung a secret. Fa, who thus far had shown little initiative, realized what panic would ensue should that secret be discovered.

The Moslems of Tatsienlu did not welcome an invasion any more than the other inhabitants of the city. They wished this whole business had never started. Their lives and fortunes had been established in Tatsienlu, and of all the people they stood to lose the most no matter which side was victorious. A number of the younger and more fanatical of them would have been happy to do battle, but this number was small. Many more were seeking ways to get out of Tatsienlu, fearing the inevitable reprisals.

Such chaotic conditions were perfect for Kareem Musa to work out his plans. A strategist of enormous capability, he would not miss the opportunity to capitalize on such an opportunity.

He began by sending Tiso Awa into the streets to "keep the pot brewing." Tiso Awa was to spread the news of the oracle's capture. This he did well, though it did not take much to get any rumor circulating through the town. Conditions became even more chaotic and it was later discovered that many of the Chinese soldiers did know of the oracle's capture.

Later that evening, the lama butcher, arrived.

"Tatsienlu is on the verge of panic," he cried, as he came running into the house where the oracle Sung was kept prisoner.

Jamtzen was out of breath, as if he had been running in many directions at the same time. His face was a brighter red than usual and this I attributed to his excitement as well as a generous supply of *chang,* which he was known to drink.

He described the atmosphere in Tatsienlu as one of volatile forces moving near each other on a collision course. The city was expecting war and there were already rumors that the

Moslems were moving south from Kansu, leaving a wake of destruction and plunder.

"Is this true?" I asked apprehensively, fearing for my family, who would surely be on that path.

"It is as true as the other rumors that are circulating. There is talk of a General Tsoa sending up reinforcements from Atunze in Yunnan. That would take about two weeks, but according to the reports, the Moslems are already approaching the north gate of the city. Confusion reigns. You may believe whichever rumor suits you. But this much is true: the blacksmiths are working late into the night, forging old swords into repair and making new ones. Ah, were all this talk of war true and I were a blacksmith. . . . Look out here."

Jamtzen led Kareem and me downstairs to the door. There he pointed down the narrow street toward the other end of town. Our eyes wandered over the flat roofs to the street of the blacksmiths. There, between bright red flashes of fire and sparks, the black smoke poured into the dark night air, giving the street the appearance of being on fire. Even over the loud crashing of the Dar Chu one could hear the hammering and banging of the smiths' tools as they forged the weapons of war.

"The blacksmith profits from war," the lama butcher lamented, half in jest. "There is little to be made from being a lama butcher."

Kareem walked back into the house. Jamtzen and I followed. The lama butcher sat down near the fire and took out his *tsamba* bowl. He helped himself to the tea that brewed over the fire and then sat back, almost falling over.

"Everything is arranged." The lama butcher smiled. "But it was a costly affair. I just had enough Moslem silver to feed the guards at the north gate. I have barely made any profit."

I assumed that he was referring to bribing the guards for Kareem had already worked out a plan to get Sung out of the city.

"Of the rupees you gave me, I have spent most of them. I have even had to cut into my commission and I may even come out losing on this venture. You know that I do not like to lose."

"He owes me at least two yakskins," I whispered to Kareem.

"What else can I offer you?" Kareem asked. "Would you take two yakskins?"

"Skins?" Jamtzen looked confused. "But what need do I have of yakskins? I am in this business myself."

"Nevertheless," Kareem came back, "according to Small Ears over here, you have shortchanged him more than once and he has had to pay that."

The lama butcher smiled knowingly.

"Yes," he admitted, "I have." Then he laughed. "But this is the way I conduct business. That was business."

"And so is this, my fat friend," Kareem said. "I have no wish to deprive you of your profit but I can do no more than what I have done. You must accept it, just as this boy must accept your count. An alternative does not exist."

The lama butcher laughed philosophically. "In truth," he said, "I am quite satisfied with what I am getting. I just thought that if there were any chance of squeezing more out of the situation, you would not think any less of me for trying."

"I would think less of you if you did not try," Kareem smiled, "and this is why I value your aid. You are motivated neither by revenge nor hatred. Emotions sometimes can get in the way of common sense. But you, my fat friend, are only interested in profit. I assume that our cause is more profitable than our enemies', otherwise I am sure that I would have lost my head some time ago."

"Yes, but your Allah has been good to you," Jamtzen said. "If you do not become offended by accepting the help of a woman. . . ."

"What are you talking about?" Kareem interrupted.

"Rinchen Dorje," Jamtzen answered calmly, "has come to your aid. And as the guards will eat Tibetan silver as well as Moslem, your affairs are arranged."

"Why would this woman help me?" Kareem stroked his beard. "I do not know her. I did not know that she knew me."

"Her generosity has a condition," the lama butcher said.

"And what is that?" Kareem asked sarcastically.

"She wants you to leave Tatsienlu. She does not want you here to stir up trouble. It's bad for business. She does not care for Fa or Sung. She will be happy to be rid of one or the other, but she wants you to leave as well."

"She wants me out of here." Kareem smiled. "Well, you may tell her when you see her that nothing would please me more. I have no more business in the infidel town while the war rages up in Kansu. Here I am in a town full of fat, weak merchants who fear the sword even before it's unsheathed."

"Then you've made a good bargain, I should say." The lama butcher smiled. "She wants you to leave and you want to leave."

"How do you know Rinchen?" I asked. "What possible business do you have with her that allows you to know her so well?"

"Ah, Small Ears. Still determined to judge me?"

I did not answer.

"I have had the most serious of businesses with Rinchen. What can be more serious than the business between a man and his former wife? Now, Kareem Musa, if we can settle our count, I will go back into the streets for more information."

A New Plan of Escape

Kareem returned from some business later that evening accompanied by another man. Tiso Awa and I were sipping our bowls of tea. Sung had refused to join us. As the two men entered the room, I noticed that the man with Kareem was limping, favoring his left leg. I recognized him to be one of the beggars who frequented the town's marketplaces and a fellow of questionable character. His name was Akbar and he was a Moslem, as indicated by his dirty white turban.

Akbar was liked neither by his fellow Moslems nor by the other beggars in Tatsienlu. The Moslems had done well in Tatsienlu, and the majority of them were prosperous and complacent. Akbar represented a disgrace, for them. While charity is the basis of any religion, Akbar was not well received by his Moslem brothers in Tatsienlu. But for a Tibetan, a beggar fulfills a worthwhile and needed trade. It is merit to give, and so beggars, who for the most part inherited their lot, are usually cheerful and optimistic with no ambition to rise out of their situation. They are necessary in the scale of things and are neither neglected nor abused.

The other beggars did not accept Akbar in their guild because he was a devious and dishonest fellow. It was true that Akbar was born with one leg shorter than the other, but it was not true that he was a deaf mute, which he pretended to be in order to gain more donations. Nor was it true that Akbar was blind, which he also pretended to be when new traders came into the town. The other beggars held their honesty with pride, and Akbar, through his various schemes, was not one of them. Indeed, among them were the deaf and the blind and the afflicted, and Akbar's imitating these misfortunes angered them a great deal. Only three days before, I had watched as Akbar was being thrashed by a Chinese silk merchant in front of his shop. The cause of the dispute was not important, for it was not unusual to see Akbar involved in some unpleasant matter. But I remembered hearing Akbar's high, whiny voice meekly call out in protest as he received the beating.

He was a tall, wiry man with an exceedingly long face that seemed to weigh down his heavy narrow eyes as if he were always half asleep. And although one leg was shorter than the other, this was compensated by his long arms, which the beggar swung freely and which aided him in stealing. There was also written into his face a suggestion that life had not been kind to him, but this too was exaggerated to help his begging.

Now, as he walked proudly alongside Kareem Musa, I could almost see a brightness come to his dull eyes. But even the sword that Kareem had given him to wear on his belt did nothing to dispel the old image of Akbar. The sword was too big and clumsy for him, and the prouder he tried to look, the more he seemed to stumble.

I must admit that I was surprised to see Akbar in the camp of Kareem Musa. But I was sure Musa had his reasons.

Akbar approached the oracle. He strained to lift the sword

from its sheath and then held it threateningly above his head as he circled the oracle, letting out all sorts of oaths in his high, brittle voice.

"You will follow this man," Kareem commanded the oracle.

Sung did not move. He folded his arms, then unfolded them.

"You will do as I say." Kareem looked directly at the oracle.

"You dishonor me with your choice of guard," Sung finally spoke. "I thought that I would rate at least someone of your caliber."

"You will follow this man," Kareem repeated. "You will do as I say."

Sung looked at me and then at Akbar who by now had put a comfortable distance between himself and the oracle. Seeing that Kareem would not be moved from his position, he unfolded his arms once more and, like a waking elephant, lifted himself from the ground.

Turning to Akbar, he said, with more than a hint of sarcasm, "Lead the way."

Once they were safely outside, Kareem turned to me. "Has he been of any help, Small Ears?" he asked.

"I'm not sure," I answered honestly.

"I know that he has powers," the Turkestani said, "and he may very well be aware of our plans, but I have no desire to tempt his ears. I must tell you that we are leaving Tatsienlu tonight."

"Tonight?" I repeated. "But why tonight and why are you with that man Akbar? You must know that he is not to be trusted."

Kareem waved his hands as he sat down on a pile of

blankets. "You are full of questions, Small Ears, but you have a great deal to learn. First of all, I am aware of the shortcomings of that beggar, but he comes from a village not far from my own. Though mine has been destroyed by the Russians and no doubt his as well, he is from my country, and so can be trusted by me."

"I hope that you are right. But why leave tonight? All the arrangements have been made for tomorrow morning."

"As I said, Small Ears, you have a great deal to learn. I have not made any arrangements. The lama butcher made the arrangements. Do you trust this man?"

I hesitated.

"Not fully." Kareem Musa answered his own question. "Nor do I. It is possible he has made arrangements with the guards to help us escape, but it is equally possible he has made a better arrangement with them for our capture. I cannot be sure. I will not take the chance. So we leave tonight—soon. Besides, the terms that he has presented us with are quite impossible."

I could see that Kareem was coming to the real reason for this sudden decision.

"The terms that Rinchen presented are exactly what you had planned," I said. "Why have you changed your mind?"

"It is not her terms," Kareem Musa admitted, "it is the aid that she gives with them. How would it look if I, Kareem Musa, prince of Urgan, the avenging angel of Allah, should accept the aid of a woman? Who would follow a warrior who relies on a woman's help to save his skin? No, Small Ears, I would rather die on the end of a Chinese sword than accept this woman's help. It is quite impossible. We must leave tonight." His serious expression changed as he fumbled through a yakskin bag and finally produced an official-looking document in Chinese script. There was an official-looking clay seal imprinted on the bottom.

"I knew this would be of use someday." He laughed. "You did not really believe that I would risk my skin to leave this city."

"I do not read Chinese," I said. "What is that paper?"

"It is the seal of the governor-general of Atunze in Yunnan," he answered, "and with it, many doors will open up to me."

"But Atunze is well to the south of here. How did you come upon this seal?"

"Some years ago, we pillaged a small caravan which was carrying some important papers to Peking. The other men were very upset at the take. There was only a little silver, no gold and some salt, but these were just stupid bandits who could not see what real value this caravan held. While they cursed and looked for gold, I found these seals. I knew that they would be of some value someday. Unlike my foolish comrades who were eventually captured one by one, I had planned to continue a life of brigandry. I did not just fall into it for lack of something else to do.

"Now the governor-general of Atunze is sending a message to Peking. The message must go by the south gate. I will have no problem leaving.

"You see, all that time that I spent with the Chinese soldier was not purely for friendship. He gave me a very good picture of General Fa's military administration. I know, for example, that the north gate does not know what happens at the south gate, and vice versa. And he gave me his uniform, which he no longer had any use for."

"What will you do with Sung?" I asked.

"I suppose," he hesitated, "I could leave him in Akbar's incapable hands. But," he smiled, "he is the official business that is going to Peking to see the emperor. We have no choice but to take him with us. For his and our own safekeeping. But he shall be returned in about six days."

But what of the Chinese merchant, I thought to myself. What has happened to him?

Kareem sensed my question.

"You are concerned about that old Chinese," he said, "but don't waste your time on him."

"I am curious," I admitted. "Did you kill him?"

"Kill him?" Kareem looked at me. "But I gave him my word that I would not. My word is not so easily broken. I believe the poor fellow drowned. There was nothing that I could do."

"Drowned?" I repeated.

"The poor man did not believe that I would do as I said. He attempted to escape by swimming across the river. That was the last I saw of him."

I decided that there was little to be gained by pursuing the matter. Perhaps the old man did, in a frantic panic, attempt the river. Perhaps he was pushed in or slipped in. As with everything else, Kareem Musa made his own interpretations of his own laws. I found out later that the old merchant was not what he pretended to be either. He was actually on a mission from the emperor in Peking. He was a lieutenant colonel who, during the first Moslem revolt, was responsible for the massacre of two Moslem villages. Whether Kareem Musa knew this or not, I cannot say. But I think not, for if he had, I doubt that death would have come as easily and quickly as it did.

"We both have our separate wars to fight." Kareem smiled ironically, as he brought his horse to be mounted. "And I doubt that we shall ever cross paths again."

"You have taught me a great deal." I smiled as I watched him climb into the saddle. "I shall never forget what I have learned."

"Ha," he laughed, "even I have learned. You will take good care of Tiso Awa."

Then he dismounted and we embraced each other. Again he began to speak and again he hesitated.

Finally, he said, "It is the custom in eastern Turkestan that if two friends should part for some time they trade hats or *tsamba* bowls. This is the custom among my people."

He handed me his dingy white woolen hat. "I would also trade bowls with you, but since you have already had *chang* and alcohol in your bowl, I cannot. Take my hat, and I will take yours. Then someday we will have to meet again—if for no other reason than to return each other's hats."

I said nothing as I gave him my Khampa hat.

He hugged me in his big burly arms and then gently pushed me away, looking straight into my eyes. "I suppose that I will never understand you Tibetans."

Then he turned the animal in a direction away from me. I felt a great sadness as I watched him ride away.

The Caravans Arrive

The Chinese themselves made Kareem's escape sure to succeed. Moslem discontent had been smoldering for some time on the verge of ignition, and the recent revolt and its subsequent bloody suppression by Chinese troops did little to abate it. In fact, the opposite occurred.

The revolt had been successfully put down from the military standpoint, but its causes—which ranged from fanaticism to legitimate grievances—had never been dealt with. The cost of war had been great to both sides. Whole towns had been leveled. There were massacres on both sides. The country was torn by rumors and threats. As a result of the war, Moslems were prohibited from living within the walls of certain cities. But this regulation was not very strictly enforced, and practically not at all in Tatsienlu.

For some reason, the Chinese military did not see the Moslems as a serious threat, and so when more wood was thrown onto the fire, there was little attempt to prepare for war. Wild rumors set the Chinese into a disorganized frenzy.

There was probably a reason for this as well. To be sure, there were some soldiers who were militarily inclined and who had gone to the proper military schools in Peking, Ichang or even Japan, but for the most part the army consisted of conscripted farmers and peasants who had no taste for war. The army was an ill-disciplined, highly unprofessional collection of malcontented farmers who only waited for the chance to get back to their farms and opium smoking, and rootless scoundrels who thought that they would give the army a try. According to Hsi Teng there were many more who were just waiting for the opportunity to desert.

Strangely enough, the following morning revealed little evidence of the panic and dread that had gripped Tatsienlu the night before. It was as if nothing had ever happened, and in fact, except for Kareem's escape, nothing had. As rumors do, the one of the impending invasion and inevitable disaster rushed through the town like a fire out of control, only to burn itself out. Fresh rumors circulated, completed their cycle and were forgotten while the people of Tatsienlu went about their business. These rumors were becoming the daily early morning discussions in the teahouses and wherever monks congregated to chat. But as the day wore on and little evidence could be found to support these predictions of doom, the people simply forgot them.

There were, of course, some who would believe anything. But the group of Chinese and Tibetans waiting at the south gate to seek refuge in the Yellow Hat monastery discovered that the monks had not heard of any invasions and did not welcome what they considered to be the real invasion. One by one, the people returned to town, some still convinced that the end was near.

The fires that had burned so brightly the night before in the blacksmiths' shops were almost cold now. An occasional predictor of doom wandered the streets warning people to save themselves, but found little audience. Even the blacksmiths, who would certainly profit by a war, seemed to lose interest in making arms.

Of the many rumors that burned through the city, two were of particular interest to me. The first concerned the disappearance of the oracle Sung. It was, perhaps, Kareem Musa's own daring which led people to take this rumor lightly. Sung, after all, was a very good friend of General Fa's, and it was unthinkable that anyone would have the audacity to abduct so important and influential a figure. Sung was known to have a number of efficient bodyguards, and the chance of any harm coming to the oracle did not seem great. Nobody could believe that the oracle had been taken. There was even talk that he had been seen near the monastery on his way to the baths only that morning.

The other rumor was more mysterious. It concerned a death at the south gate. The victim and the circumstances of his death were not completely known. Some said it was a Moslem rebel. Others talked about a Chinese lieutenant and then a Chinese private. I was not to learn the truth of this incident until a few days later.

In the meantime, the mood of the city had been completely turned around. What had brought about this dramatic change?

Very simply, the first of the major caravans had arrived for the tea season. The season had come. Instead of preparing for battle, the city was preparing for business.

The caravan was of medium size, consisting of about 150 yaks and an equal number of mules. Four stately camels marched in regal procession at the rear of the caravan. The caravan originated from a good-sized monastery in Amdo, on the borderlands of the great marshy swamps. They had not been far from Kansu, but were unaware of any new outbreak of violence.

"Were there any Moslem insurgents on the way to Tatsienlu?"

Laughter. "There was nothing like that."

"Was your caravan attacked?"

Laughter again. "Yes. In the Dze Chu pass about thirty Goloks made an unsuccessful raid where at least half of their number was killed."

"Is it true that the town of Lusar was leveled by the Moslem bandits?"

"Lusar still exists, but there is no place to have tea there, as the only teahouse burnt down some weeks ago."

There were the questions and the answers and the fresh excitement that always greet a new caravan on its arrival. Young boys gathered at all the gates, loaded down with buckets of wild strawberries which they had picked days before in anticipation of the season. They would sell these berries for one or two rupees a bucket, or whatever the traffic would bear.

Beggars suddenly appeared in every part of Tatsienlu. Some were humble and pitiful: "Kind sir, it is merit. Help a poor unfortunate. Gain merit." Others cajoled and threatened the wealthy-looking merchants, promising them any number of curses if they were not taken care of. Even in begging, there is style and inventiveness.

The whole town seemed to be taken up in the mood of trade and commerce. As the day wore on and more caravans arrived, the teahouses filled and spilled out into the streets. Rinchen's coolies aggressively seduced the caravan men, taking them off to their various haunts and, by late afternoon, there were groups of men and women who, having been well fortified with an ample supply of *chang,* marched and chanted down the narrow streets of Tatsienlu. There were the inevitable fights, the most violent of these concerning two mule drivers from Batang. This was to be expected, of course, for it is said that if two men of Batang are in the same room there is bound to be trouble. Nobody knew how the argument started, but these men seldom needed excuses to fight. No one was seriously injured, the extent of damage being a long cut on one of the participants' right arm.

I had to some extent prepared for the arrival of the season, but I never anticipated the excitement it would generate. The usual mobile population of the town was increased many times, and merchants who the night before had been

259

polishing their rifles were busy preparing their stock, trying to display it in the most inviting manner.

One by one, the large caravans wandered into the town. By midafternoon three more caravans had arrived, one from faraway Nepal with beautifully worked silver and bronze religious figures. Later that same day, the caravan from Shigatse passed through the north gate. It had passed the caravan from Lhasa, the biggest one of all, just some five days before, and estimated that by now it would probably be waiting for the snows to clear at Tcheta pass.

I realized that I would not and could not stay in Tatsienlu, but I must admit that since leaving Hor Drango I had never felt so exhilarated. I was happy to be pushed and jostled by the crowds lining the narrow streets. I welcomed brushing shoulders with mulemen who had just come off the road. I pushed and shoved my way into the crowd, eager to get a better look at the new arrivals.

My mouth watered when a caravan from Hami, on the borders of Kareem Musa's land, filed into Tatsienlu with a cargo of dates and dried apricots. I mentally made a note of what price I would be willing to pay for some Sikkimese goat wool that I knew would be entirely too expensive for me. I admired the fine workmanship of the Nepalese religious articles and watched with amusement a long bartering siege between a Tibetan rhubarb dealer and a Chinese merchant. Apparently they were old friends, the bond of trade going back many years. However, each year they went through the same ritual, alternately insulting and complimenting each other until a bargain was struck. I was told that they attracted an amused and attentive crowd every year.

I watched the rich merchants and representatives of the

monasteries file off to the various tea warehouses, where transactions involving large sums of money and tea would be made in quiet seclusion, away from the noise and bustle of the street.

Rinchen Dorje was, of course, particularly busy. Though there was no shortage of women eager to work for her, some of her old reliables were unable to work, having spent what little they earned on *chang* for themselves and some of the mule drivers. This too was the same every year, but Rinchen was becoming less and less tolerant of this behavior.

One tiny woman came in cursing and spitting and smelling of strong *chang*. She demanded that she be put back to work. Rinchen paid little attention to her ravings.

"She is usually one of my best," the head of the women coolies guild said to me, "but every year it is the same. She gets drunk. The caravan leaves. She has a baby. What am I going to do with her?"

The woman ranted and raved until she fell in a heap near the steps of Rinchen's teahouse. The big woman commanded two of her servants to bring her into the house, though one could easily have carried the little woman.

"Tomorrow she can have work," Rinchen sighed. "There is still plenty to do here."

Then she looked at me through her tiny narrow eyes. "Besides," she smiled, "it is the season, isn't it?"

I did not answer, but I knew that it was indeed the season, and in the midst of this exciting time I had almost forgotten the *migou* skin I carried under my cloak. I had almost forgotten my reason for coming to Tatsienlu and the reason that I would soon have to leave.

The Escape

I learned about the circumstances of Kareem Musa's escape quite inadvertently. Three days had passed since the attempt was made. I did not spend that time only watching the caravans arrive. There was a great deal of work to be done. I was becoming a fairly efficient tea packer, working alongside Thundup. One day I saw Akbar in the streets, playing the blind man. When I acknowledged him, he gave me a knowing wink and a smile and then disappeared into the crowd. He did not seem eager to talk to me. Moreover, I knew his information might not be reliable.

I was still sent to the street of butchers to gather the skins used to sew up the bales of tea, and it was on that street that I saw the lama butcher once again. He was sure that Kareem had left the city unharmed. When I told him that Kareem did not follow the plans they had agreed upon, he seemed very surprised.

"What is this?" he asked incredulously. "I have thrown good silver at those Chinese guards. Everything was arranged. How will I get any of that back? Why didn't he tell me?"

"He didn't trust you," I said, not sure if his concern was for Kareem or the silver.

He scratched his large head and then wiped his hand on the sides of his cloak. He was amused.

"I suppose," he said to me, "that I am not to be trusted. But I swear to you that I did not betray your friend. Nor would I betray him."

Could I believe him? It mattered little, for what did he

know of Kareem's escape? He seemed to know as much as I did, which was not a great deal.

He gave me a load of skins which we both counted together. This time, to my surprise, he did not attempt to cheat me. He smiled as he placed the last skin on the pile, scratched his head again, and laughed. "No, if I were you, I would not trust me."

Then his voice became very low, almost a whisper. "I have done a great deal for money," he said. "I have done things that even I find hard to justify. You do not know the many bad things I have done—and will do. But I would sooner cut my own throat than betray Kareem Musa."

Perhaps I had judged him wrongly. He appeared genuinely concerned about Kareem's fate, almost frightened.

"Why this admiration of Kareem Musa?" I asked.

"Tiso Awa remains in Tatsienlu," he answered calmly. "If anything were to happen to Kareem because of me, I would expect little mercy from that wild Mongol. I do not know the fate of this bandit Moslem."

He seemed to be telling the truth. When I left him, he was lamenting the loss of "all that good silver."

Rinchen Dorje, in spite of her knowledge of all the comings and goings of the town, could offer little more information. She was not surprised that Kareem had turned down her offer of aid. She cared little whether he accepted or not. She was even less concerned about the fate of the Moslem. Her purpose had been accomplished. Dead or alive, Kareem Musa was no longer in Tatsienlu.

According to her, there had indeed been a killing at the baths, and talk of a killing at one of the gates of Tatsienlu. This much she was sure of. But the authorities (in this case,

General Fa) were not eager for the details to be known. They understood that no matter what happened, it could not be good for the morale of the town. If Kareem Musa had been killed and discovered to be a bandit with a high price on his head, then people were sure to believe that the rest of his band was not far away and would come seeking revenge. If a soldier had been killed, it was even worse, as it proved the rumors of the Moslem uprising were not far from the truth. Either way, it would not be good for the town.

But I had to know. I knew that I could not leave Tatsienlu without learning my friend's fate. I knew that this mystery would haunt me like a relentless hawk that picks away the bones of the dead. I had to find out.

And I did, but in a less dramatic way than I would have expected. I had just delivered a load of skins to a warehouse. The large rambling courtyard was a bustle of activity. Bales were being packed and stacked in neat piles while the women coolies marched out one by one with fresh loads to take to the north gate, where they would be loaded on yaks for the trip to western Tibet.

A woman coolie ran into the courtyard, announcing that the caravan from Lhasa had arrived. Everyone stopped what they were doing. This caravan was the largest of all. When it had started from Lhasa eight months before, it was already large. Smaller, less well protected caravans joined it en route for mutual protection; when it finally arrived in Tatsienlu, it numbered over 1,000 yaks, mules and horses. Among the human cargo, there were at least six high-ranking monks from Lhasa, representing some of the greatest powers in the state.

Like everyone else, I ran outside to see this retinue march

into town. Although the yaks were left outside the north gate (they are not permitted in the town), there were a great many horsemen. First came the soldier monks, about fifty men who are chosen more for physical strength than for religious zeal. Following them was a long train of mules, each carrying a heavy load of wool or silver. Finally came the incarnate monks and holy men, two of whom were riding stately camels. More soldier monks protected the rear flank.

As the last group of soldier monks marched by with their tall lances topped with tufts of wool, I noticed two particularly big and mean-looking soldiers step toward me. I was not sure if they meant to do me harm. They then broke rank and came toward me like two charging yaks. What was even less understandable was the broad smile each wore on his face.

I moved this way and that, trying to avoid their path, until I realized that they were not looking for me. There were two Chinese soldiers standing near me whom the soldier monks were approaching. The men were very good friends and had not seen each other for a year. They exchanged greetings warmly, asking each other about friends in common. As I was near this conversation, I could not help but overhear what was said.

"And what of the Moslems?" one of the Chinese soldiers asked. "Has there been any trouble in Lhasa?"

The soldier monk laughed, displaying a mouth half full of teeth and a straggly beginning of a beard. Up until then, I do not believe that I ever saw a larger or more contrary-looking man. His laugh was not evil but it was tinged with cruelty, and I was sure that many had thought better than to go against this monk.

"You always have trouble here," he said to the Chinese soldier, "but they know better than to go against my monastery."

The Chinese soldier agreed that any adventure against this soldier monk's monastery would be a dangerous undertaking. "But," he added, "they are a devious bunch. Why just the other night there was a murder at the south gate."

My ears perked up. It could have been just another rumor but I was determined to hear it through. I moved closer to the Chinese soldier and pretended to be involved in the parade of a small monastery that was marching in.

"The strangest thing," the Chinese went on. "No one is quite sure how it happened, but these Moslems are not easy to hold on to. Anyway, do you remember a Manchu from Ichang, a certain Captain Yang?"

"A scoundrel, if I recall," the monk answered, "an opium-smoking thief."

"The very one," the Chinese came back, "but he is a scoundrel no more."

"Dead?" the monk asked.

"His head was cut off. In fact, it has still to be found."

"What happened?"

I moved in closer again.

"Well, Yang had the watch at the south gate. You know that he used his position to profit by it."

"He stole."

"Whenever he could," the Chinese said, "but it seems that there was a messenger with an important communication from the governor-general of Atunze. He had his papers with the official seal. He was traveling with a hooded monk of no particular rank. Yang told the messenger that there was a new tariff placed on messages being sent out of Tatsienlu. The messenger seemed like a stupid fellow, and the monk didn't seem much more intelligent. Never said a word. So Yang assured him that whatever fees he paid would be returned by his master in Atunze and that he himself would sign the receipt for it.

"Well, this fellow was not as stupid as he looked. He claimed that he did not have anything more than what he was carrying, but he had a fresh mount waiting for him and the monk past the Hilo bridge."

"Yang was not very smart to interfere with official business," the monk grunted.

"He was even less smart to accompany this seemingly ignorant messenger. The messenger promised that he would be rewarded when they reached the second mounts. So Yang committed the greatest military sin. He left his post. That was his undoing. You know Corporal Wei Heng, the one with the fat Tibetan wife. He was at the gate and he told me that he noticed something strange about this messenger. He could not stop staring at Yang, and when Yang took out a bag of tobacco he had recently acquired, the messenger's face seemed to become violent. Of course, nobody knew the reason why, and Yang followed the messenger and the monk outside the south gate. Not long afterwards, his headless body rode back on a fresh horse. There was no doubt that it was Yang but the bandit wasn't very efficient. Yang had a great deal of money, but none of it was taken."

"None?"

"That's the strange thing. The only thing that was missing was Yang's usual bag of tobacco. That's all. It had been ripped out of his uniform and there was a most perplexing note attached to his back. It simply said, 'The debt has been paid.'"

"'The debt has been paid'?" the monk repeated.

"Yes, that's all. Just a bag of tobacco."

"Well, that's the trouble with you Chinese soldiers." The monk laughed at his friend. "You do not make good soldiers. Nothing like that would ever happen in Lhasa."

"You are right," the other sighed. "I would make a much better farmer."

"And what's this I hear about the oracle Sung?" one of the soldier monks asked. "Has he disappeared?"

The Chinese soldiers laughed. "Oh, that's yesterday's rumor," one said, "but you don't really believe these rebels would attempt anything so formidable as that?"

"I don't know," the soldier monk replied, "these Moslems have no fear, it seems."

"It is true," the other Chinese soldier mused, "that General Fa has closed the baths for the last two days. A military operation, he says."

"What are you talking about?" his comrade spoke. "Why, Sung was seen just this morning near the south gate."

"Did you see him?" his friend asked.

"Well, no."

"I love Tatsienlu," the soldier monk said, laughing loudly. "Everyone knows what's going on, but nobody knows what's going on."

They all laughed, turned and headed for the teahouse on the corner. I watched them walk away. I was satisfied that I had learned the truth of Kareem's escape.

Bad Piece of Business for Tiso Awa

I had already stayed too long in Tatsienlu. It was time to go. I had spoken to the oracle Sung and now there was nothing left for me to do there. I would go southwest and find Chumbi valley. My karma would lead me to the *migou*.

But first I paid a visit to the lama butcher. He told me about the return of the oracle Sung to Tatsienlu. In the excitement of the arrival of the caravans, his return received little attention. His was not a glorious return. But he had no wish to bring attention to what had happened for his undignified entry into the city involved a serious loss of face. And his very existence depended on his aura of invulnerability. How, after all, would it appear if the oracle with all his powers could not even prevent his own abduction?

As it was he never acknowledged the rumors of his capture. Quite the contrary, he claimed to be very free and was merely escaping the routine of his busy schedule before the arrival of the Tashilumpo caravan from Shigatse.

Where had he been?

Up to the north country on a pilgrimage to an early Buddhist shrine on the upper Yalung River. He stated further, that during the ascent of a mountain in that region, his horse stumbled and he was flung from the back of the animal down the mountain. Fortunately, his cloak caught a branch which slowed his fall. In the process, however, the cloak was ripped to shreds and his supplies were lost. This explained the circumstances of his return to Tatsienlu. A local peasant had been kind enough to give him a dingy sheepskin robe and he entered Tatsienlu like any of the peasants who wait for the gates to open.

The story was a good one and I was happy that everyone believed it. For he would not pursue revenge. He would not lose face.

The lama butcher also told me about Tiso Awa's departure from the city two days before the arrival of a caravan from Amdo in the north. I was surprised but clearly the lama butcher was glad to see him go. He breathed a long sigh of relief as he talked about Tiso. He knew as much about Tiso Awa as I did but he feared him while I admired his confident ways. He had asked the lama butcher to relay a message to me about his sudden departure. As I expected, it was a vague message.

"A bad piece of business has turned up," the lama butcher said.

"A bad piece of business . . .?" I repeated.

"That's right," the red-faced butcher said. "A bad piece of business."

A Muleman in His *Chang*

I was on my way to Rinchen Dorje to say good-bye. The street was practically deserted as I walked toward the middle bridge. By now, the traders and merchants had retired to the privacy of the big teahouses, where the difficult transactions could be discussed among friends. The women porters of Tatsienlu and the men who had come on the impressive caravans were already in the midst of their distractions, which included the consumption of large amounts of *chang*.

As I was passing one of the larger warehouses belonging to a monastery in the Jyekundo region, I was stopped by a familiar voice singing a familiar song.

"'Don't ride Chinese horses, their backs are like frogs.'"

The words to the song were wrong, but I knew the voice. It was Uncle Sangsang, Little Father.

I found him lying in the muddy street as I had seen him so many times before. He was singing and laughing. Only his voice had changed. It was not the kind of change that *chang* can bring to a voice, although there was a little of that too. It was more of a whistling sound. I discovered that this was the result of a missing front tooth. Though his face was blood-stained and encrusted with mud, a faith to take things as they come shined through. He was not in any pain. Quite the contrary, he was in the best of spirits.

Taking little notice of me, he was more determined to find the words to a song which he could never remember.

"'Don't ride Chinese horses . . . on the backs of frogs they came.' . . . Oh, so it's you, Small Ears, what are you doing here? You know the words . . . come on . . . 'Don't ride' . . . come on. . . ."

I filled in the words for Sangsang and he finally made an attempt to get up. He was quite drunk, but when he managed to complete his song some sobriety returned.

As he stumbled to his feet, waving me off, he realized the loss of his tooth. A muddy hand went to his mouth and his middle finger wiggled where the tooth should have been. I was sure this would bring up his anger. But instead, he smiled. He thought for a while and looked at me. "It was Dendru, a muleman from Batang," he said. "That is how I lost my tooth."

271

"Will you go after him now?" I asked.

"Why should I?" he replied. "I already knocked out one of his a long time ago. What are you doing here, anyway?"

Sangsang listened intently as I told him all the events that had passed since I was given the *migou* skin in Hor Drango. He knew all about the strange visit of the old pilgrim and was eager to see the skin that was taking me so far away from the place where I was born. He did not react when I showed it to him. Sangsang never put much into these things; it made no difference to him. He merely wanted to satisfy his curiosity. He had been in Hor Drango only some weeks before.

"And how are things there?" I asked longingly.

"You are like me." He laughed. "You expect great changes when you are not around. But things are the same, except that everyone is concerned about you."

"And Grandmother's health?" I inquired.

"The same," he answered. "No better, no worse. I suppose that this is good. In truth, though, she urged me to 'keep an eye on things.' But you seem to be in control of the situation.

"I had also hoped to see Tiso Awa," he continued. "We have not been on the road together for years. A reliable muleman, that one."

"Yes, I was disappointed when he left so suddenly."

"A bad piece of business." Sangsang laughed. "That bad piece of business will never end."

"You know about it?" I asked.

"Nobody knows the whole story of Tiso Awa," he answered, "but this bad piece of business happened a long time ago, in Amdo. Tiso Awa once had a woman there. She went with him on the roads and was devoted to him. The only problem was that she was married to a Tangut nomad. That is why Tiso Awa seldom goes north. This nomad still hunts the wily Mongol."

"He never said anything."

"He wouldn't." Sangsang smiled.

"But what happened to this woman?"

"She died crossing Jeto pass many years ago. A landslide. The nomad blames Tiso for taking her away."

"And he is still being chased!"

"You know that these things have a way of never ending. Well, perhaps I will see him some other time. But now you must allow me to take you to Chumbi. I told Grandmother that I would watch out for you."

"Of course," I said, happy to have his company.

"And we have already fallen on a bit of luck," he said as we began to march down the street. "Just this afternoon, Dendru, the muleman from Batang, told me of a caravan going toward Nagchu Dzong. It is still far from Chumbi, but is only eight days from Lhasa. And even better luck, he has some charge of the caravan's affairs. I am to purchase mules tomorrow morning and the cook needs a helper. Not a very likable one, this cook, but you'll survive."

He looked me up and down.

"You have grown tall and strong in fifteen years." He smiled approvingly. "But first things first. We must find a place to drink *chang*. Come, lead the way."

"I am going to Rinchen Dorje," I told him. "I'm sure that there is plenty to drink there."

"Too far," Sangsang said. "She is well at the other end of the town walls. Too far."

It was dark now. After we crossed the bridge, Sangsang found the first inn. A scrappy woman porter with strong thin arms and a narrow pretty face was standing at the door. She appeared to know my uncle.

"Hey, muleman," she called, "come in here."

"Careful," he warned her. "When grass and weeds come up an old mule goes crazy."

"I have heard you before." She laughed. "Boasting is like muddy waters. Little depth."

"We'll meet early tomorrow in the town square," he whispered to me as he walked toward the woman, puffing up his chest. "Rinchen is too far away. We will meet tomorrow." Then he walked into the inn with the woman, each challenging the other's sexual prowess.

I spent the night at Rinchen's, where we talked well into the night. She was not surprised that I was going.

In the morning, I thanked Rinchen for everything she had done for me. She shrugged her shoulders. "It is merit to give," she spoke softly.

I knew that she was not the kind to display strong emotions.

"We shall never see each other again, but you are doing religion's work. Could I have done any less?"

Then, as the women coolies came in and Rinchen noisily assigned the work, I quietly slipped away. I watched her as she barked, growled and cajoled her porters. She was a majestic woman. I remember that most about her. There was no long farewell. I left her in total control of her feelings.

Could I have done any less?

Buying Mules

It was a bright morning, especially for Tatsienlu. The plant hunters who gathered medicinal plants from the upper slopes had been out for some time. Most of them only had rhubarb to sell. As usual, the supply of rhubarb was greater than the demand. There was no gold-leaf rhubarb, that one finds on the upper slopes; only the cheap variety, the worst of it smelling like yak dung. Nevertheless, optimism prevailed, and each was in the process of arranging and rearranging the leaves. As I walked by, a solitary and severe-looking Chinese was examining their stock.

Next I passed an old Tibetan woman who was gauging the quality of some musk a hunter had for sale. After running a piece of string through a clove of garlic, she dropped the end of the string into a bag of reputedly pure musk. She offered the hunter the first smell of the string. He refused, and this action alone made him suspect. Then the woman smelled the string herself.

"I smell more garlic than musk," she said with a challenge. "If your musk is top quality, why do you have to mix it with blood and liver?"

The hunter vehemently denied that he would do anything dishonest. Nevertheless, the price went down considerably.

I found Sangsang in the market, buying mules. He was in deep contemplation as he gazed intently at a group of stocky gray animals. A nomadic woman, apparently the seller, stood nearby, trying to look disinterested at each of Sangsang's reactions to her stock.

Sangsang was in his element. He nodded to me and smiled, calling me over. I followed him as he swaggered through the market. He needed only a glance to make a judgment of the stock. If he stopped, it was only to point out a serious defect in one or another animal. He made sure the seller heard him if any trading was to be done so that the full impact of his comments could be absorbed.

"Look at this one over here," he said, pointing to a large mule. "She is right in most respects. Thickset, short legs . . . ah, but the tail. Do you see how short it is? Too short. I have never seen a short-tailed mule who was a steady animal."

He walked on to another group of animals. Without a word, I followed. "The trouble with this market," he said, "is that it is too close to Szechwan and Yunnan. As a result, we see nothing but these worthless Szechwanese and Yunnanese mules. Fine if one is to approach the lowlands of China, but completely out of the question for the uplands of Tibet."

Finally, after making one more tour of the market, we returned to the old nomadic woman. Sangsang was ready to deal.

All that remained of the woman's stock were three very young mules and one very old one. The old one wore on her back the scars of many journeys across Tibet and I was sure she would barely make it out the gates of Tatsienlu. However, Little Father chose the old mule.

"Those young mules have never been on a caravan before. You can tell by how smooth their backs are," he said.

He walked over to the old mule and gave her a handful of *tsamba*. Her back was rough and bumpy.

"But this animal knows what a caravan is." He smiled. "She knows what a load and a saddle are. Those young ones

276

would buck their load every chance they got. We would make no progress at all and would lose many loads. Choose an older animal. She knows the road."

In another part of the market ponies were being sold. A number of Sining ponies were up for sale that morning. Sining ponies, while not very big, are spirited and reliable animals. According to Sangsang, they are preferred to Szechwan ponies, which have big clumsy hoofs.

A large deal had just been made. A big silver mare was being led through the market and everyone, including Sangsang and myself, stopped to admire the animal. The seller, a short stocky Moslem with great brown eyes beaming under a white turban, was proudly announcing to all that he sold the finest horses around.

Sangsang was more interested in the buyer. "That's Thugben's servant leading that horse," he said to me. "We will be on Thugben's caravan. I wonder how much the pony cost. I know that merchant; a difficult man. I'm sure that he has a great deal of Kashmiri blood in him, although he claims not to. I wonder who got the better bargain. But it is, after all, a Sining pony, and a beautiful one at that."

The Caravan Route

Although the north road, known as the Merchants' Road, has fewer high mountain passes and raging streams, it was decided that we would leave Tatsienlu by the south road, known as the Ambans' Road.

Thugben wanted to get to Litang on the south road, where

silver could be purchased considerably cheaper than in Tatsienlu. He had a merchant's mind, and weighed the cost of losing some mules on the way to the profit he could make by reselling silver in his native Sining. There had been some trouble recently in Batang, three days west of Litang. An *amban* on the way to Lhasa had been murdered by the inhabitants of Batang and talk had it that the Chinese were moving troops along this road. Thugben wanted to take advantage of this protection.

From a fortified Batang, Thugben intended to take the caravan north toward Riwoche, where an early Buddhist shrine existed, which he planned to visit. Then the caravan would follow the pilgrims' road to Jyekundo.

Jyekundo, the caravan's immediate destination, was the center of the Nyingmapa (Red Hat) sect and the last place in the west not under the total jurisdiction of the Lhasa government. It was also a large wool center.

On a brisk morning our small caravan, which consisted of 100 mules loaded with wolfskins and tea, marched through the gates of Tatsienlu bearing Thugben, his servant, nine well-armed mulemen, two lamas, a cook and me, the cook's helper.

The Climb to the Upland Pastures

Eight days west of Tatsienlu, the glorious upland pastures began. Here we met a yak caravan that Thugben had sent out the month before. Like us, they were bound for Jyekundo, the caravan town, where they would join with thousands of other yaks, forming the massive caravans that brought tea to Lhasa and beyond.

It was late afternoon, under a pale early winter sky. The sun clung stubbornly to the horizon, making blood-red streaks, as if a knife had cut into the sky.

The yaks, who had been relieved of their heavy loads, were nourished by the sturdy brown grass that crept up between patches of snow. They enjoyed the bitter winds now gaining force, which lifted and whistled through their shaggy flanks. They would move, but only reluctantly. As they rumbled down the gently inclining hills, snorting and grumbling, their drivers kept them together by hurling small stones at their backs while two large brown dogs, one leading the way down and the other scampering around the flanks, barked furiously. They stopped to eye us contemptuously, undecided if they should continue what they were doing or attack us. Fortunately they chose the former. I'm sure this was because none of us hesitated from arming ourselves with small rocks.

The yaks seemed to take less notice of the dogs than we did. Never totally domesticated—even these animals, crosses between yaks and cows—they accepted their lot with brute reluctance. Every yak on every caravan would throw off its load at least once. It is a yak's karma, and a yak driver's karma as well. Were it not for their wide, strong backs and amazing surefootedness even on ice, a more agreeable animal would have taken their job. Their one great disadvantage is that they are, by necessity, slow. The speed and progress of the caravan depends solely on what grazing is found along the way. Since this was the last good grazing between Tatsienlu and Jyekundo, the yaks had already spent the better part of six days here.

As the yak drivers marched past us in their dingy sheepskin *chubas*, Sangsang nodded to a wizened old man with a slightly bent back who eyed us suspiciously. He had a severe, narrow face and was in constant movement, whistling and shouting as he flung small stones at the stragglers. Never missing a step, he threw a constant barrage of stones at one of the yaks, while he cursed both the yak and the dog trying to help him. His eyes were dull and unhappy and his long face seemed that much longer because he did not smile. He looked like a man who would never smile, and Sangsang soon confirmed this.

"His name is Rabbit," he told me. "I never heard his real name. He never smiles. He'll drive anything but camels— yaks, mules, horses—but he doesn't like camels. It seems a camel once spat on him."

Sangsang added with a relieved expression, "I am happy that he is not driving mules this time. Otherwise he would be with us. I suppose that every caravan must have at least one."

"I don't understand," I interrupted.

"A complainer," Sangsang said flatly. "One who sees doom. Rabbit manages to see the worst in everything. Try not to pay attention to him. Nobody does. You'll see."

By the time Thugben's white cotton tent had been set up and the yaks tied together by the single yakskin rope that went around the back feet of each one, a strong and welcome fire blazed in the yak drivers' camp.

Surrounded by the odor of yak and mules, I sipped tea with strong adventurous Khampas under a shimmering early winter sky. There was no place else I wanted to be. Sheltered by large bales of tea which had been piled high in a semicircle facing the northeast, where the strongest winds were coming, we watched the night creep in around us.

I remembered how unfamiliar I had been with the road when I traveled with Kareem Musa and Tiso Awa. Now I felt at home in the company of these mule drivers. I was far from the goal which had driven me from my mountain home, yet I felt for the first time that I could relax and leave tomorrow to itself. My karma had been set long ago and I was merely to carry it out.

The feeling of ease and self-assuredness was soon to disappear. The man that they called Rabbit managed to find a danger in everything, as I had been told he would. A cloud surrounded his person, turning his outlook on the world into sheer fright. This was a demon that he bore willingly and even enjoyed. His nervousness was almost contagious, and the men who had the misfortune to travel with him were under notable stress as he predicted each new disaster.

While the rest of us squatted around the fire with warm bowls of tea, Rabbit constantly got up to check the ropes to which the yaks were tied. He took a sip, looked around and then without hesitation bolted toward the yaks with keen determination, stirring the dogs into frenzied barking. When he returned to the fire, he simply resumed his position as if nothing had happened. This anxious ritual was repeated again and again. If it wasn't the safety of the yaks, it would be something else. If the fire crackled and sputtered, he jumped. If the slightest unusual sound came through the night air, his was the first rifle to the ready.

On and on, he rambled, his monotonous drone filling the descending night. Like the others, I tried not to pay attention to his pessimistic ramblings. But when he spoke about the

Moslem rebellion in Kansu, a subject that was fresh on everyone's mind, even the most disinterested of us listened closely. Not that Rabbit knew any more than any of us; there was a great deal of conjecture about the revolt. But Rabbit collected the worst of the stories, and even rumors must have some basis in facts.

Sangsang, however, was not interested. "You worry too much," he said defeatedly as Rabbit described the Moslem bandits that waited for us in the passes ahead. "You always find something to worry about."

No doubt Rabbit had heard this before, most likely many times. One of the other yak drivers smiled at Sangsang as if to say that he was wasting his words.

But nothing could have made Rabbit happier. He enjoyed attention, even bored attention. He was relentless.

"Maybe so," he looked up from his bowl of tea, "but you know about the trouble up there in the Amdo country. . . ."

He broke his sentence and looked around like a cat in the grass. His long white hair, which rolled in straggly bunches over his hunched shoulders, moved slowly, following the jerky movements of his head.

"I don't see our Moslem mule driver around," he whispered, leaning into the fire. "But I know he's out there. No one listened to me. He's just a poor Moslem. Very well, where is he? And where is the horse he stole? We're lucky that he is not like the other one, you all said. He's not one of those crazy fanatics, not one of that Salar creed. But I still don't trust him. And another thing . . ."

He looked around to see who was listening. For some strange reason, I was.

"Did you ever know a war to stay in one place?" he asked with almost a smile. "You would think that the Moslem

282

would have learned from the last time. Do you remember what happened to the price of tea?"

He was looking right at me.

"No, you don't remember," he said, "you're too young. But I can tell you how it was. Your uncle can tell you as well. It was a bad time and . . . wait! Did you hear that?"

I only heard the fire crackle and the sounds of the night.

"And you hear things too." Sangsang laughed.

"Maybe so." The rifle was already at the old man's shoulder, the fork placed in the ground and aimed into the darkness.

"They're a daring bunch this time," he said as he swung his rifle around slowly. "Don't tell me that you didn't hear what happened in Tatsienlu?"

One of the men laughed meekly as if to say, not that story again.

"Go ahead. You can all laugh." He continued to aim his rifle in the dark. "But I heard that the oracle Sung was abducted by the Moslems. Right out from under the nose of General Fa."

The words cut through me sharply. I tried to keep a disinterested look. Only Sangsang noticed my reaction.

"And you believe everything." Sangsang reached for another bowl of tea.

"Maybe so," he went on, "but I'm not the only one to hear this story. And there's more. Tibetans were involved. General Fa is offering a sizable reward for any information. I'd like to get some of that."

He was looking directly at me again. Perhaps because I seemed to be the only one interested. How much did he really know, I wondered.

"What do you think, boy?" He leaned into the fire.

"Wouldn't you like some of that reward?"

"Yes . . . yes," I stumbled. "But I've never known a Chinese to give a Tibetan the better of the bargain."

"Well said." Dendru, another muleman, laughed and turned to Rabbit. "Leave the small-eared one alone," he said. "Must you constantly go on?"

The old man looked around the campfire. He knew that he did not have an ally but this only made him more determined and disagreeable.

"I was just wondering," he said with a half smile, "whether with those small ears he was able to hear anything about this in Tatsienlu."

"The oracle Sung abducted?" Dendru, who was a good friend of my uncle's, laughed incredulously. "Can't you think of a more reasonable rumor to circulate around the fire?"

One of the yak drivers, a quiet, sullen man named Tendon was about to bed down. "Gossip is not only the domain of old women," he said without emotion. "Rabbits make up their share."

"I'm telling you," Rabbit continued undaunted, "the Chinese have already sent out their agents looking for information about this outrage. Wars never stay in one place."

Again, he was looking right at me. I knew that if the Chinese were indeed offering a reward for the capture of the abductors, delivery would have to be made quietly so Sung would not lose face. If it were ever discovered that I had taken part in this affair, I realized that even Sangsang would be unable to protect me.

"What would you do with the reward?" the old man asked me.

"If there were a reward I would go to sleep, like everyone else," I came back, wishing for this conversation to end.

Then I turned into the sheepskin blanket. When Rabbit saw that nobody else was listening, he looked around. He decided to check the ropes one more time and then, seeing nobody cared, he, too, went to sleep.

"You handled yourself well," Sangsang whispered to me as I curled up in a large blanket.

"Did I?" I asked.

The confidence and swagger with which I had entered the camp were still intact. It was not a fragile confidence that needed reassuring. I had learned something.

I remembered my days in Hor Drango which now seemed so very far away. I remembered my father, who used to teach me the Bon scriptures. I was an impatient learner and always tried to jump ahead without conquering what had gone before. My father would never allow what some may think is the right of youth. He was convinced that certain truths are basic no matter what age, and when I would proudly read ahead, he would snap a birch branch across my wrists.

"You are committing a dangerous sin," he used to say. "Never allow yourself the luxury of feeling good about yourself."

Now I understood what he meant. I tried to sleep.

We left the yaks and their drivers early the following morning, well before sunup. They would remain only a few more days to take advantage of the lush grazing. The road ahead would be difficult even in the best of times, so this time was hardly wasted.

I watched with relief as Rabbit and his camp fell away on the dim horizon. There was a sharp chill in the air and I pulled my hat over my ears. Shivering, I told Sangsang that I had the feeling that all the time Rabbit was talking to me.

"That's because you were listening," he assured me. "But nobody believes anything he says."

"What if he's right?" I asked.

"A snake doesn't sprout legs." Sangsang laughed. "And it is Rabbit's nature to be wrong."

"Still . . ."

But by now Sangsang was no longer paying attention.

A Thief Is Caught and a Skin Is Examined

Being the cook's helper, I was usually the first one up well before the morning. One of my jobs was to gather yak dung for fuel. By the time I returned to camp, the other men were usually just stirring. The process of loading the mules was carried on quietly and efficiently. Wooden saddles were used so only occasionally was there a need to repack a load. Tents were struck, campfires blazed and as the sun came up behind us tea was served; the first tea of the day. Thugben was the last one to leave his tent and never had tea with the rest of the caravan. Most of our marching was done in the morning while the weather remained good and by early afternoon, Thugben's *sidar* (caravan leader) had already chosen a spot to stay the night.

Making or breaking a camp was done quietly. Everyone knew what was expected of him. There was little talk until the caravan was well on its way. There was no desire to inform bandits, who were always a problem, of our presence.

Once, when we were on the pilgrims' road between

Chamdo and Riwoche, one of the mule drivers was caught stealing a mule and bricks of "Go-mang chu-pa," the highest quality tea. The merchant was planning the tea as a gift to the abbot of the Riwoche *gompa*. The thief was brought to Thugben's tent accompanied by two men, each holding an end of a rope tied around the thief's neck. Thugben came out of the tent. He was a tall man with a narrow face and cold dispassionate eyes. He was dressed in a *chuba* of fine silk and there were many corals and turquoise in his hair, which was folded into braids at the top of his head. A sword thrust out of the side of his *chuba* just under his right hand. There was no question that this was a man used to taking charge.

The thief, a wretched fellow, who had been in trouble before, begged for mercy claiming that being so far from his beloved moist grazing lands had caused him so much remorse that he had no control over his actions.

Thugben ordered him to be silent. Speaking in a low firm voice, he explained that he could not punish the man for stealing the tea. By doing this, he said, the tea would assume the responsibility for the man's misfortune and how could he present an imperfect gift to the lama abbot. Above all, this was the pilgrims' road.

The face of the thief grew bright and he praised and thanked Thugben but once again, Thugben ordered him to be silent.

"However," he continued, "this does not account for a stolen mule. . . ."

He was given one hundred lashes with a riding crop and so for some time was unable to steal anything. I heard his cries well into the night, but everyone agreed that he got much less than he deserved.

"His greatest crime," Sangsang said to me, "was one of stupidity. He was actually taking the tea back to Tatsienlu where he would have only received half the value of what it would bring in the west."

The next morning, the thief could hardly move but managed a big grin to all who greeted him.

Such was the justice of the caravan of Thugben the merchant from Sining. And this was one of the few times that I saw him. He was content to spend most of his time in his tent where according to what I was told, he prayed constantly. He was not known to drink *chang* or smoke tobacco, but like almost everyone else did not disguise his fondness for snuff. It was said that he carried on his trade with the nomads fairly and as it was a profitable trade for all concerned, he did not find it necessary to cheat them as many others did.

Thugben also liked a good argument. I found out myself one morning just before we arrived in Jyekundo. I had been gathering yak dung from a nearby field when I saw a figure approaching the camp. I was about to run back and call the alarm but soon realized that it was Thugben himself. He was coming toward me.

"You are with that muleman Sangsang," he said as he approached. "I see that you are as alert as he is. Come, talk to me."

I had no idea what he wanted to talk about. He came right to the point, however.

"What is this skin you carry?" he asked.

"You know about that, sir?" I answered, looking at him.

He laughed. "I know everything that goes on here. But what is this skin? Is it truly the skin of a *migou?*"

"I'm sure of it, sir," I replied. "I carry it on my person so it cannot be stolen."

"I would like to see it," he said. "I do not believe I have ever seen such a thing. I want to see it."

"You are not afraid?" I asked.

"Of a skin?" He laughed nervously. He was afraid. "No! Show it to me."

I took the *migou* skin out from under my cloak. Thugben examined it closely. He seemed relieved.

"I know skins," he said to me. "And I assure you that you have been mistaken on this one. Have you never seen a red bear in that Khampa village you come from? That is the skin that you are carrying. I know. I know skins."

I decided not to argue for he was as convinced as I was and he was also the head of our caravan. Why would he take time out to argue with me?

This, however, had the opposite effect. He was looking for an argument.

"You are not satisfied with what I have told you but you refuse to argue." He looked at me. "Forget who I am. Tell me I am wrong if that is what you believe."

"I think you are wrong," I finally called out.

"Fine," he said. "But you are not very convincing."

"It is the skin of the *migou*," I said flatly. "There is no doubt of it. Even the oracle Sung confirmed this."

"Now you are the one who is lying." He smiled. "How could you, a boy from beyond the mountains, have an audience with Sung? You don't expect me to believe that. Not even I have seen him."

"No," I confessed, very pleased with myself. "But it is the skin of a *migou*."

"It is obviously a bear. A small red bear," he said. "And now that I have satisfied my curiosity, I know it is the skin of a bear."

I allowed him the last word. He smiled at me and walked away.

"Where have you been?" Kampo the cook began scolding me when I returned. "The sun is almost up and tea has not been started."

"I'm sorry. I was having an argument with Thugben."

"An argument with Thugben? On what subject can the two of you possibly argue? You pay attention to your work and less time dreaming of arguing with the master. What nonsense is this? What, may I ask, did you argue about?"

"Bears," I said as I began blowing on the fire.

"Oh, I see." Kampo smiled. "You and Thugben were discussing bears." With that he gave me a hard smack on my bottom. "You pay attention to what you have to do."

I smiled for it was all worth it. Nobody would ever believe that I would argue with the head of the caravan. Nobody would ever believe that I saw the oracle Sung. Nobody would ever believe that I carried a *migou* skin. I was safe and secure in the disbelief of others.

Later that day, I saw Thugben once again, just leaving his tent. He did not acknowledge me. However, as he passed by, I heard him utter one word.

"Bear."

A Shensi Merchant
Brings News of the War

After two days' march through the gradually ascending plateau, the verdant pastures were left behind. The flat, monotonous plain gave way to rocky, hilly valleys, where grazing was scarce and the opportunities for bandit ambushes many. A constant rain accompanied us, discouraging attack; even bandits do not look forward to crouching in the rain, awaiting victims.

By the middle of the third day, the clouds cleared. A dazzling blue sky broke through in big and little patches, like the scattered blue ice one sees on the rolling plains. The sun remained behind gray clouds, lighting up a small section of the sky.

We were making camp at one of the many clearings that lined the wide banks of a fast-flowing stream. The late afternoon was coming fast and we were eager to be settled in with warm bowls of tea. As we were tying up the mules, one of the men spotted a figure tramping down a rocky hillock near the opposite bank of the river. When the figure, who was well out of rifle range, saw us he most likely thought us bandits, for he turned around frantically and stumbled back up the hill. He huffed his way up, looking like a marmot spotted by an eagle. His clumsy, futile attempts to escape made him ridiculous. None of us could resist cheering him on as he reached the crest of the hill.

Sangsang volunteered to ride out on Thugben's Sining

pony to bring the man to our camp. He splashed across the stream, which, while not very deep, was quite swift. In a little while he disappeared behind the hill.

Shortly afterwards he returned with a fat little old Chinese man named Hsien Lu. He was a merchant from Shensi who was returning from Sining, where he traded heavily in musk and other medicinal plants. He was on his way to Jyekundo, where a brisk trade in musk from the Koko Nor region is carried on. Two days before, both his pony and his musk-laden mules were stolen during the night. He was relieved to find that we were not brigands, and in no time he made himself at home in our camp.

The two days without food or transportation had been very inconvenient for the poor man, but he seemed no worse for the ordeal. He was very round, with tiny sparkling eyes and wide thick lips. As he was of no particular rank, he wore the standard blue suit of his countrymen. He did not have a great deal of hair, but enough to make one short pigtail that extended just above his thick neck. He was a genuinely happy man, who took his recent losses with a degree of humor.

He told us that he had been on the Golok road from Sining to Jyekundo, and that while he had survived the journey through that infamous brigand country, he was not prepared for what happened afterwards. He made the necessary observances to the bandit chiefs for safe passage but, as he put it, "One cannot pay off every bandit in Tibet."

Hsien Lu had been in Sining when the Moslem rebellion broke out, and we were all anxious to hear his firsthand account of what was happening. After consuming many bowls of tea and warming himself by the fire, the old Chinese told us what he had seen and heard.

Indeed, there had been a serious outbreak. It began, according to Hsien Lu, as a dispute among the Salars and their less fanatic brothers. The argument raged over whether men under forty should be allowed to wear beards. When the Chinese intervened in the person of Captain Ling Tien, the rebels united and turned the war against the Chinese.

"I was in Lusar when the trouble first broke out. It could have gone badly were it not for the monks of Kumbum Monastery. The monks put on their war trousers and made a good showing for themselves. A detachment of the Central China Army from Hunam also had a lot to do with saving that place. As it was, the rebels seemed better armed and organized this time."

He was obviously a man who loved to talk and although he kept a level monotone, not emphasizing any point over another, the bloody and hard-fought battles of Kansu were amazingly vivid.

"That was in the beginning," he went on, "when the Moslems were still motivated by religious zeal, not plunder. But that didn't last long and what happened at Shen-Ch'un was tragic and inevitable."

He paused and reached for another bowl of tea.

"What happened in Shen-Ch'un?" Tendon, who usually kept to himself, asked. His interest seemed to be more than casual.

"Very sad," he continued slowly. "In the end there were no men left to defend the city. All of them—Moslem, Chinese, Tibetan—were dragged into an army. Only old men, women and children remained in Shen-Ch'un."

Tendon was now visibly upset. His eyes widened and settled on the merchant.

"What happened?" he spit out each word as he rose and hovered over the Chinese like an angry hawk.

"I was getting to that." Hsien Lu looked up. "It took them a long time, but the Moslems finally took a city of women and old men. No prisoners were taken."

Tendon clenched his fists. His upper lip tightened, yet there was as much sorrow as anger in his expression. Slowly he turned around, walked away from the light of the campfire and into the dark, cold night.

The merchant brushed himself off and attempted to regain his composure. "Not a very pleasant man, that one," he said.

"It's his family," one of the mulemen said. "His whole family lived in Shen-Ch'un."

"Oh, that is too bad," the merchant honestly lamented. "Poor man. We all lost a lot in this trouble. And he didn't hear the worst of it."

"The worst of it?" Sangsang asked.

"Yes," the answer came back. "I told you that no prisoners were taken, but that does not mean that death was swift and clean."

Sangsang stared at the merchant. "Do you really think that he does not already know that?"

The merchant did not answer. He quietly sipped his tea.

I, too, was affected by this tale. My fears for Kareem Musa were renewed. I did not think that this defiant Turkestani was capable of butchering old men, women and children. It was possible that at one time he might not have given it a second thought. But having lost his own family, he could not bring such havoc to others. Besides, Kareem Musa was never motivated by plunder.

Kareem Musa followed the will of Allah as he saw it. No

294

one could tell him if he could wear the beard which he had been wearing for years. Kareem did not interest himself in religious debates or conflicts. He was not a politician or a mediator. He was a fighter and a prince, and he needed little excuse to fight the Chinese, whom he hated only a little less than the Russians.

The talk of war permeated the thin air around the fire. So much so, that I almost forgot the *migou* skin under my coat. This skin, which had driven me from the region of my birth and set me out on a dangerous and treacherous path, rubbed close to my naked chest and I could feel its heat. Suddenly it felt like it was burning out of my *chuba*.

Our Arrival in Jyekundo

The next morning, we moved out under a dim gray sky. It was a strangely silent morning.

Even Sangsang, who mocked danger, realized that it was still some six to eight days to Jyekundo and much of the country to be passed was through narrow valleys and gorges: ideal places for a brigand ambush.

The Shensi merchant told us of the war. But the fact that the Moslem army was tired, broken and defeated only added to the sense of dread awaiting us as we approached each new canyon. As one of the mulemen pointed out, a tired, hungry and defeated Moslem rebel was probably the most dangerous kind.

However, nothing suggesting the trouble in Amdo was

seen until four days later, and then it was not at all what we expected.

We saw the first broken remnants of the Moslem army, but rather than fierce, vengeful fanatics, they were wretched and tired men who had survived the massacre of Hocheo (the Mecca of Chinese Moslems) only to fall victim to the treacherous and exacting plain. More to be pitied than feared, a group of about six of them stumbled along. Two of them, resting on the shoulders of their comrades, were badly wounded, and it was doubtful that they would continue much longer; judging from their sorrowful condition, it was amazing that they had come this far. As our caravan passed, those in their number who had the strength eyed us with a mixture of contempt and fear.

A little later, we came across the bodies of those who would go no farther. Predators from the land and the air moved from body to body like bees on flowers. It was a sight that only Tendon, who by now was almost mad with vengeance, seemed to enjoy; only he could well up this amount of hatred for dead and dying men.

Though the danger we expected was exaggerated, it was still with a sense of relief that we approached the large *mani* pile just outside the south gate of Jyekundo. This *mani* pile, according to Sangsang the largest in Tibet, was formed by a series of rocks on which the sacred mantra *om mani padme om* was written. These rocks, piled one on top of the other by travelers and religious pilgrims, made a long, wide, impressive wall.

This famed wall was only one of the attractions of this important caravan town. Jyekundo falls on every major caravan route. As well as being the trading post for the nomads from the southern shore of Koko Nor, all the caravan routes converge and disperse from Jyekundo.

Like my own Hor Drango and Tatsienlu, Jyekundo falls on the confluence of two strong rivers: the Pach'i Chu from the south, which we were following, and the Dze Chu, a tributary of the Yangtze, from the east. The town is surrounded by a high, lush pasture, another measure of its fame.

Shortly after reaching the Dze Chu from the east, the roads converge and the traffic becomes heavier. The black tents of the nomads that fringe the city become more numerous. The nomads themselves, clad in dirty sheepskins, line the road, carrying buckets of sour milk to sell to the newly arriving caravans. Monks, primarily of the Sakyapa order (which is dominant here), saunter along the road in their saffron-red robes, spinning their prayer wheels while they murmer their prayers. Wool and musk traders from Sining, with their large handsome mules and big horses, crowd the road. Lhasa wool merchants are also in number; Jyekundo is to wool what Tatsienlu is to tea.

One immediately sees the evidence of this within the walls of the south gate. Here, sitting in front of their flat-roofed homes, are the Tibetan women, spinning wool with the concentration of prayer. They sit in small groups in the bright early morning light, gossiping, sometimes singing.

When we reached the end of the main street, there was a series of small houses climbing around the smaller hill of the town. Thugben knew the abbot of the monastery on top of the hill, and he headed the caravan in that direction.

But a much smaller caravan would reach the monastery. There were many diversions for mulemen in Jyekundo, and the men fell away to their various indulgences.

Sangsang knew of a wool merchant who was reputed to have the largest ongoing game of *sho* in the area. Sangsang said that while he normally enjoyed my company, this time he wanted nothing to interfere with his luck at the dice. He told me to meet him at an inn located at the other end of town. I knew that once he became involved in a game, nothing could extricate him from the rattle of the dice. Still, I was surprised that his first thought was not of refreshing himself with many cups of *chang*, as so many of his comrades were doing.

A Busy Jyekundo Inn

A caravan town, Jyekundo boasted a number of inns. These meeting places for honest merchants and pilgrims also collected an assortment of brigands, opportunists and generally disreputable people.

The inn where my uncle chose to meet me was the loudest and most popular one for mule drivers. At one time it was a Moslem inn, where the followers of the prophet were assured that all the laws of the Koran were observed. A sign hanging from rusty hinges outside the front gate bore the teakettle and the mystic words KIAO MEN (member of assembly), indicating its Moslem past. After the previous uprising, the Moslems, like so many others, fled for the safety of Turkestan. The inn was now operated by a remaining servant, whom Sangsang described as a half-breed Tibetan-Chinese by the name of Ching.

As I approached the inn, various fights and quarrels were in progress. I wondered what it was that gave the place such popularity and why my uncle had chosen to meet here.

I could not help feeling some apprehension as I came to the creaking wooden gate which guarded the long corridor leading to an open field where horses and mules were tethered. I had to pass through a narrow, dark passage. The only light came from the kitchen at the far end and from the shafts of dim moonlight beginning to fall on the open field.

Suddenly, I was startled by a wild-eyed, dirty mule driver whom I immediately recognized as Tendon. He waved a large knife at me, but he was drunk and not very dangerous.

Tendon had never been able to figure me out. Like the others, he knew something about the skin that I carried with me. Reactions depended on the individual; for the most part, the story of a *migou* or bearskin was not discussed. I was happy for this, and as long as Sangsang was around I felt safe.

There were some, however, who feared me, believing that I had the power to reign destruction on them. Tendon, I believe, was one of them. Like him, I had a knife attached to my belt, but I thought the skin would be a more effective weapon. I motioned to reach into my *chuba* and his knife disappeared. He now permitted me to pass, cursing me as he stepped aside but obviously as happy as I that our little confrontation had not amounted to more. Later on, I learned that the poor man was killed in a fight with a Chinese soldier from Hunam.

From the large courtyard, a number of small one-room apartments lined the outer wall, their wooden doors facing inside. On the eastern section, a place was reserved for those Chinese who sink into the dreams of the purple poppy. Here they could lie and dream without fear of being jolted into reality until the next morning.

A gaunt man in a dirty but not ragged scarlet jacket of the Chinese Sining army wandered out of his room and looked aimlessly about. One of his comrades called him from inside and he returned, as if he had found his way.

A heated argument in Chinese was going on in another room; a blatant contrast to the quiet.

From still another room, a small, wiry man, with large hungry eyes and a skin that seemed stretched to its very limits, came out smiling. Although he carried an opium pipe in his hand, he did not have the look of an addict.

"Another guest." He looked at me, still smiling. "How was your trip?"

I smiled back.

"I'm Ching. You've heard of me?" He beamed. Looking slightly confused, he said, "I don't know you. Who are you, with the small ears?"

"You know my uncle, Sangsang," I answered.

"Ah, Sangsang," he said, as he pointed to a scar just above his eyebrow. His hair was cut short, almost like that of a monk, and the scar, though not deep, was fairly wide. He smiled, showing dingy, yellow teeth.

"Sangsang?" I asked sheepishly, staring at his scar.

He laughed. "A well-placed boot," he said. "But I deserved it. I was not fast enough bringing his *chang*. Oh, I have many such scars. Such are the risks of this business and the extremes of *chang*."

Just then the argument between the Chinese burst out into the courtyard. Two dirty, mud-encrusted men wrestled on the ground while their supporters encouraged them.

Ching paid little attention to the trouble. He did not seem to mind that a part of his inn was progressively being destroyed.

"Would you break up a fight between two mad dogs?" he asked me. "They'll fight themselves out. One is from the Sining army and the other from the Hunam. Each accused the other of atrocities. Ah, these wars!"

As I followed him across the compound, he realized that he was still carrying the pipe in one hand.

"Oh yes, this," he said. "Sometimes . . . sometimes I prefer serving Chinese to monks. Monks demand morality with work. But I'm happy to fill a pipe and get my share." Then he laughed, which he did frequently.

Suddenly, there was a loud roar from the other end of the compound, where three hunched figures huddled around a smoldering flame. From the moonlight and the dim light of the fire, I could easily see one figure tower over the others.

It was Dendru, Sangsang's best friend and the man who had just knocked out Sangsang's front tooth. He waved to me, smiling his own toothless smile as we approached the fire.

"Please stay with this ferocious yak, your uncle's friend," Ching smiled, "while I bring some more to drink."

Dendru was the biggest man I had ever known. Because he was from Batang, he had the reputation for being argumentative and rude. To those who did not know him very well, this may have seemed true. I found him to be a gentle and sincere man who, according to Sangsang, could always be depended upon.

Squatting on either side of the big muleman, looking like two mushrooms by comparison, were two ragged and road-worn mulemen—or so it appeared. Each wore a dingy white cap but neither had the swagger or attitudes of experienced caravan men. They seemed to be out of place.

One of them, oblivious to Dendru's apparent disinterest, continued to talk. He was very short, with watery eyes and the scant beginnings of a beard on his narrow chin.

The other emphasized his points by raising a finger. He had something of a regal appearance. His cap was not quite as dingy and he had a sharp long nose, the kind the Chinese admire. But he was fidgety and uneasy, constantly looking around, hunching his shoulders. He reminded me of Rabbit.

The two men appeared to have accumulated the dust and grime of many trips across Tibet, yet something did not seem right. I noticed as the taller one made a point by raising his right middle finger that his hands were exceptionally smooth—not at all the kind of hands you would expect to see attached to a mule driver.

Dendru was happy for an excuse to growl the two men away. His growl was severe. He was a very big man who never realized his size or strength.

As the two men sulked away to regroup, Dendru motioned for me to sit near him.

"Merchants," he said. "Moslems from Sining. They think I can help them escape."

"They didn't look like mulemen," I said as I took the pitcher of *chang* from him.

"They think I might be able to save them," he said.

"From what?"

"Ah, Small Ears. From many things. The usual brigands, those Chinese soldiers, but most of all from the brothers of their own religion. They did not take part in the last Moslem revolt and now fear that they will be sucked into this one. But what difference is it to me? I just drive animals."

He began to laugh and patted me strongly on the back, almost pushing my face into the ground. Then he scratched his greasy black hair and took a long drink of *chang*.

When he looked up his eyes became serious. This was not like him.

"I know that you are going to Chumbi," he said, almost in a whisper. "You have never been that way, have you?"

"No," I admitted.

"Well, don't expect it to be the same kind of country as this. Once you go beyond the farmlands of the Adra Dsamar nomads, you will find a very unfriendly country."

"Bandits?" I asked, sounding very brave.

"Yes, of course, bandits," he answered. "And don't take such things lightly."

He took another long drink of *chang*. "It's a bleak place. Nothing, or hardly anything, grows there. The few nomads who live there eat horses and goats."

He scratched his matted greasy hair and, speaking in his most serious manner, said, "I have advised your uncle to go with the yaks. A big caravan leaves here in five days. It will take twenty days to reach Nagchu Dzong. Go with them. Nobody attacks caravans of this size. They'll take plenty of supplies, too. It's much safer and now with these fanatic Moslems running about, I cannot understand why he considers going alone. It's madness! What is the hurry? The snow already blocks the passes to Chumbi. If it rains here, it snows there. So why does he hurry? Why not wait and go in five days?"

I had never seen Dendru so concerned. Seeing my apprehension, he quickly recovered.

"Ah, what am I worried about?" He scratched his head. "You will have two rifles, and if Sangsang plays well you will ride out on Sining ponies, for that is why he is not here drinking *chang*. Even the Dsagarnag nomads would not eat such a splendid animal.

"But what drives you to Chumbi is inexplicable. Is it that bearskin of yours?"

He laughed, poking me in the chest, hard at first but then, seeing me lose my breath, he removed his finger. Dendru too had heard of the "bearskin," but like everything else, did not take it seriously.

"It's religion," I said, having no wish to produce the skin now.

"Ah, that." He laughed loudly. And the louder he laughed, the more he laughed. Soon I found myself laughing with him.

The Merchants' Fatal Mistake

Dendru, having filled himself up with drink, now turned his attentions to one of Ching's daughters, a chunky girl with a wide smile, smallpox scars on her face and long wavy hair.

Wavy hair on a woman is considered unlucky in this region, as it is in my own, so there was little hope that Chime would marry. This, however, did not stop her from enjoying herself. She was said to enjoy the company of mulemen, even if only for a night. The caravan talk about Chime was that she was easy but unlucky.

As she came up to the campfire carrying a pitcher of *chang*, Dendru grabbed her by one of her chunky arms. Dendru was not very discriminating in his appetite for women. As with everything else, he took whatever came.

The girl giggled as the pitcher of *chang* splattered to the ground. She offered little resistance as the big muleman removed one of the silver bracelets on her wrist. She was obviously pleased with the attention.

Dendru then held the bracelet above his head with both hands as she halfheartedly attempted to retrieve it. It was like watching a fly bothering a yak.

"You want it back!" Dendru laughed. "Meet me later tonight near the gate."

"I don't want it back." She giggled. Then, taking quick little steps, she moved out of the light of the fire. Dendru, gathering all his strength and moving like a just-awakened yak, took off after her. He was not moving very fast, but neither was she.

I found myself alone, but not for long. Soon I was flanked by the two Moslem merchants who had unsuccessfully tried to enlist Dendru's help.

They sat themselves on either side of me. The regal, nervous merchant eyed the wet ground contemptuously. He probably remembered when the inn served only Moslems— and now *chang* was even being spilled on the ground.

His friend seemed less concerned. He was a round little man who had the timeworn look of survival on his face. He had survived hardships before; he always would.

A calm that comes from fatigue had settled around the inn. The fight between the Chinese soldiers ended with each knocking out the other. The scent of the purple poppy drifted toward us, mixing with the smells of horses, mules and the incense for the evening prayers. Dendru had caught Chime; in the morning she would have her bracelet back. A few dim stars managed to break through the clouds.

305

"You know the muleman well?" The survivor rubbed his smooth hands together.

"I do."

"Did he tell you who we are?" the other one asked in a frightened voice.

"Of course," I teased him. "Dendru talks a great deal."

"I told you it would never work," he whispered to his companion. "I'm sure everyone knows. And now we find ourselves with infidels, opium, *chang*. . . ."

"Quiet," his friend hushed him as he turned toward me. "Listen, maybe you can help us. You know this muleman. We've offered him a great deal. We need a bodyguard. We'll go in any direction he chooses."

"Why don't you go to Turkestan," I asked, "with the rest of your brothers?"

"Turkestan?" the regal-looking Moslem exclaimed. "But that would be the first place he would look for us. Please, you must try to understand the position in which my associate and I have found ourselves. We're just merchants. We want no part of all this trouble. Now the Chinese hate us. The Tibetans think we're responsible for the massacre at Shen-Ch'un and this madman Kareem Musa hunts us like dogs."

"Kareem Musa?" My head snapped back at the mention of his name. "Kareem Musa hunts you?" I asked, attempting to act disinterested.

"You know Musa?" The smaller merchant detected something.

"Only what I've heard," I lied. "That he is a relentless and difficult man. But from what I know, he would not waste his time running down merchants."

"Listen." The round Moslem waved me over. "Don't be

too sure about what you've heard. A lot has happened. All that trouble in Lusar. We had nothing to do with it, of course, but . . ."

"We had nothing to do with it," his friend jumped in with a pleading voice. "Kareem Musa has made a serious mistake. There are other merchants in Lusar. We were not the only ones. It's all a mistake."

"A mistake?" I asked, without expression. I was eager to find out about Kareem but knew that I would learn nothing if I appeared so.

"How were we to know about the rifles?" The tall merchant looked at me. "We deal in silk. We don't have time to check every order that comes in and goes out. He can't blame us for what happened."

"But what happened?" I finally asked.

"You mean you haven't heard?" The regal Moslem looked at me incredulously. "You don't know what has happened since the temples of Nan Hsi Si were destroyed by some of our more zealous brothers in religion?"

I admitted that most of the caravan talk had been about the disturbances in the north. I had already heard that the Central China Army from Sining had been joined by the Hunam army.

The two Moslems looked at each other, then the smaller man turned to me. "The rebels were pushed to Siao Hsia. They were battered with cannon fire. Chinese soldiers with guns and spears waited in the fields for those who fled."

"But one rebel did not flee," the regal-looking Moslem said. I could not make out the expression on his worried face. Was it pride? Fear?

"One madman has an overwhelming compulsion to sur-

307

vive," he continued. "Kareem Musa, who stays alive to hunt the two of us. He managed to get to Topa."

"Our little mistake would not have made a difference anyway," the other man spoke. "The Chinese had cannons."

"Your mistake?" I asked.

"His rifles were to be in Topa." The tall merchant rubbed his hands together nervously. "The last Moslem town—Topa."

I tried to look confused.

Now the shorter one seemed surprised. "The rifles," he answered. "Kareem Musa's rifles arrived in our shop as part of a silk shipment."

"But nobody told us to look out for rifles," his companion sighed. "To us it was just another shipment. We had no way of knowing."

"What happened to the rifles?" I asked.

"They were sent to Captain Cher Eh Feng, as part of a shipment for Chengtu," he answered in an almost inaudible voice.

"You mean that they were sent to the Chinese garrison?" I almost wanted to laugh.

"We had no way of knowing," the merchant with the long nose answered. "It was just a shipment. Another shipment of silks. Besides, the rifles were not used by the Chinese. They weren't discovered until after the siege. How can Musa blame us?"

I looked into their pleading eyes. Even if they were telling the truth, I knew that if Musa was after them there was little that could be done. Kareem Musa had been denied the man who destroyed his life. He would deny himself nothing else in his vengeance. Had they been involved in Musa's plans from the beginning, this might not have happened. They would have been expecting the rifles and would have known what to do. But not taking sides angered the vengeful Kareem Musa more than anything. He had as much use for cowards as he did for traitors, and if these men weren't one, they were surely the other.

"But that big muleman." The survivor smiled. "One would think twice before taking him on. We've offered him money. A great deal. Naturally it isn't here. You know him. Talk to him. You can't leave us to that madman."

"I'll do what I can," I said. "But I have never known him to change his mind. Tell me, did Musa have a Mongol with him? A man named Tiso Awa?"

The two men looked at each other. "If he did, we did not see him," the shorter one answered. "But you seem to know a lot about this madman."

"Only what I've heard," I said.

"Then you've heard a lot more than any of us." The regal-looking merchant tilted his head slightly.

"One hears a great deal on the caravan roads," I replied.

I had not convinced him, but what difference would it have made? There was nothing that they could do to me and there was even less that I could do for them.

"I'll speak to him in the morning," I promised.

"See," the round man said to his friend, "he'll help us."

We looked at each other. He knew it wouldn't help.

The fire was dead. I walked into an empty room. The *k'ang* protruding from the ground had not been used in some time.

Sangsang finally showed up the following morning with two fine Sining ponies. One was the gray-and-white mare that had belonged to Thugben. The other was a brown colt.

Dendru was very surprised to see the animal in Sangsang's possession. Thugben had been more than reasonable, Sangsang reported. They had no trouble striking a bargain.

"He was concerned about you." Sangsang looked at me. "I told him the country we planned to travel and he said a Sining pony is more valuable than a bearskin in that land."

He reached for the bottle of *chang*.

Toward the Great Plateau

We took the road going south and west out of Jyekundo. It led through the northern part of the Dsagarnag nomad country, which, according to Sangsang, was desolate and frequented by bandits.

Not wishing to take any unnecessary chances so early in our journey, we joined a small caravan of nomads bringing butter, cheese and dried beef to Nagchu Dzong. Caravans usually unload in this busy trading town and hire local transport to Lhasa, only eight days farther down the road.

The nomads had done well in Nagchu Dzong, but this year they complained about the increase of brigandry along the caravan roads. They said that the addition of a broken and desperate Moslem army on the trails had made traveling very dangerous. They welcomed the arrival of two more steady rifles to their number. We found them to be a happy bunch, in spite of the recent hardships they had endured. Always ready to play jokes on each other, singing or telling stories around the campfire, they made the journey pass very quickly.

We reached Nagchu Dzong without incident, thanked each other and went our different ways. They would wait some days and continue on to Lhasa. But we wanted to move faster, going due west and south toward Mount Darbo in Bangba Chugdso nomad country.

"The nomads of Bangba Chugdso still hold to the Bon religion. We can expect a decent welcome there," Sangsang told me. "We will need water and provisions to carry us through the plateau. The people of Bangba Chugdso are poor but they will sell us what they can spare. This will be the easy part of our journey. Soon you will learn to hate the taste of sand."

The southern part of the Dsagarnag nomad country was rich in farmland, but the people were suspicious and either refused to sell us anything or offered very little. The defeated Moslem army escaping to Turkestan had been there before us.

This country did not extend far, and soon we found ourselves at the edge of a vast sandy plateau. This was Bangba Chugdso.

"We should do better here," Sangsang assured me.

But he had underestimated the number of Moslem soldiers who had been here before us. We were chased away from two encampments and when we bullied our way into the third, the frightened nomads reluctantly sold us some butter only after learning that we were Bon-pos. But as they had very little water themselves, they could not sell us any.

We needed water and more provisions; Sangsang would not be deterred again. We boldly approached another camp.

A brave old man stood behind his furious dogs, waving us away with a matlock rifle. But we had armed ourselves with some sticks to keep the dogs off, and even from a distance our rifles looked formidable. When he saw that we were not Moslem soldiers (I had stuffed Kareem Musa's hat into a saddlebag) and were nothing more than a muleman and a young boy, he allowed us to enter his camp, which consisted of two tents.

It soon became apparent that he was the only one there. He told us that the two other men in his camp were out on a hunting expedition. His wife had died two weeks before and his daughter-in-law had been raped and murdered by the rebels only three days ago; I now understood what the hunting expedition was about. He went on to describe the trail of havoc left in the wake of the fleeing rebels.

"Defeat has not stopped the trouble," he said, as if he had only been an observer. "It has caused more trouble. Many of the Moslems escaped and scattered along the plains like black eagles looking for prey. Defeated yes, but they have not given up. They are full of hate and revenge and have caused our people much distress on their path to Turkestan. Many people were killed and horses stolen; you've been lucky up to now. Two rifles against those dogs are not enough," he concluded. "You should pick another time to cross this land."

Sangsang thanked the old man for his advice, but it was obvious he wouldn't take it. "If one was to fear every disturbance that occurs in this country," Sangsang explained, "one would never have the courage to go beyond the walls of the farm."

"You may do as you like," the old man said without emotion. "But you will need more than guns and horses. You will not find much water where you are going."

He then described the treacherous country we intended to cross. He omitted no danger, and finally offered to sell us the stomach of a sheep to store water. The price was very high and Sangsang told him so.

"Well, if anyone else will sell you one," the old man said disinterestedly, "then buy it."

The old man was a wily trader. He knew that we had little choice.

"Besides," the old man pointed out, as Sangsang counted out four bricks of tea, "the information I have given you is free. You still come out ahead."

Now we had water, and for another brick of tea, the old man gave our horses *tsamba* and dried peas.

Sangsang Laughs at Danger

As we left the camp and entered the vast white plain beyond, I could not escape the sense of dread that I felt followed us. I tried to express these feelings to Sangsang, but he was indifferent to danger. Sangsang enjoyed the challenge of a hazardous journey.

He was of one mind. His association with mules had added the element of stubbornness to his character. There was nothing I could do.

The laws of karma do not allow for accidents. They are exacting and demand balance. The weight of acts committed in previous lives, both good and bad, must be brought into account. It is foolish to look back and think how different things might have been. It is futile to protest. The tragedy that was to befall us was inevitable.

The landscape was even bleaker than the nomad had

described. Stretching out before us was a flat, white and desolate plateau. A pale brown horizon shimmered and danced off in the distance, buttressed by a range of mountains toward the southwest. In that clear morning light, the mountains seemed close enough to touch. I longed to be there.

I always longed for the mountains. I remember how from our flat-roofed house in Hor Drango they appeared so close in the crisp morning air. Having the boundless imagination of youth, I transformed the flat roof to the top of a high mountain from which I could see the entire valley. The cows and cattle foraging in the courtyard, the chickens scattering about them, the mud brick wall enclosing the farm—all became something else. The cattle were wild yaks, the chickens were beautiful white snow pheasants and the mud wall was a gigantic tree uprooted by Titans to block my mountain solitudes.

We passed numerous herds of gazelle, which took little notice of our intrusion on their territory. They chewed contemplatively on the short brown stubby grass that managed to creep up around the rocks, feeling no danger as they were in their eighth month. (Hunters usually seek gazelles in the third or fourth month, when their horns are in velvet.)

The tranquillity of this scene was deceptive. I could feel it. Again, I tried to express this feeling to my uncle, but again he shrugged it off.

I suppose that I never really understood my uncle. Fear was never a concern to him. He always chose the more difficult path. His easy smile and foolish courage had always pulled him through tight places before. It was perhaps this sense of daring optimism that made me admire him so much.

314

Although my father was a Bon lama, Sangsang had never been swayed by religion. He seemed to be constantly at odds with the gods. Although he never knew it, and my father would never admit it, there were many times when my father intervened on his behalf. Sangsang was a quiet heretic.

I remember a friend of his, a mule driver who used to visit us. Like Sangsang, he was a little belligerent, but unlike Sangsang he was a practicing Buddhist. Invariably, they would get into a religious argument (they both loved to argue) and it would always end the same way.

"My dear Tsering," Sangsang said to his friend, "your own Buddha has said that you are your own torch."

Tsering would answer, "As usual, there is no talking to a mule head."

Sangsang was like that. And now, as we prepared to cross this inhospitable land, I knew that I had given my uncle every opportunity to change his mind. There was nothing left to do but go with him.

Survival on the Plateau

One day is like the other on the plateau. It is not long before you are engulfed in its harsh fist. It is easy to become confused. Even now, I don't remember exactly how things happened.

Trees had disappeared days ago. The last of the nomads were also far behind. There was nothing to stop the wind; the treacherous, penetrating wind that swept across the plain like an angry phantom, pursuing us relentlessly. We crouched with our ponies, watching the sun disappear over the reddish-brown horizon. Sangsang wrapped himself in a heavy woolen blanket. I placed the *migou* skin around me. We sat silently waiting for the endless night to turn to morning.

The next day was deceptively calm. In the afternoon we saw a herd of *kyang,* probably the animals who had left tracks the day before. Or was it the day before when they rambled over the plain in front of us and soon fell off the horizon?

Sangsang now began to talk of the wind as a necessary inconvenience. The plain was warning us to move faster.

As we rode on, we came across the remains of another ill-fated caravan. The skeletons of men and horses were strewn across the earth, almost blending in with the white sandy soil. Three or four riders had been separated from the main caravan. The results of that error had been fatal.

Sangsang walked through the cemetery of bones, looking each one over. Then he looked at me, and for the first time I could see concern in his eyes.

"Look here." He pointed to a skull. He bent down and picked it up.

He held the skull in his hand, showing me the part on the right side that had evidently been bashed in. A closer inspection revealed a bullet hole in another skull. This was the work of bandits.

"But this must have happened a long time ago," I said, trying to assure myself.

Sangsang laughed ironically. "Yes, a long time ago," he said.

From then on Sangsang became increasingly cautious and observant. If bandits were in the area, they would not take us by surprise.

We found the tracks of a single horse the next day, and soon found that another horse and yet another had joined the first. The tracks were fresh and the wind had not yet obliterated them.

We spent another cold night. The next day the tracks had melted into the earth.

All the lakes on the plateau are saltwater, but there is an occasional exception, a tiny finger of some great river trickling through the sand. It was late morning when we approached one of these small freshwater streams. It was surrounded by tall grass. Sangsang halted us a good distance from the water.

"I smell bandits," he said.

But by then it was too late.

A shot rang out and whizzed past my left arm, almost throwing me from my horse. Then there was another shot and the poor animal crumpled under me.

Sangsang dived to the ground, holding his pony's reins. He grabbed his loaded matlock and started shooting without even setting up the antler horn fork to rest the rifle.

"They are over there," he whispered, pointing to the tall grass. "I can't make out how many there are, but I'm sure there are enough of them."

The rifle was already reloaded with rapid precision. He fired a shot into the tall grass. Then, taking his horse we moved back, hoping to get out of range.

It was incredibly still. The crackle of gunfire echoed in the air. We waited.

"If there are more of them," I asked, "then why don't they rush us?"

"We have nothing for them," he answered. "Except this

horse. Even a bandit can recognize breeding. As long as this horse lives, we have a chance."

He fired another shot into the grass. We saw a horse's mane come up from behind the grass, and Sangsang, already having reloaded, fired again. This time there was a low moan and the sound of grass crumpling.

"You got one of them," I smiled.

"Don't be sure," Sangsang warned me.

"Hey, in there," Sangsang called out. "We have nothing you want. We are only poor pilgrims on the way to holy places. Would you deter us from doing religion's work?"

There was no answer, only another crackling shot, way off its mark. The shot made a red burst of flame in sharp contrast to the green grass.

Sangsang shot again and we heard a weight tumble in the grass. "This time I got him." Sangsang laughed.

We waited again. It seemed like forever. Sangsang had calmed his animal, and we knew that with night coming we would have to take action soon.

"Hey, in there," Sangsang called again. "You are interfering with religion. You know of the special place in hell for those who obstruct religion."

Two more shots rang out and Sangsang's horse began to break free. Then, before I knew it, Sangsang had mounted his animal from the side and charged into the tall grass. It was too late to stop him. I watched him ride away, crouched in the saddle with his rifle blazing.

A few more shots rang out. One hit Sangsang in his arm, but he kept going until he disappeared behind the tall grass.

"Sangsang," I screamed. "Sangsang!"

I watched the grass rustle and suddenly two of the bandits

emerged, running to their horses as fast as they could.

Now all the horses scattered. I watched Sangsang's pony gallop away.

Suddenly it was quiet again. I didn't know what to do.

"Small Ears," Sangsang's voice called me. "Come, the danger has passed."

I crept along the cold hard earth with the taste of sand and battle in my mouth, until I came up to the tall grass.

"Small Ears," Sangsang's voice called me again.

And then I saw him. The body of one of the bandits lay across him. Two other bandits lay dead nearby.

"Pull him off, please." Sangsang smiled.

As I pulled off the bandit's body, I saw that he had been stabbed with his own sword. I also noticed a large wound in Sangsang's chest.

"See, you were right." He pointed to one of the dead bandits. "I did get him the first time." He smiled. "We gave them a good fight."

"Yes, we did." I tried not to cry.

"You must go on to Chumbi," Sangsang said. "You are doing religion's work."

Sangsang laughed. "I suppose that these cowards never had to face Khampas before."

And then he was dead.

I sat there with my uncle in my arms. I had almost forgotten the wind which was now laying claim to the land. Surrounded by the tall grass, I watched the sun disappear in the distance. I sat there and waited for the night.

A Meeting with the King of the Vultures

By the next morning, the air was clear and the sky was totally unobstructed. The vultures appeared in the distance and sped toward us in a whir of flapping wings. It was not difficult for them to pick up the scent of tragedy. Nor was it difficult to spot the black king who led them. He was a vulture of enormous size and was regal even as he clumsily landed away from me and waited patiently to be called.

I moved Sangsang away from the bodies of the other men and placed him prominently on the flat white plain. Slowly backing away, I left the birds to their sacred duties, their timeless occupation, their part in the celestial interment.

I said the prayers that my father had taught me and tried to instruct my uncle to better rebirths. When I was far enough away, the black king of death moved in. Another bird landed, and then another. They would have their turn. Their feast had begun.

I remembered what my father had taught me: "The life of all living things is like bubbles on the water."

My uncle was devoured quickly, indicating that even with his indifference to religion, he was a good man and would enjoy better rebirths.

Of the bandits, only one had led so shameful and evil a life that he was not touched until much later, and then hardly at all.

Nevertheless, I prayed for the better rebirths of all these men. I repeated the Bon mantra and walked around the bodies from right to left in the Bon fashion.

As I was circumambulating the black king of the vultures spotted me. I looked into his cold wet eyes. He understood what was expected of him. Or was it that I, too, would fall victim here? I couldn't be sure. He quickly went back to his work, chasing two smaller birds away as he did.

My situation was not good. I had my choice of rifles and plenty of ammunition, but I was without a horse. Even more serious was the loss of the water carried on Sangsang's gray-and-white pony.

By now the wind was whipping and snarling around me. I took two of the best rifles and as much ammunition as I could carry in my *chuba* and began the long march.

I cannot say how far I walked that first day. One place seemed like the next. Tracks disappeared almost as they were made. There was no path, and the sun, which had shined so brightly that morning, took refuge in an increasingly cloudy black sky. Still, I tramped on. I had no way of knowing where I was going. I just knew that I was being pulled in a direction. I couldn't stay where I was. I kept seeing the eyes of the king of the vultures.

"Am I going to die?" I asked myself. "Will I fall here on this haunted plain, and only the black king of the vultures will know what happened to me?"

I remember wrapping the *migou* skin around me as night slowly fell. Black, cold night.

Somehow I fell asleep.

Alone on the Plateau

The next morning, as I woke from a heavy sleep beset by dreams of death and vultures, I was greeted by a welcome sight. Standing only a little distance from me was Sangsang's gray-and-white Sining pony. He had been patiently waiting for me to get up. Stretched across his back was the sheep's stomach at least half filled with water.

We greeted each other like brothers. I took some water and gave it to the pony. There was not a lot there, but used wisely it would last a few days, by which time we could find more water. But optimism quickly faded, for the animal was not well. His tongue was light blue and his eyes were cloudy. Apparently he had galloped in every direction when he felt the exhilaration of freedom, but finding no grazing or water (and yet smelling water), the poor animal ran himself out. He was very tired and certainly in no condition to be ridden.

"But you are a Sining pony," I spoke to the horse. "Your class will show. You cannot be defeated by this."

The horse looked at me with quiet soft eyes. He understood, but it was beyond him to go on. He was just too tired. In fact, he even slowed my pace. But I would not leave him behind. I hoped that the water and perhaps some of the stubby brown grass would restore his health.

Finally there was nothing that could be done for the poor animal. By late afternoon he stopped, lay down and died.

"The people there eat wild horses and goats." I remembered Dendru's words.

There was no sense in trying to start a fire. There was

322

nothing to burn. Even if there were, the wind would quickly put out any fire.

I cut the horse open. The flesh was still warm. I remembered the black king's eyes as I began to eat.

The Death of a Moslem Soldier

I wasn't sure how far I'd come as I slowly tramped south. I knew that Dam was behind me but I cannot really remember what happened during the next few days.

Demons lurked on my trail and placed obstacles in my path. They were unseen obstacles that made everything seem heavy. My steps became slower; putting one foot in front of the other became more difficult.

I felt weighted down, as if I were carrying huge boulders on my shoulders. I wanted to glide over the plain the way a lama glides from shrine to shrine, moved by the power of religion. I wondered if my own faith could see me through this. I wondered if my quest were any less religious than theirs.

I don't remember when or how I lost the first of the two rifles. I do remember a certain exhilaration, as if some of the weight were taken off my shoulders. When I discovered the loss I reacted by tossing away the other rifle. The heavy ammunition I carried also fell away. I was free, unencumbered, almost blissful, with a sense of indestructibility.

At one point, I saw gleaming spears shining off in the distance and I believed that Golok bandits were coming for me. I suddenly wondered what I had done with my rifles. I knew very well that a rifle could offer little resistance if the bandits were intent on robbing me. I realized the enormous distance between us. I knew that any shot would fall far short of the mark. I even knew, somewhere inside me, that I was at least three weeks from Golok territory. Yet knowing this did not subdue my fear and anxiety. Reason is inevitably the first casualty of desperation.

When these gleaming spears rumbled across the horizon and finally fell off into nowhere, I realized that I had seen a herd of wild yak. What I thought were shimmering spears were actually shiny white horns picking up the sun.

I tried to laugh.

Suddenly, I noticed what appeared to be a small tree not far off in the distance. It must have been in view for some time, but I was so preoccupied with thoughts of immediate survival that it went unnoticed.

A tree, I believed, was a good sign, and some evidence that the local gods were taking an interest in my safety. A tree indicated that water could not be far away.

I stumbled and fell, got up again and ran with whatever strength I had left toward this hope in the wilderness.

As I approached my goal, I realized that it was not a tree at all, but a nomad's hut. A small *mani* pile of perhaps forty stones had been set up near it; the strips of material on which the sacred words had been written fluttered in the biting wind.

This is a religious place, I thought to myself, and so I would be safe. Yet I was unable to heave a sigh of relief, for I was swept by the overwhelming feeling that I was being observed. A chill ran through me. I was sure now that a bandit, a Moslem soldier or a demon was waiting for me in that hut.

I wanted to turn back but realized that I had no place to go back to. I approached cautiously.

"Come," a weak voice called to me from the hut. "Come before the storm fiends devour you."

The voice was weak and followed by choked laughter. There was an urgency in the tone that frightened me. I backed away.

"Come, what possible harm can I do to you?" the voice called out again.

"Who are you?" I shouted.

I waited for an answer but none came. "Are you a demon?" I asked. Having asked the question, I realized how foolish it was.

There was weak laugher again, a strange kind of laughter that sounded as if it came from another place. I jumped to the ground with my face resting on a rock and my arms stretched out in front of me.

"I am not a demon," the voice came back. "But who are you?"

"I will tell you nothing," I called out. "You will not learn what charms to use against me."

"Come, little Tibetan who fears demons. There is room in here for you. Come, before the storm fiends find you. I will not harm you. I will not harm anyone."

The wind was coming up strong now. Sand swirled around my eyes. I knew that I would not be able to endure the ferocity of the black clouds that were quickly descending with the coming of night. I had my *migou* skin and I wrapped it around me. I wanted to be in that hut. It would lessen the bitterness of the night wind. I was unable to move one way or the other. I was paralyzed by my own fear.

"Would you stay out there all night?" the voice pleaded. "Would you stay out there and let a poor wounded man die alone? Please come. I have a task for you."

"Are you wounded?" I asked trembling.

"Come in here. My time is short," the voice answered. "There is something that you must do."

A bloodstained white cotton jacket was flung out of the tiny opening flap of the hut. The wind picked it up and blew it toward me.

"An honest wound, my friend." The voice was still weaker. "A wound of battle."

I still could not be sure that this wasn't a trick. I clutched the jacket in my hand. It is strange how one's survival can outweigh one's feeling for compassion.

My father often told me that compassion is something that must be learned and nurtured. It is difficult to attain. And when adversity strikes, the time compassion is most needed, there is usually little of it to go around.

This is how I felt about the stained garment. I hoped it was the blood of a man. I wanted to find a wounded man in the hut, for it meant that he could not harm me. It would have been easy to blame the wind, the plateau or the *migou* skin, but I knew that these feelings came from me. All I could do was escape into remorse. Soon this remorse turned into daring. I stood up and walked toward the hut.

As I entered, I saw a man lying across the sandy floor, surrounded by the blood that was slowly pouring out of a small hole in his stomach. He wore the billowy white pants of a Turkestani. He wore nothing above his waist and seemed almost proud of his wound. He was a very tall man, with deep black eyes and long sinewy fingers. His hair was rolled up under a dingy gray turban.

"You see." He smiled. "I cannot harm anyone. Soon I go to Allah."

"Who are you?" I asked again, softly.

"I am unimportant. I am from the ill-fated army of the prince of Bukhara, the feared and chosen one of Allah. I am from the army of Kareem Musa."

"You served with Kareem Musa?" I asked.

"Yes." He smiled. "And had I fallen with him at the battle of Topa, this would not be necessary. But it was not written that way."

"Kareem Musa is dead?" I asked, already knowing the answer.

"Many died at Topa. It was our last stronghold. Kareem Musa implored us to fight on. Even those who gave themselves up to the Chinese were cut down. Yes, he is dead. He fell beside me in that place. . . . But why such concern for a Moslem rebel?"

"I knew him," I answered.

"Let me see you." He smiled brightly. I moved toward him. "Allah be praised, for only Allah could have such a sense of humor. It is you. The one with the small ears and the . . . *migou* skin."

"Then Kareem Musa spoke of me?"

"He wore your hat when he died. He spoke of you a great deal."

"How did he die?" I asked.

"Chinese cannon fire. He fell under the barrage. It was just as well. . . ."

He stopped to catch his breath. "Just as well," he repeated slowly. "After the outer walls of Topa were destroyed, many thought they could escape during the night, when the Chinese have no taste for war. But this was a bitter time. It was just as well that Kareem Musa did not see his own men running away in the night like old women. The cowards were easily picked off. The massacre at Shen-Ch'un was still fresh. The Chinese had a taste for revenge. It was better that Kareem Musa did not see the mosque of Topa destroyed. It is better that he did not see the destruction of his army."

He paused and struggled to raise his head. "What chance did we have," he continued. "The Hunam army under General Wei was quartered in Chen Hai Pu. The Sining army was only eight *li* beyond, near the river Heh Tsui Tsi. They had infantry, cavalry and, worst of all, they had cannons. Kareem Musa was in one of the towers surrounding Topa. It was a direct hit. He fell under the barrage. But I am wasting time . . . there is something you must do."

I looked at him quizzically. It was obvious that he did not have much time left.

"Can't you recognize a dying man?" he asked. "Would you deny a dying man a last request?"

"I do not have tobacco," I said apologetically.

"Tobacco?" He returned my look with a stern glance. "I am a Moslem. Would you have me die with tobacco in me? No, that was Kareem Musa . . . I am not he. But we are wasting time. You must kill me so that I do not die of a coward's bullet."

Now blood began to trickle from the edges of his mouth. I was surprised he was still alive. "Had I fallen in battle beside my friend, this would not be necessary, but yesterday I was attacked by bandits. I shall not reach Turkestan. I have no wish to come back as a ghost to haunt this place."

He tried to get up but his head fell back. His eyes rolled and I thought that he was dead.

"I am not dead yet," he whispered. "Not yet. Lust has been

my constant companion in this life and I fear that I am too weak to dispel the demons that have entered my wound— your Tibetan demons. But you are a full-grown boy. You are capable of performing the task I have asked of you. Smother me. Smother me as your butchers would smother a yak for slaughter. Kill me so that I do not return as a ghost."

I had never killed a man before, and was afraid that I could not perform the task without error. He sensed my apprehension.

"Come, Tibetan. I am a comrade of Kareem Musa and you have a *kata* in that bag. Or is all you keep in it that *migou* skin?" He caught his breath. "No." He waved his hand in front of his face and laughed. "I have no desire to see it. Not now, anyway. . . ."

He swept his hand slowly around the mud brick hut. There was a sheep's stomach half full of water, a chunk of dried mutton and some butter. There was no horse, but there was enough to survive.

"Take these things I leave here. They're yours. Dispose of them as you wish."

I took the *kata* that Grandmother had given me out of the bag. The Moslem looked at it.

"Silk?" he exclaimed. "But that is too good for the likes of me."

I held the *kata* in each hand as if prepared to make an offering. He smiled. His eyes brightened for an instant.

"Come, small ears." His words fell slowly. "Come, make haste. 'There is one god—Allah. . . .'"

I said nothing as I placed the *kata* over his face and nostrils. Blood was beginning to pour profusely around his mouth. I walked behind the dying man and wrapped the *kata* firmly around his head. Then I turned it, and as his eyes rolled back in his head, I could feel the breath leaving his body.

A Phantom Soldier

Although the man who had just died assured me that I would be safe, it is known that death attracts demons. I knew that I had to move the body out of the hut and as far away as possible.

I was sorry that I did not know a proper Moslem prayer to say for the man. I hoped that by repeating the Bon mantra many times, he would have a chance for a better rebirth. This was out of my hands, as his acts in this life would determine where he was placed in the next. Nevertheless, I felt compelled to say something.

As I struggled with the body, pulling, pushing and dragging it over the cold rocky earth, I remembered all the questions I wanted to ask.

I wondered if this Moslem rebel, a comrade of Kareem Musa, knew anything about Tiso Awa. I wanted to ask the man about his home; had he ever been to Hor Drango? There were many questions that would go unanswered.

The body was heavy. I had some difficulty moving it away. When I turned to see how far I had come from the hut, it was a disappointment to see that I had not come very far. And now the wind itself seemed determined to stop me. It whipped around me, looking for a place to throw me back.

But I was just as determined. Finally, I got the body to an incline near a dried-up stream. I felt it was far enough away.

"Yours will be a celestial interment," I said to the dead man, half expecting him to answer. "I apologize that I do not know the proper procedures of your faith. But at least you were not dumped in a stream like a leper or a beggar. I did not know you for very long in this lifetime. You were a friend of Kareem Musa, so this speaks well for you. I leave you now to the black eagle and his brothers. I pray that your next life will be less difficult than the one you left."

Night had already descended around me. I had become oblivious to the penetrating bite of the wind as it snapped across the flat plateau. It was a dark night. There wasn't any moon and only a few dim stars lit the sky. I had the feeling of being enveloped in darkness.

The next morning, the sky was cut into sections; the top was cold and gray, while a bright red ribbon stretched over the horizon in the east where the sun was just appearing.

As I left the hut I was horrified to see a tangle of arms and legs just outside the door. The wind had blown the body back toward the hut. In the outstretched arms of the dead man was the *kata* I had left with him. He was giving it back to me. I wondered if his god had rejected him in his infidel trappings, or was the bloodstained *kata* meant for someone else?

I took the *kata* and put it in my yakskin bag. There was a strange expression on the dead man's face. It was as if death had taken him completely by surprise.

I looked into the sky. A few crows had already taken their places. I waved them away. Should a crow be the first to partake of a body, it would be bad luck.

I waited as the sun's morning warmth crossed my face and the black eagle swept over the horizon, leading the hungry birds. I took whatever food and water I could carry, turned around to see the black king and his subjects begin their feast, and walked away. I wondered if the man would keep his promise not to haunt me. I had only done what he asked. Would he now follow me across the plain?

As I marched determinedly across that desolate place, a familiar feeling swept over me. I stopped and looked around. The land stretched away monotonously in each direction. The dead man and the vultures had become specks on a cold gray horizon. I again felt as if I were being watched. I began to walk again, turning around suddenly, expecting to see the dead soldier lurching for me.

This never happened. Still, I was sure that out of the corner of my eye I glimpsed a smiling Moslem soldier.

I came to a small freshwater stream trickling through the short brown grass; an unexpected gift. The stream took a little rise in the ground farther along its course. Tucked in the tall shrubs, a bull yak peacefully contemplated past and future lives.

Numerous birds that I had not been aware of before—ring-necked ducks from Mongolia, bright-colored birds, renegades from the Himalayas—all seemed to have appeared from nowhere. Marmots chattered noisily around their mounds. It was midafternoon and I was tired. I was glad for an opportunity to rest, and felt myself lucky to have found such a good place. I placed the *migou* skin over my head like a tent.

Occasionally a mischievous wind swept up from nowhere to blow it off me. As I quietly fell off to sleep, I was feeling good about myself, which, of course, is a luxury that few of us can afford. And given my questionable situation, I had no reason for such confidence. I remember birds chattering with what sounded like anger as I found myself quietly drifting off to sleep.

I was awoken abruptly as the *migou* skin flew off with a powerful gust of wind. Jolted awake, I ran to retrieve it. It had dropped near a group of large, shiny blue crows, who took little notice of me or the skin. They were more concerned with a yakskin bag of *tsamba* which they had stolen while I slept.

The greed of each of them was to my benefit. Each time one bird would go for the bag, the others attacked it in a flurry of wings and feathers.

They were a brazen lot; a bluster of blue feathers and shrill voices. They hardly stirred as I ran toward them. I had to throw some rocks before they were willing to give up their booty. Even then, one bold bird would not be denied. I fought with him over the bag as he attempted to fly off with it. I caught a part of it just in time, but the bird was relentless—the damage had been done. The bag ripped and handfuls of *tsamba* scattered to the earth. A gentle breeze blew up as I attempted to cup as much as I could in the palms of my hands, folding it into the ripped bag. The crows, who scattered around me like blue-black stones, waited as the food was blown toward them. I could hear Big Father's words: "Never allow yourself the luxury of feeling good about yourself."

Was it Big Father's voice in my mind's ear? Or was I hearing the Moslem soldier? Could it even have been my own voice? As the days wore on, the voice continued to be with me. Rather than be afraid, I began to enjoy the company. I remember asking the Moslem soldier what crops were grown in his country, and he talked about melons.

I also remember singing for him all the verses of "Don't Ride Chinese Horses," but was surprised to find that, like Uncle Sangsang, I had forgotten much of the song.

I did not know where I was going but it didn't matter. Something was pulling me in a direction.

One morning, however, I woke with an uneasy feeling. I didn't know where I was. I had no idea how far I had come or how far I had to go. I felt alone again.

I longed to be in Hor Drango. I wished to tumble into the path of whatever it was that carried me from the place I was born. As I took out the *migou* skin and wrapped it around me, I tried to think back.

A tall figure in a saffron-red monk's habit suddenly loomed over me.

"Are you from Lhasa?" I heard a voice that sounded far off. Was it my voice?

The Mysterious Lama

"I am the Lama Amchi Kesang," a voice announced.

The sudden appearance of this tall figure took me by surprise. I had not heard his approach or that of his two mules. At first, I believed that I was in the midst of a dream. It was easy to understand why. The bright morning sun which flashed across my eyes, the strange appearance of the lama who loomed over me, his commanding voice—all added to a sense of unreality that gripped me.

The lama walked around me. His penetrating dark brown eyes hardly blinked, as if they had a life of their own, like the Moslem women of Balkhash whom Sangsang had often described as "floating through the streets like eyes without bodies." His eyes had the intensity of the eyes of the *migou* who had stared at me that night on the road to Tatsienlu. I

334

felt my hands involuntarily go for my ears. He was looking at them. I felt uncomfortable being so closely scrutinized with emotionless eyes. Still, it never occurred to me to run or clap my hands and make the dream go away. The lama's effect was overwhelming.

It was not a dream. The cold, dispassionate plain, the relentless wind, my own anxieties for survival may have distorted what I saw, but it was not a dream.

I recognized him to be a member of the Kagyurpa sect. His hair was worn long and was topped with the characteristic knot that some of his sect wore. His robes were the color of sheep's liver, made of heavy dark red cloth.

He wore a thin coral ring in each ear, and an amulet set with an amber stone. (I learned later that the amber helped improve his eyesight.)

I judged him to be about the same age as Grandmother, although he had not one strand of silver hair. I suppose it was his long angular face. He carried his age around his eyes. These eyes sparkled with religious intensity, but they were set very deep.

There was something commanding in the way he moved. I had no doubt that he was well versed in tantric tradition. I recall Big Father telling me that some of the Kagyurpas were wizards, some with powers even beyond his own.

"I am on my way to the Chumbi valley." He waited for me to get up.

"I am going in that direction," I said quickly. "I am Yungdrung. I come from Hor Drango in the state of Chango, in Khams province."

"I know. I know." He waved his hands in front of me. "It's not important."

No more was said. He knew that I would follow him. He

335

spoke very little. His silence did not appear to be hostile.

I knew that he was no ordinary man. If I had to point out a single feature that suggested this, I couldn't. I did not have to be told what my mind's eye had already seen.

The following morning we were awoken by a light snow. The wind fiends of the west and north, fighting for dominance, stirred up the powdery snow, swirling it into transparent shapes so it appeared as if our campfire were surrounded by ghosts.

Lama Amchi had just given each mule a handful of dried peas and barley mixed with a little butter. We finished our *tsamba*, licked our bowls and fingers clean and placed the bowls within the folds of our *chubas*. I threw another yak chip into the fire.

"I watched you last night," the lama spoke softly. "Before you went to sleep you took out a skin and unfolded it. It is a *migou* skin, isn't it?"

"Yes," I admitted. "I am to take it to Chumbi. But you knew this already, didn't you?"

He looked at me intently. "There is no magic involved here." He smiled. "When I first saw you, I wasn't sure. You are a Bon-po and that surprised me. But your small ears . . ."

I looked at him. He could tell that I was more confused than ever.

"I've been to Chumbi." He smiled. "In Chumbi, there is a story about a small-eared boy who will bring religion to the *migou*. You are that small-eared boy."

The fire sputtered and hissed. A chill ran up and down my back. I felt the *migou* skin near my chest. Before I could take the skin out he waved his hands in front of me.

"There is no need," he said. "I have already seen the skin of a *migou*. I have seen the *migou* with the skin on."

My hands went back. "You have seen the *migou?*" I asked anxiously.

"I have," he said. "When you have traveled as extensively as I have, you hear some stories. But this really happened."

"I have only seen two green eyes suspended between dark trees," I said. "I knew it was the *migou.* But where did you see a *migou?*"

"In the Chumbi valley," he answered. "I was with an English doctor. We made camp in a narrow valley just on the other side of the Am Machu River, near Yatung. We were there to collect plants. I was just coming up from the stream when I heard sounds. They seemed to alternate between screams, laughs and screeches. Then I saw a *migou,* no bigger than yourself, rambling through the camp.

"The Englishman was more worried about his plants than anything else. But the *migou* was not interested in plants. He went to the fire, kicked the broiling lamb off the coals, and juggling it in his hands wandered out the other side of the camp. The doctor tried to convince himself that it was a bear. But I have never seen such a bear.

"I remember that he turned around before taking to the mountains with our dinner. And now you carry the skin of such a creature to Chumbi. But don't you know why?"

It had been in front of me all the time.

"I'm carrying the skin of a *migou*—my own skin from a previous life—back to Chumbi," I said. "I must go to Chumbi."

"No." The lama looked at me. "Not yet."

Why We Didn't Go to Lhasa

The loading and unloading of each of the lama's mules, I learned, was only done by the lama. The one time that I tried to help him with his mules, he brushed me away without a word.

Of his two mules, one was loaded with the usual necessities: an image of the goddess Tara, bags of barley, bricks of tea and rolled-up blankets. The other mule, however, was loaded with four wooden boxes with strange markings stamped across their sides. They must have been heavy, for the lama alternated the boxes each day from one mule to the other.

I knew better than to ask what these boxes contained. I knew that my questions would not be answered. My strange companion, I felt, would not tolerate open curiosity.

One morning, as I was stoking the yak-dung fire for our tea, a large particle of dust flew into my eye. I tried to ignore it, but it lodged itself well in my eye, causing it to sting and water.

Suddenly, I felt the lama's eyes on me. He sat near the four heavy wooden boxes which had been piled two by two near the fire to block some of the wind.

"You are the cook." He smiled as he waved me over. "You must expect to get soot in your eyes."

I tried to make light of my discomfort.

"Come over here," he commanded again. "Or do you want to view the world through soot?"

I couldn't tell for sure, but there was almost a laugh in his voice.

He was looking through one of the wooden boxes. After a careful search, he turned around, holding a small bottle which contained a clear liquid. I took this to be water.

Without a word, he shook some of the liquid onto a cotton cloth and softly massaged around my eyes. It was not water. It burned my eyes and at first made me wince. It had the smell of charred wood.

"From what flower does this come?" I asked, now feeling that I could talk. "Is it a flower that grows in Tibet?"

Now he actually did laugh. "It does not come from a flower," he answered as he put the bottles away. "It is English medicine. Have you ever seen an Englishman?"

"No," I confessed.

Then he looked at me with his penetrating brown eyes. It was the kind of look that Grandmother used when she wanted me to do something. "Say nothing of this treatment to anyone," the lama said. "It does not look good for a doctor to have foreign cures. I seldom use them."

I suddenly felt an overwhelming compulsion to see the contents of the wooden box.

The lama closed the box quickly. "Your eye will feel better now," he said.

Nothing more was discussed that day.

"You might as well know who I am," he said to me the following morning.

"But you don't have to . . ."

"No," he said, "I do have to. It surprised me that you are a Bon-po. I wasn't sure, but there is little doubt."

"I don't understand," I said.

"I'm not sure that I do either," he came back. "But here we

are. You have never been to Lhasa, but I am sure you've heard of the Ragyapas."

I had. The Ragyapas were the wretched beggars and vagabonds of Lhasa who cut up the bodies of the dead and fed them to the dogs and vultures. They are a dirty lot, who live in homes made of ram and sheep horns. They are looked down on by every segment of society and are placed on the same level as butchers.

"But what do they have to do with you?" I asked, sensing his answer.

"I was born in a house of sheep and yak horns in Lhasa," he began. "Both my mother and father carried the bodies of the dead to the cemeteries. So I was familiar with death at an early age."

I found myself immersed in his words. He spoke with a soft voice but the pride underneath was unmistakable.

"One learns a lot about human beings when dealing in such a trade," he continued. "When I was three years old, I remember watching bodies being cut up. Like a child, I was curious and had little understanding of the circumstances. But childhood is a short period of time in the Ragyapa district of Lhasa, and my curiosity did not pass with it. In fact, it increased.

"It was never enough for me just to watch the bodies being cut up. I wanted to know why things were like they were. What made one finger move and not another? Why did one man have a liver as black as charcoal when another didn't? So I observed. I observed closely.

"I remember begging near the hill where the Chokpori school of medicine is located. I envied those monks and their learning but I had not wasted my time. I, too, had learned a lot.

"When I was nine years old my parents died. Most of the children I had grown up with had already been carried to the hill. When I was twelve, I got into trouble and had to leave Lhasa. I have not been back since. This is foolish isn't it? Anyway, I left Lhasa, crossed Chumbi and went into India, to a place called Darjeeling. Perhaps you've heard of it? That is the name marked on the boxes."

He looked at me, paused and took a deep breath. "In Darjeeling I worked in the kitchen of an English army doctor. It was my curiosity that immediately brought me to the doctor's attention.

"One day, under the guise of dusting, I went into his office, simply to look. I remember standing there surrounded by bottles of many colors lining the shelves. I thought how little I really knew, how much more there was to know. So I just stood there in the middle of that sunny white room, looking.

"I didn't even hear the doctor come in. I thought that I would be thrown out if not beaten. But he smiled at me. He said he had watched me for some time, and that my interest in medicine was evident. He liked that. From then on, I was moved out of the kitchen and worked alongside the doctor. He called me his assistant. Our relationship developed into that of student and teacher. He was surprised that I knew as much as I did, and he was just as curious about our Tibetan medicine as I was about his. He took a particular interest in our plants. We spent many afternoons in the hills around Darjeeling looking for plants. We also made two excursions into Chumbi.

"He taught me to read and write the queen's English, and I tried, not very successfully, to teach him Tibetan. When he returned to his country nine years later, I was sorry to lose such a good friend.

341

"He gave me the boxes of medicine you see."

He stared into the fire. "I returned to Tibet," he continued. "In Chumbi, I met an old man, a Kagyurpa monk who asked me to travel with him. I stayed with him until his death fifteen years later. We traveled to every end of Tibet. I shall not tell you which initiations I received. It is not important."

The flame was flickering down. Unconsciously, I tossed another chip into the fire. A small burst of flame seemed to light up the whole morning sky.

The lama had finished speaking. I knew there was much more to tell, but there would be time. I was to learn a great deal from the Lama Amchi. It was difficult to be patient.

The Rumblings of Another War

Now that Lama Amchi had found me, I believed my goal was in reach. I was sure he'd lead me to the mountain in Chumbi valley where I would return the skin. My journey would end. I would discover which forces had drawn me from my home in Khams.

But the lama insisted there was plenty of time for me to go to Chumbi. And when the time came, no one would have to show me the way.

I stayed with the lama for five years, and traveled throughout the south and west of Tibet. I can't say where we were at one time or another; but Lhasa and Chumbi were avoided, each for its own reason.

In the Female Earth Rabbit year, I returned to my home in the Khams for the last time. That reunion with my family was a melancholy one.

Only my mother greeted me. Unfortunately, Big Father had left only a few short days before to "beat the drum" for a recently deceased nomad chief. Although I waited two full moons, I was not to see my father again. The unlucky timing of my visit filled me with great remorse. My mother told me that Big Father already knew of Sangsang's fate. This didn't surprise me.

Grandmother, who had now become very old, sat in front of our "God Room" spinning a prayer wheel and telling her beads. She hardly recognized me. The fire in her eyes, which once illuminated her face, had disappeared. I left her there immersed in religion's work.

It was perhaps just as well. For she more than anyone would not have liked what was happening in the Khams.

The Chinese were everywhere. Soldiers were followed by settlers and at least two hundred soldiers from the Chentu regiment were now quartered in Hor Drango.

I learned the ritual as well as the life of an itinerant lama. The lama offered luck-bringing services to the farmers and herdsmen of the region. We lived by the seasons, following the barley harvest from the low valleys to the high plateau. Even in a very bad year, one had the right to glean a field for the last of the crop. And the farmers and local people were generous. For uttering a prayer or incantation, there was always a bundle of grain waiting when we left. We were often invited into the camps of herdsmen where the lama read from the scriptures and offered prayers. We were always assured a bowl of buttered tea and usually we were given meat as well.

However, the lama did not require a great deal of either food or other things, and I found myself adopting his rhythm of life. I required less. I thought less of what I had.

One can easily overcome the inconveniences of making a

body function, but the mind is another matter. This was perhaps my most difficult time. My goal was just out of reach, and the *migou* skin felt as if it were burning through my body. The dream that I had when I was given the skin recurred. I kept grasping for a rope to pull me up into the sky. I awoke, asking myself who I was.

When I told the lama the dream, he was more convinced than ever that the time was not right for me to go to Chumbi.

"You must develop patience." He spoke to me sternly. "Everything is impermanent. Everything. Even your impatience is impermanent."

As time passed, I felt less compelled to hurry to Chumbi valley. While I never forgot the *migou* skin I carried, it did not consume my energies or cloud my meditation. The dream stopped.

Then, in the late summer of the Year of the Water Hare, Chumbi valley suddenly became important to all of Tibet. There was talk of the British coming through Chumbi and taking over the country.

We were in the Zbungru region, in Tsang province of western Tibet, when we heard the first rumblings of war. A herdsman we knew, Dresu by name, welcomed us into his camp. He had just returned from Chumbi valley and was quite distressed over the situation that was quickly developing there.

"How do you tell a yak not to eat grass?" he complained. "How do you tell them the grass on one side of a rock belongs to the British and on the other side to Tibet?"

We agreed that the problem was serious, particularly for herdsmen.

"You know what I've heard?" he continued, as he handed each of us a large chunk of lamb. "I've heard the British fear the Russians and the Russians fear the British." He paused and laughed ironically. "And the herdsman loses good pastures."

This was the war that the oracle Sung had predicted. And it wasn't long before there were other signs that a war was not far away. An enormous caravan, said to be carrying his holiness the Dalai Lama, was reported to have left for China late one night.

We had our own firsthand experience with war fever when we met a Khampa division under the leadership of a big confident man from Batang. "Now that the Khampas are coming into it," he assured us, "the British will soon be licking their wounds."

But the signs from Lhasa and from oracles around the country were less positive. I believed that now that religion was in danger, it was time for me to go to Chumbi. I wanted to talk to the lama about it but I did not want to appear impatient. I suppose I knew that it still wasn't the right time.

A few long weeks after our conversation with Dresu, we were camping by the Tsang Tsangpo. An autumn chill was in the air. It would be a true Tibetan night.

The lama looked at me across the fire. He seemed to know what I was thinking.

"Our country is in danger," I said, trying to lead up to the subject of Chumbi. I waited for the lama to say something. I didn't expect him to say what he did.

"Tomorrow morning," he spoke calmly, "I leave for Chumbi valley. I will be going alone."

"I don't understand," I said, without disguising my immense disappointment. "I must go to Chumbi. I must bring the skin back. I must. . . ."

"Of course you must," he interrupted, "but not just yet.

345

You may feel that you are ready for the final part of your journey. You may very well be. But now Chumbi is not ready. There is a war in Chumbi. Wait a little longer."

"But how long?" I asked, feeling impatient again.

The lama looked at me kindly. "The war will not last long," he said softly. "Not much longer."

"Will we win?" I asked. "Will we throw back this threat to religion?"

"In war," he answered, "only hatred wins. That is why I must go to Chumbi. Compassion is the first casualty in battle. But you cannot come with me. You must know by now that your karma does not lie with the world of men."

I knew what the lama was talking about. I could not resist the force which took me from Khams and would eventually lead me to the summits of Chumbi valley. I knew I would be a hermit.

"Your entire life," the lama continued, "has been in preparation for your meeting with the *migou*. Everyone you have encountered has helped clear the path. So now your karma can carry you to the upland slopes, beyond the inaccessible passes. You will return the *migou* skin and teach the *migou* religion, just as someone before you has and someone before that. You are concerned with waiting longer—a year, five years. Even a hundred years are nothing. Time is insignificant. Religion will always be constantly threatened. You must help keep it alive on the summits of our country."

The lama paused and threw a yak chip into the fire. He methodically rolled out his sheepskin blanket and lay down. I knew that he would not say anything more. But what more could have been said?

I don't remember falling asleep that night. I do remember

346

dreaming that I was back in Hor Drango, in my familiar place near the *k'ang*, yet my family was not there. I heard the sound of mules, and Lama Amchi's voice. "No, don't get up yet," he said. But I was already at the gate. "I do not give you my mules," I heard the lama's voice again, "or anything that you can sell." Then I closed the door and found myself outside.

"You must conquer solitude, and this you can only do by yourself." This time, it was my voice.

When I awoke, the lama and his mules were gone. I was not surprised, but nevertheless I wanted some evidence that the last five years had really taken place. I found it just near my head, on the edge of the blanket—a bottle of English medicine from Darjeeling. It was the medicine Lama Amchi had used when I had soot in my eyes.

The war didn't last very long. The British proved a strange, powerful enemy. By the time they reached Lhasa, the Dalai Lama was in China. They couldn't find any Russians, so they stayed for a while and then went home. Still, many Tibetans perished in the war. Among the more than four hundred who fell at Dhari Zhong was Lama Amchi Kesang. I learned this news from the herdsman Dresu, who lost a brother there. The news didn't surprise me. The lama had known what would happen before he went to Chumbi. I sensed that the night he told me he was leaving.

And now he had cleared the path a little bit more. I would follow the last of the barley crop that season from the high plateau to the deep valleys around the Himalayas. No one had to tell me that it was time to go.

It was early spring. The war had been over for a year. I would be in the Chumbi valley by winter. There was a mountain somewhere in that land pulling me toward it.

The Lama Yishey

As I marched toward the Chumbi valley, I saw the usual assortment of pilgrims, traders and lamas coming and going.

Some four days out of Chumbi, I encountered a rotund lama who had apparently been on the road for some time and we formed an immediate friendship. I met this lama—or I should say, we bumped into each other—on the circular path around one of the small lakes on the road. The lake itself was small and did not have the same waters that one would find farther in the valley. Nevertheless, it was considered quite sacred. Its small size enabled it to house many of the serpentlike *nags* who guard the wealth of the underworld. It was considered as beneficial to make observances here as it was to bathe in the waters farther down the valley.

The lama, whose name was Yishey, was walking around the lake in the direction that follows the sun, in accordance with his Buddhist beliefs, and I, a Bon-po, was going in my direction, which was exactly opposite. A collision, therefore, was inevitable.

As we marched around the lake, murmuring our prayers and immersed in religion's work, we almost knocked each other down. We both laughed. As it turned out, Lama Yishey was returning to his monastery, which was at the northern end of the Kambo valley in Chumbi. We agreed to travel together after completing our observances.

After a two days' march through a constant light sleet, we emerged onto an open plain. There were other travelers on the road, and Lama Yishey appeared to know most of them.

He knew the region well and was an invaluable guide as well as an interesting companion.

His face was moon shaped and round in every respect. In fact, from his chubby fingers to the round chin from which the scant beginnings of a beard appeared, he looked as if he would roll away if tipped over.

He was a totally likable man with very strong Buddhist beliefs and an innate unsophisticated intelligence that he credited to his nomad heritage, of which he was very proud.

"I know that when I am not around," he told me, "some of the other monks have a good laugh at my accent. I have never mastered the Lhasa dialect, nor do I care to."

I laughed, for as a Khampa I was often subjected to the same kind of ridicule because of my accent.

"I am Amdowa. My people are the Panik tribe who surround the sacred Koko Nor. Many years ago, a delegation from the monastery came for me, claiming that I was an emanation lama and an incarnation of the recently deceased abbot. They said the monastery was small and not very well known, but the poet-saint Milarepa was said to have slept on the spot where it was built. It was a great honor for my family as well as for my tribe, but I must confess I cannot say for sure if I am indeed who I am supposed to be. Even now in my older years, I wonder."

He was airing his doubts to me, a stranger, secure that no bad luck would come of it; for we had met on the circular path where weapons are never drawn and where sworn enemies unite in the common bond of prayer. Still, he was surprisingly candid. Totally committed to the dharma of Buddha, he nevertheless questioned the validity of oracles.

He told me he had been visiting the lake where we met for

some time, hoping to find something in its waters, which were believed to be oracular. Unfortunately, very little was revealed to him.

After another day's march we arrived at the northern end of the Kambo valley. Here our directions split: Lama Yishey was returning to his monastery and I was going on into the valley.

It was a fresh morning; the air was unusually clear for autumn. The blue mist that usually descended from the mountains appeared content to remain above. As Lama Yishey had pointed out, one could see with perfect visibility to the ends of the sky.

"There are caves in these mountains," I told him as we sat down for our last tea together. "Your monastery maintains five of them. But they are not here; they begin at the western end of the valley. From the higher caves you can see most of the Chumbi valley. Yatung spreads out on the banks of the Ammo Chu."

"But how did you know?" He lowered his voice. "Have you been here before?" I did not answer. "If only I had the same confidence in my own direction," he said. "Do not misunderstand me. I do not waste time on questioning the validity of an oracle's predictions. I believe the dharma of the Buddha, for if nothing else, one cannot dispute the truth of his teachings. Life itself has shown me that. But what am I saying? You are a Bon-po aren't you?" He didn't wait for me to answer. "Well, no matter," he said. "I am sure that our abbot would allow you the use of one of the monastery caves, although your being a Bon-po may present him with an interesting religious dilemma. Our abbot is a remarkable man, and not given to the pomp and ceremony that one usually associates with such rank. The caves are open to any or all who would use them in the interest of religion. But you are a Bon-po, and so you go in . . . well, the wrong direction. You would be doing and undoing religious work. Will the good luck balance the bad?" These questions seemed to amuse him.

"There will be no need to put your abbot through the ordeal of such a decision," I told him. "I will make my hermitage beyond your caves."

"Ah, you know that, too. You know where you're going." He laughed. "Well, it would have been interesting. There are not many challenges."

He looked at me as if I were an old friend. "I shall not see you again. Our caves are well hidden in the mountain. I have only gone farther up once before to participate in the installation of new prayer flags on Jelap pass. If there are caves even farther up I do not know of them, nor do I have the strength or the courage to find them out. I have not been given the benefit of a dream to help me answer these questions of divination. But that is my problem and not yours. Is it not?"

I said nothing.

"The abbot would never have let you use one of the caves." He finally smiled. "You see, of the five caves, three are in use at this time. You or anybody else—Buddhist, Bon-po or Moslem—would be the fourth. Four is an unlucky number and so it would be very bad luck. The abbot would have had no choice but to say no."

"But it would be lucky for me," I pointed out. "Even numbers are lucky to a Bon-po."

"By the sacred volumes," he laughed as he got up, "you

Bon-pos are a defiant lot." He extended his hand to help me up and then we each went on our own way, praying our own prayers.

The Hermit's Cave

I climbed a good part of that bright blue day. By late afternoon, I left the last brave tree trembling below. I walked through a descending mist of soft clouds onto snowy glaciers. The sun, which had illuminated the day so brightly, was falling over a distant mountain, taking with it the day's warmth and light. I was entering the world of eternal snow. As I slowly and cautiously tramped up the mountain, breathing became an effort. My judgment became cloudy. Mistakes at this altitude can be fatal. A hesitant step, a wrong turn, the accidental dislodging of a pebble could be disastrous. More dangerous is the sense of security the mountain can lull you into.

Suddenly my eyes were drawn to something rising above the snow. At first it could have been mistaken for a lump of snow itself. But the sun had one final gasp of brightness, and in that burst of red glow, the object seemed to have a radiance of its own, as if challenging the sun itself.

I moved down the mountain to get a closer look. I had not gone very far when I dispelled all doubt. It was a boot in the snow; a beautiful boot.

I was anxious now as I scrambled down the mountain, tripping over myself, falling and picking myself up. As I stumbled down, I passed the one brave trembling tree I had seen that afternoon. It was like seeing an old friend in the wilderness. The boot seemed to be burning in the snow and I wondered why I had not seen it before.

And then, just as I was about to get a closer look, I felt the ground give way under me. I found myself falling through a narrow crevice in the snow, one of those dangerous soft spots that look safe but are deceptively treacherous. I fell, without much dignity, into a cave.

The boot was outside the cave. I had seen such a boot once before, a long time ago, on a strange old pilgrim who passed through Hor Drango.

It was not red anymore, but had turned almost pure white and was frozen in the ice. I tramped through the snow and found other things on this site which indicated to me that my search had ended. A broken prayer flag with faded, barely legible script and a number of headless arrows were scattered on the ground. The ground was also littered with many flat rocks, some with the swastika—symbol of the powerful *garuda* bird, the Bon diety who flies for the victory of religion.

This was my cave. I had been here another time. I knew that this was where I would stay, in this religious place.

After investigating the cave and the area around it, I blessed and thanked the gods. I thanked the soil gods and the gods of the atmosphere. I prayed, too, to our Lord Shenrab who was the founder of my Bon sect. I repeated the Bon mantra many times before finally giving in to the most blissful sleep I had ever experienced.

Then my first winter in the mountains came. It was the Year of the Earth Dog. That year, an unusually long and severe winter began early in the mountains.

There were warnings. The first was the early migration of the mountain goats to their winter pastures below. Even more unusual was their leaving the upland slopes when there was still a great deal of pasture available. But they were racing the snows that would soon close the valleys.

I watched them as they marched past my cave. The leader was a large blackish-gray fellow with numerous scars on his hindquarters. These he wore proudly, as they were the result of a dispute between a leopard and himself and so were well earned.

He took his responsibility seriously, and from time to time came back to see if all stragglers were accounted for. He was the undisputed leader and would be until he was too old to fight. That time, unfortunately, did not seem a long way off. More than one predator had been crushed under his strong hoofs. More than one rival had been banished into the wilderness and inevitable doom after tasting the determination of his long curved horns. But that was a long time before. I wondered if he knew it.

There was a dignity to his departure, none of the panic that one sees in animals fleeing a burning forest. The danger was no less imminent, as there are as many cold places in hell as there are hot. Yet there was a military precision to their leaving that could only be described as orderly.

As I watched the last goat rumble by I noticed the old fellow doubling back again to check on any last-minute stragglers. He had never understood what I was doing here, and now, sensing winter closing in, he was even more perplexed that I wanted to stay. We caught each other's eye. He sauntered over as if to say good-bye, and I tied my blood-stained *kata* around one of his horns. Even now I cannot say what compelled me to do this.

I remained where I was. I had no intention of being chased by the snows.

Nymgal, a Friend, and the Night of the *Migou*

That very night, the snow began to fall.

It seemed that the wind challenged the snow for the mountain. But the snow continued and gained momentum. The wind fiends, angered by this, blew with uncontrolled ferocity, eventually blowing themselves out. The snow continued. The wind fiends, who usually dominate the mountain, had to concede until they were able to gather the strength for a fresh challenge. Still, the snow continued. I watched it as it covered the scant and sturdy grass that grew near some scattered rocks. I saw a marmot poke his little head from his hole in another rock. The snow had apparently caught him unprepared and bewildered him. But he was a round little creature, and had stored up enough fat to help him survive the long night that is winter. He was lucky, as well, for he did not have to venture far from his hole to find food. A snow rabbit scurrying across the snow to his nest was less fortunate. His fat gray body against the white snow made a perfect target for the eagle who swooped him up in his talons. Both the marmot and I looked up and then the marmot, screeching nervously, returned to his hole near the rock. Soon the rock was buried in snow.

Only some days before, a local farmer, a simple and devout man named Nymgal, had brought me enough provisions for a long winter. Nymgal belonged to the Nyingmapa sect of Buddhism. There has been a long-standing enmity between Bon-po and Buddhist. But these matters did not concern us.

Nymgal was a simple man; thankful, as he put it, to be cast into the human world and not to be one of the lower forms of existence. He did very well at farming, leading a life of good actions and thereby gaining enough merit to secure an even higher existence in his next life.

When I explained to him that I was not a lama, having never been in a monastery or undertaken any initiations, and that in addition I was not even a member of his sect, he laughed good-naturedly.

"You are a sentient being," he smiled, "and your life is an example for those of us in the valley who seek release from the wheel of endless existences. You are my lama. I ask nothing more than for you to allow me to see to your bodily needs so you will have more time to pray."

And so while I discouraged visits from the unworthy, the curious and the self-serving, I looked forward to seeing Nymgal. It was always difficult to comprehend that this man wanted nothing more than to make sure that I was getting enough to eat.

Nymgal had another name in the valley—Three Chins—because of a disease he had brought with him from his home in Bhutan. In this affliction, another chin grows out from the neck and the neck itself disappears. One who is afflicted also has bulging eyes and seems to be carrying two extra chins on his neck. I never questioned Nymgal about it, although it was his most striking feature. However, he occasionally would joke about himself.

When he had come up to see me a few days before, he

laughingly pointed to his chins. "The lamas in the valley predict a long and terrible winter," he said, "and so I have stored my chins with all manner of provisions. I will not visit my lama with empty hands or empty chins."

I handed him a bowl of tea. "A lama in the Yatung Monastery suffers from the same condition, you know," he continued. "He is Bhutanese, from the Korbo valley like me. He wears his robes almost up to his eyes. But I have nothing to hide. The result of previous deeds has brought this to me."

He got up and walked to the entrance of the cave. "I am still waiting for those two new servants I engaged. They are coming up here with some dried yak meat and bags of *tsamba*. Do you have enough tea?"

He stamped impatiently. "What is taking them so long? They must be aware that winter will soon be on us. It would be an honor for me to share your hermitage, although I have no wish to disturb your solitude. But for them . . . well, I am sure that they would not survive. Small hearts. Yes, they are men with small hearts."

The servants finally arrived and dumped the provisions at the entrance to my cave. They looked me over carefully. One, a sturdy old man, was genuinely curious, and as he attempted to look the other way he could not resist eyeing me. The other was simply afraid and I did not get a good look at him. When I growled for no apparent reason he turned around and bounded down the mountain. The other followed, and Nymgal and I stood laughing.

And now, as I chewed a piece of dried yak flesh, I thanked Nymgal for his kindness. As the snow continued to rise around my cave, I blessed this man who never asked for anyone's blessing.

Later that night, I was awoken by an unusual sound. At first it sounded like newborn snow tigers. It was a screeching, yelping sound, but I knew of no tigers in the area. They seldom came down this far on the mountain. And besides, the sound was very loud, much louder than any newborn cubs could make.

The wind had once again taken control outside the cave and I assumed that it was what I was hearing. But I wasn't sure, for the sounds did not seem to come from the wind, but rather were carried on it.

I listened again. It was a mournful cry. Some days before, a covey of snow pheasants had scurried by the cave. I thought for a moment that they were now making the sounds, but I knew, in the part of me that knows things, that they were not.

The cries continued and I began to recognize a strange and insistent pattern. At one point, I thought that the sounds were coming from within the cave; that somehow I involuntarily was haunting myself. It was a strange sensation. I put my hands over my ears to block out the cries, and they stopped. I removed my hands and the cries were still to be heard.

I looked out into the black night. Everything was white and black. In spite of the heavy snow that was falling all around, there was still a moon in the sky, and it highlighted the surrounding hillside. But I saw nothing.

The sound continued and then I began to realize something about its pattern. It was almost as if whoever—or whatever—was making these cries was praying.

I did not sleep that night. I could not. I felt that I was at the edge of the purpose that had brought me to this mountain. I would have to be just a little more patient.

Just as dawn was beginning to break, a shadow fell over the entrance to the cave. A *migou*, carrying a white bloodstained *kata* in his outstretched arms, appeared.

That was a long time ago.

The Years Pass

I live by the seasons and I am growing old. I expected somebody by now. Some confused yet determined traveler, carrying a *migou* skin, who would climb the steep slopes beyond the clouds.

I cannot say how long I've waited. I can barely remember when I began to wait.

How long have I been living and meditating in this small cave, with its strong smell of *migou?*

Another spring approaches, and the *migou* has already begun the climb to the isolation of the eternal snows. Spring chases winter's white protection from the valleys. The *migou*'s food—the mouse hares, foxes and other small creatures—already fled the insecurity of the lower slopes. The *migou*, like the farmer, the herdsman and the hermit, lives by the seasons.

And so I wait for winter. The *migou* will come, just as he has come every winter. Religion has been accepted reluctantly. Only one *migou* returns to my cave to hear about religion. Only one *migou* understands compassion.

It is fall. My friend Nymgal comes to see me, always bearing quantities of food. I tell him that I am only one and there is enough *tsamba* for many. But he smiles and says there are many birds and animals around the cave and they, too, are sentient beings worthy of compassion.

We have learned that Shenrab, the founder of Bon, and Buddha can fit into each other's skin. Why argue forever about who said what first. It is a needless, endless argument, when all that really matters is compassion. Compassion is religion. That is what I've tried to tell the *migou*. Nymgal understands this. He cannot read or write. He is old now and often forgets the words to the prayers. But no one understands religion better than he.

The climb gets more difficult for him each year. I fear we will not have many more times together. No more time to allow ourselves a simple indulgence, a chance to look back.

I wonder why no one has come.

I have written down a record of my experiences in both the Tibetan and Zhang Zhung tongues. I will give them to my friend Nymgal when he comes to see me. I will tell him to bury these papers on the plateau in a place where men of ease and comfort, trapped by material possessions, will not find them.

Someone will come.

Last night I had a dream. The old pilgrim who had come to me in Hor Drango was climbing the mountain. Although neither of us spoke a word as she approached my cave, I knew she was coming to take the skin back. We smiled at each other.

We are like pebbles, I thought, dislodged from snug river bottoms by late summer rain, caught up in the cosmic flow.